FRONTIER LADY

Books by Judith Pella

Frontier Lady

The Russians (with Michael Phillips)

The Crown and the Crucible
A House Divided
Travail and Triumph

The Stonewycke Trilogy (with Michael Phillips)

The Heather Hills of Stonewycke
Flight from Stonewycke
Lady of Stonewycke

The Stonewycke Legacy (with Michael Phillips)

Stranger at Stonewycke
Shadows over Stonewycke
Treasure of Stonewycke

The Highland Collection (with Michael Phillips)

Jamie MacLeod: Highland Lass
Robbie Taggart: Highland Sailor

The Journals of Corrie Belle Hollister (with Michael Phillips)

My Father's World
Daughter of Grace
*On the Trail of the Truth**
*A Place in the Sun**
*Sea to Shining Sea**
*Into the Long Dark Night**
*Land of the Brave and the Free**

*Michael Phillips only

FRONTIER LADY

Judith Pella

BETHANY HOUSE PUBLISHERS
MINNEAPOLIS, MINNESOTA 55438

Cover by Dan Thornberg,
Bethany House Publishers staff artist.

Published by Bethany House Publishers
A Ministry of Bethany Fellowship, Inc.
6820 Auto Club Road, Minneapolis, Minnesota 55438

Printed in the United States of America

Library of Congress Cataloging-in-Publication Data

Pella, Judith
   Frontier lady / Judith Pella
      p. cm.
     1. Frontier and pioneer life—Texas—Fiction. 2. Texas—History—Fiction.   I. Title.
PS3566.E415F76   1993
813'.54—dc20   92–43516
ISBN 1–55661–293–1   CIP

To

Michael Phillips,

Friend, brother in Christ, and mentor.

*"Greater love hath no man than this, that a man
lay down his life for his friends."*
John 15:13

Thank you, Mike, for being so generous with your
talents, your wisdom, and your encouragement.

JUDITH PELLA is the author of five major fiction series for the Christian market, co-written with Michael Phillips. An avid reader and researcher in historical, adventure, and geographical venues, her skill as a writer is exceptional. She and her family make their home in California.

CONTENTS

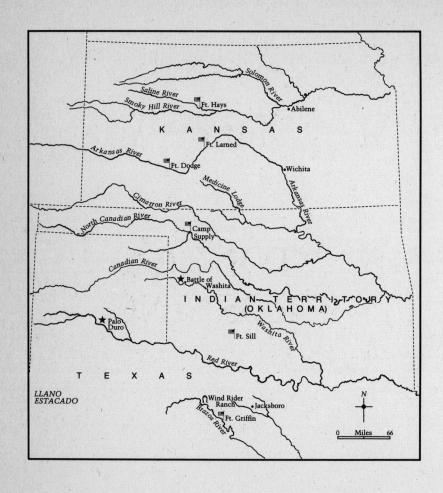

Solomon River

Saline River

Smoky Hill River

Ft. Hays

• Abilene

K A N S A S

Ft. Larned

Arkansas River

Ft. Dodge

• Wichita

Medicine Lodge

Arkansas River

Cimarron River

North Canadian River

Camp
Supply

Canadian River

★ Battle of
Washita

I N D I A N   T E R R I T O R Y
(OKLAHOMA)

Washita River

★ Palo
Duro

Ft. Sill

Red River

T E X A S

N

LLANO
ESTACADO

Wind Rider
Ranch

• Jacksboro

Brazos River

Ft. Griffin

0   Miles   66

PART 1

STONER'S
CROSSING

1

THEY WERE BUILDING A GALLOWS in Stoner's Crossing. The two men commissioned for the job perspired and grumbled as they set nail to wood under the searing Texas sun. The temperature was no less than a hundred degrees on that midsummer day. A brilliant yellow sun reflected against the stark blue of the sky.

Wiping a grimy red handkerchief across his damp brow, the older of the two builders, a man with more gray in his tangled hair and beard than brown, stood back and surveyed the results of his labors.

"Should be done on time," he observed.

"They better have that free whiskey for us when we're done, that's all I can say," replied the younger fellow.

They would earn two dollars each and a bottle of whiskey for their work—no less than a king's ransom to the ne'er-do-well drifters. But they could have commanded any price for the nefarious task, since they were the only ones in the dusty, ramshackle excuse for a town who had the stomach for it.

Having arrived in Stoner's Crossing only a few days earlier, they had never known Leonard Stoner. To them he was but a victim, murdered in the prime of life. To them, his killer should pay for the crime by hanging. That was the law. They didn't know the victim; they didn't know his murderer, and they didn't much care about either. Still, they were not completely heartless.

The older man mopped his drenched brow again. "You know, Tom, I don't feel altogether settled about taking that there money."

"Me neither, Wash."

"Wash," otherwise known as Eli Washburn, slowly shook his head as he aimed his hammer at another nail. "I reckon someone was bound to take it, though, if it weren't us."

"I suppose you're right there."

"You ever hanged anyone, Tom?" Without waiting for an answer, the older man continued. "It ain't a pretty sight. I seen tough fron-

11

tiersmen carry on sorely aforehand. It ain't easy sticking your neck through that noose."

Momentarily sobered by Washburn's unpleasant statement, both men fell silent.

The steady clank-thud of their hammering dominated the stifling air, without even a flutter of a breeze to dull the haunting sound. Oddly, the town was quiet just then, the two or three hundred residents, apparently occupied indoors, showing no interest in the solitary activity around the ominous wooden structure. Occasionally the sound of a snorting horse or a raised voice at one of the saloons penetrated the silence, but for the most part only the tattoo of the hammer and the grunts of the workmen broke the grim quiet.

The sun arched higher in the sky, its movement almost visible, if anyone had the kind of mystical vision that could peer directly into that blazing light. But even a blind man could *feel* the sun's inevitable climb toward its apex.

High noon.

That hour would not pass this day without note. The cloistered citizens of the town would surely not neglect to attend the upcoming event. Even if their hands must stay free of actual blood, their curiosity was another thing. It had to be appeased.

Like the no-account vagrants they had hired to do their dirty work, the residents of Stoner's Crossing wondered. Some had seen a hanging before. Some had even participated. Often, in that untamed wilderness, the affair involved nothing more than pitching a sturdy rope over a stout tree branch and then kicking the victim's horse out from under him. The scions of law were often too far removed to await that nebulous thing easterners labeled "due process." The rope and the gun were often the only law an honest man had available to him this far west of the Mississippi. One could not be fainthearted. Too many who had let a desperado walk away from a crime later ended up receiving a bullet in the back as thanks.

Hangings were not uncommon, but trials were. In fact, the recent trial in Stoner's Crossing was somewhat of an anomaly in this lawless land. But that's how Caleb Stoner had wanted it—all nice and legal. And Caleb usually got his way. It was his town, after all.

Shading his eyes with a calloused hand, Tom gazed up at the sky.

"I figure that there sun's as high as she's going to get."

Washburn pounded the final nail into the structure.

"Yeah. Told you we'd finish."

The two dirty drifters scrutinized their work once more. Fifteen feet high, the gallows had taken them nearly two days to build, and was a handsome piece of work. The steps were even, except for one near the top, where an ill-placed nail had split the wood, leaving it rough across the center. It shouldn't pose a problem, though. Most folks climbing a gallows were moving slow enough. The framing was strong, too. Washburn gave it a couple of heavy-handed blows to be sure. It wouldn't do to have the thing crashing down prematurely. He'd seen something like that happen once, only it had been a tree branch, and the criminal managed to escape in the confusion that followed.

Tom hauled a sandbag up the steps. It weighed only about fifty pounds and wouldn't be a true test of the structure's soundness, though Washburn didn't think it would have to take much more stress than that. They only needed to test the trapdoor. For this procedure the two men tied the bag to the rope Washburn had already fastened around the crossbar of the framing. Tugging at the rope, Washburn pulled the bag to the top.

Washburn wondered why they were going through all this trouble. A tree and a horse would have served as well, even if it would have meant he'd be out two dollars and the bottle of spirits. He decided the sheriff must have figured these unusual circumstances warranted a more formal approach.

"Let 'er go!" Tom yelled.

Washburn released the rope. In a flash, a mere twinkling, it was over. The bag fell smoothly, with a dusty thud, through the trap. Everything worked fine. You couldn't have found a better gallows, even in New York City.

Tom set down his hammer and strode over to the sheriff's office to tell them everything was ready.

But the older drifter didn't look entirely satisfied with his work. He let his eyes roam over the structure as if looking for some flaw, almost hoping he'd find one, forcing a postponement of the imminent event. He tried to tell himself he wasn't squeamish. He'd fought Indians and Mexicans and grizzly bears; spilled enough blood, both his own and that of others, to know it wasn't that. But there was one thing he hadn't done before and, old and seasoned as he was, he still couldn't say if he had the stomach for it.

Washburn squeezed the moisture from his handkerchief, and retying it around his sunburned neck, turned to his assistant who had just returned.

"You know, Tom, I ain't never—"

But his words were cut off as all at once the stifling midday air began to stir with voices and movement.

They were coming now, the sheriff and his deputy with their prisoner sandwiched between them.

The prisoner was a woman.

She was barely twenty years old—so young, yet years of strife clung to her as closely as the sultry air. She walked with a sure step, her shoulders hitched back, her chin, despite its delicate line, firm and proud.

It was time for the hanging to begin.

2

HER FRAME WAS SLIGHT COMPARED to the two men walking on either side of her, but somehow she gave the appearance of towering over them, as if she, not her captors, were in control. The two men gripped her arms, but obviously not because she needed their support. If her knees trembled at all on this her last journey in life, she gave no outward evidence of it. She appeared ready to meet her fate—indeed, almost eager to do so, in spite of the pallor of her skin that seemed but a continuation of her colorless gray muslin dress.

The sheriff, now striding grimly at her side, had been amazed at her calm demeanor. She had spoken not a word all day, mostly sitting very straight and prim on the edge of the cot in her cell, with her slim hands folded in her lap. She ate her last meal with meticulous care, finishing every crumb. Sheriff Pollard had known men, hardened outlaws, who couldn't even choke down a cup of coffee on their execution day. But the woman ate as if it meant something more than just appeasing her hunger. She ate as if she defied even her appetite to accuse her of weakness. Pollard would never have expected it of her, being the genteel eastern-bred woman that she was, although he supposed he'd had a few previous hints of what kind of woman might be inside that feminine frame. She had behaved the same way during the trial, too. Never once did she break down, never shedding a single tear, even with her family and neighbors accusing her like they did.

And more than that, she never showed a shred of remorse for her deed.

The jury had been unanimous in its decision. However, Pollard had to admit that finding twelve objective jurors was no easy task. Caleb Stoner owned the town and everything and everyone in it. But, in the sheriff's opinion, the evidence was pretty incriminating all by itself, and that's what he had testified to the court. She'd been found standing over her murdered husband's body with Leonard's Colt 44 in her hand. If her own father had been on the jury, he couldn't have argued with that kind of evidence.

When the judge, a circuit rider from Austin, asked her, "Did you kill your husband?" she had replied with a single quiet word: "No."

She hadn't said much more than that through the whole of the trial, and she just didn't sound convincing enough. Almost every criminal denied his guilt. No one ever listened much to denials unless they were accompanied with ample emphasis and insistence.

Pollard did not take well to hanging women. But he figured a woman ought to be grateful to hang rather than spend time in some state prison—a living death for anyone, much less a lady like Mrs. Stoner.

Still, Pollard remembered when she had come west two years ago. The way Pollard heard it, her father and brother had been killed early on in the war and she had been left alone. Because of some connection between the two families, Caleb got her to come west from Virginia in order to marry his eldest son, Leonard. She arrived in the spring of '63, at a time when it was no easy matter to travel through the South. Pollard didn't know what could have driven her to make such a trip in the middle of a war, but then again, it wasn't any of the sheriff's business. Anyway, regions more to the west, Texas especially, avoided most of the heavy fighting that ended up devastating the South. Stoner himself managed to avoid even what fighting there was. His younger boys were too young to be expected to join the Rebel army, and he was essentially too old. His eldest son, Leonard, he contrived to get into a Home Guard unit that had been formed to protect the state from the ever-present threat of Indian attack. Thus he had been able to maintain his place as a loyal Texan and a Confederate, while at the same time cushioning himself in the event the South lost their cause. Now that the war was over and Texas was being "reconstructed" by the North, Stoner's fancy fence-straddling was serving him well.

Of course, avoiding national political struggles didn't spare him any personal troubles. The Stoners had enough "civil war" right in their own house. How much of it was on account of the girl, the sheriff didn't exactly know, but it sure hadn't begun with her arrival. Maybe she was just like the slavery issue in the war. The war didn't start because of it, but it was the match that lit the fuse. That's how he thought Mrs. Stoner was.

Sheriff Pollard had been on hand that first day she had arrived on the stage from Austin. Caleb and his sons didn't even come to meet her; they sent one of their hired hands. On first glance Pollard thought she looked rather fragile, surrounded as she was by her stark black mourning clothes. But her skin showed the high color of one acquainted with the out-of-doors. Beneath the bright prairie sun, the few strands of hair escaping the confines of her black bonnet looked like pure gold. Even then she had seemed in command of herself, despite the natural apprehensions of coming to a new place. She was a beautiful girl, but sitting as she was, so straight and solemn, she seemed beautiful like an ancient statue, not like a real flesh-and-blood woman. Maybe if she had smiled . . .

But Pollard never did recall seeing Mrs. Stoner smile. It would have done wonders for those blue eyes of hers. They were like the kind of sparkling blue pools you didn't often see in Texas—only most of the time hers looked as if they had been caught in an early frost. It was those eyes, however, that first indicated what was inside that solemn young woman. When Caleb's man stopped the wagon to drop off the mail he had picked up in the capital, Pollard got a good look at her eyes and immediately forgot his initial assessment of her as a frail southern belle. One look, once you got past the sadness, gave the sheriff a hint that this lady, for all her beauty, all her femininity, was made of steel.

He had never known her to be harsh or mean or even hard. To his knowledge, she was always as soft-spoken, as dainty, as gentle as any woman he'd ever known. Whatever could make a woman like that gun down her own husband, Pollard didn't know, though enough had come out in the trial to convince the jury that she was unhappy in her marriage. But unhappy enough to kill to escape it?

That's what the jury thought.

Pollard wasn't sure. If only she hadn't been found standing over the body like that.

Still, Pollard had tried to make a case for self-defense, but no one would listen to him. Since Stoner had been unarmed and shot in the back . . . well, there were some things you just couldn't fight. In the end, the decision wasn't his, anyway. He was just the sheriff. His job was not to convict the guilty but to carry out what was decided by others. That's what he had to do now, though he didn't especially like it.

They were halfway to the gallows. Glancing around, Pollard noted that the residents of Stoner's Crossing were beginning to show their faces. Word had spread quickly that it was time and, like rats crawling from holes, the people were coming. Alone, or by twos and threes, they crept toward the place of execution. The spectators were all men. What few women there were in town would not breach propriety by venturing out to watch, though some of them had raised damning enough voices against the accused during the trial.

By the time the prisoner and her escorts reached the gallows' steps, some fifty or sixty had gathered to witness the proceedings. The crowd was quiet and subdued; the festive air that often accompanied such an occasion was absent.

Pollard paused and scanned the throng for one important face. Not finding it, he turned to his deputy on the prisoner's left side.

"Doc, you hear anything from Caleb?"

"I did not. He should be here." The man called "Doc" also perused the gathering, but to no avail. An annoyed grimace flickered across his face. Doc Barrows was not only the town's sometime deputy, but also its physician, barber, dentist, undertaker, and preacher. He had a very busy schedule and wasn't happy about a delay, even if it was caused by Caleb Stoner himself. Doc considered himself indispensable enough to be able to show some backbone toward Caleb, at least when the man was absent in body.

Pollard shuffled his feet, indecisive. He figured Caleb would have been at this hanging, not only early, but with an eager relish. Maybe he was planning on making some grand entrance, although the sheriff saw no point in that now. It would be just like Caleb to use this as another means to further enforce his hold on the town. Squinting, Pollard glanced up toward the sun and muttered a curse under his breath. On top of everything else he didn't fancy standing around in the heat. But then Caleb did like to see his people sweat, didn't he?

He heard the wagon, raising a cloud of dust as it approached. It was Caleb, all right, with his son Laban at his side.

Mrs. Stoner turned to watch the wagon, too. Her impassive expression did not change except perhaps to grow somewhat harder around the edges. If you could read nothing else in that woman's stony countenance, thought the sheriff, hatred, at least, was clearly present as she beheld her father-in-law.

The wagon stopped on the fringes of the crowd. Caleb did not speak, and no greetings were exchanged. But Pollard knew it was time to begin.

17

He gave his prisoner's arm a little nudge. "You ready, Mrs. Stoner?"

She said nothing, replying only with a barely perceptible nod of her head. Then they began the ascent. There were six steps in all, but it seemed to take inordinately long to traverse them. Pollard thought he felt a bit more tension against the hand that held the woman's arm, as if the full impact of what was about to transpire had finally dawned upon her.

Even steel must bend occasionally.

Reaching the top, Pollard led his prisoner into position under the dangling noose.

"You got any last words, Mrs. Stoner?" the sheriff asked, fully expecting her silent shake of the head in reply. "Then Doc here will say a prayer for your soul."

For the first time, she looked directly at the sheriff and spoke. "I want no prayers," she said coldly.

The sheriff swallowed nervously and took a frayed breath. It would have been nice to maintain some atmosphere of spiritual decorum. What was a hanging without a prayer? Yet, he wasn't about to deny a woman's last wish, as it were. He rubbed his whiskered, unwashed face and ventured a glance over the heads of the spectators toward Caleb's wagon. If he had hoped for some intercession from the town patriarch, he got none. Caleb Stoner focused on the gallows with a fixed, imperturbable gaze. No wonder he and the woman hated each other—they were too much alike.

Pollard cleared his throat. "Well, then, let us proceed."

He nodded toward Washburn, who shuffled forward and took up the dangling rope, hesitating only a moment before he slipped the noose around the woman's slim, pale neck.

Doc, not to be put off by the woman's wanton rebuff, stepped up to the prisoner. He wasn't about to be cheated from his own moment of glory in this momentous event.

"Let us pray!" he said grandiosely. But he couldn't look into the woman's eyes. " 'Our Father which art in heaven, Hallowed be thy name. Thy kingdom come. Thy will be done in earth, as it is in heaven. Give us this day our daily bread. And forgive us our debts, as we forgive our debtors—' " The doctor's voice gave particular emphasis to that final sentence before continuing. " 'And lead us not into temptation, but deliver us from evil: For thine is the kingdom, and the power, and the glory, forever. Amen!' "

When the doctor and part-time preacher was certain his words had had time to make their fullest impact, he began again in his most

18

pompous tone. He even ventured a brief look at the prisoner. "Mrs. Leonard Stoner, I commit your spirit into the hands of the Lord. May God have mercy on your soul!"

Washburn tightened the noose. Pollard noted the drifter's hands were shaking. The sheriff was feeling a bit queasy himself. The sound he thought he heard next must be his over-wrought imagination. In fact, if he were a man of mystical bent like the doc, he could almost have believed that the Grim Reaper himself was thundering toward town to claim his prize personally. Of course, Pollard knew that was pure bunk. But . . . it did sound like horses approaching, several of them.

3

THE CROWD HEARD TOO, AND HEADS began to turn toward the sound. It wasn't the sheriff's imagination. Horses *were* coming, and at a full gallop!

In another minute the riders appeared in the billowing clouds of rising dust, cutting a swath of horseflesh and noise right down the main street of Stoner's Crossing. There were eight of them, all with rifles and pistols drawn. Washburn gave a low whistle and lowered his hands off the noose. If this was some kind of rescue, he didn't want to be caught in the villainous role of hangman. He slithered back into the shadows. The sheriff couldn't blame him and would have liked to join him, but instead stood his ground, though his mouth was gaping at the sight.

The crowd frantically spread apart as the galloping horses showed no sign of slowing. The riders, all masked with bandanas pulled up over their noses, did not rein their mounts until they reached the foot of the gallows where they thundered to a halt. Immediately the drawn weapons were trained all around the throng of townsfolk, with two rifles aimed directly at the passengers of Caleb Stoner's wagon. Another gun was leveled toward the sheriff, still standing dumbfounded on the gallows' platform.

"Well," said the bearer of that weapon, "looks like we got here in the nick of time!" He was a rugged-looking man, perhaps even somewhat handsome under the layers of trail dust. His crooked nose, notable even beneath the taut kerchief, mediated between eyes filled with acid humor. He sat on his horse straight and tall, giving no doubt as to who commanded the band of riders.

"What do you boys want with us?" asked the sheriff, his voice none too steady—though who could blame him with a cocked rifle pointed at his head.

"I'll tell you, Sheriff, my feelings is just plumb hurt, that's all. Here you are having this fine hanging, and me and my boys wasn't even invited."

"You didn't need no invitation. Nor them—" Pollard cocked his head toward the weapons.

"Well, it's too late now," said the tall rider. "Our feelings are hurt too bad and ain't gonna feel better till we spoil all your fun. Right, boys?"

The other riders responded with several wild hoots and a few shots fired into the air.

"If you interfere with the law, you won't get away with it," said the sheriff lamely. He well knew he could do nothing to stop the man. The masks couldn't completely hide the fact that this was the Lampasas gang, and their leader, whose real name Pollard didn't know, had gained a reputation for rustling, bank robbery, and general cain-raising before the war. During the war they concentrated their larceny on the Union Army, perhaps to their credit; but in those months immediately following the war they had returned to their old targets, namely anything that offered the promise of making them a buck. No one could get a positive identification on them, and thus far they had enjoyed full rein in Texas and the territories.

Thus, the outlaw leader laughed boldly at the sheriff's words. "Try and stop me, Pollard!" His eyes were bright with challenge, seeming to want nothing more than an excuse to make use of his gun.

"And if we call your bluff?" A new voice rose, filled with menace and challenge. It was Caleb Stoner, and the force of command he projected was every bit as strong as the outlaw's, though it was raised in volume only enough to carry across the short distance that separated the two men.

"I reckon then, Stoner, you'll be the first to die!" replied the outlaw. "And you'll still be robbed of the pleasure of seeing your daughter-in-law hang."

"Why are you doing this?" asked Stoner, ice infusing his words, fire glinting from his eyes.

"I'm just a regular killjoy, that's all!" The outlaw laughed again. "You ain't hanging no one else, Stoner, as long as I can help it." He had lost two of his men by the rope last month because of Stoner, who had strung up the boys out on the range without benefit of trial or even listening to their side of it. Maybe they had rustled a couple of cows, but at least the outlaw's boys had never murdered anyone; he couldn't say the same for Stoner.

"You'll die for this!" spat Stoner, the edge of his reserve crumbling in his fury and in the knowledge that he would indeed be deprived of his long-anticipated revenge.

The outlaw leader threw back his head and howled. "The Texas Rangers wanted to hang me before the war, Stoner; now it's the United States Army; and I reckon half the lawmen in three territories wouldn't mind getting their hands on me. So, pardon me if I don't tremble at your threat."

He then focused his attention toward the sheriff. "Okay, Pollard, take that noose off the lady's pretty neck, and cut them ropes on her hands."

Pollard hesitated only a moment, wondering whose wrath he ought to fear more, the outlaw's or Caleb's. Well, reasoned the sheriff logically, the threat from the varmint with the gun was far more immediate. There might still be a chance to later wheedle his way back into Caleb's good graces if the outlaw didn't put a bullet in him. Of course, no one had ever proved Caleb *had* any good graces, but who would blame Pollard for obeying the outlaw with an arsenal of weapons ready to blow his and a score of other heads off—not to mention Caleb's head, too?

Pollard lifted the thick noose from around the woman's neck and, with a knife supplied by the doctor, sliced away the cords that bound her hands.

The sheriff didn't expect what happened next. Instead of showing relief at her rescue, the woman actually shrank back.

This was no less a surprise to the outlaw rescuer. He arched a single bushy eyebrow. "Uh ... ma'am, you are welcome to join us. That is, unless you prefer to take the trip Caleb had planned for you."

Still, she did not move.

"You don't have to be afraid of us, you know," the outlaw continued, though it was plain that fear was the last emotion discernible in the woman's eyes.

In another moment she seemed to make her decision and, stepping clear of her guards, approached the gallows' steps. The tall outlaw motioned to one of his men, who bounded up the steps, gave the lady a hand, and escorted her down and to his leader's horse. The outlaw leader reached down a long, muscular arm, grasped her firmly by the waist and hitched her up onto his horse. When she was settled in front of him, he returned his attention to the townsfolk.

"I don't figure any of you are crazy enough to follow us," he said, "but be warned, my men don't miss when they shoot, so at least eight of you are sure to die right off. If you're sure you won't be one of those unlucky ones, then come ahead."

His words sank in, and no one moved as the outlaws thundered away in another choking wall of dust. Mrs. Stoner was just one woman, after all, and no one was willing to risk his life just to see her die in the end, anyway. Even Caleb Stoner did not move, though his dark, foreboding eyes shot hate like venom after the retreating riders.

4

THE TORPID PRAIRIE SUN HAD DIPPED low in the sky before the gang of rescuers began to show signs of pausing in their flight. A couple of hours before, they had slowed their pace to a leisurely trot. But as confident as the imposing outlaw leader appeared, he knew it would take many more miles before they were adequately insulated from pursuit.

Tall yellow grass seemed to stretch endlessly out before them, sometimes flat, sometimes in low undulating hills that rolled like a golden sea. Occasionally broken by a stand of trees, a misplaced boulder or the gorge of a dried stream bed, the grassland went on for miles in every direction.

Travelers feared the prairie, and with good reason. There were plenty of stories about lost men who would follow their own tracks in circles for days, thinking they had happened upon another traveler who would lead them out of the grassy maze to civilization, only to die by a landmark they had passed several times. More than this, however, the heat and the scarcity of water plagued even the ablest of frontiersmen.

Griff McCulloch, seasoned outlaw, was not afraid of getting lost or of dying of thirst. He knew the land well enough, as one whose life depends on such knowledge must. He knew exactly where he was going and where to find the best water along the way. His main concern at the moment was far more perplexing—namely, what was he to do with his pretty little prize now that he had her. A woman was bound to slow them down eventually. And, besides all the other hazards of this land, they were in Indian country. There would be Comanches for certain, and Kiowa and Shawnee. This being the hunting season, they might also run into some Cheyenne, who had been none too friendly of late. Griff might be a cold-blooded outlaw, but he wouldn't leave a helpless woman stranded on the prairie. Despite the fact that this particular woman looked like she might be able to handle an Indian, he figured even she would be hard pressed in a pitched battle with a Comanche warrior.

"We'll be making camp shortly," McCulloch said, mainly to hear something besides the sounds of the horses. The woman hadn't said a word since leaving Stoner's Crossing. He reckoned she'd talk when she was ready, but he couldn't wait that long. It was too much having a woman that pretty so close and not even to be able to talk to her. "By the way," he added, "I'm Griff McCulloch, if you're interested."

She must have been tired of the silence too, because she finally responded.

"Where are we going?" she asked.

"I got me a hideout up by the Red River. It'll take a spell to get there."

Another long silence followed. Griff had always believed women to be powerfully curious creatures, and full of talk. He'd had an Indian squaw for a while, and even she could have talked the horns off a buffalo. He did not think it possible that a woman could be silent for four solid hours. It was enough to drive him to distraction.

"You want some water?" he asked.

When she gave her usual silent nod, he reached down to his saddlebag and got the canteen. It was nearly empty, and he hoped the spot where he planned to make camp still had water. He hadn't been there in a while. The woman drank a short swallow and handed back the canteen.

Another quiet, monotonous hour passed before the party of outlaws drew up to a grove of cottonwoods clinging to the edge of a spindly chocolate-colored stream. They'd just have to make do. They dismounted, and while three men were dispatched immediately as lookouts, the others began to set up camp. The horses were picketed and guarded, a small fire was built, and a pot of coffee set over it. McCulloch didn't like building a fire and tried to take care that it was smokeless. He wasn't too worried about a posse from Stoner's Crossing, for he felt certain his doubling-back maneuver a few hours ago had thrown them off—at least he had seen no sign of them. He was more concerned about Indians. Since the Sand Creek massacre in the winter of '64 when Colonel Chivington's Colorado Volunteers had slaughtered over four hundred peaceful Cheyenne, all the Plains tribes had become restive and dangerous. Griff hadn't seen any fresh Indian signs, but they had passed a sizable herd of buffalo a couple hours ago, and at this time of year you could almost count on Indians being where the buffalo were. He didn't want to take any chances, but he had been craving a cup of coffee all day and thought the risk was worth it. He stamped out the blaze the minute the coffee grounds had made a good, strong brew. The remainder of their dinner consisted of hardtack and dried beef.

He brought a tin plate of food and a tin cup of steaming coffee to the woman. She took it without comment.

At last his patience gave way.

"I suppose a fine-bred woman like yourself is too good to say thanks to a no-account varmint, even if he did save her life!"

"Thank you, Mr. McCulloch." Her voice was even, her tone contained little gratitude.

"Well, you are dad-blamed welcome!" he shot back, hardly mollified.

She spent a moment nibbling on the hard biscuit and sipping at her coffee. Then she looked over at McCulloch, who had seated himself on the ground a few feet from her with his own plate in his lap.

"Why did you do it, Mr. McCulloch?" she asked.

He knew she was talking about the rescue and not her dinner; he did wonder why it had taken so long for her to get around to it.

"It seemed like the thing to do at the time," he answered, his previous ire somewhat softened.

"You do not even know me."

"But I do know Caleb Stoner." He paused and, deciding to take advantage of the woman's uncharacteristic talkativeness, went on again. "Maybe you can answer me a question, Mrs. Stoner?" He didn't wait for her permission, doubting she'd give it. "You didn't seem none too anxious to leave that gallows today, and I been wondering why. I figured it was because you was feeling guilty over killing your husband and took it in your head that you deserved to die. But that

Stoner bunch is as ornery as you'll find, and I'll lay odds that Leonard Stoner deserved shooting."

"Are there any innocents in this world, Mr. McCulloch?"

"Some more'n others." He bit off a large chunk of jerky and, talking around it, continued. "Now, take me for instance. I've rustled my share of horses and cattle, and knocked over a bank or two, and a few Union pay shipments. And I reckon if they ever catch me I'll hang for what I've done. But I ain't never killed no one who didn't rightly deserve it, and I ain't never hurt no woman before, either. I ain't never been ornery just for the sake of being ornery."

One of the men who had been listening in on the conversation chuckled. "You're a regular saint, you are, Griff! Ha! Ha!"

"Aw shut up, Slim! I'm trying to have an intelligent conversation here."

"Now that's something I got to hear from you!" Slim laughed.

Griff was not amused. He had more in mind than mere talk with the woman and didn't like his plans interrupted, nor did he like being made to look foolish in front of the lovely lady whom he hoped to seduce. He drew his gun and aimed it at Slim's head.

"Seems to me, Slim," said Griff, with a low growl, "that it's your turn to take lookout."

"I was just having a little fun, Griff. No need to get touchy!" Despite his protests, Slim lurched to his feet and stalked away.

Griff holstered his gun and quickly returned his attention to the lady. "So, you see, ma'am, you don't need to feel remorse over what you done. Any man that hurts a woman ought to be shot."

"What makes you think he hurt me?"

"You don't look like no cold-blooded killer, ma'am. You would have had to have a good reason for what you done."

"The court did not take that into account."

"That's because they was all in Caleb's hip pocket. They believed what he wanted them to believe." Griff drained off the last of his coffee, spitting out a mouthful of grounds. "So, you really did kill him, then. . . ?"

"I thought you already knew the answer to that."

"Well, I assumed . . ."

"As did Caleb's court."

"Then you didn't?"

"Does it matter, Mr. McCulloch?" She paused, gazing into the fading embers of the fire. When she spoke again it was in a faraway tone, as if she had forgotten anyone else was present. "It would have

25

been better if it had all ended on that gallows. It would have been better for everyone—"

"Now, don't go talking like that, ma'am! I'm gonna start regretting sticking my neck out for you."

She seemed to focus with effort on her companion. "You shouldn't have, Mr. McCulloch. You may have brought yourself a great deal of trouble, for Caleb will not rest until I pay for what happened to his son."

"I ain't no stranger to trouble, ma'am." In that brief moment his flippant tone deepened and became almost introspective.

Mrs. Stoner asked, "And it's not something you enjoy, is it?"

Griff's voice softened. She had struck a tender spot in him. "You mean what I do for a living?" She nodded and he continued. "I never thought about it like that before. I mean, I didn't get into this business on purpose. It just sort of happened." He paused and poured himself another cup of coffee. He offered some to her, and when she shook her head, he sat back on his haunches and went on.

"Once I owned me a pretty piece of land down by Houston. My well went dry, and I had to dig me a new one. I had to borrow some money from a banker to do the job. Now, in Texas they say no one can take away a man's land for debts. Only that ain't exactly true; bankers have plenty of loopholes, as they call 'em. And this here banker used a lot of legal fine print to swindle me outta my place the first minute I fell behind in my mortgage. I had me a girl, too, and was all ready to get married; but when things went sour, I told her to find someone else, since I had nothing to give her. And she did, too.

"I was pretty mad at that banker. I got me a couple of friends, and we robbed that bank. There was no turning back after that, because we sure didn't want to go to jail. Anyway, it turned out I was pretty good at that line of work. And, believe me, it was a far-sight easier than slaving away on a piece of dirt for nothing but grief."

"And you have never known grief as an outlaw?" asked Mrs. Stoner.

"You know them two friends that helped me on the first bank job? Well, one of them is Slim over there; the other one Caleb Stoner hanged last month for rustling a couple of his cows. He was my closest friend."

"I'm sorry."

"I guess I got me some small revenge today. I been looking out for an opportunity. Rustling Stoner's cows just wasn't personal enough. What I did today got him real good. Why, I reckon it was even better than shooting him. Everyone knows what store he set by his oldest son. Not to get proper vengeance for his death—well, that must've hurt like the dickens."

"You can be certain of it, Mr. McCulloch."

They fell silent for a moment; then Mrs. Stoner asked, "What will you do with me now?"

The frankness of her question took him a bit unawares, despite the fact that he had been giving that issue a good deal of consideration all along. But he had not yet come up with a solution to the problem. He took off his soiled wide-brimmed hat and scratched his matted brown hair.

"I reckon we're stuck with you for a while."

"I could leave."

Griff laughed outright at that. "Ma'am, we're in the middle of hostile Indian country. If you try and make it alone, you'll just be saving Caleb the price of some rope. Besides, since you're here, I reckon we can make the arrangement mutually beneficial." He grinned in her direction, then said benignly, "I suppose you know how to cook and help set up camp so as to leave more of my boys free to scout and hunt and such like."

"And that is all?"

"Now, ma'am, what do you take me for?"

"You are an outlaw."

"Well, if you want to put it that way, Mrs. Stoner, it seems to me that now you're an outlaw, too."

For the first time since he had laid eyes on Deborah Stoner, a hint of amusement tempted the corners of her lips. It was no more than an ironic twist of the lips and far from a real smile, but the slightly twitching mouth and the brief glint in her luminous blue eyes was close enough.

Griff thought he was getting to her and decided to press his advantage. "I ain't never had the need to take a woman against her will, Mrs. Stoner, and I don't reckon to start now. But you just might soon enough find my charms irresistible." He gave what he hoped was an inviting grin, full of that promised charm.

"I am in mourning, Mr. McCulloch." Any humor that might have tried to invade her solemnity faded, replaced not by anger, but by a kind of desolate emptiness.

She seemed suddenly to retreat back within herself, leaving no doubt to the outlaw that the conversation was over. She turned her shoulders slightly away from him and gazed off in the opposite direction. Griff shrugged and rose to his feet. They would have plenty

27

of time in the next days on the trail to resume their dialogue and get more familiar with each other. He had no lack of confidence, either with a gun or with the ladies. But, he did think that for both his and Mrs. Stoner's sake, he ought to stake his claim on her soon. For the moment, his boys assumed he'd have first crack at the lady, but they wouldn't wait on him forever. He didn't trust some of his gang to know how to treat a lady proper-like. There was always a bad apple or two, especially in a gang of outlaws. And it had been a long time since any of them had had feminine company. Deborah Stoner, lovely as she was, posed too great a temptation.

Women did indeed cause more problems than they solved. Maybe Mrs. Stoner was right when she said he'd probably brought a heap of trouble with her. Griff ambled over to where the horses were picketed and gave his palomino an affectionate pat. Glancing back toward camp, he shook his head. She didn't look so strong and self-assured now with her knees hugged to her body, staring into the dead coals of the fire. She looked sad and lost and alone, and Griff felt more than a twinge of sympathy for her. Maybe she would have been happier to have died that day.

5

DEBORAH STONER HAD BEEN prepared to die that day in Stoner's Crossing. Though Doc Barrows, in his capacity as preacher, might have questioned her spiritual preparation, and perhaps she could not argue that point. She had convinced herself that death, even if it meant languishing in hell, was an improvement over the path her life had taken thus far.

And sitting there now, under a dim, moonless sky in the company of notorious outlaws, fleeing for their very lives, seemed only to emphasize the fact that nothing had essentially changed.

She had been acquainted for so long with pain and loss and misfortune that she had nearly forgotten there had once been a time in her life when she had known peace, even happiness. But in four years the memory of such times had all but vanished from her grieving mind. Sometimes, though, vague snatches of those days would try to torment her by returning in her imagination, occurring at odd moments with a carelessly spoken word, or at the sight of an insignificant object, or in a familiar look on a stranger's face—all conspiring to keep alive within her desolate heart a long-forgotten past.

Once a display of buttons in the general store had conjured up memory of another similar collection, kept in a basket at the foot of her mother's favorite rocker. Young Deborah loved to sit at her mother's feet and sort and count those buttons. But the sweetest memory was when Deborah was a few years older and she became the honored student of her mother's patient instruction in needlework. She could never decide what she loved more—hearing her mother's soft, gentle voice or watching the dear woman's nimble fingers move expertly over a piece of cloth, turning even a pair of socks into a work of art. Deborah never became as accomplished in her own work, for those beloved lessons had ended abruptly with her mother's death less than a year after they had begun.

A box of buttons in a store . . . it was too cruel.

Always a close family, the death of her mother, Carolyn Martin, only strengthened the bonds between Deborah and her father and older brother. Josiah Martin owned a prosperous farm in Virginia, and the family enjoyed a place among the notable gentry of the area. Mr. Martin and his children spent much leisure time together, pursuing their passion for horses, whether it be riding, breeding, or racing. Deborah and her brother Graham were expert riders, and Graham had brought several gold cups for racing to the family archives. The birth of a new foal was a family event, accompanied by as much pomp and celebration as Christmas or the children's own birthdays.

Deborah had laughed back then, giggling with delight as she'd watch a newborn colt's gangly efforts to stand on its four spindly, delicate legs. She thought there was nothing in the world more beautiful than a new foal, with those larger-than-life eyes, limpid and innocent. And though there were plenty of hired hands in the stable, Deborah and her brother were always given the responsibility for the foals. Mr. Martin taught his children a reverence for life through the wonders of God's awesome creation so vividly portrayed in the growth of those magnificent creatures. Many times he would tell them, "Remember, children, in the wonders of nature, God is revealed to the wise but hidden from the foolish."

In this loving atmosphere Deborah grew into a beautiful, sensitive young woman. Her protective ramparts had not yet been constructed, except perhaps in one small part of her that still mourned a mother whose love she had never had enough time to fully experience. But she still had her father and brother, and to them she opened her innocent heart, fearless and bold, unaware that the capacity to love is often measured as much by sorrow as by joy.

Deborah's fondest memories were of the stables and riding all over the enchanting Virginia countryside, to the extent that some neighbors chided Josiah that he was raising a tomboy. But she also remembered quieter, domestic moments. Deborah's father was a learned man and put much store by literature and poetry, and he passed this appreciation on to his children during the frequent evenings they spent together reading. Even now, so long removed from those days, Deborah could still close her eyes and hear her father's deep, resonant voice imparting Dickens or Scott or even the Bible. Almost as delightful as the reading were the lively discussions afterward, when Josiah encouraged both of his children to freely voice their views.

But without the presence of a woman in the house, Josiah was greatly challenged in the raising of his daughter. At fourteen she went to the Young Ladies' Day School, where she learned the art of southern gentility. Manners, attire, and decorum were taught fastidiously, and Deborah became a fine Virginia lady in spite of her frolicking out in the countryside. The more intimate aspects of a woman's lot, unfortunately, were sadly ignored. But Deborah had no concern for such things while she was within the sheltering arms of her family.

The War Between the States intruded cruelly upon all this. When her brother went away to fight in the summer of 1861, Deborah did not think a girl could feel so lost and lonely. Looking back from her present perspective, she could see how naive she had been, but that was the first time since her mother's death that she had to bid even a temporary farewell to a loved one.

Graham was her closest friend, for Deborah had never been one to open herself up to others. Her father was dear and she enjoyed his company, but it was not the same. He was not as eager to spur his mount into a pitched race with her as Graham was. When her father did, she knew he always let her win. Graham was fiercely competitive; when she won, she knew it was a victory of which she could be proud. Graham did not care about condescending to her femininity. He expected as much of her as he did of himself, which was a great deal. She loved him especially for that. When neighboring boys began to take more than a childish interest in her, Deborah could always speak frankly with her brother about these things and receive from him honest and loving advice.

She wished she had known that day when he rode away, looking so gallant and dashing in his gray uniform, that it would be their final farewell. Somehow she would have made more of those last days together, perhaps taken one last ride on their favorite horses upon the beloved estate. At least she would have wept more when he departed. But like so many foolish southerners, she had been caught up in the glory of the cause and the thrill of watching the heroic soldiers march away to war.

She had not even a vague premonition of what was to come. Like everyone else, she thought the war would be over in a few months and they could return unscathed to their horses and races.

But Graham was killed in the very first battle of the war. Bull Run might have been a technical victory for the South, but for Deborah it was no less than a jarring defeat. To lose her brother and best friend in one terrible instant was nearly devastating. Lost and empty, she could not even assuage her grief upon the back of her horse— that only deepened her pain as it made her recall the many happy hours she and Graham had spent riding. Josiah Martin attempted to sustain his daughter with his great faith in God. She tried to listen to her father's gentle admonitions, often accompanied by his own tears, that God works all things for good to those that love Him. She tried to believe that her father's God had some great purpose for calling her dear Graham home. And she tried to find hope in her father's faith. But as great a man as Josiah Martin was, as devout a believer, and as strong as his faith was in the ultimate victory of Christ, *his* relationship with God was not enough to carry Deborah's burden. She knew her father's God, but she was only vaguely acquainted with the personal God of Deborah Martin.

Instead of using her father's faith as fertilizer for her own, she began to resent it.

"I thought you loved him!" she once railed at her father in her pain. "But you seem to go on as if nothing happened."

"I go on because I must, Deborah. I go on because it would be an even greater injustice to Graham's memory to allow his loss to consume and destroy me. I go on because there is comfort and peace in the knowledge that he is in a better place now."

Deborah could find no such comfort for herself. She simply could not come to grips with a God who would so senselessly take away her friend and brother. Given time, her father's loving witness might have eventually worked its way into her spirit. But in a way, Josiah

31

did end up letting his grief consume him, and thereby also consume his daughter. It drove him to an act of pointless self-sacrifice.

Josiah Martin was not a political man. Like his friend and neighbor, Robert Lee, Josiah had never been an enthusiast for secession or war. He was not a slaveholder, and he abhorred that heinous institution. Yet he could not turn his back on his native state or on his friends who were marching off to war. This sense of loyalty became even more profound after the death of his son. Graham had died for this cause, his life snuffed out by the Union tyrants who would dominate a sovereign state's right to self-determination. Suddenly Josiah Martin became a zealous Confederate and joined Lee's regiment as a staff officer.

When he told his daughter of his decision to join the Confederate Army, she simply could not understand. "Haven't we sacrificed enough for that stupid cause?" she cried.

"I know it is hard for you to understand a man's duty, my dear. But it is *because* of Graham that I must go. How can I refuse the cause he saw fit to die for?"

She wanted to be brave, but her foundation for such a response was built more on sand than rock. And in the fall of '62, the pilings were knocked out of even that fragile foundation. Josiah Martin was with Lee during the Peninsula campaign when the South valiantly repulsed McClellan's attempts to take Richmond. He was at Antietam in the fall for Lee's first major defeat. And there, Josiah Martin himself fell, thus bringing further grief and pain to his daughter's life.

Lee himself had come to her to extend his sympathy and to assure her that her father had died bravely and nobly, but Deborah saw neither heroism nor pathos in Lee's account of Martin's last days. To her it was all pure futility. She felt as if her loved ones had been human sacrifices to a cruel and vengeful God who, instead of leveling wrath against sinners, did so against the just, the good, the gentle. Because her father was not there in her time of crisis to represent to her the true nature of God, and because she refused to hear it from anyone else, she allowed herself to believe the worst about her father's God.

With her growing despair she began to hate even the sight of the beloved estate. The horses, which her father had always believed so mirrored God's awesome love, brought pain instead of comfort. Yes, they reminded her of God, but the reminder tasted like ashes to Deborah.

Caleb Stoner was a distant relation on Deborah's mother's side of the family. How he learned of the tragedy in the Martin family

Deborah did not know, but men like that had ways of knowing things that would benefit them. He had traveled west in the early '40's, made a fortune in the California gold rush and used his wealth to start a vast ranch in Texas. He maintained loose connections with relations in Virginia, and even before the war had made overtures to Josiah Martin about the possibility of a union between their two children. Martin had turned Caleb down without even consulting his daughter, ostensibly on the ground that he could not bear to have Deborah live so far away. He felt no need to voice his further reluctance— that he never had liked Stoner, who had a reputation in the family as a hard, cold man.

Unfortunately Deborah was not privy to any of this insight. Upon learning that the beautiful daughter of Josiah Martin was not only still available but orphaned as well, Stoner again pressed the suit. Suitable women were simply too scarce in the West, and he wanted the best for his son. The fact that Deborah would now also bring a sizable inheritance into the marriage was of no small interest to Caleb.

What Deborah recalled of that first visit of Caleb and Leonard to Virginia were the fanciful insights of a young girl. Caleb was stern and rather intimidating, but Leonard was handsome, with striking, if a bit sharp, features. To Deborah's romantic naivete, his dark eyes were mysterious, and his aloof maturity worked to charm her rather than warn her. It did not occur to her that he was but a younger version of his austere father.

Caleb's offer represented what she was most looking for at the time—an escape from the war and from the constant reminders of her shattered world. Against the proof of harsh realities, she tried to convince herself that she might yet find happiness in that faraway land of Texas, married to a rancher's son. She did not hesitate to accept the offer.

However, from the vantage of an outlaw's camp, the shadow of the gallows only recently removed from her life, Deborah wondered at the utter fool she had been, thinking she could run away from pain and grief. Oh, how God, if He did indeed exist, must be laughing at her now! As if the death of everyone she had ever loved was not enough to teach her, a tiny spark of hope had still tried to ignite out of the dead coals of her life. She actually had thought she could find a new beginning as Leonard Stoner's wife!

What she found was a new kind of nightmare.

6

THE RAMPARTS AROUND DEBORAH'S heart were sturdy, but because they were built of sorrow and not stone, they were not entirely impenetrable. Try as she might, she could not shore up all the cracks. She desperately wanted to be hard, cold, unfeeling and numb to all the anguish and discouragement. If part of her was made of steel, there was yet another part, often buried deep in the core of her being, made of a softer fiber. And she could not completely quell her innately sensitive nature, the very part of her that made her able to feel her losses so deeply.

That first night in the outlaw's camp Deborah cried herself to sleep; mute tears heard by none save the God she had repudiated in her suffering.

Deborah hated herself for those tears of weakness, as she defined them. That was the kind of vulnerability that made her fair game for others to hurt. How else could Caleb and Leonard Stoner have so destroyed her?

She should have sensed her peril the moment she arrived in Texas and found only a hired hand there to meet her. Yet she had already begun to insulate herself against false hopes. If she expected nothing from these people, perhaps they in turn would expect nothing of her.

Nevertheless, their casual reception when she arrived at the ranch did prick the tender part of her nature. She was young, after all—only eighteen, and vulnerable. A portly Mexican woman opened the door for Deborah and ushered her into a spacious, well-built house. Obviously the man who had constructed it must have had great things in mind for it, and for himself. The furnishings were simple and rather austere with a decidedly Spanish flavor. That it was a home occupied solely by men was clearly evident, and in truth, no woman had lived there for over ten years.

The servant led Deborah into a parlor, then went in search of the *patron.* Deborah waited fifteen minutes before the master of the house appeared.

Caleb's first words to her were, "I see you continue to wear mourning."

Unprepared to respond to this blunt, unexpected comment, her face flushed with pink as she floundered for a proper response.

"My—my father has not been . . . gone a full year."

"No bride of my son's will wear black."

"Of course. I do not intend to wear black on my wedding day."

She began to gather back her wits, remembering that she had not been raised to cower before others, even a stern prospective father-in-law. How many times had her brother told her she was as capable as any man?

"My son will receive you at supper this evening, and I expect you to be dressed as befits such an occasion. In the meantime, Maria will show you to your room where you can rest and partake of some refreshment."

Only hindsight revealed to Deborah that this was a fitting introduction to what lay ahead.

She wished she had had some of that same hindsight that first day. Perhaps she would have thought better of her behavior, subduing her natural tendency toward independence. But she instantly rebelled at Caleb's heavy-handed welcome. The moment he turned on his heel and strode from the room, she decided she must stand up to this man immediately or forever be bullied by him. So she appeared for dinner that evening in black. Granted, the neckline was cut low with a sheer black inset, and she stretched her strict mourning even further by adding her mother's cameo to the ensemble, but the message was clear enough.

If Caleb silently fumed at this brazen disobedience of his orders, his son was quite enchanted with his father's choice of a bride, the black notwithstanding. In fact, the contrast of the somber color tended to set off to better effect the finely chiseled delicacy of her lovely features, especially the golden tones of her hair, pulled back into fetching ringlets, tied with a black velvet ribbon. He thought he was getting a fragile southern belle, indeed.

Leonard Stoner himself was a strikingly handsome man, tall and strong, with a muscular frame. His brown hair and brown eyes should have softened his angular face, but his eyes were penetrating and hard. At twenty-four, he physically resembled his father; even his charming manner could not entirely hide the innate arrogance common to both men. But it was this charm, and the ready smile accompanying it, that fooled Deborah at first. She did not notice then that his smile was empty of warmth. He inquired of her needs and her wishes, especially in regard to the wedding. He seemed most willing to put her at ease. He gave all appearance of being the perfectly bred southern gentleman.

Present at that first meal also were Leonard's two younger half brothers, Jacob and Laban. They were both half-Mexican, the sons of Caleb's second wife, who Deborah later learned had died when Laban was five years old. Laban, the younger of the two, was not yet fifteen, while his older brother was Deborah's age. They were dour, quiet young men. It became quickly apparent, even to a newcomer like Deborah, that these sons were held in far less esteem by their father than Leonard. Caleb never had a positive word to say to them, if he had any words at all. Leonard all but ignored them.

Dinner did nothing to soothe Deborah's tension. And later that evening, when three men from town stopped by for a visit, the tense atmosphere only thickened. When the men ambled into the parlor for brandy and cigars, Deborah naturally followed them. After all, they said they had come to welcome her! But, barring her way at the door, Caleb turned on her.

"What are you doing?" he asked in that throaty voice that ever sounded like a volcano about to erupt.

"I—I did not want to be rude to our guests," she stammered. Somehow Caleb always managed to reduce her to a babbling idiot.

"You are not needed," he said flatly, as if she were his house slave.

"Oh, let her come, Caleb!" said one of the men. "We so seldom get the pleasure of a pretty face around here."

Grudgingly, Caleb conceded, though he made it clear it was for the sake of his guests and not for her.

Most of the talk was of the war, in which Deborah had absolutely no interest. But when the conversation drifted to ranching, she perked up. This was a new realm to her, and she thought she ought to learn more about it if she was about to marry a rancher's son.

"I have always been curious why Texas has never thrived in the slave market," she said, speaking for the first time. "It might well be the rest of the South could learn something from you Texans."

Caleb flashed her a lethal look. She squirmed, thinking she had unwittingly stepped into a touchy issue.

"Darkies ain't very profitable for the cattle business," replied one of the guests. "The eastern part of the state has its share for the cotton crop, though."

"What exactly does it take to raise cattle?" Deborah asked again.

"Lots of grass!" laughed one of the men.

"I'm surprised you haven't made more of the cattle trade then." Deborah was perhaps getting carried away, considering Caleb's displeasure, but she felt as if this was the first intelligent conversation she had had since coming to Texas and she couldn't stop.

"No market." The guests were enjoying watching this beautiful young lady as much as she was enjoying talking. "We sell some in New Orleans, and even a few went to California before the war."

"The way they're multiplying on the prairies," added another guest, "something's going to have to give eventually."

"Have you ever considered foreign markets?"

"Don't pay. We lose too many cows in shipping."

Thus the exchange flowed for another half hour, during which Deborah forgot all about Caleb. But when the guests departed, he accosted her immediately.

"Your behavior tonight was appalling!" he said.

"My behavior? I—I don't understand."

"I thought you had been bred better than that, young woman! Parading before our guests as if you were a cantina hussy. Shameless!"

"I was merely conversing. I see no harm—"

"I'll not have our friends and neighbors thinking we are bringing a loose woman into this home."

Deborah gaped, speechless.

It was Leonard who stepped in with a conciliatory gesture. "What my father is saying, Deborah, is that in this home we observe a certain decorum."

"I was just talking!" she sputtered.

"You are young," Leonard said. "You'll learn." There was no gentle entreaty in his voice—rather, the words almost sounded like a command. But by comparison to Caleb, Leonard sounded like the voice of reason, and Deborah allowed herself to think he was different.

"She had better learn quickly," said Caleb. "The circuit rider will be here on Sunday."

"The circuit rider?" said Deborah, bemused.

"Yes," said Leonard, "for our wedding."

7

DEBORAH ATTRIBUTED NOTHING more than normal youthful jitters to that initial panic she felt upon hearing Leonard's sudden revelation of their wedding date. If only she had taken it as a sign and fled Texas at her first chance.

If nothing else, she had hoped to have time to acclimate herself to the new environment and the new people before her wedding took place. Yes, she had come in order to marry, fully realizing it was a marriage of mutual convenience, not love. Yet she had hoped, in her youthful romanticism, that she would have the opportunity to fall in love with this stranger before she began to share her life with him. Now she had only five days! Even for a young girl, that was hardly time enough to stir the emotions she was seeking. Yet she managed to convince herself that Leonard was handsome and charming, in his own way, and it would not be so difficult to fall in love with him eventually. She resigned herself, therefore, to the set date, and in the whirlwind of activity involved in making plans for the affair, she forgot her initial panic.

Caleb, for all his asperity, was not opposed to a festive celebration—especially if he could use it to affirm his esteemed place in his community. The marriage of his son to a genteel lady from Virginia proved such an opportunity. And, from the beginning, Deborah felt distinctly that she was on display, not as a person of worth, nor even as a gentleman's lady, but rather as a prize, a trophy, an object of no more worth than one of Caleb's thoroughbreds. And what was worse, she soon sensed the father's attitude in the son.

She wore her mother's wedding dress, which she had brought along for sentimental reasons and because she knew that wartime privations would probably prevent her from purchasing a new one. If she had looked lovely in black, then in the oyster white satin wedding gown, trimmed with antique lace and studded with pearls, she was stunning. The black had given her a fragile appearance; the white, almost an angelic one. But this was a vivid angel, with skin that glowed, hair that shimmered, and eyes that sparkled. For that day at least, she let herself forget her mourning and the emptiness she still felt when she thought of her lost loved ones. That day was one of the few times the citizens of Stoner's Crossing saw what a smile could do for the new Mrs. Leonard Stoner. And Deborah had to admit, it felt good to smile again, even if it did not completely well up from her heart but came more from her intellect, which told her that a girl ought to smile on her wedding day.

When Leonard slipped his arm through hers and they turned to face the guests for the first time as husband and wife, she truly believed her life was about to turn around. When her new husband kissed her lightly on the cheek, she detected a pride in his eyes, if not love, and she thought she could accept that. But a disquiet crept over her at the same time that she could not trace until later. For she noted something besides pride, something disturbing, making her smile momentarily fade. His penetrating brown eyes also wore a look of triumph. As quickly as the feeling of disquiet came, she shook it away. She was being trivial and overly sensitive. Men behaved stupidly around women and were apt to strut; that was their way. Leonard was a bit arrogant, she fully realized, but she told herself she preferred that to a coward or a bore.

It did not take a month for all her illusions to be shattered; it did not take a week. It happened that very night.

She was, of course, totally ignorant of the relations between a man and a wife. Maturing without the guidance of a mother had left her without a female confidante. And certainly such things were never discussed at the Young Ladies' Day School.

Was it possible. . . ? Did men commonly turn into animals when intimate with a woman? No other words could describe Leonard Stoner that night.

He led her into his bedroom, closing the door behind them firmly and turning the key in the lock. He nudged her immediately to the bed and began groping at her dress, never saying a word.

"Leonard, be careful. I don't want to tear my mother's dress."

How odd, that her first thought was of the wedding gown when her heart was pounding with fear and her body trembling.

"To blazes with your dress!" He yanked at the fabric, making buttons pop.

"Leonard, please!" She tried to move away, but his hands held her firmly. "Wait just a moment while . . . I get ready." She had no idea how one prepared for such a thing, but she was desperate for more time. She had begun to consider the possibility of fleeing.

"I've waited a week . . . watching you . . . that lovely, lovely body of yours move and tempt me. I have waited long enough!"

"I—I don't know what to do!" she blurted out, frantic. But if she hoped for a sympathetic reprieve from her new husband, it was an empty hope.

He laughed—a hard, dry laugh. "That's the beauty of it, isn't it?"

Then followed one of the most horrifying experiences of her life. Even the prospect of hanging from a gallows had not equaled it, and death certainly did not frighten her as much as the mere thought of intimacy with Leonard Stoner.

He ravaged her that night. He took his prize and had his way with it, deaf to her pleading, to her screams, to her anguished tears. And when he was done with her, he left the room and she spent the rest of the night sick and alone, her flesh feeling like filthy rags. Even the bath Maria drew for her in the morning did not fully cleanse her, though she scrubbed her flesh nearly raw.

The next night he came to her room, but she was ready this time when he came at her with that vile stain of lust in his eyes.

"Leonard, I am not feeling well tonight."

"You look perfectly sound."

"Please, I am just not up to it tonight."

"Are you refusing me?"

She shuddered at the stark accusation in his tone. She began then to realize that people did not refuse the Stoner men—at least not Caleb and Leonard.

"Of course not." Her voice shook weakly, unconvincingly. "But I . . . I just thought—"

"It is not your place to think, my dear. Leave that to the menfolk, for whom God intended it."

A brief smile flickered across her lips. Surely he was jesting!

"Are you laughing at me?" he demanded.

"You cannot be serious about women not being able to think," she replied. "Such ideas are becoming antiquated."

"Not in this house! And it is best you learn that quickly. Here, a man is still master of his house and his wife. Your place is only to look as lovely as you are and to service my needs. Remember that, and you will be happy."

"I have a mind, Leonard, and I plan on using it," she retorted, finding courage in her utter astonishment at his medieval attitude. "I am not your nigger!" She had never before used the derogatory term for Negroes, but it was the only way she could describe her husband's behavior toward her.

His hand shot up so quickly she did not even see it coming. The blow hit the side of her head, not her face, and it made her ears ring and her vision go black for an instant. She fell back against the bed, but she was stunned more from the shock of the unexpected attack than from the pain. It was the first time in her life that anyone had ever struck her. This was almost as shocking as his maltreatment of her on their wedding night. But when the initial shock faded somewhat, a new insight occurred to her. Perhaps Leonard was as ignorant about how to treat a woman as she was toward a man. If she could but suggest to him what could most make her happy, that might be all he needed.

"Leonard, this is all so new to us," she began, choking back the knot that had started to rise in her throat. "But it seems to me that gentle treatment might be more appropriate at a time like this. A woman responds much better to a gentle hand and a kind word."

"You would like that, my dear?"

"It would greatly help."

He snorted derisively. "My father was right about you. He called you a spoiled, strong-willed vixen. Give you a 'gentle hand' and you will ride all over a man. On the contrary, what you need is to learn quickly who is in control."

"That's not true!"

"Every word you speak tells me the opposite. Your very first act here was to defy my father. And now you would defy me. Deny me my marital rights, would you? Ha! Yours is a spirit that must be broken quickly."

And he had the power, the brute, physical strength, to do so. She could not fight him, at least not on a physical level. She had to surrender her body to him, but she clung desperately to her spirit. She refused to allow him to destroy it. Although at times she felt it had been crushed beyond help, still a spark always burned within her. She would not let Leonard or his father control her.

There were moments when she considered running away, or even killing Leonard, but those were acts for which she did not think she was desperate enough. After all, she was married to the man. Other women had survived unhappy marriages without disgracing themselves. So could she. She soon found that life could be somewhat tolerable if she kept her "place," as defined by her husband. And when he came to her at night, though she cringed, grit her teeth and had to choke down nausea, she found she could survive the ordeal.

Actually, it was harder for her outside the bedroom, in public, to maintain the unnatural ruse. One evening when several male guests came to dinner she carelessly spoke up during the discussion of politics. Later, out of the public eye—he was always careful about the image he projected to others—Leonard railed furiously at her for behaving like a "brazen hussy." How could this be the same man who had offered the voice of reason before their wedding when Caleb had blasted her for the same offense?

At first she retained a hope that Leonard could be won over by her feminine charms, that deep down she was more than an object to him. If only she could win him away from the corrupting influence of his father. She believed this probably because she had to believe in something; she had to have some hope that she was not locked into a life of misery. In time, Leonard would lose his youthful inse-curities that were no doubt the reason he felt compelled to control her.

But it was not long before even that slim hope was dashed.

One morning she arrived at breakfast with a bruise across her face where Leonard had struck her the night before. Caleb was there alone. He studied her, particularly noting the bruise.

"You will stay inside, today," he said.

"I had planned on shopping in town—"

"I said you will stay in."

"Are you afraid for people to see what he does to his wife?" She could not help the smug satisfaction the words gave her.

"Most men around here would applaud him for keeping a rebel-lious and self-willed wife in tow," he answered evenly. "It is to pre-vent your own shame that you will not go out into public."

Deborah could not believe he really cared a whit about her honor. His cool "fatherly" advice to Leonard when he came to the table seemed to confirm this.

"Leonard, do not strike your wife on the face again."

"She tried to tell me she had a headache again last night."

"There are other ways to deal with such behavior so neither you nor she is shamed."

Deborah could not help the glimmer of hope Caleb's words stirred in her. Perhaps she had misjudged Caleb. Maybe at last, he would instruct his son on the proper way to treat his wife.

"Never strike your wife so the marks can be seen," Caleb said. "It is very distasteful."

When the two men went off alone to Caleb's study, Deborah had no hope at all that their session together could possibly benefit her.

That night, as if to demonstrate his newly acquired skills, Leonard struck her several times. She had no visible marks afterward, though her whole body ached.

More than this, she realized that with his father goading him, indeed, *encouraging* him, Leonard would never change. She might have to resign herself to this abhorrent life forever.

8

A MONTH AFTER HER MARRIAGE, two things happened to offer Deborah a brief respite from her misery. First, Leonard went away. Second, she found a friend.

Leonard had been home only on an extended furlough from his duties in the Home Guard. When Indians on the frontier began harassing settlers, he was called back to duty. Deborah bade him farewell with all the decorum she could manage, only barely concealing her great relief at his departure. She felt as if a huge weight had lifted from her shoulders. She understood now what a runaway slave must have felt as he approached the Ohio River and freedom.

She fairly sang the first morning she awoke free from his sickening touch. She almost found herself smiling at breakfast and was hardly perturbed by Caleb's sour reaction.

"What are you so cheerful about?" he demanded, as if such behavior were an abominable crime.

"I don't know." She immediately tried to dull the obvious.

"Just remember," growled Caleb, reading her motives, "he'll be back."

She secretly hoped her husband would stop an Indian arrow and never return, but Deborah did not even want to admit that to herself.

She ate her meal quickly and hurried outside, hoping that Caleb's dark, grim eyes were not following her.

Ever since her arrival she had heard about the Stoner Ranch's stock of fine horses. At first the memories of home were still too sore for her to show much interest, but the love of horses was simply too deeply ingrained for her to stay away forever. When she made her first trip out to the stables, Leonard had reprimanded her for it.

"The stables are no place for a lady," he told her firmly. "If you would like to ride, one of the servants will bring a mount with a sidesaddle for you."

Deborah loved the environment of the stables as much as the horses themselves, and she hated to ride sidesaddle. She determined that in this, at least, she would have her way. After all, she had made her share of sacrifices for her husband. But with so many other adjustments to deal with, she put off further visits to the stables. When she discovered he was going away for several weeks, it seemed as good a time as any to get these people used to her presence in that area. Discovering how much she knew about the raising of horses, they might even come to welcome her.

Thus the first day of Leonard's absence, she took a handful of sugar cubes from the kitchen and headed directly for the stable. But with each step she resented her stealthy, back-glancing movement. One of the hired hands was in the corral saddle-breaking a chestnut filly. Resting her arms on the wooden rail, Deborah watched, entranced. The animal moved with such fluid grace it seemed a shame to confine her. The filly bucked several times as if to indicate her displeasure at the weight on her slender back, but the rider held on, and in a few more moments the chestnut took several spritely steps. She then pranced around the corral with only an occasional buck, finally settling down into an even gait. *Another Stoner filly was broken.*

She didn't hear the footsteps approach from behind. The voice startled her, even though it sounded friendly.

"I wondered if you would come out to see my father's horses."

It was Jacob Stoner.

Deborah had hardly spoken more than a few words to him or his brother in all the time she had been at the ranch. The two brothers were present only at an occasional evening meal, and even then were noticeably silent. Most of the time they managed to be gone. Deborah did not think they had rooms in the house—at least they never slept there, as far as she knew.

"Leonard does not think it fitting for a lady," Deborah replied, attempting to keep any rancor from her voice. She had no idea if this Stoner son would carry her complaints back to Caleb, who would no doubt find a way to make her pay for them.

"My brother does not think a woman is fit for anything but—" He stopped abruptly, suddenly embarrassed at his near-impropriety.

"My own father raised horses," Deborah said quickly to soften the awkwardness.

"Yes, I know. That's why I am surprised you stayed away so long."

"My brother and father and I found much pleasure together in our horses," said Deborah. "When they died, I did not think I wanted to look at a horse again. It brought too much sadness. I suppose that, along with Leonard's discouragement, was enough for a while."

"But once you love these animals, it is hard to get them out of your blood for long."

"Yes, exactly."

Deborah attempted a slight smile in her brother-in-law's direction and gave him a closer appraisal. He did not sound or act like the elder Stoners. His tone, the acerbic edge to his voice when he mentioned his father and brother, indicated that he had no great love or admiration for them. He was only three or four inches taller than she was, furthering the impression that he was not cut from the tall, lanky mold of his elders. Stocky and muscular, he was obviously no stranger to hard work. That, too, could be seen in his ruddy, sun-weathered complexion, though how much of that was from his Mexican heritage, Deborah could not tell. His black hair and eyes indicated that his mother's blood was dominant in him. His facial expression as he spoke to her was warm, almost gentle. She realized that her impression of him as a sullen, dour young man might well have been due only to the fact that she had seen him solely in the company of Caleb and Leonard. That was enough to make anyone sullen!

"Do you break all of your colts directly to the saddle?" Deborah asked, not wanting this pleasant exchange to end.

"That is the western way. There is often not time for extensive pre-training. But I think the cowboys consider it more manly to ride the buck out of a horse."

"Oh, you western men! You will set civilization back hundreds of years!"

He chuckled softly at this—by no means a hearty laugh, and rather tentative, but nonetheless sincere.

"I will show you the stable if you like," Jacob said.

"Oh yes, I would!"

As they started away from the corral, Deborah instinctively glanced over her shoulder toward the house.

"I saw my father take the wagon into town a few minutes ago," said Jacob. Pink instantly flamed across Deborah's face, and he added, "Don't worry, I understand . . . I am his half-caste son." The poignancy of his tone made Deborah's heart quake.

"I—I'm sorry." It was all she could say past the sudden ache that rose in her throat.

"Thank God for the horses," he said in a rather poor attempt at levity. "They help one forget. Come on." He took her arm, nudging her into motion.

He was right, of course, and she knew now why she had finally sought out the animals she so loved. They did make her forget, and they almost made her happy again.

Jacob spent the next hour showing her around. There were two thoroughbreds that had won cups in local competition, but Deborah had to do some probing to learn that Jacob himself had been the one to ride both horses to victory. He deprecated his feat with a casual shrug, saying, "Because I'm small I happen to make a suitable jockey." Deborah knew it took more than size to make a good jockey and told him so.

Besides these and several other fine stock horses, there was a new foal, only a week old. Deborah rubbed the new colt's fuzzy bay coat and fell in love immediately. She gave the foal's proud mother a lump of sugar and an affectionate pat on the nose. She and Jacob stood for several minutes, silently observing mother and son together.

"I never tire of watching them," she said.

"I'll bet you never tire of riding them either, eh?"

"Oh, Jacob, do you think I could?"

"Why not?"

She did not miss the irony in his tone as he asked the simple question. But that's why she had come out in the first place, to show her husband that he could not control her life as if she were his property. The fact that he was miles away, as was his father, did not lessen the boldness of her act. She had no doubt that her actions that day would somehow be reported back to Leonard and Caleb— though she felt certain not by Jacob.

It did not take long for Jacob to get two horses saddled. Deborah regretted that she had to ride sidesaddle, but she had not come dressed to ride and dared not return to the house to change, lest by some ill chance Caleb were there and tried to stop her. At that point, she was simply happy to be on the back of a horse again. When they rode out of the ranch house compound into the open country, Deborah had such a sense of release that she actually threw back her head and laughed. Suddenly she realized just how much of a prison that house had become, how much of a captive she felt. She also realized how lovely this country was, though vastly different from her home in Virginia.

She had passed her time during her journey west reading inform-
ative books on the subject of the frontier. In one book she had read
a poem that, until now, she had glossed over as mere poetic over-
statement.

These are the Gardens of the Desert, these
The unshorn fields, boundless and beautiful
For which the speech of England has no name—
The Prairies. I behold them for the first,
And my heart swells, while the dilated sight
Takes in the encircling vastness. Lo! They stretch
In airy undulations, far away,
As if the ocean, in his gentlest swell,
Stood still, with all his rounded billows fixed,
And motionless forever.

How well she could relate to that foreigner's words now! How
faithful, how accurate was that man's description! Others may have
spoken of the monotony of the prairie, but on that bright May morning, none of the dreary tedium stood out in Deborah's mind. To her,
the flat, open expanse offered freedom, where she could ride forever
and never tire. And the wild flowers! They speckled the low grass
with many shades of brilliant color. Jacob pointed out the Texas blue-
bonnet and the vivid Indian paintbrush. Deborah believed she could
live with Leonard Stoner for eternity if she could just ride every day
upon this fair prairie.

Later she would learn of the loneliness and desolation of these
plains, and of their dangers; but now, riding with a man who evidently
knew them well, she felt secure, content. When Jacob paused for a
rest beneath a small cluster of oaks, she was out of breath from pure
exhilaration.

That evening, however, she had to pay for her excursion. She had
managed to keep out of Caleb's way when he returned from town,
but he accosted her the moment she came down for supper. She had
reached the last step of the stairs as he was exiting the adjacent study.
Nothing short of a blind flight could have spared her a confrontation.
She would have to face him at supper, anyway, so she determined
not to back down from him. What could he do but browbeat her?
Could anything possibly be worse than what his son did to her every
night?

"Good evening, Mr. Stoner," she said promptly, her head high, her tone defiant.

He focused such a cold gaze at her it made her shiver.

"You were at the stables today?" he said.

"I was."

"And you rode?"

"I did."

"I believe my son made it clear such behavior was not acceptable."

"I see nothing wrong with it. It is the one thing around here I enjoy." Although she quailed inside, she leveled an unflinching eye at him.

"My son will be married to a lady, not some saddle tramp."

"Your son is stuck with me as I am with him." Then a deliciously wicked thought popped into her mind and nothing could prevent it from escaping her lips, nor could she prevent the spiteful grin that accompanied it. "If he doesn't like it, let him divorce me!"

Caleb's hand shot up, clipping her heavily on the side of the head. She winced and gasped at the sudden shock of the blow, though her aroused anger quickly blotted out her pain.

"You dare!" she seethed, almost speechless in her fury.

"Be assured, Deborah, that in this battle of wills, you will be the loser. There is no way you can win except in submission."

"Will you beat me to death if I don't submit?" she retorted.

"I do not think it will come to that." His tone, however, implied that he would not be opposed to such measures.

"Well, I *will* ride and go to the stables! The only way you can stop me is to hold me prisoner."

She did not wait for him to reply; instead, she strode away as if she had every confidence that she had indeed won. And, suppressing her burning urge to retreat to her room, she went to the dining room and sat in her usual seat. She refused to give him the satisfaction of watching her run from him. He joined her a few moments later, and Maria served the meal despite the silent tension.

Deborah ate every morsel, regardless of the knots in her stomach.

When she wasn't appalled and horrified and frightened by her impossible situation and her disastrous marriage, she was simply mystified. How could two men possibly behave so inhumanly? Sometimes she wondered if it wasn't somehow her fault, that if she knew better the mysterious ways of marriage and knew the right things to say, perhaps Caleb and Leonard would respond differently. She had never had to worry about such things with her father and brother,

48

though perhaps it was different because they were family, her own blood. But with Jacob she had no need to calculate her every word and action. Perhaps it was different with husbands and fathers-in-law.

As Maria served coffee at the end of the meal, Deborah found that confusion had begun to overcome some of her anger. Perhaps she just had not tried hard enough with Caleb. He had to have some sense of reason.

"Mr. Stoner," she began contritely when Maria had departed, "I believe I have somehow displeased you—not just today, but almost from my first day here. If that is so, I truly wish for peace in this household, as I know you must also. It is not too late for us to start over again. I'm sure we can work out a mutually agreeable relationship."

He seemed to ponder her statement, his eyebrows slightly arched in a mixture of surprise and satisfaction. Perhaps she was coming around after all. He said, "You have but to assume the role of the submissive and dutiful wife, Deborah, and we will all be 'mutually' benefited."

She struggled to keep her tone even. "I realize I can be strong-willed at times, Mr. Stoner, and I have no doubt I have room for some change. But I do think the same can be said for Leonard."

"He is your master, Deborah. It is you who must change to suit him."

"That's ridiculous!" she snapped, all her attempts at contrition instantly dissolved. "Why, you and your son make Genghis Khan appear tame! I wouldn't change for you if . . . if my life depended on it!"

She pushed back her chair, knocking it over in her haste to jump up. Now she wasn't fleeing in fearful retreat, but rather escaping because she could no longer trust what she might say or do next if she remained.

Caleb's ominous rebuttal stopped her at the dining room door.

"Don't let it come to such extremes, Deborah."

She spun around, glaring at him. "And just what does that mean?"

"Life and death are relative terms," he answered. "You are married to my son for life. It is entirely up to you if it will be a living death, or a life of contentment."

"There are other choices!"

"If you are thinking of running away, be assured you would never get farther than town before you are stopped. And if you try to take any other direction, you would not last a day alone in this country, even on my swiftest horse. Besides, I don't think you would want to live with the shame for the rest of your life."

Maybe he was right. She didn't know. Maybe she ought to give it up, do what they wanted her to do, though she wasn't even certain she could. Maybe fighting it did only make matters worse. Perhaps Leonard would treat her better if she gave in to him. Yet these thoughts of submission only made her feel as if the prison doors were closing in on her again.

It wasn't fair! They were asking too much.

Then she had a peculiar thought. How did slaves do it? She had seen many slaves in Virginia, even if her family owned none themselves. They shuffled along so docilely, peacefully, by all appearances; sometimes they even looked content, happy. How did they manage it? Surely it was not possible that they really were happy in such straits, no matter how benevolent their masters might be. It must have taken years and years, even generations, to control those poor creatures. Perhaps given a few years in this house, she, too, could manage it. A creature could be beaten down only so much before breaking. She pictured herself ambling along like a dispirited slave, kowtowing to her husband with an empty grin on her face.

Could that really be what he wanted?

It seemed impossible. Even more impossible was the notion that she could actually behave so. Somehow she must find a way of surviving without losing the essence of who she was. Escape might be out of the question, for the time being, at least. Caleb was right about that. But she could survive, and perhaps even win a battle or two in the process.

9

IN THE DAYS THAT FOLLOWED, Deborah found at least temporary means of survival in the horses and the open prairie. And, oddly enough, Caleb did not confront her about it again. Perhaps even he realized a person could be pushed only so far. Or, perhaps, he was just waiting for the return of Leonard, who had a far more effective means of crushing her impertinence. Whatever the reason, Deborah took full advantage of her new freedom.

For several days Jacob joined her on those delightful, long rides, made even more pleasurable with his presence. It had been so long since she had been able to converse on an intelligent and friendly level with anyone. She did find Jacob to be quite intelligent, for all his lack of formal education, and he was an extremely sensitive man. In personality, he was unlike Deborah's brother, Graham, yet a relationship began to develop between her and Jacob similar to what she had once had with her brother. It was growing into a true friendship. Suddenly she did not feel so alone, so stranded and desolate.

He talked freely about himself, as if he, too, hungered for such a friend.

"My mother was the daughter of a great *patron* down in Mexico," he told her one day. "She was very beautiful and could have chosen from among many caballeros for a husband."

"Why, Caleb, then?" asked Deborah, hardly able to fathom how a woman could be attracted to such a man.

"Twenty years ago, Caleb was a very handsome man. Sometimes women just assume such a man must have a heart to match."

Deborah looked away. "Yes," she finally sighed. "Leonard also seemed like such a gentleman before we married. I suppose I saw some hints of his father's sternness, but I didn't think much of it because he was so good-looking. Sometimes he was actually charming."

"Of course he was," Jacob replied caustically. "He wanted to snare his genteel southern lady. He wouldn't do anything to risk you changing your mind. Being so congenial, even for a week, worked quite a hardship on him though, and more than a few of the peons on the ranch felt the lash of his heavy hand during that time."

"How could I have been so blind?"

"I wish I had warned you, but at the time I did not know you and did not give it thought. It seemed impossible that there should be a repetition of such a thing."

"I wouldn't have believed you, anyway," said Deborah.

"At least you can take comfort, Deborah, that you are not the only woman to be deceived by a handsome man," he said, full of sympathy.

"There are some good-looking men with hearts to match," said Deborah. "You are proof of that, Jacob."

He gave a self-effacing shrug, but she could tell by his eyes he appreciated the compliment. No doubt he received very few.

"I don't understand one thing, Jacob," Deborah continued after

51

a brief pause; "both Caleb and Leonard seem none too tolerant of other races. They treat you and Laban almost as badly as they do their servants, which is no better than demeaning and condescending. Their Mexican servants and hands fare even worse. Why would Caleb marry a Mexican woman, considering his intolerance?"

"Very simple. My grandfather offered a large dowry, including several large sections of this very ranch. And back then women were even more scarce in Texas than they are now. By lowering his standards a little, Caleb got much—many pesos and cattle, land, a beautiful wife, and two more peons—my brother and me—to work his land. The shame of two half-breed sons is a small price to pay, eh?"

"I'm sorry for you, Jacob. You don't deserve to be treated so."

He reined his horse to an abrupt stop and swung around in his saddle to level his dark gaze fully on Deborah as she came up next to him.

"Don't feel sorry for me, Deborah! It's the last thing I want from anyone—especially you!"

"It was a foolish, thoughtless thing for me to say. I guess I feel as sorry for you as I do for myself."

The momentary fire in his eyes softened. "You should get out of here, Deborah, while you can."

"I could say the same for you."

"My grandfather is dead and his lands are gone, or maybe I would go to him. Where else would I go? I like the ranch and the land here. It will never be mine, but if I stay perhaps I will get some inheritance. Anywhere else in Texas I would be nothing more than a Mexican peon, a greaser. So why not stay here where at least I have some small hope of getting something? Besides, I could never belong in the East with all those people. I have thought about California . . . maybe someday. In the meantime, Caleb is my father, the only family I have. It's not so easy to turn your back on family. And then, too, there is Laban. I wouldn't want to abandon him like that."

"He ought to go also."

"He wouldn't go."

"For the same reasons as you?"

"Who can tell? Laban is a puzzle. He doesn't talk much. You would think we'd be close, being in the same boat and all, but it's not so. He is as closed and unreachable as a faraway planet." He paused, then asked, "And what about you, Deborah?"

"Leonard is my husband. I have to keep hoping, too."

Jacob frowned, and a dark look of remembered pain flickered

52

across his countenance. "You should go," he said flatly, then spurred his mount into a vigorous trot.

After a week of these rides—the best week Deborah had known since her brother's death—she began to sense it would be unsuitable for her and Jacob to continue to ride together so frequently. She knew the countryside well enough now and, using this as a convenient excuse, thanked Jacob for his patience with her and released him from further obligation of attending her. He seemed to understand her real motives, and believing them to be wise, did not protest. Yet both experienced an overwhelming emptiness from the severed friendship.

It wasn't long, however, before Jacob "accidentally" began to happen upon her on the trail. They both knew almost at once that it was more than mere chance that brought them together. They hungered for companionship, especially Deborah who, all her life, had known only warmth and kindness and love from those close to her. She began to look for Jacob while she rode and was disappointed when he did not show up. Soon, they began to plan their meetings, finding secluded places where no one would chance upon them. It was all innocent. They were friends and nothing more, but both knew Caleb and Leonard would never be able to understand such a friendship.

When Leonard returned home a month later, Deborah needed Jacob's friendship more than ever. Leonard was furious with her for defying him about the stables. As with Caleb, she held her ground and declared she would continue to ride when she pleased. He made her pay for her impudence that night in bed. She was bruised all over from his rough and demeaning treatment, but the marks were not in places that could be noticed by others.

He locked her in her room for two days without food. When he let her out on the third day, she went to the stable and saddled up. He chased after her and fairly dragged her back. When he pushed her once more into her room, something happened inside Deborah. Perhaps it was the beginning of that "breaking" Leonard wanted, but she was too desperate to care. She fell on her knees before him.

"Please, Leonard! Let me ride and work with the horses . . . I beg you!" She wept like a slavering servant. "I will do anything if you will just do that. Please!"

Leonard may have hoped for such contrition from his wife, but when it came, it was unexpected nonetheless. His initial surprise, however, was quickly replaced with a gleam of triumphant cunning in his hard eyes.

"*Anything?*" he said softly, as if even then he could not believe his good fortune.

"Yes!" she answered without hesitation. If she must live in misery, at least she'd have her one island of pleasure.

In the next months Deborah played her part well, living up to the letter of her bargain. When guests came to the house she was the demure, meek wife attentive to her husband's needs and to those of the guests, who were mostly male. When the conversation turned to subjects that interested her and on which she had a valid opinion, she clamped her mouth shut. Once a rather progressive Texan ventured to actually ask her opinion.

"I understand, Mrs. Stoner, that your family was acquainted with General Lee. Will he be able to carry the South to victory?"

Instinctively, she opened her mouth to give an intelligent reply. She knew Lee and knew him to be a great general, but the South needed more than great generals to win against northern economic might. But just before the response slipped out, she glanced at Leonard and saw an expression that almost dared her to give him cause against her.

So, instead of the answer she wanted to give, Deborah giggled inanely. "Oh, fiddle-de-dee!" she tittered. "However should *I* know such a thing?"

If she had hoped by submission to gain a reprieve from Leonard's abuse, she was disappointed. She gave him less overt cause, but she soon learned that Leonard enjoyed violence for its own sake. He needed no logical reason; he received pleasure from controlling others, and when he could dominate them physically as well as emotionally, all the better. This was apparent in the abominable manner in which he treated their servants. Luckily they had no slaves, for Deborah shuddered to think what their lot would have been like on the Stoner Ranch.

Her daily escapes to the stables and her rides on the prairie did make it somewhat bearable. Her friendship with Jacob infused sanity into an otherwise demented situation.

The new foal also brought an unexpected joy to her life. She took the colt under her wing, naming him "Prairie" because his sandy coat reminded her of the surrounding land in the midst of a blazing summer. Jacob laughed, but never derisively, at how she pampered the horse. He said it was about time someone on Stoner's land got a little pampering. And, as she had hoped, the stable hands even came to respect her equestrian knowledge. She won over the head groom entirely when she cured a mare of kicking the side of her stall just before feeding time.

"Get a child's ball, no larger than the size of my fist, and tie it with a short, soft cord to her fetlock joint," Deborah suggested. "She'll get the message soon enough when that ball hits her joint every time she kicks."

It worked, and it wasn't long before the man came to her for other advice. The stable became her haven, the one place where she not only had respect but some measure of control as well. After hours of playacting with her husband, it was a release to come to a place where she could be herself and remember how it used to be. Ironically, she had come to Texas to escape the painful memories of the happy life the war had destroyed. Now, in desperation, she grasped almost frantically at those memories. She *needed* to remember that happiness was possible in this grim world.

10

ONE SUMMER MORNING, AFTER Deborah had been in Texas a little over a year, she took Prairie out to one of the pastures for some exercise. He was still a colt, only a year old, and had several more years of growth to go, but already he showed signs of becoming a fine animal. Because he had been handled from birth, he was good-natured and fearless of humans. His quickness in training marked him as quite intelligent as well. Deborah recalled a verse from the Bible her father was fond of: "Hast thou given the horse strength? Hast thou clothed his neck with thunder?" To Josiah Martin, such beauty was one of the most profound testimonies to the love and grace of God. And Deborah, on that clear, clean summer day as she watched her colt prance over the grass with such elegance, could almost believe again in her father's God.

But the shadow of her present life, never far from her even on a pleasant day like that one, proved too strong for more than a glimmer of light to penetrate her private fortifications. Deborah could not help but contrast the verse from Job with something from Shakespeare more apt to her present situation.

"A horse! A horse! My kingdom for a horse!"

Well, what if *she* had sacrificed her very self for a horse? Even God, if He cared at all, could not deny her this one pleasure. Prairie was well worth the sacrifice.

Her attention was momentarily diverted from the frolicking colt when she saw a rider approach. It was Jacob. She wasn't surprised, since a place where they often met was nearby. She smiled and waved an enthusiastic welcome.

"Ah, the 'little prince' is looking good!" he said when he saw the colt.

"He is grand, isn't he?" She grinned like a proud parent.

"Thanks to you, Deborah."

"Only if love makes a fine horse."

"You'd be surprised how much good a little love does."

She turned suddenly solemn. "No, Jacob, I wouldn't be surprised at all."

They both grew pensive for several moments. Clearly they were not speaking only of horses.

When Jacob broke the heavy lull, his voice was more intense than usual. "Let's go down to the creek, Deborah. I want to talk."

The colt followed along as Deborah and Jacob steered their mounts to the creek gully about a quarter of a mile away. Even that early in the summer the water in the creek was low and muddy, but there was a healthy clump of cottonwoods along the edge and the ridge of the stream bed somewhat concealed the horses when they were tied to the branches of the trees. Deborah and Jacob dismounted, secured their horses and Prairie, and sat under the thin shade of the trees.

"Deborah, I have been thinking about many things, lately," Jacob began without preamble.

"So, that's why I haven't seen you all week," Deborah replied lightly, trying to offset his intensity.

"I am going to leave the ranch."

The unexpectedness of his statement and its sheer bluntness made Deborah's stomach lurch as if her world had once more been yanked out from under her. She had often thought that for his own good he should go, yet now that they had become so close, she did not think she could survive without him. She simply could not respond to his words without all her own selfish motives confusing the issue.

"Deborah," he went on, "I want you to come with me. It would be the perfect solution to everything."

"Jacob—"

He broke in quickly, afraid of her refusal. "I am in love with you, Deborah! I cannot bear for you to be with my brother another minute."

She closed her eyes to force back the tears that suddenly rose in them. But the tears squeezed through anyway. It was inevitable; she and Jacob needed each other too much for it to have remained as simple friendship for long. It did not surprise her to realize her tears were mostly of mourning and loss, for now they would end up with nothing.

Jacob reached up his hand and gently brushed away the tears from her cheeks. When had Leonard ever touched her like that? Before Deborah knew what was happening, she was in Jacob's arms. He did not grab her or pull her as Leonard would; instead, they just seemed to flow together in an embrace of mutual hunger and passion. And Jacob's was the touch of a man who cared for her, not as an object, but as a person of value. When their lips met, it was with tenderness, and she felt a kind of reverence emanate from Jacob's being. She did not want it to end. She wanted always to feel his strong, gentle arms around her, and his tender lips against hers.

But she knew it must end.

Not only was it wrong, against all the moral fiber that had been built into her since childhood, but she knew that if Leonard ever found out, he might well kill them both. She had never wanted to admit it, but she knew that deep within herself she was terrified of her husband. She already knew in part what he was capable of, and no doubt he had many more heinous ways of making not only her life miserable, but Jacob's as well. Were a few moments of pleasure worth destroying two lives for?

In spite of all her reasoning, it was only with great effort that she pushed herself away from Jacob. It surprised her that Leonard's abuse had not soured her completely on the prospect of physical closeness with a man. But perhaps such needs were too elemental to be eradicated completely. Thus, though her whole body trembled with desire, perhaps even with love, she turned her face away from the force of his kisses. For a brief, terrifying moment, when he did not immediately stop, she feared he would *compel* her to comply. How could she be certain that was not the way with all men?

But Jacob did stop. Despite the pain and regret in his eyes, he fell away from her, and for several moments neither could speak or even move. Deborah continued to weep, her tears now completely from self-pity.

Finally, Jacob spoke, his voice filled with bitter irony. "My brother has everything! I hate him, Deborah. God forgive me, but I hate him!"

"Jacob, he doesn't have my love. He never will."

"What does it matter? I *would* fall in love with an honorable woman!"

"I doubt it has anything to do with honor," she replied, her tone mirroring his bitterness. "I just can't give him the satisfaction. He would destroy us both."

"He is destroying us, anyway."

"Jacob, how I wish it could be otherwise!"

"Do you, Deborah?" Hope once more infused his words.

"Oh . . . it is so tempting."

"Maybe it is wrong—perhaps a sin. But do you think God wants you to live always in such misery? Isn't what my brother does to you a worse sin? Let him pay for a change! Imagine his shame when it gets around that his wife ran off with another man—his own no-account Mexican half brother! Let Leonard suffer for once."

"I fear that what we feel for each other, Jacob, is too mixed up in what we feel toward Leonard."

"I love you, Deborah—because of *you,* not in order to get back at my brother. But I'd feel no sorrow if that were the effect."

Slowly Deborah shook her head.

Jacob went on, more emphatically now. "I will tell you something, Deborah, before you make your decision. I have made no mention of this because I didn't want to frighten you too badly. But now perhaps you need to be frightened into seeing just what kind of place this is." He paused, appearing reluctant to continue, but he did so with great resolve. "You have never asked how my mother died. But I will tell you now. She took her own life. Do you hear me, Deborah? She killed herself! She took a knife and cut the veins in her arms until she bled to death."

"Jacob, no!"

"I don't know all of the horrors you suffer with Leonard," Jacob went on in a strained voice, "but I know a little of my mother's. Caleb treats his horses better than he treated her. I was only a boy, but many mornings I would come upon her weeping in her bed. I did not understand why she should be weeping, but I beheld her haunted, ghastly eyes. My mother was a devout Catholic. But Caleb would have none of that papist apostasy in his home. She always kept her faith secret, but she never gave it up. To her it was a mortal sin to take her own life, but she was willing to risk the fires of hell rather than spend the rest of her life with my father. She left me a note when she died. She put it where she knew I'd find it but not Caleb. In that note she begged me to forgive her for deserting Laban and me, for leaving us alone with him. She said she could not go on any longer, and must place us in the hands of God." He paused, taking a ragged, anguished breath. "That, my dear, sweet Deborah, is what lies ahead for you if you stay here."

Empathizing with his pain, she could hardly speak, but now, more than ever, she had to convince herself of the logic of going on with her marriage. And she tried to convince Jacob, too. She argued that it was different for Jacob's mother, who was Mexican. No doubt a white wife would receive better treatment, although even as she spoke she knew by experience how lame that reasoning was. But Leonard was not Caleb, and she was Leonard's first wife. There was still hope of changing him. Jacob just listened, sadly shaking his head.

"Come with me, Deborah," he entreated, "before it is too late!"

"I can't."

"How can you still be faithful to him? He doesn't return the favor to you. I have seen him go to the cantina in town and visit the women there."

"All the men go to the cantina—"

"After all you have been through, you cannot yet be so naive."

She shook her head dismally. "It has nothing to do with that. Jacob, I am expecting Leonard's child."

He responded with a stunned gasp. "Dear God, no!"

"You see why I must stay. I can bear my own shame, but not my child's. And I think it will make things better. He wants a child; it'll make him happy and maybe think better of me."

"It did not help my mother," Jacob replied.

"For all his faults, Leonard is not as cold and hard as your father." Oh, how she wanted to believe that!

Jacob said no more. If she must stay, why should he destroy her hope, flimsy as it was? She would have nothing else to comfort her. But the pain his silence caused ripped like a blade through his soul.

"Will you still go?" Deborah asked at length. She hated herself for asking, but she desperately hoped that somehow they could remain as they had been before.

Jacob knew that was impossible. "How could I stay now? I fear I would kill him if I saw him hurt you again."

"I knew my happiness could not last forever—"

The sudden sound of a galloping horse forced her to stop. She and Jacob exchanged a panicked glance. The approaching horse was heading right for the gully.

11

JACOB JUMPED UP WHEN LEONARD'S mount crested the ridge of the gully. Jacob's and Leonard's eyes met—hatred and challenge on one face; fury and accusation on the other. Deborah pulled herself up to stand beside Jacob. Her legs were trembling. She did not see how this could end in anything but tragedy.

Leonard swung from his horse and loped down the side of the gully. He was wearing a gun, but it was that look in his eyes, not the weapon, that frightened Deborah most.

She shuddered when that cutting, chilling gaze focused on her.

"So, in addition to everything else, you are a tramp as well!" Leonard spat.

Jacob stepped forward, his hands knotted in tight fists. He had never stood up to Leonard before. It was time he started. "Take care what you say, Leonard!" he warned.

"You will come to the defense of your cheap lover—how noble! And you nothing but a half-breed bastard."

Jacob knew his brother meant that final word in all its truest meaning. He would never be more to his brother, or to his father for that matter.

"I don't care what you say about me," Jacob rejoined as calmly as he could, "but if you speak that way against Deborah again, I swear I will kill you!"

"Ha! You don't have the nerve. All you are good for is making my wife into a common whore—"

Jacob had no weapon, but he didn't need one; his years of pent-up hatred were enough. He sprang on his brother with animal fury, knocking him down, pummeling his face with unrelenting blows. The speed and surprise of his attack was sufficient to give Jacob the advantage for a few moments, and he made the best use of it. Before Leonard gathered back his wits, his face was streaked with blood.

But the next time Jacob aimed a punch at his brother, Leonard grabbed his wrist and repelled the blow forcefully, pushing Jacob's solid body back far enough for Leonard to roll away from him. Immediately both men leaped to their feet, but Leonard was first to launch a counter-offensive, charging Jacob. As Leonard's full weight fell against him, Jacob stumbled back, but he did not fall. Instead, he sprang toward his foe, fists flying. He landed two or three more punches, but Leonard was far from beaten. He came back at Jacob with a barrage of punishing blows to his face and midsection. Bent over, gasping for breath, Jacob didn't see the boot aimed at his face. The blow shook his teeth and brought blood spurting from his mouth. The force of the kick knocked him into the shallow creek. He had barely hit the water when Leonard flew bodily at him.

They struggled in a vicious clinch for several moments before Jacob finally gained the advantage, buffeting Leonard fiercely from the right and left. He thought he felt Leonard's body go limp beneath him, and he eased his attack.

That was all Leonard wanted. Unseen by Jacob, Leonard's hand moved to his side.

Deborah screamed. "Jacob, his gun!"

But it was too late. Leonard drew and fired. Jacob fell back, blood dripping from his arm. Leonard took aim again, this time unobstructed by Jacob's close attack. The pistol was aimed squarely at Jacob's head, the hammer cocked.

Deborah ran to her husband. "Leonard! Please don't! Let him go."

"It is my right to kill him," Leonard panted, his eyes glazed with the fury of a crazed animal.

"There was never anything between us but friendship," she insisted, although she knew Leonard would never believe her.

"Ha! I have heard about you sneaking off together."

"Don't hurt him, Leonard. I beg you!"

"And with what will you seal *this* bargain, my dear? I don't think you have anything left to bargain with."

He was right. She had nothing. Leonard's power over her was complete, and because of her utter helplessness, Jacob would die. How she despised her weakness! But in those brief moments of despair, a resolve began to form in her. Somehow she would not let Leonard Stoner defeat her! She would win, and she would never be helpless again. That sudden resolve, however hollow and absurd, did manage to spark in her, if nothing else, a physical rush of strength. And that was all she needed to gain a brief instant of mastery over her husband and secure Jacob's safety.

She bolted at Leonard.

She was not heavy enough to knock him down under normal circumstances, but because he was balanced on one knee in the water, with his gun aimed and most of his attention focused on Jacob, the force of her attack effectively pushed him off balance. He toppled into the water.

"Jacob! Run!" Deborah shouted. When he hesitated, she cried once more, "Go, now! You must. And don't come back—ever!" The words seemed to excise her heart as she shouted them, but she knew it was the only way.

Jacob realized the truth of her words and forced himself to respond. He ran to his horse and mounted. But before he rode off, he turned back to his brother. "If I ever learn you have hurt her, I will come back and kill you!"

Then he bolted away at a gallop, his horse cutting a dusty swath in the yellow grass.

Leonard could have fired at his retreating brother, for Deborah was hardly strong enough to stop him. But he did not. Whether it was from a sense of mercy, or brotherly loyalty, or the simple practicality that shooting a man in the back would tarnish his reputation, Deborah did not know. Nor did she care. If he was wise enough not to come back, Jacob would be safe. Though she had lost her best friend, she could take comfort in that, at least.

Leonard scrambled to his feet and holstered his pistol. Then he reached out a hand to Deborah. There was no warmth in this gesture, and his face, bruised and bloodied as it was, remained cold. His simple effort to assist her was probably no more than sheer reflex, yet Deborah was immediately struck by the fact that this was the first time her husband's touch was intended to help and not hurt her. If his action held any deeper significance, she certainly could not fathom it, and later events did not show it to be a precursor to change.

They rode back to the house in silence. After returning Prairie to his stall, she went directly to her room to change out of her wet things. An hour later, as she lay on her bed resting from the emotional ordeal of the day, Leonard came to her room, entering without knocking as was his habit. He was also in clean, dry clothes; the wounds on his face had been washed and tended, with a small bandage on a particularly nasty cut over his left eye.

"What do you want?" she asked coldly.

"Do I have to give a reason for visiting my own wife's bedroom?"

"No. You usually have only one reason."

"Indeed!" A sly grin slipped across his face.

"Then get it over with. I'd like to go to sleep."

"Is that how you received my brother?"

"You will never know!" she retorted icily.

He raised his hand to strike her, but she managed to block his attempt with her arm. It was a paltry defense. He instantly grabbed her wrist and forced her arm against the bed. The viselike grip of his hand hurt terribly, but she bit down a cry of pain. When she tried to claw at his fist with her other hand, he imprisoned that one also. She could not budge, and yet he was hardly exerting himself.

"It seems we are going to have to begin our lessons in submission all over again," he threatened ominously.

Oh, how she wanted to hurt him back! Then the perfect weapon occurred to her. She had hoped before that it might be used to repair their marriage; now she only wanted to lash out at him with it.

Using all the scorn she could summon as she lay there at his mercy, she spoke, "I guess you may as well know, I am pregnant."

"Whose brat is it?" He was challenging her, not asking her.

She was tempted to drive her weapon into him, to leave him ever tormented with doubt. But just in time, before she further degraded herself, she realized he was not a man to suffer inner torment over anything. He would assume the worst, and only their child would suffer for it in the end.

"It's yours." She nearly choked on the words, especially as it fully dawned on her that she was indeed carrying *his* baby—this man whom she looked upon as little more than a monster.

"And I am supposed to believe you?"

"In spite of what you wish to think, there was never anything between Jacob and me. How I wish to God it was his baby! But God is not abundant with His blessings toward me."

"Well, we will know eventually, won't we? If that baby has but one black hair on its head, I will kill both you and it."

"I really don't care anymore, Leonard."

And with that only partially true declaration, she relaxed her arms, which she had been struggling to free. She closed her eyes and tried to close her mind as well to all emotion and feeling. As Leonard bent over her, she wondered if this was how Jacob's mother had felt before she ended her life. Overwhelming apathy, with but one singular desire—release.

At least Jacob was free. That was one good thing to come out of this dreadful day. She berated herself many times over for not going with him.

Oh, her stupid honor!

And her misguided desire to bring her child into a proper home!

63

What kind of home was it when it made her think more about dying and murder than living? And what kind of child would she raise in such a place? What if it turned out like Leonard, as Leonard mirrored his own father?

Still, what if there was a small chance that it might not turn out so? Perhaps a child would bring out the humanity in her husband. Children had changed other men, or so she had heard and read. It was possible!

She sighed miserably. Why did she bother to hope at all?

12

AFTER JACOB'S DEPARTURE, Leonard made Deborah more of a captive in his house than ever. He went so far as to post guards at the doors to insure she did not leave. He said it was because he could not trust her until he was certain Jacob was far away. Deborah hardly cared to go out anyway. Again, the stables brought her painful memories. She forgot all about the young colt, Prairie.

And it only added to her distress when Laban accosted her shortly after Jacob's departure. He did not touch her—he didn't have to. His scathing speech and accusing look were as sharp as a knife thrust through her heart. His trench-out glare was more effective than all of Leonard's abuse.

"This is your fault. You have forced my brother away!" He leveled the words like an attack. She was too stunned to wonder at his sudden concern for his brother, for even Jacob had commented on Laban's aloofness. Perhaps that had only been a protective shield. Maybe Laban was more like her than she had thought. Maybe he cared so deeply for Jacob and needed him so much that he had been afraid to admit it for fear of losing him.

She only gasped at the sting of his words. "I loved Jacob; he was my friend." But she spoke weakly, despondently. No one would believe her. These people did not understand anything as pure as friendship.

"He would not have left if you had not come," he accused.

For the first time, Deborah really looked at Laban. She had never done so before; she had barely spoken to him. He lived with Jacob in a line cabin on one of the more distant ranges, but he made an even more pointed effort to stay away from the house than his brother had. Now, she saw how young he was. In the stark devastation of his grief she saw he was but a boy, only sixteen. What had made him appear deceptively older at times was the hard, silent sullenness of his eyes. He had no doubt been hurt even more deeply than Jacob by the early loss of his mother, the only person who could have given him the tender love he needed. But what was even more apparent— frightfully apparent—was his strong resemblance to Caleb. Except for his dark coloring, there could be no doubt whose son he was. Jacob had definitely taken after his mother, which no doubt was why Deborah had warmed up to him so easily. Similarly, because of Laban's likeness to his father, Deborah had never reached out to him. She pitied him more for his similarity to Caleb than for his present grief.

Nevertheless, Deborah wanted somehow to comfort him. She could understand better than anyone the desolation he must feel. Even though he now leveled hatred at her, she wanted to show him the gentle compassion he'd find nowhere else. But everything she could possibly say sounded hollow, as empty as her own soul.

There was only one thing that might appease him, and since she suddenly believed it might be the truth, that is what she said. "You are probably right, Laban. It is all my fault." Then she turned and shakily made her way up the stairs to her room.

She wept for many days. She did not leave her room for a week. What did it matter? She was a prisoner anyway. She did not eat or bathe. Dark circles ringed sunken, dull eyes. The healthy tan she had begun to acquire from her time outdoors faded beneath a perennial pallor. Even the wine she began to take with increasing frequency gave her little solace, but it did provide welcome numbness.

Eight days later, Deborah had a miscarriage.

Deborah could not even summon the strength to feel guilt about the immense relief she felt at the loss of the baby. Always that image of Laban would appear in her mind and she dreaded the prospect of being responsible for producing another incarnation of Caleb. She feared she would never be able to love such a child.

It took Deborah several weeks to recover both physically and emotionally from both the loss of the child and of Jacob. In the end, she only did so because Leonard threatened her.

"I do not want people to think we are starving you out here!" he shouted one day. "Either you clean yourself up and start taking nourishment, or I will hire someone to force feed you. It will not be pleasant, but it is no more than you deserve for purposely losing that child."

"I would have thought you'd be happy about it," she retorted, though halfheartedly, to his untrue accusation. "Now you won't have to wonder whose child it was."

"You are right about that. Next time there will be no question."

His reference to "next time" made her sick at heart. But she knew he wanted a child—not, of course, out of any sentimental desire; he merely craved someone else to control. Deborah was desperate to prevent it. But when she locked him out of her room, he kicked in the door.

She began to seriously consider running away. She believed she had nothing to lose. If she must live her life in shame, so be it. At least there would be no child to also taint.

Perhaps she could find Jacob, although at the same time she prayed he was far away from there. But she realized that her feelings for Jacob had only been another escape, and she could benefit neither of them by seeking him out. Even if she could find him, she would only endanger him further. It was best that he start a new life far away from Texas.

Striking out alone became more appealing to Deborah. Dying at the hands of Indians on the frontier seemed a small risk compared to spending the rest of her life here. However, chance of escape was now more impossible than ever. The guards at the house were more vigilant than before. Leonard was taking no chances of his philandering wife disgracing him again.

Deborah decided to revive her earlier performance of the dutiful wife. She hoped to deceive Leonard into lowering his guard and thus providing her more opportunity to get away. It was a thin, shallow attempt at best. It hardly fooled her husband, but he did see the benefit in rewarding such behavior in order for it to continue. Thus, that winter he allowed her to go into town occasionally. The guard, however, always accompanied her. She never went anywhere alone.

She had considered finding a confidante in town, some objective party to whom she could go for help. Perhaps Leonard could be arrested for what he did to her. There were only a handful of women—decent women, not saloon girls—in town. One day she chanced to meet one of these in the store. She was the banker's wife and seemed nice enough, and even invited Deborah to tea.

"You simply mustn't bury yourself out there on that ranch. We women have to stick together, you know!" the woman said warmly.

Deborah went to the woman's house, and while tea was served, after some small talk between them, she forced herself to broach the subject of her marriage. This woman was a stranger whom Deborah had met only once before at her wedding; yet she was a woman, and a chance like this might not materialize again. It wasn't easy and Deborah spoke only in the vaguest terms.

"I'm afraid my marriage isn't all I'd hoped it would be," she said tentatively.

"None are, my dear."

"Has your husband . . . that is to say, is it common for a husband to strike a wife?"

"I've heard of it happening," the woman replied with some measure of kindness in her tone. "Though, heaven forbid, my husband never would. For some men it is the only way they know to control an unruly wife. It is a small price for a woman to pay, I suppose, for the security of a home of her own." She paused, then her eyes widened as the full implications of Deborah's query dawned upon her. "Dear, are you saying that your husband has struck you?"

Deborah nodded. Even then she could not come right out and verbally admit it. She was suddenly ashamed, not only of Leonard, but of herself also. The prim southern woman beside Deborah did nothing to dispel that shame.

"Deborah," the banker's wife said with more innocence than rebuke, "you must just try harder to please him."

That was the end of Deborah's ill-fated attempt to seek outside help—especially when, on the heels of it, Leonard confronted her with it the next night.

"How dare you flaunt our marriage before friends and neighbors! But don't think it will get you anywhere; I am too well regarded in this town for anyone to pay you heed. But just in case you should get any ideas of repeating your impudence—"

His fist flew at her, striking her over and over, giving no care even to making marks. When he finished beating her, he raped her viciously. She spent three days healing from that attack, locked in her room the whole time. As usual, Leonard told Maria that Deborah was ill and not to disturb her. He would tend his wife's needs himself—ever the attentive husband.

Somehow after this Deborah contrived another trip to town. There she made a purchase that helped to cement her determination to free herself, one way or another, from this miserable life.

67

When she arrived home, the house was empty; even Maria was gone. Deborah hurried to her room and dropped her packages on the bed—except for one, which she carefully unwrapped. She picked up the small object inside, feeling an awe as she stared down at it. The storekeeper said it was called a derringer. It fit in the palm of her hand and it could fire only two bullets. She doubted she'd ever have need for more.

Carefully she loaded two bullets from a box of ammunition that came with the weapon. She almost smiled at the little deception she had used with the storekeeper, telling him it was to be a Christmas gift for her husband and that she'd appreciate it if he kept it their little secret.

Deborah hid the gun in a small drawer in her bedside commode. She did not know if she could ever use the weapon, either on Leonard or on herself. But somehow knowing it was there gave her a kind of strength. In the dreary days and weeks ahead she frequently imagined using it. She even dreamed about it. How sweet was the image in her mind—the look on Leonard's face as he came at her and she lifted the gun hidden in the folds of her clothing. Ah, the stark shock and fear, especially fear, he wore as she pulled the trigger and a circle of blood soaked his chest.

Yes, the derringer gave her strength; it gave her a sense of control. She did not always have to be a victim.

But it also gave her the prospect of another kind of release. More than once that winter, she sat at her dressing table with the little gun grasped in her white-knuckled hand, pointed at her own head.

She never knew or understood what kept her from pulling that trigger. She never considered that a force beyond herself had spared her for the future life that still lay before her. She did not let herself recall her father's loving words about a caring, omnipotent God, a God who did not cause evil, but who was ever ready to lift a rebellious soul from the mire of a godless world. It would have been so easy to surrender to this Deity, to appropriate that peace and love from His hand. But she was too caught up in blame and recrimination to accept gifts from the one she considered responsible for the deaths of those she loved.

So, Deborah did survive, for whatever reasons, through that winter. And spring came to mark her second year in Texas. She marveled that it had been such a short time. But two years in hell was easily a lifetime.

That spring of 1865 also marked another milestone—the end of the War Between the States. Deborah greeted the news of the surrender at Appomattox Court House with apathy. The war had touched her once, given her grief, driven her from her beloved home. But for the last two years it had been like a distant memory of a dim dream. If it could not change her present circumstances, it did not matter that it was over. She did feel a twinge of sorrow for poor General Lee. He could have been the commander of the Union Army, for rumor had it he had been asked, and he could have now been a great hero. But instead he had fallen in disgrace. Some rumors circulated that he would be arrested and perhaps executed, but even the North respected him too much for that. At least one good man had survived the war.

Unfortunately, so had Leonard. His father had adroitly kept him out of the Confederate Army. How convenient it would have been for some stray Yankee bullet to end all Deborah's misery. But even the Indians had not been able to provide her freedom.

Life continued as always, war or no war. Deborah could not have known that when her hoped-for release finally did come, it would be by way of a hangman's gallows.

PART 2

THE COMPANY OF OUTLAWS

13

THE OUTLAWS CUT A GENERALLY northwest route, though McCulloch was careful not to veer too much to the west where the wild, unsettled regions of western Texas invited Indian attack. Keeping the western rim of the Cross Timbers more or less to their right, they steered a fairly direct course across the rolling, mesquite and grass covered plains until they crossed the Brazos River. Then they adjusted their course to a slightly more eastward direction, through a corner of the timbered land.

They encountered Cheyenne and Kiowa hunting parties. Luckily the Cheyenne party, which had twenty or thirty warriors, didn't see them, and the outlaws passed without incident. Only a few shots were exchanged with the Kiowas, but there were only six or seven in that band; they quickly realized they were out-gunned by the outlaws and retreated back to their hunting. Other than that, the outlaws passed the days of their journey uneventfully. They saw no sign of a pursuing posse from Stoner's Crossing. McCulloch decided his trick, heading south toward Mexico before turning sharply north, carefully covering their tracks, must have fooled the law.

That sheriff would be expecting them to go to Mexico. He was probably already across the Rio Grande trying to track them through Coahuila—that is, if he had the nerve. More than likely he had given them up for a lost cause. Caleb Stoner would raise a ruckus over that, but even he couldn't make a man—especially a soft, spineless one like Pollard—risk his neck in Mexico. Those banditos down there were nearly as bad as the Indians.

The woman remained a puzzle to McCulloch, although she was beginning to take a little more interest in her surroundings and maybe even her future. He still didn't know what to do about her.

Last night there had been a bit of a scuffle in camp over her. He'd noticed a couple of the boys looking at her pretty keenly. One was Sid Miller, an ornery brute. Griff didn't know why he kept him

73

around, except that with a cuss like that it was better to have him in your sights than off sneaking up behind you. Griff had no doubt that he could handle the other boys, but Miller was new to the gang and it had not yet come to a test between him and Miller. Griff felt in his gut that it was only a matter of time.

He smelled trouble the minute Miller sidled up to the woman while she was drinking coffee after supper.

"Howdy, ma'am," Sid said in a slippery, sweet tone that sounded about as much out of place from him as a snarl would have from Mrs. Stoner. "You don't mind if I set here a spell and pass the time of day with you?" He didn't wait for an answer before plopping down on the ground right next to her.

Mrs. Stoner scooted away from him.

"Ma'am, I sure hope you don't take me wrong," Sid said, affronted. "I just want to be neighborly."

She sighed wearily. Griff expected her to maintain her usual stony silence, but she answered Miller in a sharp, icy tone. "You can do that just as well from a distance."

"I figure I got a little more coming to me. I risked my neck to save yours." He paused and, lifting her hair with one calloused, grimy paw, ran the fingers of the other hand up and down the length of her slim, soft neck. "It shore is a right pretty one, too."

She closed her eyes and cringed with revulsion. Griff wouldn't have been surprised if she had hauled off and slugged Miller.

She didn't.

She tensed and inched away. Somehow McCulloch hadn't taken her for the type of woman to meekly accept such lurid advances from a man.

When Miller moved in close again, Griff watched, tense. He didn't want trouble over the woman and so wasn't quick to interfere.

Miller leaned even closer, his fetid breath blowing strands of her hair. He put an arm around her. Griff wondered how much she would take; and how much he, Griff, would let her take.

"Please, no!" she said in a strained, anguished tone.

That was all Griff needed to hear. "That's enough, Miller! Don't you see she ain't interested?"

"Aw, you just want her for yourself." Miller made no effort to move.

Griff pulled his gun. "I said get away from her!"

"Try and stop me, Griff! You ain't gonna shoot one of your own boys."

Griff fired. The bullet blasted a hole in the dirt not more than two inches from Miller's leg.

The outlaw jumped up, cursing. "You're plumb crazy, McCulloch!"

Griff replied with a steely menace in his voice, "You ever touch the woman, or go near her without her permission again, Sid, and the next hole I make ain't gonna be in the dirt, and it ain't gonna be in your leg—it'll be straight through your heart!" McCulloch swung around to glare at the others observing the altercation. "And that goes for the rest of you varmints, too!"

Later, McCulloch was out smoking a cigarette on the edge of camp, watching the horses. He didn't actually hear her light footstep but somehow he sensed her approach. He turned and was struck again at how pretty she was, especially with the moonlight glowing over that golden hair of hers. It made him ache that he couldn't have her, but it made him even more sick to think of someone like Miller pawing her.

"Ma'am," he said in greeting, tipping his hat.

"I hoped I'd find you out here," she said. Her tone was softer than usual, more as it should have been. "You often visit the horses when we camp."

"These critters are our life. If we lose any of 'em, we'd be goners, way out here in the wilderness like we are." He masked his surprise at this rare attempt on her part to initiate conversation. "Besides," he went on, "I kinda like to listen to 'em. They're peaceful-like, you know."

"Yes, they are. I have thought of laying my bed by them at night."

"You don't want to do that, ma'am! Even this is too far from camp to be safe. I've known Indians to get right up to a man's campfire without him even hearing them till it's too late."

"Thank you for the advice." She paused, seeming to consider her next words carefully. "I also want to thank you for what you did for me before."

"Well, ma'am, I don't want no trouble." Now, it was his turn to pause thoughtfully. "Can I give you some more advice, ma'am?" She nodded, and he went on. "Well, if I hadn't been around back there, I don't rightly know if the other boys woulda done anything for you. I guess what I'm saying is no one would think the less of you if you defended yourself."

"Would it have done any good, Mr. McCulloch?" she said bitterly.

"Well, I always figured if I was gonna go down anyway, I'd rather do it shooting from both barrels."

75

She actually smiled at him—nothing bright, or even very cheer-ful, but at least sincere.

"That's good advice, Mr. McCulloch, I'll remember it."

Yes, the woman was a mystery. One minute she was hard and tense like a coiled spring. The next, she seemed about as helpless and vulnerable as a newborn fawn. Then she'd turn right around and smile, though not too often; but when she did, even the prairie in springtime wasn't prettier or more pleasant. Griff figured she'd had some kind of hard life to end up killing her husband. It would take time for her to get over all that, but when she did, he thought she'd make a fine woman.

Until then he was stuck with her. He only hoped he didn't end up killing one of his boys over her. He didn't think she needed more of that in her life, and he knew he didn't. They'd be getting to his cabin soon; maybe then something would work out. It was possible that once the boys got used to having her around, they would ignore her. It would be nice for a change to have someone around to keep things clean and make some decent meals. Griff was right sick of Slim's cooking.

14

THE MORE DEBORAH SAW OF THIS country, the more she liked it.

She had read somewhere that people either loved Texas or hated it, with nothing in between. She should hate it, but in spite of the misery she had known here, she still could appreciate its innate qual-ities. After all, it wasn't the land that had harmed her. In fact, the only happiness she had ever known here had been in large part because of this very land and her many hours riding freely over its broad expanse.

Yesterday, the rolling plains had begun to give way to a stretch of timber Mr. McCulloch had called the Cross Timbers. He had identified blackjack and post oak as the predominant trees in the area, though there was still an occasional clump of mesquite on the landscape.

She had lost track of how many days they had been traveling. More than a week, to be sure. Except for the pleasure of being on horseback once more, and the grandness of the country, it would have been a grueling progression of heat, dust, tasteless food, and leering, ominous stares from the men.

Griff McCulloch seemed a tolerable enough sort for an outlaw. His company, at least, was far more preferable to what she had left on the Stoner Ranch. She could not picture herself spending the rest of her life with a band of outlaws. But for now she had no complaints as long as they continued to heed their leader's threat regarding her. She feared being the cause or the object of further violence.

She remembered once resolving never to be helpless, not to allow Leonard to defeat her. In the time that had followed, especially while she sat in jail, that resolve had broadened to encompass more than Leonard, who by then was dead and could no longer dominate her. She had always considered herself a strong and independent person. Two years with the Stoners proved what a frivolous impression that was. She was, after all, only a woman. Any man could have anything he wanted from her by sheer physical prowess. She *was* helpless. Her inner determination did not matter a whit.

Her present predicament was proof. She needed these outlaws. There was no way she could survive in this wilderness alone. She could not even shoot a gun, either to defend herself or to hunt food for survival. She could ride as well or better than many men, but she had no idea of direction, nor of how to find the right trail. She could not endure on sheer stubbornness alone.

But couldn't she learn?

Maybe she'd never be as strong as Sid Miller, but she was certainly more intelligent. If an oaf like that could learn to get about in the wilderness, why couldn't she?

"Mr. McCulloch," she said suddenly riding up beside him, "when we reach your hideout, would you teach me how to shoot a gun?"

"Uh ... did you say 'shoot a gun'?" This took him by complete surprise.

"Yes."

"I don't see why not, *if* you promise never to shoot me." He chuckled.

"I promise."

She almost laughed at herself for her silliness, yet her request made her feel good at the same time. It was similar to the way that derringer had once made her feel. In the end she hadn't gotten any actual use out of it, but it had given her a sense of control.

She *would* learn to take care of herself.

It might not happen right away, but one day she would have control over her own destiny. She would not need a man. She would not need anyone.

That afternoon the crooked line of the Red River appeared on the horizon. The dull river snaked its way lazily between its sandy banks lined with oaks and some elms and cottonwoods. The riders picked their way carefully down a little-used trail that led down a rocky ridge toward the riverbank. Keeping within the cover of the trees, they followed the water course along the south bank, eastward, for several miles until they came to the best place to ford the river.

Griff was glad to note the area was as deserted as it had been the last time he was there a couple years ago. He commented to Deborah that the war had pretty much slowed down settlement this far west. There were some settlements farther east, downriver, but thus far, no one but a few trappers and mountain men had been adventurous enough to disturb this particular valley. Unfortunately, it wouldn't be long before people would begin to discover the redeeming qualities of this wilderness.

Deborah had never seen such a wild and lonely place. She imagined savage Indians hiding behind every tree. If Griff McCulloch had a hideout here in the middle of nowhere, she wondered how safe it could be. But she had long ago decided she feared Indians less than the life she had just escaped. Moreover, the outlaws' guns offered a fairly substantial protection against attack by Indians armed with more primitive weapons. They had certainly outmatched those Kiowa several days ago. Would her first lessons in the use of a gun be in an Indian battle? The idea both frightened and exhilarated her.

Reaching the north bank, the party of riders continued on for another two hours. As the sun dipped down behind the flat-topped hills in the west, Deborah began to think they would have to make another camp before reaching their destination. Now that they were so near, she was anxious to have the long trek over with. She had no idea what she'd find at the end of the trail, how rustic or primitive the hideout was, but she was nevertheless ready for a long rest. As much as she loved being on horseback, her bones and muscles were aching from the continuous jostling over rough terrain.

"Here we are!" announced Griff. "Just beyond that ridge."

Deborah could see nothing even closely resembling a human habitation. They had to climb a narrow trail, around the steep ridge, with tall trees on either side. And then, there it was! It was an ideal location for a hideout. Unless you were looking for it, or stumbled upon it by accident, it was doubtful anyone would venture along this roundabout path. The cabin was set back against the rock of the ridge, with trees growing almost up to the very walls of the log structure. The clearing surrounding it was small, but large enough for a dozen horses to graze comfortably.

"I found this place about five years ago," said Griff to his passenger. "Used to be a trapper's cabin, I reckon. Can't imagine anyone else settling way out here—and, of course, back then it was even more hostile out here than it is now."

"And you are the only one who knows about it?"

"Far as I know. I ain't never seen no sign of disturbance, not even by Indians. We still have to keep a lookout, though. You just never know."

"How long has it been since you have been here?"

"Two . . . three years—"

"Two years, Griff," interjected one of the outlaws named Longjim Sands, a short, muscular man with a black beard and coal black eyes to match. "Remember, it was just after that Butterfield job when you took a slug in your—"

"Oh, yeah," said Griff quickly.

Though it was obvious Griff wasn't particularly keen on having an embarrassing story repeated, especially in front of a lady, Longjim continued, "That whole job was a botch, weren't it, boss? All along we were thinking it was gonna be a simple stage robbery until we found ourselves face-to-face with a company of Union cavalry. Turned out that stage was carrying a Union gold shipment. We hightailed it outta there at a dead gallop. But we didn't get away before one of the passengers, some easterner looking for glory in the wild west no doubt, emptied his shotgun at us. Don't see how you could forget, Griff. Why, you couldn't sit for—"

"Don't bore the lady, Longjim," Griff said gruffly, reining his horse sharply away from his talkative associate. "Let's quit the yammering and get unloaded. I want some real cooking tonight."

After one look inside the cabin, Deborah decided it would be days before it would be fit for cooking—or any other kind of civilized living. The few furnishings, all coarse and spare, were covered in a thick layer of dust. A table with benches cut from an unfinished log split in half sat in the middle of the one-room cabin. There was a small work table, built in the same rustic style as the big table, against a wall, with two shelves above it containing an assortment of dusty tin dinnerware and various black iron kettles. The only cabinet in the room, with a door hanging off its hinges, displayed a supply of tin goods, equally covered with dust and cobwebs. A hearth, built of stone, was the only attractive thing in the room; whoever had built the cabin had taken some care with it, at least. Deborah realized this was not only the source of heat for the place, but the cookstove as well.

One of her first thoughts was how these cramped quarters could possibly accommodate eight outlaws and her. Apparently Griff had given this some thought also. He strode over to where a dingy brown curtain hung across a section of the wall. Pulling it aside, he revealed a small alcove, no larger than the bed which was wedged into it.

"You can bunk here," he said. "Me and the boys'll sleep out under the stars."

Deborah walked to the bed and laid a hand on the mattress. To her astonishment, it was stuffed with feathers and invitingly soft. It would be a great improvement over the bed of hard earth she had occupied over the last days. A stack of wool blankets sat at the foot of the bed. There were no pillows or sheets, but otherwise she felt she could be quite comfortable there. She didn't argue about getting the only bed in the place. Most of the men would sleep outside, anyway.

"Now for supper!" said Griff, eagerly rubbing his hands together. He grabbed a kettle from a shelf, wiped his hand around inside, and plunked it down on the worktable.

"Mr. McCulloch," said Deborah, "all of these things will have to be washed before they can be used."

He looked at her for a instant as if she were completely mad, and seemed about ready to respond in some negative fashion. Then he thought better of it. "Hey, Slim, come here." He grabbed a blanket from the bed, spread it on the dirt floor, and began dumping the dishes and cooking things into the middle of the blanket. When it was full he gathered up the corners of the blanket into a bundle and shoved it at Slim. "Take this stuff down to the creek and wash it. I'll get a fire going."

Deborah smiled apologetically. "I am sorry, Mr. McCulloch. I'm not much accustomed to the . . . rustic life."

"No . . . I don't reckon you would be. Just remember what my daddy used to say to me. 'Son,' he'd say, 'just plan on eating a couple of cups of dirt afore you die. It's good for the constitution.' "

"I will try to keep that in mind, Mr. McCulloch, but it will take some getting used to."

Then she set about trying to put the room in some order so as to expedite the preparation of supper. First, she found a bucket in a corner. Cobwebs crisscrossed its interior, but otherwise it seemed sound.

"Where is the creek, Mr. McCulloch?" she asked. "I need to fetch water for supper."

Griff looked up from where he was laying out wood for a fire in the hearth. "Let the boys do that, ma'am. They need to stretch after riding all day, anyway." He yelled out the door and flung the pail at the first outlaw to respond.

Deborah peeked in the cabinet. By the look of the size and appetites of her outlaw rescuers, she did not think it would take long for them to consume what was there. It could easily be gone by tomorrow. That raised another question that had been nagging at her for some time, although it was only now, faced with the tangible prospects of the cabin, that she ventured to voice it.

"Mr. McCulloch, how long do you plan to stay at this hideout?"

Griff leaned back on his haunches. A fair blaze was crackling in front of him. "There's plenty of good hunting around here, ma'am. And there's timber for heat, and I think a couple of the boys might be able to risk going to one of them settlements downriver to pick up a few other supplies. It wouldn't be a bad place to winter in."

"Everyone?"

"Naw. The boys will be wanting some action. They'd go crazy if they had to hole up in a deserted place like this for long."

"Then you think I can stay here alone?"

"That wouldn't work either, now would it?" He rubbed a hand over his face. "We'll work something out, ma'am. I mean, it's kinda our responsibility, seeing as how we saved you and all."

"Perhaps I can go to one of those settlements?"

"That's no good, Mrs. Stoner. They'd ask too many questions, and right now that's the last thing you want. Anything suspicious is liable to leak down to your father-in-law. This is a big state, but news travels fast." He tossed a chunk of wood on the fire, causing a spray of sparks to shower the dirt floor. Griff stomped the sparks out. "Your best bet is to hide out here for a spell, at least until folks start to forget about you. News of your hanging did get around some." He picked up another piece of wood. "You got some problem with staying here? If you're worried about the boys—?"

"No, it's not that. I believe they will heed your warning." She paused, uncertain of how to proceed. A southern lady just did not discuss such things with men; but then, how many southern ladies had ever been in such a situation? There were no rules of etiquette to fit her present plight. Sighing, she continued, "It is just that ... well, Mr. McCulloch ... I believe you ought to know that ... I am ... with child."

A loud crash punctuated her words as Griff dropped the log he had been about to toss on the fire. He said nothing for some time. Slim came in and deposited the utensils he had washed, and exited while Griff still sat with his mouth ajar. He lurched to his feet but said nothing when Mitch came in with the water.

"Hey," Mitch said, "when's the grub gonna be done? I'm starved."

"Aw, eat the rest of the jerky!" snapped Griff. "It's too late to cook. And stay out of here for a while—the lady wants some privacy."

Grumbling with disappointment, Mitch stomped back out. Silence continued to hang over the little room.

Deborah finally spoke. "I'm sorry," she said, unable to say more. She meant so much more in those simple words than could appear on the surface. This was the first time she had spoken of her secret to anyone, the first time she had even allowed herself to think of it. Through the trial and all those days in jail, she had almost, but not quite, forgotten.

"Ma'am, this is just a surprise, that's all." Griff paced a few times across the floor, then stopped. "You know about this all along?"

"Yes."

"Do you know that they wouldn't have tried to hang you if they had known? Even Caleb Stoner wouldn't have killed his own grand-kid."

"I know that."

Griff shook his head. "I suppose you had your reasons."

"What would they have done to me, Mr. McCulloch? Thrown me into prison instead of hanging me—or until I gave birth, after which they'd still hang me? Then the baby would have been placed into Caleb's care. I couldn't allow that. I didn't know what else to do."

"I guess I knew them Stoners were bad, but I never imagined ..." He let his words trail away unfinished. Even he, man of the world that he was, couldn't fathom such evil.

"I did not want Caleb to know."

"Like I said, you probably had your reasons. And it don't make no difference to me. And I guess it don't change nothing, either. You still gotta lay low for a spell, now more'n ever."

"When my times comes—"

"You can't expect no help from any of us. Birthing young'uns ain't something we're experienced in!"

His tone, edged with panic, brought a slight smile to Deborah's lips. The idea of Griff McCulloch and his gang delivering her baby was both amusing and appalling.

"I was thinking," she said, "that one of those settlements you mentioned might have a midwife, or even a doctor."

"There ain't nothing like a doctor there. You'll maybe find a couple of trading posts, and a few saloons, some trappers. Maybe a family or two, so there might be a woman." He paused and gave her a studied appraisal. "How long do you think we got to chew this over?"

"About five months."

"Then we'll work something out." He gave the fire a final kick with his boot, then bid Deborah good-night, and strode out.

She hated being the cause of so much trouble. How much simpler it would have been if they had just left her to hang on that gallows. Yet even as the thought occurred to her, she realized her apathy was gone. Now that she was free from the grip of the Stoners, she began to see that she really did not want to die. For two years she had been as good as dead, but now, as freedom lay before her, she saw herself as having been raised from the dead.

What was it her father used to quote? *"Once I was dead, now I am alive."* She no longer had to dread the coming of a new day. She no longer had to be afraid. She could live again. Perhaps it would never be as good as it had been in Virginia before the war. She was probably too scarred and wounded for that. But at least she could look forward to tomorrow.

The child was another matter. She was still uncertain how she felt about it. One thing she did know: The baby had been spared along with her, perhaps for some reason she could not possibly fathom. She wasn't ready to go so far as to admit God had some eternal plan in these events in her life, but she could not deny the witness of reality. The baby was alive, and she would never do anything, of her own accord, to harm it. She only hoped that when the child came, she could look at it and love it.

15

THE FOLLOWING SUCCESSION OF WEEKS were interesting ones for Deborah, and in many ways they were fulfilling and restful. The living arrangement worked smoothly, especially as the men grew accustomed to her presence and she ceased to be a novelty. She learned to cook in the primitive kitchen, and the outlaws most likely did not care to risk the pleasure of tasty, hot meals for the appeasing of baser appetites.

Most of the time, however, they were gone. Deborah did not ask where they went or what they did. But they might be gone for days, even weeks at a time. Griff had put by a good supply of dried meat for her during their absence. He had cut enough wood to last the winter and had purchased, or somehow procured, a few other precious supplies—coffee, sugar, flour, even some tea, much to Deborah's delight, for she had not had tea since leaving Virginia. Griff also once brought back some reading material for her—a few books, two old issues of *Goodies Lady's Book,* and three old newspapers. Deborah was especially delighted with the newspapers. She remembered when she had once asked Leonard for a paper.

"There's no need to fill your head with such matters," he told her.

She had even tried to bribe Maria into getting her one when the war ended, for she had been starved for news. But the loyalties of the housekeeper, an employee of the Stoner men for years, were solidly set against Deborah.

When Griff was around, he began to teach Deborah the rudiments of using the rifle that he left with her for protection during his absences. Oddly, though, she never felt in any danger so far out there in the wilderness. The quiet peace of the place and the freedom from Leonard easily lulled her into a sense of security. But she had other reasons for wanting to learn to handle a gun, and thus, she was a good student. Her lessons were few, for Griff didn't like firing too many shots for fear of drawing attention to their presence. Still, she learned quickly and even began to think about doing some hunting, but Griff firmly discouraged her.

"Don't you leave this cabin when we're gone except to get water. I don't want you to lose your scalp."

Her first inclination was to rebel at being ordered around again, but reason showed her he was simply concerned for her safety, and the fact that someone should actually care about her for her own sake rather touched her. In this way, the concern shown her by a rough-hewn outlaw began within Deborah the beginnings of healing from the years of abuse from her husband.

Thus Deborah was able to accept Griff's warning. But even if she had been inclined to ignore his admonitions, her pregnancy was progressing noticeably, and she realized it was no time to be traipsing over the countryside, especially alone.

Strangely enough, as the child grew within her, she began to feel a kind of protectiveness toward it, and when it quickened in her womb she felt a thrill—if not of love, then at least of affection for it. The baby may have been Leonard's, but it was also hers. There was no reason why she might not find something about the child to love. If nothing else, she became more open to such a possibility.

In the beginning the frequent time alone in the cabin was a balm to her frayed and wounded emotions. She avoided deep reflection by reading and rereading the material Griff brought. She remembered the many pleasant evenings listening to her father read and the lively discussions they would have afterward. Caleb Stoner's home had been noticeably devoid of reading material. So, now, after the dearth of the last two years, she found the time enjoyable and stimulating, even if she often had no one to discuss the books and articles with.

Once she tried to engage Griff in a discussion about something she had recently read.

"I read this most intriguing statement by Carlyle this morning, Mr. McCulloch. Listen: 'The oak grows silently in the forest a thousand years; only in the thousandth year, when the axeman arrives with his axe, is there heard an echoing through the solitudes; and the oak announces itself when, with far-sounding crash, it falls.' I wonder if he meant that man's crowning achievement in life is destined to coincide with his death. Or, perhaps it is death itself?"

Griff scratched the unshaven stubble on his face and screwed up his face in thought. When he spoke, it was as if he had come to a profound conclusion. "Seems to me, ma'am," he said, "that what that feller means is when an oak tree falls, it makes a powerful racket."

Perhaps Griff was not as intellectually stimulating as her father, but she was nevertheless content. However, as summer slipped away into autumn, Deborah began to feel restless, or just a bit bored. She wanted a change of scene, some excitement, a break in the routine. She was still young, only twenty, and she still had a youthful, eager, adventurous spirit that even the Stoners had not broken. But when she mentioned her restiveness to Griff, he told her to count her blessings because the only excitement he could think of in these parts was an Indian attack, a storm or a flood, or the arrival of the law—none of which he would recommend her wishing for.

When a break in the routine finally came, it happened to fall within the scope of one of Griff's dire predictions.

It was late October, and most of Griff's boys were spending a lot of time at the cabin. Deborah saw them more than once huddled outside, heads together, in some intense discussion. She had no idea exactly what they were talking about, although she could hazard a fairly good guess. Griff had alluded to getting a little "nest egg" together for winter. Deborah assumed they were planning one last job before bad weather set in. From the intensity of the conference Deborah thought it must be a big undertaking. She asked no questions, however, for she did not want to know.

Occasionally, one or two of the boys would ride off, be gone a day, or a few days, and, when they returned, there would be another discussion. When Slim and Mitch returned from one of these forays, something most unexpected occurred. The two outlaws did not return alone. A stranger rode between them and, by the look of it, he was their prisoner.

When Deborah heard the commotion outside, she went to the cabin window to watch. The stranger was about the same age as Griff, around thirty. His hands were tied behind his back and his face was almost entirely covered by a bandana acting as a blindfold. Slim removed the bandana once they stopped in the yard, revealing a rather pleasant-looking man whose ruddy, freckled visage appeared both rugged and warm, even in spite of his present predicament. The longish hair curling in an unkempt fashion under his worn, wide-brimmed hat was reddish brown, and his several days' growth of beard contained far more red than brown. He wore buckskin breeches that had seen much use, and a similar buckskin coat with a faded blue bandana tied around his neck. As he dismounted, Deborah noted he was about two inches taller than Griff, but they were otherwise equally matched in brawn. At first Deborah wondered why she immediately compared the stranger to Griff, but she quickly realized that it was because both men emanated an impression of command. If this situation ever turned into a showdown, it would certainly be between these two.

For the moment, however, the stranger was firmly in tow and actually showed no sign of resistance. In fact, he seemed to be taking everything in his stride.

"What you got here, Slim?" asked Griff as he strode into the yard. His casual tone indicated more curiosity than alarm.

"Found him creeping around, boss, just over the ridge. Woulda shot him instead of hauling him in, but he weren't wearing no gun."

"You're too soft, Slim," railed Sid Miller.

Griff glared at Miller, then said to Slim and Mitch, "You did right, boys. No sense killing the man till we find out what he was doing nosing around here."

Griff gave the man a careful appraisal. "So, what you got to say for yourself—?"

But as he spoke, Mitch, who was rummaging through the stranger's saddlebag, interrupted. "Hey, Griff, lookee here at what I found." He held up two items—a six-shooter in a holster and a black book. "He's got hisself a Holy Book!"

It was indeed a Bible in the man's saddlebag, its black cover worn and apparently much used.

"What you got that for?" asked Griff. It wasn't every day one found a man on the frontier with a book, much less a Bible.

"That's one of the tools of my trade," answered the stranger in an easy Texas drawl.

"Which is?"

"I'm a minister of the Gospel of Christ, a circuit rider in these here parts."

Griff eyed the newcomer again with renewed interest. "You don't look much like a circuit rider, nor sound like any preacher I ever heard. You look more like a cowboy. Maybe a lawman. . . ?"

"I'm afraid there ain't much I can do 'bout that." The man spoke with great confidence. If he was afraid, he did not show it; Deborah believed, from the slightly amused glint in his eyes, that he was almost enjoying himself. "I guess I got more of my schooling in the saddle than at some fancy eastern university."

Dissatisfied with the progress of the interrogation, Griff turned his attention to the pearl-handled Colt .44. He took it from Mitch and turned it over in his hand a few times. It was a fine specimen, as was the holster, which, though worn, was of quality Mexican craftsmanship.

"This here—" Griff motioned with the gun. "One of the tools of your trade, too?"

"I reckon I'd have to say it's a necessary evil. The Word of God says to be gentle as a dove and wise as a serpent. It would be foolish to roam around in hostile Indian country unarmed."

"And can you use it?"

"I can, but not without a mighty good reason."

"So, who are you? And what do you want?"

"My name is Sam Killion. I'm riding over the country tending the Lord's flock wherever I may find 'em. I saw a bit of smoke in the sky—"

"Hey, boss!" broke in Longjim. "Don't that there name sound familiar? Killion . . . where'd I hear it. . . ?"

"I know!" said Sid. "I shoulda figured it out right away. Sam Killion—this here ain't no preacher; he's a dirty Texas Ranger!"

All the outlaws tensed and, though Killion was unarmed, every hand eased toward a gun. Griff pulled his six-shooter and pressed its barrel against Killion's cheek.

"Okay, pardner! I think it's time you started talking straight." Griff spoke evenly, without raising his voice, but he left no doubt about his seriousness. "You that Killion fella?"

Killion nodded.

"And this preacher business is just a smoke screen? You're really Sam Killion the Ranger?"

"I'm an ex-Texas Ranger and a current preacher."

"The Rangers are all supposed to be 'ex' now that the Union has taken over the State—but that don't mean there ain't some still operating. Ain't you the Ranger that gunned down them Mexican banditos back before the war?" asked Longjim with unabashed admiration in his tone. "Griff, you heard 'bout that, didn't you? Way I heard it was them greasers had Killion pinned down in a deserted barn out by the Pecos. All Killion had was his loaded six-gun, no holster and no spare ammo. There was six Mexicans, and Killion was the only one to walk away alive. He had six bullets and made each one count!"

"That's quite a piece of shooting," said Griff.

Killion shrugged. For the first time, though, his expression grew solemn. "I killed five and wounded one," he said grimly.

The brief silence that followed was broken by Sid Miller's gruff voice. "Well, what are we gonna do with him? He knows where the hideout is now, 'cause no blindfold is gonna stop a Ranger."

Several of the others voiced similar concerns, with the consensus among these being that the Ranger had to be shot. But Longjim and a few others protested.

"You know what they'll do to us if we kill a Texas Ranger? The Union may have put them outta commission for a spell, but they're still a clannish lot—and dangerous!" reasoned Mitch.

"If I gotta hang anyway, I may as well get something worthwhile out of it," said Sid.

The two factions debated heatedly for a few minutes, ending in a stalemate. Killion watched calmly as if his life didn't hinge on the outcome of the argument.

When Griff estimated his boys had argued the issue into the ground, he spoke up. "Sid, you're being a hot-headed fool," he said in a perfectly cool tone. "Right now the law just wants us on general principles. But if we kill a Ranger, we may as well slit our own throats and have done with it. Them Texas Rangers'll move heaven and earth to get us; they won't rest till we're all dangling from a rope."

"I think you're getting soft, Griff!" railed Sid.

"I'm getting smart," said Griff, "like a serpent, right, preacher?"

"I don't have no argument with that," Killion replied.

"And what about tomorrow?" said Miller.

"Nothing needs to change," answered Griff. "We'll tie up Killion real good and leave him under guard. Then when we get back, we'll take him downriver and leave him by one of them settlements. By the time he can do anything about it, we'll be long gone."

"What about the hideout?"

"So, we have to find another hideout—no big deal."

"I don't like it," Miller grumbled.

"Well, you ain't boss of this outfit," retorted Griff, "and until you're man enough to take over, you do what I say."

"So be it!" Miller barked, more challenging than conceding. "But when this blows up in your face, it will be me the boys choose as leader."

"Yeah, when they get a partiality to polecats!" sneered Griff, swinging around with his back pointedly toward Miller, holstering his gun almost as an added insult. He added to Slim, "Get some rope and bring it to the cabin."

Griff nudged his prisoner toward the cabin door, shoving it open and pushing Killion inside. The ex-Texas Ranger's look of imperturbable confidence momentarily faded into consternation as he first noticed the pregnant woman standing by the window.

16

DEBORAH IGNORED THE STRANGER. She thought she detected a look of pious judgment in his appraisal of her, and thus she wanted no part of him. Without comment, she swept past him back to the table where she had been kneading bread dough before the interruption.

Griff led Killion to a corner of the cabin, shoved him to the floor, and proceeded to bind him firmly with the rope provided by Slim.

"You ought to be comfortable enough here for a few days—" Griff began.

"A few days!" exclaimed Killion sharply, revealing his first note of dismay since his arrival. "You don't expect me to sit here all trussed up like a roasted goose for days!"

"It's either that or letting old Sid out there fill you with lead."

Killion shrugged resignedly. "I see what you mean."

"Mrs. Stoner'll see that you get fed proper-like. And Slim will guard you."

"Me, boss?" protested Slim. "But I was planning to go with you to—"

"Put a lid on it, Slim. If our guest here finds out too much, we may just have to kill him."

"Sorry, boss. But why do I have to stay behind? It ought to be Pablo or even Sid. I been here longer than them."

"Yeah, but I can trust you, Slim. And, don't worry, you'll get your full share."

"Okay," Slim drawled reluctantly, "but I don't like missing all the fun."

"Maybe Mr. Killion will entertain you with his preaching," Griff taunted good-naturedly. "If'n he really is a preacher."

Slim groaned in reply. Then, swinging a leg over the log bench he sat down rather dejectedly at the table. He stared wistfully at Griff's back as he exited the cabin.

Killion smiled. "I'd be happy to oblige you."

"Anything but that—please!" pleaded Slim.

"What do you got to fear from the redemptive mercy of our Lord and Savior, Jesus Christ?" said Killion. His amusement faded into an earnestness. "He has the gift of everlasting life to offer you, brother— a gift, I might add, given freely to any who'll just turn their hearts to Him."

"My pappy used to tell me to be wary of Greeks bearing gifts," said Slim smugly.

"Then you got nothing to fear, for Christ is no Greek."

"Aw, you know what I'm getting at! There's nothing in this world that's free."

"Except the love of Christ—a fact that the entire Gospel of salvation hinges on."

Slim eagerly changed the subject. "You really a preacher?"

"Yup."

"How'd you switch from Texas rangering to preaching?"

"It's a long story, but I'd be happy—"

"Never mind!" Slim wasn't dumb; he saw when he was getting lured once more into one of Killion's religious tirades. He hitched himself to his feet. "I'm going out for a spell. Mrs. Stoner, you holler if he tries anything."

Like a spooked rabbit, Slim darted out the door.

Deborah continued kneading her dough vigorously on the table. She was feeling as uncomfortable as Slim had with the stranger. The last thing she wanted was to be preached at, and she had no doubt that if this man was a genuine cleric, he'd find no loss of recriminations against her—that type always did, attacking *appearance* without regard to truth. Deborah's father may have presented a moderate, balanced example of Christianity, but Deborah had been exposed to enough other types to support her suspicions. Virginia had its share of itinerant preachers, hollering about hellfire and damnation and the wrath of God. In fact, their own local parson was of that ilk. How Josiah Martin managed to retain his gentle outlook on religion, Deborah never knew. But she came to believe it had more to do with Josiah's innate personality than with God's character. Josiah Martin saw goodness in everything and everyone, so it was not surprising he'd attribute such qualities to God. Deborah found it easier to recognize the wrathful, avenging Deity who sends His judgment upon the just and the unjust alike.

Thus she averted her eyes from the stranger, concentrating on her work. She placed the dough in a bowl, covered it with a cloth and carried it near the hearth, setting it down by the emanating heat. She had to pass in front of Killion to do so, but she paid no attention to him. Completing her task, she returned to the table to clean up and prepare supper. All the while she was acutely aware of Killion's eyes on her, following her every movement.

Finally, the preacher spoke. "I hope you'll forgive me, ma'am, for watching you. It's just been a long time since I've watched such a homey scene. You know, kneading dough, making bread, all that. I ain't been home for a long spell."

Deborah remained silent, absorbed in measuring water from a pail into a large black kettle.

"I guess I'll never forget," the preacher continued, undaunted, "how my ma would make bread and then how I'd get a big, thick, hot slice spread with her boysenberry jam." He took a deep, dreamy breath as if the aroma of his mother's bread was filtering past him. "I don't reckon you got any boysenberry jam here, do you?"

In spite of herself, she glanced up at the innocuous question, wondering what it would hurt to answer it. Instead, she dumped a measure of beans into the kettle.

"Ma'am," said Killion contritely, "have I offended you in some way?"

Deborah lifted her eyes once more in his direction. "No" was all she said.

"Whew! That's good. I wouldn't want to do that. 'Course, there's no reason you got to be friendly. But if we're to be holed up here together for a few days, there's no sense in it being unpleasant. I'm afraid I have to admit I'm a man who likes conversation. I like to think I have some of the more spiritual gifts like wisdom, or prophecy, or faith; but one thing's certain, I got an abundance of the gift of *gab*. I just have to believe God knew what He was doing when He gave it to me." He paused. As much as he liked to talk, he preferred a *two*-sided exchange to listening to his own voice.

Silence filled the room once more. Deborah hung the kettle of beans over the fire and then found some other trivial tasks to occupy herself. She wondered if it was necessary for Griff's prisoner to be kept in the cabin. She supposed it gave the outlaws more freedom in making their preparations outside for wherever they were going tomorrow. She also supposed it was too cold outside for a man to be bound, immobile, to some tree. But she was not looking forward to the next days at all.

Apparently having had enough of the penetrating silence, Killion ventured to speak again. "I couldn't help hearing a couple of the boys calling you 'Mrs. Stoner.' You wouldn't happen to be Leonard Stoner's wife?"

For the first time Deborah realized the danger using her married name could pose. Alone, here in the cabin these last months had insulated her, but now faced with the possibility of this man carrying back news of her whereabouts to Caleb, she saw what a foolish oversight it had been. If she ever left this place, she would have to do so with another name. In the meantime, she began to wonder if Sid Miller might have been right about eliminating this man. He posed a threat to all of them.

She turned cold eyes toward Killion. "You talk too much, Mr. Killion."

"I told you, it's a blessing and a curse! My curiosity just got the better of me." He paused thoughtfully. "You don't have anything to worry about from me, though, ma'am. I'm in the business of saving souls, not damning them."

"Even a sinner's soul?"

"We're all sinners, ma'am. Even Christ didn't condemn the woman caught in adultery—"

"That's very magnanimous of Him!" she broke in harshly, full of her own recriminations.

"I didn't mean—"

"I know what you mean, Mr. Killion. You spout a lot of words about love and forgiveness and mercy, but inside you are nothing more than a hypocrite."

"You got me all wrong, ma'am!" His voice rose slightly in indignation. "I'm as much a sinner as the next fella, and the last thing I'd do is judge you. I made a poor choice of scripture for an example, that's all. Whatever you do is between you and God. I'm not a lawman anymore, and besides, I think you'll get more justice from God than the likes of Caleb Stoner."

Deborah shrugged as if to say she didn't know what to make of his statement but was less willing now than before to accept this man. And she was in no mood to discuss anything further with him, so she picked up the water pail and left the cabin.

Down by the creek, she was filling the bucket when she heard two or three voices nearby. She set down the pail, stood, and listened. The sound was coming from about fifteen yards away, and the speakers were hidden from view behind a thick growth of gorse, but she recognized Sid Miller's growl and Pablo's Mexican accent. The third man was one of Sid's cronies, whose name she did not know. They could not see her, but she moved to the cover of a tree trunk nevertheless, and stood very still. She immediately sensed these three could be up to no good. There had always been a tension between them and Griff, and it did not bode well for them to be conversing in low tones, obviously out of sight of the others.

"We're all agreed, then?" said Sid.

"Sí, but we better be careful. I do not want to lose my cut in the holdup," Pablo replied.

"No one's going to lose nothing," assured Miller. "That's why we gotta wait till after the job to put a slug in that Ranger. Why should we suffer 'cause Griff's gone soft?"

"You think Griff's gonna let one of us go along when he dumps Killion?" asked the third man.

"How's he gonna stop us?"

"Yeah, I guess you're right 'bout that."

"I'm right. And I'm gonna kill that lousy Ranger, even if I gotta put a few holes in Griff, too. Come to think of it, I might shoot Griff anyhow. He's getting a mite too big for his britches."

The parley apparently over, the three left their hiding place and ambled back toward the cabin. Deborah stood still for several moments before she ventured back into the open; then she retrieved the pail and returned to the cabin. She wished she had never heard Sid's plans. Of course, her next logical step was to tell Griff. But she believed, and with reason, that such an action would only precipitate violence ending in the death of either Sid or Griff. Aside from the fact that she tended to like Griff as a person because he treated her decently, she well knew what his loss would mean for her. Without Griff as a buffer between her and the other outlaws, especially those of Sid's bent, she feared what they might do to her. Escape from here was now more out of the question than ever. Not only was winter fast approaching, but her condition made travel alone in the wilderness insane.

So, in order to prevent a confrontation between Sid and Griff, she remained silent about what she had heard. She had time to decide what, if anything, to do about Killion. But she was already beginning to realize her only other option.

17

THE OUTLAWS RODE OUT THE following morning, seven of them. Slim stayed behind, none too happy, to guard the prisoner, who needed little encouragement to impart the gospel to any who showed even the slightest interest.

Deborah tried to go about her routine as usual, but with the two extra people in the small cabin, that was hardly possible. She kept to the curtained alcove when she wasn't occupied with cooking preparations. She had been looking for a change, but this was not exactly what she'd had in mind. Moreover, she was not happy about the added burden of decision Killion's presence placed upon her. For, while she lay in bed that first night, unable to sleep because of the snores of either Slim or Killion—she couldn't tell which—she had determined her course of action.

There was only one way to prevent violence, and that was for Killion to escape. Of course, that did carry with it another set of dangers, but it seemed the best of two evils. She couldn't stand by and watch Killion murdered, no matter how his death might benefit her. If Killion were gone, then no one would get hurt, although she tried not to think of what the outlaws might do to her for her part in his escape.

She had to help the preacher get away. She would have to think of some way to get rid of Slim for a while. He was being especially vigilant. He wouldn't even untie Killion's hands so he could eat; instead, he made Deborah feed the man. He said he'd have the devil to pay if the Ranger got away. Deborah wondered how *she* would pay for the deed, but she shook the frightening thought from her head the instant it tried to intrude. Her mind was made up. Besides, she was certain they could do nothing more terrible to her than had already been done by Leonard. Even killing her would not be worse.

It took all that day for her to formulate what she hoped was a viable plan. And although the plan itself was simple, most of the time, she hated to admit, was spent in getting up her nerve. Realizing she had to act soon, for Griff could be returning any time, she finally took advantage of a brief moment alone with Killion while Slim was out feeding the horses to explain her intentions.

"You have to escape from here, Mr. Killion," she said bluntly.

"That's sure stating the obvious," he replied lightly.

Doesn't he ever take anything seriously? she thought, frustrated.

"I overheard some of the men making plans to kill you when they returned."

"I ain't surprised."

"Griff would probably try to stop them, getting himself killed as well." She supposed she mentioned this to impress upon the preacher that her concern was not simply for his benefit.

"I always try to see the best side of folks, Mrs. Stoner, but I hardly think Griff'd risk his life for me."

"It wouldn't take much for Sid Miller to kill him," said Deborah. "Anyway, I don't think it's worth taking the chance. That's why I'm going to help you escape."

"You?"

"Yes . . . tainted woman that I am."

He raised a bushy eyebrow as if he would defend himself again, then shrugged off the urge. She would think what she wanted no matter what he said.

"Mrs. Stoner, it's right charitable of you to offer to rescue me, but I can't let you do it. It would put you in too much danger."

"I'll be all right," she said with more confidence than she felt.

"Tell me something," said Killion, "and I ain't judging you or condemning you, but are you . . . Griff's woman?"

She bristled at his crassness, practically spitting her reply at him, "I am no man's woman!"

"Now, don't get all riled," he replied calmly. "I'm just trying to point out that otherwise, you ain't got no guarantees concerning your own safety when they find out you helped me fly the coop. Unless—" the idea occurred to him even as he spoke, and he seemed pleased with his resourcefulness in thinking of it, "—unless you escape with me."

That possibility had not occurred to her, but if it had she would have rejected it out-of-hand. She felt far more secure about her chances with Griff than she did about the scripture-spouting ex-Texas Ranger who would no doubt badger her to death trying to win her soul. That is, if he really *was* a preacher. They still hadn't confirmed

96

that beyond doubt. Going with him might be tantamount to turning herself over to Caleb Stoner.

"Don't worry about me, Mr. Killion." She paused as she thought of a new concern. "My one hesitation in helping you is the possibility that upon escape, you will go directly to the law with what you know about this cabin and Griff and me. Once you are gone, of course, we will abandon the cabin and no one will find us here."

"I told you, I ain't a lawman anymore."

"But you are a law-abiding citizen."

"I try to be." He paused thoughtfully. "But in this case, you have my word that your generosity will be rewarded with my silence. Griff's gang will no doubt have to reckon with their crimes eventually, with no help from me. As for you—" He stopped and studied her closely with a look of conflicting pity and admiration on his face. "I don't reckon I wish to be the cause of further suffering in your life."

Deborah did not like the pity she detected in his visage, but beyond that, she could not deny a definite sincerity in his eyes. Maybe she had misjudged him. Something about him made her instinctively want to trust him, to believe the words spoken with such genuine candor. It helped ease her anxiety about letting him go.

"Well, I have no choice, I suppose," she said. "I can't stand by and allow them to kill you."

"I still wish you'd agree to come with me—"

But the conversation ended abruptly as Slim entered. Deborah returned to finishing her preparations for the midday meal. Casually, she picked up the water pail and told Slim she was going to the creek for a minute. She had hoped he would offer to go in her stead, but since no such offer was forthcoming, she'd have to invent some other way to get Slim out of the cabin. He might have gotten suspicious if she had simply asked him to do the task. She never asked for help of any of the men unless absolutely necessary.

Ten minutes later she returned to the cabin, jogging as fast across the yard as her cumbersome girth would allow. She was all out of breath when she flung open the cabin door.

"Slim!" she panted. "I saw something down by the creek!"

"What in blazes do you mean? A mountain lion? A bear?"

"I . . . I think it was an Indian!"

"Coming this way?"

"On the other side of the creek. He was running away."

"That's mighty peculiar, 'less he was gonna warn others." He hitched his spare, lanky frame off the bench. "I better have a look."

Deborah watched at the window as Slim trudged down the rocky path that led to the creek. The moment he was out of sight, she sprang into action. Grabbing a kitchen knife, she hurried to Sam Killion and began slicing at the rope binding his hands and feet. It was a task more tedious and time-consuming than she had anticipated. Once, she heard a sound outside and glanced up in a panic, but Slim did not come. She knew, however, as the last rope fell loose, that time was running out.

"You'll have to help me take care of Slim," she said when Killion was free.

" 'Take care of . . .' " he questioned with a raised brow.

"I am not planning to kill him," she assured. "You have to help me tie him up. You'll never have time to get away if he's loose." She retrieved Killion's saddlebag, which was sitting by the door, and removed his Colt. "I can hold the gun on him while you tie him."

"We'll need more rope; this ain't no good anymore."

"I'll check the horses. You wait here with the gun in case he comes back."

"This ain't going to make him happy."

Deborah shrugged. "It's too late now."

Not two minutes after she returned with a new coil of rope, Slim ambled up to the cabin.

"I didn't see a thing," he said as he opened the door. The next sound out of his mouth was a gasp as the barrel of the Colt .44 was thrust into his face.

"I'm sorry to have to do this to you, Slim," Deborah said as Killion began knotting the rope around him, "but Sid is going to shoot Killion and probably Griff as well if he remains around here. I just want to avoid anyone getting hurt."

"And what's gonna keep Griff from hurting *me* for letting Killion get away?" sputtered Slim.

"Don't worry, I'll explain everything."

"You mean you're staying?"

Slim's brows shot up at that revelation, and he seemed to regard her with renewed esteem. He had figured her to be a feisty female ever since seeing how she had stood up on that gallows so defiantly. But here she was helping a prisoner escape, with no fear of her own safety. Why, he almost talked himself out of ringing her neck once he got loose of that rope!

When Slim was secure, Deborah replaced the gun in the saddlebag.

"I still wish you'd reconsider coming with me, ma'am."

"I will take my chances here, Mr. Killion."

"Why, ma'am, I almost think you're more afraid of me than them!" he said. "Is it me, Mrs. Stoner, or my religion?"

Because it was, in fact, his religion she feared, and he had nearly guessed it, she ignored his question. Instead of answering she wrapped up some dried meat and bread in a cloth and deposited it in his saddlebag along with the gun and black Bible.

"You had better get going, Mr. Killion. You only have a few hours of daylight left."

"I won't forget this, ma'am. And I figure to repay you one day if we ever meet again."

"Just repay me by keeping your word about remaining silent."

"My word is as good as gold," he said with that frank honesty that convinced Deborah far more than his words. "But I still am beholding to you."

"Goodbye, Mr. Killion."

"Adios, Mrs. Stoner—and I mean that in its truest sense."

She closed the door firmly after him and did not pause at the window to watch him saddle his horse and disappear down the trail. She just hoped he got far away before Griff returned, for there was no doubt what would happen to him if the outlaws encountered him on the trail. Would her actions be as futile as everything else she had ever done? After all her effort, would she still be the cause of Sam Killion's demise? She had only done what she believed was the best thing—for Killion, for Griff, and perhaps even for herself. She supposed it was just up to Killion's God to protect him.

18

McCULLOCH WAS NOT HAPPY when he returned to the cabin. He cursed Slim in no uncertain terms and might well have resorted to a more physical venting of his anger had Deborah not interceded.

Slim, still bound with the ropes, was stammering, "But . . . Bu . . . Boss. . . !"

McCulloch was shouting and raving too much to listen to his hapless associate. Only Deborah's quiet voice managed to pierce his tirade.

"It's my fault, Mr. McCulloch."

"What—?"

"I helped Mr. Killion to escape."

"You what!" Griff spun around, switching the force of his fury toward Deborah.

She tried to remain calm. "I could not stand by and watch him get killed."

"You knew I wasn't planning to—"

"I wasn't worried about you. I overheard Sid Miller and a couple of others making plans to kill him when you returned."

"But I told them what we had do with that Ranger!"

"They were determined to disobey your orders," Deborah replied. "I believe your life also would have been in serious danger if you had intervened."

"Why, them dirty snakes—!" But he stopped in his angry exclamation and took a more careful appraisal of Deborah. "What did it matter to you? Did you make some kind of deal with Killion?"

"I am tired of all the violence, Mr. McCulloch," she answered simply, earnestly.

"And you thought that was gonna help? Why, Killion could have half the lawmen in Texas here in a few days! You talk about violence, lady—that could mean a bloodbath. At least my way, everyone coulda walked away from here alive."

"We can still get away."

"He's got two days on us. How far could we get? Not far, with the law trailing us."

"Mr. Killion gave his word he would not go to the law," she attempted with a lame, sick look.

"And you believed him?"

Though she knew how foolish it sounded, she told the truth. "Yes, I suppose I did. Nevertheless, Mr. McCulloch, your way was not going to work if Mr. Miller had his way, and you might well have ended up dead yourself."

"Don't be so sure about that." But Griff saw the logic in Deborah's statement, and though he still wanted to skin her hide, he knew there was a more immediate problem to be dealt with. He took a sharp breath, glinted at Deborah and said, "I ain't finished with you yet!" Then he turned and charged outside.

Deborah followed fast on his heels. Realizing all her futile efforts

100

to allay violence were about to collapse, she still hoped to interject some reason into the forthcoming confrontation. Poor Slim, still bound hand and foot, yelled after the retreating figures to untie him. But no one listened. Griff was screaming Sid's name too loudly to hear. Deborah felt a twinge of sympathy, but not enough to pause; she knew how long it could take to loosen the ropes. Slim would probably be better off where he was anyway, out of harm's way.

Griff did not have to go far to find his erstwhile outlaw accomplice. Miller, having heard some of what happened, was storming toward the cabin to vent his own anger.

"I told you something like this was gonna happen!" Miller yelled. "I always said you was a lily-livered fool, Griff, an' now there ain't no doubt about it!"

Before Griff could respond, Deborah spoke up. "It's my fault he got away, not Griff's," she said. "Griff had nothing to do with it. I let him go because you were planning to kill him."

"Me? Why, you lying, murdering little tramp!" As Sid spat out his accusations, he quickly covered the short distance between him and Deborah, punctuating his words with a stinging slap across her face.

The force of the blow was enough to jar her head roughly, but she was accustomed to such abuse and held her footing, even though the pain brought tears to her eyes. She made no other acquiescence to the pain and stared at him as if she defied him to strike her again. And no doubt he would have if Griff had not intervened.

"Leave the woman alone!" he ordered, stepping between Sid and Deborah. "Your problem's with me, Sid, and no one else."

"She is the problem," retorted Miller. "She's got you wrapped around her finger. Maybe she ought to be the boss of the outfit. Maybe she's got more guts than you!"

"Don't push me, Sid! I ain't got much more patience left," growled Griff.

"I'm shaking in my boots." Sid's coarse, ugly face twisted with mocking fear. "I said before, if your plan with the Ranger blew up, I was gonna take over."

"Ha, ha! That's a real laugh." Griff's steely gaze did not change. If he was worried, Deborah could not tell. "You couldn't take over a henhouse."

"Maybe it's about time we found out."

"What's that supposed to mean?"

"I'm calling you out, Griff!"

This brought a mixed reaction from the men who had gathered around the scene. Most didn't particularly like Sid, but it had always

101

been the unspoken policy among them that the strongest man would lead them. If Sid was tough enough to stand up to Griff, and if he was fast enough to beat him, then he ought to lead. Some recalled a few years back when Griff had called out Monty Parker. It had been a fistfight then, and Monty, a muscular hulk of a man, outweighed Griff by fifty pounds and towered over him several inches. Griff laid Monty flat in less than ten minutes, and even Monty had conceded to Griff's superiority, staying with the gang despite his defeat because he admired Griff's courage. Monty had been caught rustling some of Caleb Stoner's cattle and, with Griff's best friend, had been hanged.

Somehow, though, even the most optimistic among the gang did not believe this present contest of strength would end as amiably as it had with Monty. Sid was mean and ornery, and there had always been bad blood between him and Griff. If it hadn't been this incident with Killion, it would have been something else. They had nearly come to blows on the recent job over a minor dispute. It was seemingly destined from the beginning for their relationship to end in violence.

When Griff answered Sid's challenge, all anger was gone from his voice. But his tone was lethal.

"I'm gonna give you one chance to back down, Sid, and walk away from here alive. Just start walking, and I don't never want to see your face again."

Sid laughed. "I ain't afraid of you, McCulloch."

"Okay," said Griff coolly, "name your game."

"Six-guns."

"You sure about that? I've been known to be pretty fast."

"Prove it."

"This is foolishness!" pleaded Deborah.

"Back away, Mrs. Stoner," said Griff. "This ain't got nothing to do with you anymore." Then he gazed at Sid as he took his Colt from his holster, spun the chamber to assure that it was loaded, and slipped it back in. "I'm ready, Sid."

They moved out into the middle of the yard while Deborah, helpless to stop the inevitable, moved toward the cabin. The other men scattered to safer positions.

"Mitch," said Griff, "count for us. We want this fair and square."

Then Sid and Griff began pacing away from each other. They had agreed to a ten-count.

Deborah watched tensely as Mitch counted off. *One . . . two . . . three. . . .* She knew what would become of her should Griff lose the gunfight. She silently counted along. *Seven . . . eight . . . nine . . .*

She did not know why her eyes shifted toward Sid at that moment. An instant later, and it would have been too late, but as it happened, she was in time to see Miller begin his move on the count of nine, his hand touching his gun as his body turned.

"Griff!" she screamed.

She covered her eyes, unable to watch the outcome as two shots in quick succession exploded in the still air. Slowly she removed her hands from her face, but only when she saw Sid's prostrate form did she let out her held breath in a relieved gasp.

"You weren't worried, now, were you, ma'am?" said Griff with a grin. He was not even flustered. He slipped his Colt into his holster. "I never figured Sid would make it all ten counts."

"You knew?"

"Just an educated guess, but thanks for the warning all the same. It helped, and I owe you one."

He turned his attention to the men. Some had cheered at his victory, especially touting Griff's skill in being able to outdraw someone even when the other man had a head start. But a few others were stunned. They had fully expected Sid to be their new leader by now, and they were suddenly very worried about their friendly association with Miller. It was to these that Griff addressed his next words.

"Anybody else thinking 'bout leading this gang?" he challenged. "What about you, Pablo? You think maybe you're faster than me?"

"No, Señor Griff, I am content," said the Mexican humbly.

"Good. Now that we got that cleared up, we got work to do." He strode to where several of his men were bent over Sid. Shaking his head with regret, he added, "He woulda been a good man if he weren't so ornery. Guess we better bury him. Then we gotta get some shut-eye, boys. We gotta hightail it outta here at first light."

Deborah watched the scene, shocked at how quickly and casually everyone put the terrible incident behind them and went about their business. Three or four men carried off Sid's body, while a few others went to tend the horses that had been hurriedly deserted when the altercation had begun. No one seemed disturbed that one of their number had died. And Griff showed no remorse at the fact that he had just killed a man. Was this, then, the wild West, where violence and death were so common they hardly broke up the established routine?

She had begun to have a taste of this in Stoner's Crossing, but she had naively hoped it might be isolated to the oppressive, calculating Stoner clan. Were these the attributes one must acquire to survive in this land? Was Leonard Stoner merely a product of a harsh, cold society? Would she also have to resort to violence in order to survive? The idea was frightening, but each day she lived in the West she became more and more certain it might be as inevitable as the showdown between Griff and Sid.

Griff noted the perplexed frown she wore and sidled up to her. "Ma'am, is there something wrong with you?"

"No one seems to care that a man has just died."

"No sense tearing your hair out over something we can't do nothing about no more."

He was so matter-of-fact about it. She wondered if she could ever respond in the same way to such things.

Griff continued. "Here in the West, ma'am, there usually ain't time to mourn your dead proper-like. Not that I'd be likely to grieve much for a varmint like Sid, but too often the business of staying alive don't give you no time for luxuries like mourning." He paused, seemed about to leave, then stopped and turned back to Deborah. "I'm sorry you had to witness this business, Mrs. Stoner. It weren't right for a lady to be present. But . . ." He hesitated briefly before forging ahead. "Well, ma'am, if you don't mind me saying, you're mighty squeamish for a woman who shot her own husband."

She knew he was fishing for information, for some confession or denial of her guilt. He had always been curious. But she did not yet want to think about what had happened three months ago in Stoner's Crossing.

"Whether or not I killed my husband," she answered, "it wouldn't necessarily mean I am a cold-blooded killer."

"And neither am I, ma'am. Sometimes you just gotta do what has to be done."

"Yes . . . I suppose so."

"Well, Mrs. Stoner, I reckon I best get my horse tended. If you don't mind and feel up to it, the boys and I'd appreciate if you'd fix a hot meal for us. We had a long ride today."

"Of course."

"And you'll be ready to ride out in the morning?"

"I still think Mr. Killion will keep his word."

"Better to be safe than sorry," Griff answered. " 'Course, if you want to stay behind, that's your privilege."

A long, arduous horseback ride at her stage of pregnancy was not something she looked forward to, but she knew she was not yet ready to survive alone.

Would she ever be?

19

AT LEAST SID MILLER'S DEATH released a horse for Deborah to ride alone. Yet even as the first light of dawn pierced the cabin window and the men outside were starting to stir, Deborah had not yet fully resolved to join the outlaws in their hurried retreat.

She had received much needed rest and respite here in the cabin and could not easily give it up. She had also counted on the settlements downriver to aid her during her time of confinement. If she went with Griff, she would again be thrust into an uncertain—and most likely dangerous—future. But could she truly count on Killion's word? He was little more than a stranger and a confessed lawman. All his religious prattle might well be a cover, a "smoke screen," as Griff had suggested. If Killion brought the law back to the cabin and they found her here, alone or otherwise, there could be no doubt of her fate. Most certainly she would go back to jail, even if her advanced pregnancy spared her the gallows. That was a fate she was no longer resigned to accept.

But if Killion could be trusted, it might mean she'd be able to finish the term of her pregnancy in the secluded peace of the wilderness cabin. Of course, neither Griff nor any of his men would be available to fetch help from the settlements when her time came.

So, finally realizing that the risks of remaining outweighed the risks of leaving with the outlaws, Deborah determined to join them. Sid's horse was an added affirmation of her decision. Thus, before the pink and orange of dawn had faded from the overcast sky, the party of eight riders departed the isolated clearing surrounding the little cabin. Deborah cast only a brief backward glance. This was no time for wistful attachments.

The air was chilly that morning and smelled of impending rain. Deborah was thankful again to Sid for the use of his sheepskin-lined leather coat, which she now hugged close to her body. The coat was oversized, easily accommodating her expanding waist, but it had a foul odor that made her nauseous. She knew, however, that the time would come when its warmth would surpass that inconvenience. Already summer was a distant memory, and winter lay immediately in their future. She had no idea where Griff was leading them or how long they'd be traveling, but it was very likely winter could catch them on the trail.

They followed the Red River west until a suitable place for crossing presented itself, then struck out north across the plains. They were in the Indian Territory now, each mile taking them farther and farther from Texas. Deborah never thought it possible that she could be so far removed from the Stoner Ranch. Now she was many days' journey from it, from that nightmarish world that had held her captive for so long. Had Caleb Stoner given up on her after all this time? As much as she would have liked to believe it, she knew otherwise. Caleb was not the sort to relent easily. In fact, Deborah fully expected to live the rest of her life under the shadow of his vengeance. No matter where she went or what she became, she would always have to take care that he did not find her. She was hundreds of miles from Stoner's Crossing, but was that even far enough?

Caleb's whole life had been his son—his eldest son. If such a man could take joy in anything, it was in the promise that this beloved son would carry on his name and identity. He would search the depths of hell itself to avenge that son's murder; and the grim irony that now his only heirs were the half-breed sons he disdained would feed his hate all the more.

For the first time in a long while, Deborah thought about Laban. He hated all of them, including herself for her part in Jacob's departure. But now Laban stood a good chance of being heir to the Stoner kingdom. Jacob would never return; he had done the only thing he possibly could. During her trial, Deborah had harbored a flimsy hope he might come to her rescue . . . but of course, that would have served no good but to get them both killed. Jacob was gone forever, and though she cared for him and thought of him as a friend, she knew her feelings went no deeper. She was glad he had escaped. Only an occasional gnawing fear—that he had stayed away from the trial because he was dead—disturbed this hopeful wish. If that were so, or he simply never returned, then Laban would definitely inherit Caleb's wealth, and that was perhaps the greatest irony.

Deborah found a small comfort in the fact that Caleb would end his days knowing his heritage would pass to an heir who despised him. Odd, how the only one to benefit from the tragedies of the last two years was quiet, sullen, withdrawn Laban. Well, Deborah was happy for him; he deserved something for all his years of pain.

Riding at a fast pace, the travelers struck the Washita River in a day and a half and crossed it under stormy skies. It rained all that day after the crossing, and foul weather threatened on the third day with cold temperatures and biting winds. They camped early that day when they happened to find a campsite as well-secluded from the inclement weather as they were likely to find on the open plains. Griff built a fire and made coffee, not caring about alerting Indians. Anyway, he said, the Indians were most likely wintering and not looking for a fight. But he set two lookouts just to be sure.

Mitch took first watch and found a position southeast of the camp, on a little rise that afforded a good view of the trail south of the river. He was leaning back against a rock, waiting for someone to bring him a hot cup of coffee, when he saw the movement way off in the distance. He shot to attention. But even with his good vision, the riders were too distant to reveal details. He was certain of only one thing: they weren't Indians. Wasting no more time with speculation, he raced back to camp.

"Riders approaching from the south!" he exclaimed as Griff was pouring his first cup of coffee.

Griff held the pot in midair. "Riders? Indians?"

"Ain't Indians, that's for sure. It's white men; I can tell from how they ride."

"Soldiers?"

"Nope. I'd a been able to tell the uniforms. There's a good dozen of 'em, though, and they're moving fast."

Griff jumped up, took a brief, wistful look at his coffee, then dumped it on the fire along with what remained in the pot. Dousing the fire, however, was probably a futile effort.

"It's gotta be the law riding like that," he said. "Looks like they finally caught up with us."

"You don't think it was Killion?" asked Mitch.

Before answering, Griff inadvertently glanced at Deborah; then he gave her a regretful shrug. "Mighta been," he said noncommittally. " 'Course, it could be a coincidence."

"You need not soften the blow, Mr. McCulloch," said Deborah acidly. "I was wrong, and I am sorry. I only hope I haven't brought trouble upon all of us."

"We ain't done for yet," said Griff. "There's still a chance we can outride them." He didn't add *unless they're Texas Rangers,* but that's what he thought. His tone remained optimistic. "Let's mount up. We got a couple more hours of daylight to burn."

They covered a lot of ground in that time and continued even after sunset as long as the ground was fairly level and the trail clear. Longjim, a seasoned mountain man who had lived some years with the Crow Indians, knew this country well and made a good guide, but even he had to stop when thick clouds obscured the light of the half-moon. They pitched a cold, dismal camp that night, made even more so by the eerie howling of wolves. It made Deborah shiver, and she cast a worried glance at Griff. He assured her he had never known a wolf to attack a man unprovoked, but he set an extra guard around the horses. They slept little, wondering if they were truly being pursued or if the riders were simply independents, outlaws like themselves, perhaps. But regardless of who it was behind them, Griff still would not chance giving away their presence. Even outlaws posed a danger, and he knew a few in particular that would be especially interested in the booty Griff's boys carried in their saddlebags. Contrary to popular lore, there was little honor among thieves, especially in the West.

The next morning, two hours before dawn even touched the sky, they broke camp and mounted. Deborah was sore and weary after the hard ride yesterday afternoon and could hardly face another day of the same. But Griff set an even more demanding pace that day— a pace which became nearly frenzied when they paused about an hour after crossing the Canadian River for a short rest. Griff saw their pursuers in a gorge only an hour or two behind them. Mitch said that was about how far away they had been when he first saw them.

"They musta rode all night to keep that pace," said Mitch.

"Anyway, it's a sure bet they ain't back there by coincidence," said Griff, shaking his head. He looked around at his men. "I hoped we could stay together for protection against Indians, but if they catch up to us, we gotta scatter in groups of two or three. Mrs. Stoner, you stick with me."

"I sure hope they ain't Rangers," said Slim, voicing all their fears.

"Come on, let's ride!" said Griff, spurring his palomino into a gallop.

They couldn't keep going at that rate indefinitely, much to Deborah's relief. Though she was an excellent rider, no woman in her condition could be expected to take such a punishment. At midday, they had to stop for a rest, not so much for Deborah's sake but because they would kill their horses otherwise. They ate a hurried, cold meal while the horses drank from a stream and nibbled grass. Griff paced the whole time, stopping only to shade his eyes against the gray glare of the sky to survey his pursuers. They seemed to keep coming on, never stopping, never resting. Who were they that they could keep this up? It was impossible that Sheriff Pollard from Stoner's town would have that kind of stamina. Even Griff's more recent enemies couldn't be that persistent. They had to be Rangers.

Deborah wondered the same thing. And from listening to the talk of the men, and from what she already knew of Texas Rangers, she, too, was convinced they were the ones who trailed them so relentlessly. Sam Killion, ex-Ranger, itinerant preacher and hypocrite, had betrayed her. But it was her fault for being so trusting. Hadn't the Stoners taught her anything? Would she ever be rid of that gullible optimism that seemed determined to dog her existence? She should have let Sid Miller shoot Killion. Now, she and Griff and six others would die because of her stupidity. If she ever saw Killion again, she'd kill him herself!

After only a fifteen-minute rest, they were climbing back into the hard saddles. They traveled many miles that day, and when night came, they had to sleep, if only for an hour. Griff reasoned that the Rangers had to sleep sometime, too. They had to!

So, as night descended, the outlaws fairly tumbled out of their saddles. They slept for three hours, not even bothering to set a watch.

Griff awoke first with a sickening start. He had intended to take lookout, but he had fallen asleep moments after sitting on the ground. He roused his companions with difficulty, having to threaten and cajole them mightily to make them move. They discussed splitting up right then, but it was finally decided that until it became absolutely necessary, they were still better off together. Griff said he was going to keep his eyes open for a good place for a showdown, for it was better they choose it than their enemies.

He never got the chance.

It was slow progress for the weary outlaws the rest of the night, picking their way carefully over the terrain with their exhausted animals, trying to cover their tracks as they proceeded. By the light of morning, there was no sign of pursuit, but everyone was too tired to cheer or do anything but trudge doggedly onward. At least they held some hope that their pursuers were indeed human beings, and not some sleepless, tireless other-worldly creatures.

Three hours after daylight, the outlaws had veered quite a bit to the east, hoping that by traveling in a more erratic pattern they would throw off the Rangers, or whoever it was tracking them. And they thought their plan was working. The grassy plains had gradually begun to give way to the valley of the Cimarron River with its swath of cottonwoods and other deciduous trees breaking the dreary landscape. Instead of wasting time trying to find a place to ford the river, the outlaws turned east along its bank.

Then the sound of pounding hoofbeats exploded upon them. Moments after the outlaws descended the bank, a dozen riders appeared at the top of the rise. Somehow they must have found a shortcut, for they could not have ridden for three days without sleep. But whatever the case, there they were, guns firing as they swooped, like vultures, down upon the outlaws.

Griff and his men had no choice now but to cross the river, hoping that the water would be shallow. In a frantic chaos of gunfire and the noisy protests of skittish, fatigued horses, the outlaws clamored into the water, which, at its deepest, reached the backs of the horses. Keeping her head low, Deborah was nevertheless amazed at how she and the others were escaping the barrage of bullets. Perhaps these lawmen weren't Rangers after all, for Texas Rangers were reputed for their marksmanship. Then, as if to mock her momentary optimism, she heard a sharp cry and saw one of the outlaws fall into the water, a widening pool of red surrounding his body.

Those who reached the shore first paused to return fire, covering their companions. But when all were on dry ground, they continued their flight, pausing only occasionally to fire back at the lawmen who lost some ground as they, too, forded the river. The gap was only momentary, however, and much too soon the lawmen were again within firing range.

They could no longer outrun the lawmen. Griff frantically surveyed their surroundings to find suitable cover for a pitched battle. But nothing was at hand but spindly trees and a few small rocks. It was time for the outlaws to scatter. Their only hope now was to divide the strength of the lawmen, if that's who they were.

Deborah had every intention of keeping her eyes on Griff and staying with him as he had instructed her. But just as he made a sharp veer to the left into a grove of cottonwoods, Deborah felt a stabbing burst of pain in her right shoulder. The suddenness of the gunshot and the shock of the initial blow broke her intense concentration and nearly blinded her. She could no more keep her eyes on Griff than . . .

Smack!

She did not see the low tree branch. It clipped her against the chest and dragged her from her horse. She landed with a thud on the ground and had only a blurred image of horses galloping past before blackness engulfed her.

20

THE BLACKNESS DID NOT go away. Deborah wondered if she was still unconscious or if her fall had blinded her. Several alarming moments inched by before she realized it was night. She must have been passed out for several hours, for it had been early afternoon when she had fallen from her horse.

But where was everyone? Why had they left her? Weren't even the lawmen interested in capturing her?

Her numbed mind cleared slowly, but eventually she became alert enough to speculate on what must have happened. First of all, she knew she lay in the same spot where she had fallen because when her eyes grew accustomed to the dark, she could see the branch that had unseated her. Possibly no one had even seen her fall. The lawmen, intent on pursuit, could have charged past, completely unaware of her presence. As for Griff, he certainly had been in no position to come back for her. She didn't expect it of him and, in a way, was glad he hadn't, for it would have been one more debt she owed him. Most likely he assumed she had been killed in the gun battle. Perhaps Griff himself had been killed. That thought saddened her a bit in spite of herself. She wanted no attachments, especially to men; but Griff, for all his coarse ways, had been decent toward her and, even if he was an outlaw, he had been a good man.

But, as Griff himself had once told her, the West did not allow one the luxury of grief. She had her own survival to attend to. She could not help Griff whether he was alive or dead, but there was still a chance for her.

She tried to move. The pain shooting through her shoulder nearly sent her into another black swoon, but she gritted her teeth against it and tried once more. This time she was ready and braced against it. She sat up. Much to her relief, her legs and left arm functioned properly. Nothing was broken. The next concern that leaped into her mind was soothed almost immediately as a heartening kick within her womb assured Deborah her baby lived.

Having confronted the more urgent matters, Deborah was free to contemplate the broader implications of her predicament. She was alone in the wilderness, she had no food, no horse, and no knowledge of where she was or in which direction she should go. Oddly enough, the hopelessness of her position did not panic her. She wished she had listened closer to Griff, but she had picked up a few things from him. Perhaps she was a fool to believe the little smatterings of trail lore she had chanced to glean from the outlaws could suffice her now, but it was all she had, and she was not ready to give up. Three months ago she might have done just that, for she had been beaten and defeated, willing to accept death as a welcome release. But the ensuing passage of time had restored her somewhat, giving physical strength if nothing else. She could also sense a kind of hope springing again within, even though it was only a hope born of stubborn refusal to allow Caleb Stoner to win. If for no other reason, she would endure and triumph over this new trial just to prove that there were some things, some people, in this world that Caleb could not control. Ironically, for her continued survival, he could never know of her victory over him, but that wasn't important—*she would know*. And that would have to be enough.

With that determination burning inside, Deborah dragged herself to her feet. The dull night spun before her eyes and nausea assailed her, but, clinging to a nearby tree trunk, she straightened her shoulders in spite of the coursing ache in the right one, and pushed out her chin. She peered through the dark almost as if she thought Caleb might be watching. Then she took a step on wobbly, weak legs, feeling like a newborn colt—not at all like a woman with a purpose.

Suddenly Deborah stopped and smiled to herself. Despite her determination, she had no idea at all where she was going. Even seasoned outlaws were cautious about traveling at night. As much as she wanted to proceed, common sense demanded that she wait until daylight. But how would she know, even by the light of day, which direction to take? Griff was going north, but where was north? It would be a fine victory over Caleb if she ended up inadvertently going back to Texas. Oh, how he would gloat as she stumbled back into his snare!

"Think, Deborah!" she said out loud to the silent night.

In books, sailors always plotted their course by the stars. Unfortunately, the present clouds did not permit her to see many of those heavenly guides. If she could but locate the North Star, she'd be all right. She and Graham used to "star gaze" in Virginia and had been able to find many of the constellations. The Big Dipper, Orion, Gemini ... they knew them all. Of course they had a spy glass to help them, and even they could not locate stars on cloudy days.

But she had one sure guide—the river. She knew she was on the north bank of the Cimarron River. If she made sure not to recross it, she ought to be all right. True, the river had many bends and curves, and if she set off at a point directly perpendicular from the bank, it could take her east or west—but that would be better than south to Texas. She could follow the river in the direction of the setting sun, which would lead her west. Curiously, Deborah had no desire to go back East even if it meant returning once more to Virginia. Somehow she was already sensing her future lay in the West, and, moreover, she was becoming more and more attached to this broad, free, wild land. It suited her, and it suited the person she knew she was becoming.

With the problem of her direction settled in her mind, Deborah all at once felt fatigued. The other problems could wait until morning, not that she could do anything about them anyway. She had no weapons to hunt food, though she recalled reading in some story how a man had shaped a crude spear from a branch and caught fish. She could not quite picture herself, skirt hitched up around her thighs, stalking a trout through the river. But if she meant to survive, she would be forced to do many things contrary to the upbringing of a proper Virginia lady. She had already strayed considerably from that mold. A little more distance would not harm her.

"You weren't going to think about food now, Deborah," she chided herself as her stomach began to rumble. "It's time to sleep."

With the tree trunk supporting her back, Deborah slid to the ground. She did not like succumbing to her fatigue, but she reminded herself that she had lost much blood from her wound. She had had little or no sleep over the last two days and she was supporting a new life. If she hoped to get anywhere tomorrow, she needed sleep. But the sound of howling wolves drove the notion of sleep even further from her mind.

Then she recalled Griff telling her wolves wouldn't attack humans. That helped comfort her a bit. Perhaps it was a blessing the horse had gone; its odor would surely have attracted the dangerous beasts. So she finally closed her eyes, not fully convinced, even as tired as she was, that she'd find any rest lying on the hard earth in the chill of the night.

Glaring sunlight woke her the next morning. She had slept soundly for hours. Her body ached, but Sid's sheepskin coat had kept

113

her fairly warm. A little stretching removed the kinks from her bones and muscles, though her right shoulder continued to radiate pain. Tearing apart her petticoat, she made a crude bandage and sling for her arm, which helped tremendously as she stood and moved about. A close inspection of her wound revealed that the bullet had traveled clean through her arm—a good sign, from what she knew of medical matters. If she kept it clean and free of infection, it should heal properly.

Next, Deborah began to think of breakfast. She had not eaten any food since yesterday morning, and that was only dry, tough jerky and stale biscuits. Oh, what she wouldn't give for some of that now!

The idea of spearing fish began to look more and more appealing. She cast about beneath the trees for a suitable branch, found one, then spent nearly an hour peeling away the smaller branches from it until she had a fairly clean, straight pole. The narrow end was still rather blunt even after she attempted honing it down with a sharp rock, but it might work.

Feeling a little foolish, she removed her shoes, then carried her stick to the water's edge and stepped into it quietly. Several fish swam past her feet as she lifted the spear in readiness. But one quick thrust did nothing but cause her to lose her balance and slip on the slimy riverbed. She went down with a splash, legs in the air and skirt billowing around her face. Sputtering and spitting water, she almost giggled at the sight she must have been; only a sharp pain in her arm upon impact sobered her. Undaunted, she scrambled once more to her feet and began all over again. By the tenth futile try she had muddied the water so badly she could not have seen a whale if it had floated by.

Her groaning stomach urged her to keep at it. Carefully, she moved away from the muddy water, then waited for another prey. It came—a nice ten-inch trout. She lifted her stick, took aim.

Thwack!

Great was her surprise when she lifted the stick and saw the wiggling creature impaled on its end. She laughed out loud and waddled out of the river.

What faced her now was perhaps the most difficult part of the whole task. She had no implements to clean the fish, much less cook it. It was raw fish for breakfast, or nothing. Deborah eyed the thing distastefully. Was she really that hungry? In response to the silent inquiry, she almost threw the thing back. But practicality forced her to pause. Perhaps she could skip this meal, but she would have to eat eventually, and she might not be so lucky to catch something next time. This pathetic morsel might be her only sustenance for days. It would be a sin to waste it.

She waited until the creature ceased its struggle with life. She found her sharp rock and managed at least to decapitate the thing and give it a cursory cleaning. Then, taking a deep breath, she raised it to her lips.

Somehow she choked it down and kept it down, drinking deeply from the river afterward. She hoped she would not get hungry again for a very long time.

After that ordeal, she needed a good, long rest. It was almost midday before she began her trek. The river proved a reliable guide, and she felt secure with its sure presence on her left side. But she did not walk down in the river gorge; rather, climbing up the ridge, she paralleled it from higher ground. This way she had a better view of her surroundings, making it less likely for anyone or anything to come upon her unawares. She had no idea what she would do if she was accosted by some unfriendly creature, human or otherwise, but she instinctively knew it was more advantageous to see danger approach than to be caught unawares. She glanced at the stick she carried. It might have more uses than merely hunting food.

Once a mountain man had stopped by the ranch. He was dressed all in buckskin, with a foul odor emanating from him, and tangled, matted hair beneath a beaver-skin cap, rotten teeth, and a bushy unkempt beard. He had come down from the isolated enclave he called home to look for a wife. Deborah had regretted that she had not been available! Now, thinking about him, Deborah wondered if she might not be mistaken for some kind of mountain woman in Sid's old coat, her tattered, dirty dress hanging damply beneath it, and her grimy body under that. The image was surely furthered by the dusty slouch hat she wore—Griff had loaned it to her—combined with the smudges and bruises on her face, and the primitive spear in her hand.

But as bizarre as her appearance might have been, it somehow seemed more real to her than the ribbons and laces and hooped skirts of a southern lady.

115

21

DEBORAH TRAVELED THUS FOR two days, hunger and fatigue her close companions. Only once did she see a sign of another human. On her second afternoon of travel, much to her delight, she spotted a large herd of buffalo in the distance. So enthralled was she at the sight that she dared to leave the security of the river to draw closer.

There were at least several hundred of them grazing placidly on the grassy plain. They were magnificent, with their great shaggy heads and bodies at least as tall as she was, although she did not venture close enough for an accurate measure. She had read accounts by explorers like Lewis and Clark and John Fremont, describing the herds as being so vast as to darken the entire country with their numbers, like a huge, moving forest. This sight made her a believer in what many called wildly exaggerated reports. She had also read how Indians stalked these mighty beasts with nothing but a bow and arrows, or a spear. That was harder to believe, though it must be true since guns were still not plenteous among the Indians. Yet how could a mere shaft of wood bring down such a gigantic creature? If she had anything of value to give, she would not hesitate to sacrifice it in order to witness such a contest.

All at once, as if her unspoken wish were being answered, several riders approached the herd. There were perhaps twenty of them, and there could be no doubt they were stalking the herd, which suddenly lurched into motion at the first hint of pursuit. And of another fact there could also be no doubt: the riders were Indians!

Too captivated to heed her own danger, Deborah stood in the grass shielded by nothing more than some spindly prairie gorse. She was, nevertheless, a great distance from the scene, and even a far-seeing Indian was unlikely to notice her unless he chanced to gaze directly at her. She did not move for several moments. The buffalo were trotting at a fair clip now, but the hunters, on their sleek mounts, were keeping pace. She could discern little more detail than that, but could tell when one of the Indians made a successful kill, for a mighty buffalo would stumble forward as its forelegs crumpled under it; then its body would crash to the ground. Two or three fell in this way, some impaled by arrows, some dropped by rifle fire, before the herd had stampeded across the plain, almost out of sight.

When the Indians returned to butcher and pack their kill, Deborah suddenly realized her danger. No longer occupied with the intensity of the hunt, the warriors might take a closer note of their surroundings. It never occurred to her that they might be a source of help, and thus, she dropped quickly into the grass, hoping her foolish curiosity would not be her undoing. She carefully crept back to the river and down beside the cover of the ridge. There she waited, hardly moving, hardly breathing, for what seemed like hours.

Finally she crawled back up the ridge and toward where she had witnessed the hunt. Standing and gazing all about, she saw nothing. The prairie was as empty of man and beast as it had been during her previous days of travel. The buffalo and Indians might have been nothing more than an illusion, a mirage born of her weariness.

With every passing hour, as she continued her journey along the course of the Cimarron, she became more and more amazed at the wonders around her. The lovely green forested Virginia countryside had given her a taste of the marvels of nature. Her happy days riding the Texas prairie with Jacob had begun to instill an appreciation of the peculiar beauty of this new land. But now the land became a part of her as never before. Her very life depended upon it. Either she could fight it as if it were her enemy, reaching out to crush her at first opportunity, or she could flow with it, not as an adversary but as a friend, a companion. If she starved here on these wide, grassy plains it was not because they willed it, but rather due to her own ineptitude, her inability to truly become one with the land. It offered plenty to succor all her needs: fresh, clear water, abundant food, and beauty to soothe her soul. Only her lack of ingenuity prevented her from partaking fully of it.

She remembered how the maps in her childhood school books had always labeled this huge central swath of the United States "The Great American Desert." In reality, it was no desert. True, when you wandered too far from rivers, it was dry, dusty, and burning hot in the summer. Much of it was flat and treeless—so, of course, those travelers accustomed to a forest-based society might find little to recommend it. But Deborah found only openness and freedom. If she had one of her father's lively thoroughbreds, she would give it

117

full rein and fly like the very wind over its length and breadth.

On the morning of her third day of travel, at sunrise, Deborah climbed a small rise a hundred or so yards from the river. She sat quietly and watched the sun ascend over the flat plain stretching out below her. The clouds and gray of previous days had cleared and, though a chilly wind blew, the day promised to be a fine one. The pale blue sky, streaked with wispy strands of pink, seemed to offer her a pleasant greeting. She was tired and weak—sometimes she wondered if she could take another step—but the sight refreshed her as surely as if it had been a hearty breakfast. It made her think of her father and Graham, and that alone was food for a weary soul.

Josiah Martin had passed on to her and her brother his awe for the wonders of nature. How many times had she heard him say, "There is beauty in all of creation, children, even if sometimes you have to search a bit to find it."

And he was always quoting scripture to them. "The earth is the Lord's and the fullness thereof." And, "The heavens declare the glory of God; and the firmament showeth his handiwork."

Deborah suddenly began to believe he might be right. It was impossible that this land could have sprung up in a random fashion with no direction, no design. Nothing supported more eloquently the existence of a Master Creator than nature itself. It gave proof of a God who cared enough to spare nothing of His creative energy in order to provide such a varied and vibrant world. Sitting there completely alone, with no sign of life within miles save a jackrabbit or two bounding across her path, Deborah could almost feel as if she were the sole recipient of this heavenly gift. Odd to think God would give *her* gifts! She knew well that she deserved none. How often had she repudiated Him, railed at Him, even cursed Him? She had never truly denied His existence, though, for to do so would have invalidated everything her father stood for, everything he was as a person.

Still, if God were responsible for the beauty of nature, was He not then responsible for all aspects of His creation? For death and pain, and the cruelty of men like Caleb and Leonard Stoner? But how could the same God who brought her such suffering also bestow upon her the inestimable gift of what now surrounded her? Even Deborah's father had found no adequate answer for this question. When Graham had died, Josiah had only been able to say that God had some purpose, that He would somehow bring good out of the tragedy of death.

What good had come out of it, anyway? The death of her father? The disastrous marriage to Leonard? Her near execution? An unwanted pregnancy?

Could she possibly believe that good was yet to come her way? She glanced up at the sky where the display of color had gradually given way to the pale blue of morning. She was not so naive as to believe that she ought to have a perfect life with no troubles; no one on earth had such a life. But if she were expected ever to embrace God, believe in Him in the way her father had, she must understand Him first. She must be able to trust that she was not merely the victim of the whims of some almighty tyrant—some heavenly Caleb Stoner. She would never—*never!*—subject herself to such an existence again. And even if God did somehow prove himself to have her best interests in mind, she wasn't sure she could even then submit her will to another again.

She was finally free, and this untamed wilderness only verified that sensation. Ironically, if this land were God's gift to her, it also stood as an obstacle to the most profound gift He would give her— true freedom that went far beyond the mere shedding of physical shackles, a freedom from the bondage she herself had laid upon her own spirit. The keen external release this land gave her blinded her, at least for the time being, to her deeper need. She simply could not see how submission to God was not the same as subjection and bondage and abject slavery.

"I might believe," Deborah murmured into the wind, "but I will never submit. If you are truly not a tyrant, you will accept that."

She sat there for some time before she found the inner will to rise and leave that peaceful spot, to face again her arduous and seem- ingly hopeless journey. But at last she struggled to her feet, plodded down the hill and, fixing the position of the river to her left, began once more. Often she traversed no more than six or seven miles a day. She stopped frequently, sometimes lying down right where she was and falling asleep. Once in a while she heard the cries of wolves, but she was too tired to be afraid. She had made peace with the land, if not with the Creator of the land, and she was ready to accept the fate it held for her. She might well die here in this lovely wilderness. She had always known that sheer grit and determination were not enough to sustain the frail physical shell that contained them.

And each day that shell became weaker and weaker. The wound in her shoulder began to flame and fester. It needed soap and water and a clean bandage. But she dared not bathe in the river, for the cold water and cold air might well give her pneumonia. She had been lucky to have suffered no ill-effects from her first dousing, but now she was much weaker, and it would not take much to bring her down. Twice more she had speared raw fish for food, but when she tried a fourth time she became sick, vomiting what little food was in her stomach and heaving bile for hours afterward. The mere thought of fish, raw or otherwise, made her want to retch. She could not go on much longer.

She began wondering if following the river was such a good idea after all. Perhaps it was taking her away from civilization rather than toward it. She knew so little of the geography of this area; not many whites did. They weren't interested in this so-called wasteland—that's why thirty years ago they had designated it Indian Territory. She knew of no white settlements here, but she thought parts of the Cimarron River were close to the Kansas border, where there were certainly settlements and army posts. But even if she was only fifty miles from Kansas, it could mean many days' journey at her present speed. Without food or medical attention she could be dead long before that.

If she did dare to leave the river course, she risked dying of thirst, for water would be scarce. She gazed off toward the north. Griff had intended on going that way. He never said if he had another hideout somewhere out there, or if he was heading toward a town. There would be water if Griff planned to go that way, yet distances between water holes on horseback were far different than for a weak, sick woman on foot. At least by the river she could be certain of water, if nothing else.

She cast one final, wistful glance northward, then continued to follow her previous path along the river. She thought of those Indians she had seen the other day. They would have food and shelter from the cold wind, and maybe even some medicine to ease the ache in her shoulder. Perhaps it would not be so bad to be found by Indians. Oh, she had heard the horror stories of white women taken captive by them. Caleb had told her a few to frighten her out of running away. They amounted to tales of women mutilated and ravaged, forced to live in filth as slaves and chattel to brutal, savage warriors.

Something like what I escaped in Stoner's Crossing, Deborah thought with bitter irony.

She would give anything to see but one human face—any face, be it red or white. Or, was she really that desperate? Would she give up her freedom? Fortunately, Deborah never had to make such a choice.

Around midmorning of her fourth day, the winds, always constant on the plains, doubled in velocity as they decreased in temperature. Deborah had heard of these icy blasts—they called them "Northers" in Texas, probably because they seemed to be blowing directly from the North Pole. Deborah's progress had slowed, sometimes even

120

stopped altogether as she plowed her way against the wind like a ship sailing into a gale. Many times she was buffeted to the ground, and it took all her reserve of strength to rise again to her feet, only to be knocked down once more after a few steps. Often she just crawled along the ground, which turned into mud when the rain began. Rain and wind lashed violently at her, while splattered mud blinded her. After an hour of this unrelenting struggle, she wanted only to stop, lie down where she was, and rest. But instinct told her that if she stopped now, she would find only a rest from which she'd never awaken. As long as she kept in motion, she was alive; soon that became her only way to discern between life and death.

22

DEBORAH NO LONGER KNEW IF she was going in the right direction. She could not see the river through the downpour. But she no longer cared.

Before, she had had some hope she might survive this impossible situation. The land had been hospitable, friendly. She might have found the strength to continue for a few more days at least. Now Deborah did not know what to think. The prairie had suddenly turned on her, become hostile. It no longer held welcoming arms out to her, but struck her instead with heavy fists. Like everything else in this life, it wanted to crush her, break her spirit, control her, kill her, destroy her.

"Don't hit me! Please, Leonard! I will try to be a better wife."

Deborah clawed her fingers into the muddy earth in a pathetic attempt to propel her feeble body along. But the hard ground, the driving rain, the icy wind, were no longer substantial entities. They were monsters with huge, yawning mouths and sharp, icy teeth, ready to devour her.

"The earth is the Lord's. . . ."

Was that, then, His answer to her? Plucking His gift from her hand because He could not have complete control of her being?

"Oh, Papa, how could you have been so wrong?"

Soon other monsters loomed in Deborah's path. She could not shut them out, for she was no longer able to tell the real from the imagined. Was it the cold sting of the rain, or the vile touch of her husband? And that sound—the howling wind, or . . . or Caleb Stoner's accusing rasp?

"You killed my son, and you will pay!"

"Haven't I already paid? How much more must I suffer before you are happy?"

But Leonard was dead. Why did the suffering continue? Would she never be free? For so long she had thought only of his death and the release it would bring. She had bought that gun, praying—praying!—for him to give her cause to use it. But it hadn't turned out as she planned, as she had hoped. She still wasn't free, not really.

"Don't you know, Deborah, I will always control you! Remember, it is my baby you are carrying."

The whine of the wind turned into evil laughter as the specter of Deborah's dead husband hovered before her, nightmarish, frightening.

He had deserved to die. No honest court would have convicted her. He had deserved that bullet in his back. But Caleb had twisted everything, turned lies into truth and truth into lies until even she had ceased to know what was true. And the whole town believed him; and in her confusion and guilt, she could not convincingly refute them.

"Yes, sir, Your Honor. She come into my store and bought herself a derringer. She said it was to be a present for her man, so for me to be mum about it." The storekeeper's damning testimony.

"Looks like she'd been planning to kill him for months."

"It don't matter if she ended up using a different weapon. Derringer or six-shooter, the husband's just as dead."

"She said he struck her." Even the banker's nice wife! *"But I never saw any mark on her."*

"She and my brother Jacob were seeing each other secretly." Oh, Laban! Not you, too!

During the whole of the trial there had been no one to speak on her behalf. Even strangers accused her. That woman from the cantina—Deborah had never laid eyes on her before the trial, yet what a gleam of triumph radiated from her eyes as she testified.

"I was acquainted with Señor Stoner, as I am with all the regular customers." She was an attractive Mexican woman, three or four years older than Deborah. What could she possibly have against Deborah?

122

"He was very distressed over his wife's behavior. He did not say she had been unfaithful, but a woman can tell these things. I could see he had been shamed by his wife."

"He spoke freely with you?" the judge had asked.

"No more than anyone speaks in a saloon. Once when he had more to drink than was good for him, he did say she had locked him from her bedroom and threatened to kill him if he touched her."

Lies! All lies!

Why did no one testify about the splintered door or her strangled cries of agony? But Leonard had always been careful. It was possible even Maria did not know everything. She did not live in the main house, after all, and most of Leonard's abuse took place long after she had retired to her cottage.

"Sí, the door was broken one day." Yes, Maria had testified. *"But, Señor Judge, what is a man to do when a wife will not perform her duties?"*

"Were there fights?"

"Never was a pleasant word exchanged between them, Señor, but I did not ever see Señor Leonard Stoner harm his wife."

No, of course you did not see. No one saw.

"What of the guards?"

"After the trouble with Señor Jacob, Señor Leonard could not trust his wife any longer. He wanted a child of his own, Your Honor. What man doesn't?"

Yes, it all made perfect sense. She had every reason to kill him, but none of the reasons stated in court added up to self-defense. She was an unfaithful wife who wanted out of a constricting marriage. She had committed premeditated murder in order to indulge freely in her immoral ways.

Caleb's lies had not helped either.

"I sensed from the beginning that she would bring my son nothing but grief. She was headstrong and spoiled. Even on their wedding night she had refused him his due. He confessed this to me in total desperation."

"It's true," verified one of the wedding guests. *"I was just partaking of a last brandy with Caleb when Leonard joined us—not an hour after . . . well, you know."*

"What was his state of mind at that time?"

"He didn't look none too happy. Not like you'd expect a fella to look on his wedding night."

Everyone saw what they wanted to see. She was a wanton hussy, a murderer. There was only one thing to do with such a person. No one protested when she was sentenced to hang. And neither did she.

She had killed Leonard, as surely as she had probably killed Jacob, even Griff. One she had willed dead, the others she had sent to a sure death by her poor judgment. Did it matter if her finger pulled a trigger or not? That's what Laban had meant with his accusations the day Jacob left. She gave him no argument then, so why should she now? Everyone she loved was dead. To protest now might only place Leonard's true murderer on the gallows, and Deborah could not face causing yet another death. At the time it seemed only right to let it all end with her. Life had become too much of a burden, anyway.

A heavy, heavy burden.

As heavy as a soaking wet sheepskin coat dragging down upon her shoulders. Dragging her down . . . into the mire, the filth. The burning pain in her right arm slicing through her entire body. A woman can be expected to fight for only so long.

"Oh, God, am I to die out here?"

But it was fitting, wasn't it, to die here, alone, in this place that had been kind to her? She could ask for no better coffin than this spacious, grassy prairie.

The prairie.

Prairie . . .

"You are a grand horse, clothed with thunder. . . ."

"Oh, Jacob, why didn't you come to rescue me? . . . You must be dead. . . ."

Deborah's body relaxed. She could move no more. She was glad that in the end the wind and the rain had conquered her rather than Caleb Stoner. She'd never see his gloating face over her final defeat. He'd never even know for certain if she was alive or dead. He'd always wonder, never certain.

It would make up for his dead certainty when he found her standing over Leonard's body with her husband's Colt in her trembling hand.

"You murderous tramp! You have killed my son!"

"No! I saw someone . . . he might still be out there . . . I took the gun. . . ."

But what was the use? No one believed her. Perhaps she had imagined it, after all. Maybe this was the dream, and what she had always thought to be the nightmare was the reality. The dream that so often haunted her sleep did seem so real. Only in it she held a derringer in her hand, not a Colt. But that look of disbelief on Leonard's face could not have been more real.

"Put that gun down, Deborah."

"Beg me, Leonard! Beg me to spare your life!"

"Don't be foolish."

"Get on your knees and beg for mercy." She lifted the little gun, leveling it at his head. *"You only have to beg for your life, Leonard. How many times have I had to plead for my self-respect, my very soul?"*

"You unfaithful hussy! You deserved what you got."

"Then die, Leonard! Die . . . die . . ." Whoever said vengeance wasn't sweet?

And her hand no longer trembled as her finger squeezed the trigger. But did that horrifying explosion wake her from a tortuous dream, or did it merely usher in the true nightmare?

What truly happened the night Leonard Stoner was killed?

She was so certain she had seen someone. Maybe they were right. Maybe she *was* crazy, maybe she *was* a murderer.

Maybe . . . but she was supposed to have used the derringer, not the Colt. What did it matter? A Colt, a derringer . . . her husband was dead just the same.

And still she wasn't free. Not yet. But soon . . . soon she would be. The beautiful prairie was waiting to receive her, to take her at last to where she could know peace. She had finished fighting. She was tired.

"God, I am sorry I could do no more than believe. I am sorry it wasn't enough."

All she wanted now was to rest, like at Griff's cabin, only longer. *Longer* . . .

Soon Deborah did not feel the sting of the wind or the icy fingers of rain against her face. She felt nothing at all. But she felt no peace, either. In her delirium she continued to struggle, writhing on the ground for some time until a troubled unconsciousness overcame her.

At least death, or oblivion, or whatever it was, had stopped the terrible rain. The next sensation Deborah felt was of looking up, through distorted vision at a blue sky. Then a shadow passed over her.

No, not a shadow but a face.

"Griff, is that you. . . ?"

But the voice that replied was not Griff's, and the words it spoke were mumbled, foreign.

A few hazy moments passed, allowing no further consideration of what was happening. Deborah passed again—into oblivion, if not rest . . . into unconsciousness, if not peace.

125

PART 3

BROKEN WING

23

THE SHAMAN, CALLED CROOKED EYE, had received a sturdy pony and a fine bull buffalo hide for his services. A substantial payment when the patient was a stranger. He had accepted the gifts even though he saw that the sickness was perhaps too serious even for his strong medicine. He looked at his wife, Gray Antelope Woman, who assisted him. She wore a solemn expression and shook her head slightly. She was concerned for the unborn infant, as was understandable since Gray Antelope had never borne a child of her own. Her heart went out to such a great loss, should the baby die with the mother.

She handed her husband the potent concoction of sweet grass mixed with ground juniper and dried, pulverized mushrooms and powdered bitterroot. Crooked Eye sprinkled the mixture over the fire in the lodge, and its pungent aroma permeated the air as it purified the shaman and his patient.

Then followed the ritual for driving the evil spirit from the lodge. Crooked Eye chanted a powerful invocation while shaking his sacred rattle, made by his father many summers ago from the mighty snake he slew after it had tried to attack Crooked Eye's mother. This held strong medicine; the bad spirits would obey.

This ceremony completed, Gray Antelope Woman gave the patient a tea of healing herbs. The sick woman was, most of the time, in a fitful, troubled sleep. Sometimes she mumbled incoherently. Sometimes she opened her eyes, but she did not see. When the poor woman cried out, Gray Antelope Woman did not know if it was from fear or pain. Thus, the woman swallowed some of the tea but choked and sputtered some of it. She took enough for the tea to do its work. It would calm her, perhaps bring peace to her sleep. It might heal her also, for in it was a very potent herb. But Crooked Eye would not trust only the tea. He knew the woman's illness went deep.

Crooked Eye glanced at his small audience in the lodge. Broken

Wing, who had brought the woman to the shaman, his brother Stands-in-the-River, and his sister-in-law Stone Teeth Woman, were watching carefully, expecting the best effort for their payment, even if the patient was only a white woman.

Hovering over his patient, the shaman paid particular attention to her inflamed right shoulder. He bent low until his face was very close to the injury, and made motions as if he were sucking the offending disease from the arm. Then he raised up and with great flourish, brought his hand to his lips and instantly a small feather appeared in his hand. His audience nodded with approval. The feather, of course, was supposed to be the cause of the woman's sickness, and with its removal from her body she would recover. But more chants were still sung, and Gray Antelope administered more tea and rubbed a poultice of the same herbal mixture over the wound.

Now only the passage of time would tell if the woman would return to this life or if she would travel the Hanging Road over the Milky Way to the place of the dead.

Gray Antelope shooed the visitors from the lodge so the patient might receive the best benefit from the shaman's skill. Broken Wing lingered, and with sad eyes turned toward the pale, sick patient, all but swallowed up within a mound of Crooked Eye's best hides.

"Don't worry," said Gray Antelope, "you will have your captive back."

"I did not capture her; I found her," Broken Wing replied with more than a little pride in his tone.

"Of course, of course," said Gray Antelope patronizingly. "A gift from *Heammawihio* himself." She only mocked him halfheartedly. Perhaps his tale was true.

"I was seeking a vision," the young warrior said.

"And you found the white woman."

"It is a good sign."

"If she lives."

Crooked Eye sidled up to the pair. "Do you doubt my skill, woman?" he asked with a raised brow.

"If she lives, it will only be *because* of your great skill, husband."

Crooked Eye smiled. He had married a smart woman, even if she could not bear children.

Gray Antelope finished clearing the lodge. Crooked Eye left also, leaving his wife alone with the patient. She sat on the dirt floor next to the woman, studying her carefully. The tea was taking effect, for she seemed to be sleeping easier, not fighting as much against it, or against whatever evil spirits were haunting her. Beneath the dirt and grime of the trail, Gray Antelope thought there was a beautiful woman—at least by the standards the white man had for such things. Her skin was pale and her face was thin, but perhaps with health and good food that might change. Her golden hair, too, would probably shine like the sun when all the filth was washed from it. She had only one other time seen hair as yellow—it had been hanging from the scalp belt of a warrior called Little Left Hand.

But this woman would keep her hair. Broken Wing was being very protective of his "find." In fact, if anything happened to the white woman, it would be Crooked Eye's hair that would be in more danger!

Nevertheless, Gray Antelope thought it might still be worth her while to try to buy the white woman from Broken Wing. She might then have the baby to raise as her own, especially if the woman herself died. However, the woman must not die yet, for the baby did not appear to be grown enough to survive on its own. Regardless, Broken Wing would not let her go cheaply.

Could it be true that *Heammawihio,* the Wise One Above, did indeed send the woman as a sign to Broken Wing? It was an unusual sign, but Broken Wing had spent his young years with a mountain man and had learned many of the ways of the whites, so perhaps such a sign was not as peculiar as it seemed.

The white woman stirred but did not awaken. She would remain asleep for some time.

"If the Wise One Above wills it, you will live," murmured the Indian woman to the prostrate form. "If he does not and you die, maybe you will not mind so much if I raise your baby."

Gray Antelope rubbed more poultice on her patient's shoulder. It was obviously a bullet wound. Could other Indians have shot her, perhaps while raiding her people as they traveled across the plains to the land on the other side of the far mountains? But Crooked Eye said the wound was made with a pistol, a kind the Indians did not often use. Was she then shot by her own people? It was not like even the white men to shoot their own women, especially those with child. The woman said many words in her sleep, but Gray Antelope did not have the white man's language so she could not understand. Perhaps she would let Broken Wing listen. He had learned some from the mountain man.

An hour later Gray Antelope emerged from the lodge. Although it had been light hours ago when she had entered the lodge, it was dark now. There was no moon tonight, but several fires burned about the camp, giving enough light for her to see the approaching figure in time to avoid colliding with it. She smiled to herself. It was Broken

131

Wing. He must have been waiting outside the lodge the whole time, or was watching it closely from his own lodge across the way.

"Is she well?" he asked anxiously.

"Not yet."

"But she will live?"

"I think so. She fights."

"That is good. The Wise One Above is with her."

"It is not for me to say." Gray Antelope Woman cast a shrewd eye toward the young warrior. "The white one is very sick. It takes strong medicine to heal her."

"That is why I brought her to Crooked Eye."

"He did not know at first how much it would take to mend her."

Broken Wing cocked an eyebrow at the older woman. He was young, but he was not a fool. "Was my gift too small?"

"For a sick white captive, no. But for one who is a sign from *Heammawihio*. . . ?" She pursed her lips together and nodded meaningfully, allowing him to draw his own conclusions. This was not difficult for him to do.

"I will give him another horse—a very good one that I captured wild myself."

"Crooked Eye needs no more horses."

"Ha! What Cheyenne has no need for horses?" He realized now that the woman was speaking for herself and not for her husband.

"I want the white woman's baby," Gray Antelope said flatly.

"The whites do not part easily from their children. In this way they are much like us. Take my horse, Gray Antelope Woman; it will serve you well."

Gray Antelope sighed. She knew Broken Wing, for all his youth, was right. She knew also that she would not have had the heart to take the child from its mother, anyway. It had been a tempting idea, though. There was still the chance the woman would die, for many white women were too frail for the hard life on the plains. Then she recalled the look on the white woman's face and thought otherwise. That woman would not die easily. Her outer shell might be delicate like a hummingbird's, but inside, she had the marrow of a buffalo. At least that is what Gray Antelope thought. Time would tell.

24

DEBORAH WAVERED ON THE EDGE of consciousness for three more days. But even when she appeared to be awake, fever and delirium were never far from her. Not until the sixth day after her arrival in the Cheyenne camp north of the Cimarron River did she finally depart the netherlands of fever and exposure and near-starvation.

When she awoke at last, the play of eerie nighttime shadows reflecting from the fire in the lodge dulled the line between waking and sleeping. She was very warm, and her first conscious thought was that summer must have come to the prairie, that it had been months, not days, since that terrible rainstorm. But then she moved, and the fresh ache in her right shoulder affirmed that only a short time must have passed. But if it was winter, why was she so warm? Had some settler found her and taken her into his cabin? It was an odd cabin, with walls that seemed to tilt inward all around, coming to a peak at what should have been the ceiling.

The covers that contributed largely to her warmth were odd, too. They were heavy, a bit scratchy and with a gamey odor. But they were warm and gave her a peculiar sense of security.

"Where am I?" she asked, but in a drowsy tone as if she didn't really care one way or another if she received an answer.

Several voices spoke at once, but she didn't understand a word. She tried to peer through the semidarkness of the lodge; then someone tossed a log on the fire and the flame flared up, sending fingers of erratic light about the room. She caught her first glimpse of her companions.

Indians!

She knew she should be frightened, but she wasn't. She felt too warm and secure to be afraid.

A woman knelt down beside Deborah, holding a hollowed-out gourd in her hands. She spoke, but Deborah could not understand.

133

The woman touched Deborah's lips with the gourd, apparently wanting her to drink. She looked at the contents of the cup—some white, creamy-looking substance. Then she looked at the woman.

She was several years older than Deborah, perhaps in her late thirties. Her dark skin was not lined except for fine crows' feet about the corners of her eyes and lines framing her long, thin mouth. She had large black eyes that, as they reflected the flames of the fire, looked strikingly like burning coals. She spoke in a deep, resonant voice, both sad and vibrant. Deborah at once felt no fear in accepting the strange offering in the gourd.

Deborah drank deeply. It was a chalky liquid, rather tasteless, and though it wasn't exactly unpleasant, she had the distinct impression it was medicine of some sort. When she finished drinking, she lay back, content to sleep again.

The Cheyenne lodge was illuminated with sunlight when Deborah next awoke. This time there were no voices, no movement of others, no comforting warm fire. She was alone.

She slipped out from under her heavy covers. Her shoulder still ached, but not as badly as she remembered. Her body was stiff but seemed willing to cooperate with her as she gingerly moved each limb, one at a time. Everything seemed to be in working order, and she felt her baby kicking. She tried to get up—not an easy endeavor considering she had been flat on her back for days and there was nothing nearby she could use for support. She lay down again, out of breath from her efforts. But now that she was fully awake, she was unwilling to remain inactive. She wanted to know where she was, who she was with, and if she was a prisoner or a patient. Rolling onto her side, she struggled to her knees, crawled like an ungainly porcupine to one of the tent supports and, grasping it, pulled herself to her feet.

She was no longer wearing her gray muslin dress, she realized—the same dress she had worn continuously, except when she removed it for washing, since that day Griff had rescued her from the gallows. Now she wore a plain brown shift, made of some animal hide that hung straight and shapeless to about her mid-calf. It struck her as significant that the gray dress was gone, but she did not pause to ponder the implications of this. She was too anxious to answer other more pressing questions.

On rather shaky legs, Deborah walked to the lodge entrance and lifted the flap. The air was several degrees cooler outside, but the sun was bright and the sky was blue. No trace could be seen of the storm that had assailed her. There were many other lodges scattered along a narrow waterway. She could see several dozen from where she stood, all in the tepee shape she had read of and viewed pictures of, but had never actually seen. This was, truly, an Indian village. The busy residents, mostly women and children, with long, black hair and walnut brown skin, and wearing their buckskin garb, gave ample proof. Deborah watched the activity for five minutes, entranced. Children were playing—girls with dolls made of sticks and hides; boys with small bows, wrestling with one another or playing chase. Deborah noted one little girl riding a stick horse with her buckskin doll perched in front of her; both were having a grand time parading around the open ground between the tepees.

Women were engaged in cooking, sewing, and doing other activities completely alien to Deborah. One woman shooed a barking, frolicking dog away from an object that looked similar to a quilting frame except that it lay stretched out low on the ground and held a sleek hide. The scene that greeted Deborah was pleasant, inviting, and she found herself smiling in spite of her personal trouble and uncertainty.

Instinct told Deborah this place held no danger for her. Even when, one by one, several of the nearby villagers began to take note of her presence, stopping their labors to stare, Deborah did not feel threatened.

Before long one of the women looked up from where she was bent over a large animal hide. Deborah vaguely recognized her. That face had floated before her while she lay half-conscious, and she realized this woman had nursed her during her illness. Deborah remembered the warm, sad face, broad and unaffected and beautiful in its simplicity. She recalled, too, those eyes that had seemed to burn with intensity, though now, by the light of the sun, they were softer, yet no less intense. The woman rose and approached Deborah.

"Hello," Deborah said. "I'm feeling better now."

The woman replied in her Indian language, but Deborah did not understand. Using signs that were almost more expressive than words, the woman made it clear that Deborah should not be walking around, that she should return to her bed.

"But I am better," said Deborah, accompanying her statement with her own attempt at signs. "I believe I have you to thank for caring for me."

The woman shrugged her lack of understanding, then called one of the children and gave him some instructions, upon which the child dashed away. Turning back to Deborah, the woman firmly nudged her back into the lodge and to her bed. Not wanting to cause a stir at this early date, and feeling she owed the woman that much at least, Deborah obeyed. She was starting to feel rather shaky, anyway.

The woman brought Deborah a bowl of food, a thick soup with bits of meat and roots that tasted like turnips. Deborah tried to sign a request for a spoon, to which the woman replied with an encouraging nod. Deborah waited for a moment, but no spoon was forthcoming. The woman continued to nod, apparently urging Deborah to eat. Finally Deborah realized she was expected to use her fingers. She had done worse things since her wanderings had begun and was too hungry to bother about niceties, so she dug in, picking up the larger chunks with her fingers, drinking the rest. Whatever it was, it was tasty and she nodded and smiled her approval. The woman recognized the compliment and seemed pleased by it.

While Deborah was finishing her soup, the child the woman had spoken to returned, spoke to the woman, then skipped away. The woman tried to explain something to her guest, but when Deborah shook her head, apologizing for her ignorance, they both gave up in frustration. The woman took the empty soup bowl and, through signs, urged Deborah to sleep. This she did willingly, for though she had been awake less than an hour, she was fatigued. Another hour passed before she was wakened once more from her slumber, this time by muted voices in the lodge.

She peeked out from under her buffalo hide covers. Daylight still shone outside, and Deborah could clearly discern three figures in the lodge, all seated in a semicircle by the low-burning fire. With the woman from before were two men. One appeared older than the woman by several years; his wide brown face, which Deborah saw only in profile, was creased by many more lines and wrinkles. His left eye, which happened to be turned toward Deborah, was distinguished by a scar that traced its way along the brow and down the outer corner, making the eye droop in a somewhat sinister fashion.

The other man—younger, perhaps in his early twenties— glanced toward Deborah, and she saw a striking face that immediately impressed her with its unusual mingling of honest sensitivity and fierce strength. His large broad nose reigned like a conqueror over softer, expressive dark eyes, earnest lips, and a firm jawline. The face was framed with shining black hair, one side flowing freely over his buckskin-clad shoulder, the other bound in a braid wrapped in fur and ornamented with a silver disk attached to a lock of hair, much lighter in color than the man's own.

Though he did not smile when he saw that she was awake, he seemed pleased. He motioned to his companions. The older man was talking, and he stopped immediately. He nodded approvingly, nudging the younger man, giving him a smug, almost conceited look. The older man spoke, and though Deborah could not understand him, she had the distinct impression he was taking credit for her recovery.

Deborah pushed aside her covers and started to rise, but the woman began to protest, hurrying toward Deborah. For the first time Deborah became a bit alarmed. This woman's protectiveness seemed somewhat out of proportion to necessity. Was she merely concerned for Deborah's welfare, or was she actually afraid her prisoner might escape?

The younger Indian spoke for the first time. "Gray Antelope Woman wishes you to rest."

Deborah raised startled eyebrows. "You speak English?"

"I spent my childhood with white mountain man," answered the young warrior in somewhat stilted English.

"Would you tell . . . Gray Antelope Woman that I am much better," said Deborah. "Also, thank her for caring for me."

The young man conveyed this message, but it was the older man who replied, apparently disgruntled about something.

"Gray Antelope Woman accepts your gratitude," said the young warrior, "but it is her husband, Crooked Eye, you should also thank. He is great shaman . . . medicine man. He brought you back from Hanging Road."

Deborah turned to the medicine man and bowed her head respectfully. "Thank you, Crooked Eye. I am in your debt." This the young warrior translated, to which the shaman beamed in reply, the alarming scar on his eye now taking on an almost benevolent appearance.

Deborah again addressed the warrior. "What is your name? And where am I?"

"I am Broken Wing," said the warrior, seeming to draw up more erect and proud, if it were possible, than he was before. "You are with *Tsistsistas* . . . 'The People.' " He paused in thought as if trying to find the right words in the foreign tongue. "The white man knows us as Cheyenne. We are of the southern Cheyenne, in Black Kettle's band."

"My name is Deborah. And again, I am grateful to you all."

Broken Wing studied Deborah for a long, somewhat disconcerting moment, and she found that though his eyes were sensitive, they could also be incisive and shrewd.

"You have no fear?" he said at length, with no small astonishment.

"You have given me no reason to fear," she answered.

An amused glint briefly sparked in his eyes, though it did not quite reach down to his solemn lips. "You are welcome in this camp as a guest."

"Thank you."

"When you are well, you are free to leave."

"I have no place to go."

Broken Wing's eyebrow cocked upward at this unexpected response. "You have no one?" Deborah shook her head. "All dead?"

"I suppose you could say that."

"When I found you, I saw no signs of others."

"You found me?"

Broken Wing nodded. "You are alone. How did this happen?"

Deborah sighed but hesitated only momentarily before answering. "It is a very long and complicated story. For now, I can only tell you that when I started out I was alone and I am still alone. I have no family, no one to go to."

Broken Wing pondered this for a long while, finally replying, "You may stay here."

"Thank you. The others won't mind?"

"Why should they?"

"Because I am white."

"Some white men are our enemies, it is true, but some are our friends." Broken Wing stopped abruptly and rose to his feet. "Now, you rest. Gray Antelope thinks you are tired."

"She is very kind."

"She is concerned for the baby."

"I am most grateful."

"She wants the baby."

"What?" Another mild alarm sounded in Deborah's head, but she was certain she had merely heard wrong.

"Do not worry," said Broken Wing matter-of-factly. "She will not take the baby without your leave."

"Well, I—I . . . couldn't—"

"It is well. She understands."

"Oh." Deborah wasn't sure *she* understood, but it seemed safe for the moment to let it pass. The woman who had nursed her to health seemed harmless.

"I go now," said Broken Wing, turning toward the flap.

"Please!" called Deborah quickly after him. "Will you be far? How will I communicate with Gray Antelope Woman and Crooked Eye?"

"My lodge is not far."

He turned and left the tepee. Gray Antelope followed him.

The warrior and the shaman's wife walked several paces from the lodge. Broken Wing paused when he realized Gray Antelope Woman wished to speak with him.

"What did the white woman say?" Gray Antelope asked.

"She said she has no family, no place to go. She is alone."

"So far from her people?" queried the Indian woman. "Why was she out there?"

"I don't know. But I think she wishes to stay here."

"Here?"

"She is not afraid of us."

"This is not like any white woman I have seen."

"I have told you, *Heammawihio* sends her."

Gray Antelope nodded her head. The warrior's story seemed more and more credible.

Broken Wing spoke again. "This is good for you, Gray Antelope."

"Why?"

"The white woman has no family, no place to go. If she remains, she will need a lodge, a family."

Gray Antelope Woman brightened considerably as the full implications of Broken Wing's words dawned upon her. She considered herself too young to be a grandmother, yet she did see that such a ready-made family could fulfill some of the void her childlessness had left in her life. But she immediately questioned Broken Wing's generosity. Yes, he was generally a thoughtful, considerate man, but surely he could not be willing to turn his captive, or whatever he considered her, over to her free of charge.

"How many horses do you want for her, Broken Wing?"

"I will take three, which I will return to you if I decide to court your new 'daughter.' "

Gray Antelope smiled. "I see now why you do not take her into your own lodge." She paused, but only for effect; her decision had been made the moment Broken Wing had set forth his proposition. "You will come now and look at my horses and the horses of my husband and choose any three you wish."

139

25

THE NEXT DAY DEBORAH WAS much improved, and even Gray Antelope Woman consented to allow her to be up and around. The Indian woman escorted Deborah about the village, introducing her with great pride to her friends. They managed to communicate, at least on a rudimentary level through a rather crude sign language, but Deborah had many questions that simply could not be answered without language.

Late that afternoon while Deborah was watching a woman cure a buffalo hide, Broken Wing appeared. She was glad for the prospect of some verbal communication in her own language.

"You are well," he said. She couldn't quite tell if he meant the words as a statement or a question.

"Yes, I am."

"It is good. Do you wish to talk?"

"Thank you, I would."

"Come."

He reached a hand down and helped her to her feet. They walked together toward the camp perimeter. A chilly wind blew over them, and though Deborah had for the most part lost track of time, she sensed it was still too early for snow. Yet it would come soon, she knew.

"Where exactly are we, Broken Wing?" she asked.

"This is Indian Territory, the most north part. We are camped by Bluff Creek. The white man's fort called Dodge is to the north."

"When I was alone out there," said Deborah, "I saw no sign of white settlements, or of any settlements at all. I suppose I didn't have too much farther to go."

"I carried you a full day's journey from where I found you to our camp. Alone, you would have died before you came to the fort, which was a journey of perhaps four days for a strong man on foot."

"I am lucky you came along, then."

He said nothing in reply, and they walked in silence for some time. The rocky ravine of the creek stretched out to their right within a stone's throw of where they walked. The water shimmered as it caught the reflection of the setting sun's rays; amber, orange, and coral wove into the shadows of the bare cottonwood branches over-hanging the water's edge. The wind stirred the scene enough to give it a kaleidoscope effect, very vibrant and alive in spite of the proximity of winter. In the silence, Deborah tried to put her current circum-stances into perspective with all that had happened to her thus far. Was she once again thrust into a position of helplessness, under the control of forces stronger than herself? Surely her futile wanderings after her separation from Griff only proved her inability to survive alone in this country. And now, here she was at the mercy of more strangers. Was she doomed ever to be in such straits?

Broken Wing had told her she was free to go. How far away was Fort Dodge? It was quite possible that these Indians would give or lend her a horse to take her there; they might even escort her there themselves. But at Fort Dodge she would still be placed at the mercy of other strangers. And there, she would undoubtedly have to face tedious questions. It was even possible the legal authorities would have been alerted to her escape.

At least the Indians appeared willing to keep her—in fact, Gray Antelope seemed almost eager to do so. Broken Wing said the woman wanted Deborah's baby. Could that mean danger to her? She sensed none from either of them. Perhaps Gray Antelope was anxious for her to stay simply because she hoped to have the child around to help with. Deborah judged that her time of confinement should be in less than two months; beyond that, she knew absolutely nothing about having babies or caring for them. The presence of a woman like Gray Antelope would be nothing less than a godsend when her time came. As strong and independent as Deborah desired to be, the thought of being alone or with crude, coarse men at such a time frightened her. In Virginia, she had once or twice been among older women when they discussed such matters. An elderly aunt, who had visited occasionally from her plantation in South Carolina, had tried to acquaint Deborah with some of the mysteries of womanhood. But for the most part these delicate subjects had been avoided among the genteel ladies. She supposed had she asked, she might have forced the information from a lady who pitied the poor motherless girl, but Deborah had never been too interested in anything except horses. From what little she had gleaned in these scanty conversa-tions, and from what she had seen in her experience with animals,

141

she knew that the child-birthing ordeal was not a pleasant one. It would be a comfort to have a woman, even an Indian woman, with her.

Yet, was she fooling herself about these Indians, allowing her harrowing experiences with her husband to blind her to other real dangers? If only half of what she had heard about the "savages" of the West were true, then she ought to be wary. Indians, perhaps these very ones, had been involved in massacres of settlers and pioneers. The stories of scalpings—that was certainly not Indian hair attached to the bauble in Broken Wing's braid!—and other horrible atrocities could not be entirely fabricated. She shuddered to think that this man walking so placidly beside her, who appeared on the surface to have a sensitive nature, might have actually bent over a fallen white man and—

She could not even complete the thought, it was so repulsive. But she cast a covert, sidelong glance at her companion. Was she as naive and gullible as Griff thought her to be? Was she crazy to boot, to believe she could sojourn here with these Indians?

"You are troubled, Deborah?" said Broken Wing, his softly spoken query startling her from her appalling train of thought as if it were a blow.

"I'm sorry." She did not know why she should apologize to him, but she almost felt as if he might have read her unkind thoughts. "I suppose I am concerned about my future."

"You are welcome here. Gray Antelope Woman and Crooked Eye are willing to take you in."

"Why?" She stopped walking and looked fully at him. "Why should you or they do this? Aren't white people your enemies?"

"As I said before, some are, some aren't." He gave a shrug, though his words were by no means flippant. They were accompanied by a brow creased with introspection. This was a topic he had apparently wrestled with before. "Some Indians are my enemies also," he went on. "The Pawnee and the Crow steal our horses and women and we steal theirs and fight them often. The Kiowa and Comanche used to be our enemies, but now we are at peace with them. Are you at peace with all your people?"

Deborah smiled ironically at this. "Hardly," she replied. "That is why I am reluctant to go to the white settlements. I believe I may have more to fear from them than from you."

"Is your husband dead that he does not protect you from your enemies?"

My husband was my greatest enemy, Deborah thought bitterly.

She said out loud, "Yes, he is dead."

They started walking again. Deborah shivered, feeling the chilly air through her buckskin shift. She vaguely wondered what ever happened to Sid Miller's sheepskin coat. The sun was low in the sky and radiating too little warmth to penetrate the wind.

Broken Wing noted her reaction to the cold. "Gray Antelope will make for you a warm winter robe."

"I don't understand why she would do this for me," said Deborah.

"Gray Antelope has no children. This gives her . . ." He paused, searching for the appropriate English word. "It gives her reason . . . purpose. My stepfather, the mountain man, used to say often that he wished not to be 'beholding' to anyone. For this reason, he lived alone in the wilderness, depending only on his skill and the generosity of the land for his life. I tell you this because I think this is the white man's way, and you might think the same. Feel not this way with Gray Antelope, for as she gives, she also receives."

"It is a generous notion, Broken Wing. I think my debt will always outweigh hers, but it will help a little to keep that in mind."

"Tonight there will be a council," he said, changing the subject. "Do you wish to attend?"

"It is acceptable for women to attend such things?"

"Anyone may attend. Women do not often take part, but they have great influence. Women have wisdom, and it is good to hear them."

"Well, I am sure I won't have anything to say, but I would be honored to attend. Is the council being held entirely for my benefit?"

"Our chief, Black Kettle, has returned from big council with white soldiers and made treaty with them. We will learn tonight of these things."

"So you are at peace with the white man now?"

"Who can say? We were at peace with the soldiers when they attacked our camp on Sand Creek. Black Kettle hung the flag of the white soldiers and a white flag in front of his lodge to show we were friendly, and still they attacked." Broken Wing's voice momentarily grew hard and tense. "Sixty warriors were killed and almost a hundred squaws and babies. My mother was among them. Black Kettle's wife was shot nine times by soldiers, though she did not die."

"That's terrible, Broken Wing. I am sorry."

"You were not there; you have no reason to be sorry."

"I suppose just the color of my skin gives me reason enough. It shames me."

"And Black Kettle feels shame because he thinks he betrayed our people by trusting the white man."

143

"And still he makes another treaty?"

Broken Wing's voice filled with deep pride as he spoke. "He is the great peace-chief of our tribe. He believes peace is possible."

"But you don't?"

"I will follow Black Kettle. It is the only way. The white men are many; we are few. They have many guns."

————

That night Broken Wing took Deborah to a large lodge situated close to the center of the camp. He told her that in summer the sides of the tepee were often removed so everyone in the village could gather and hear the council of the tribe's elders, but the cold weather made that impractical tonight.

This night's meeting did not include all the tribal chiefs, for the tribe was divided into some ten bands scattered all over the plains. This was an informal gathering of some of the chiefs present at the recent treaty signing, including Seven Bulls, Black-White-Man, and Bull-That-Hears. Also crowded into the lodge were many of the warriors from this Bluff Creek camp, some Arapahoe, and a few braves from nearby camps. Many of them looked exceptionally dire and hostile, especially toward her. Deborah felt as vulnerable and helpless as ever, this uneasiness only heightened when she considered the fact that all that stood between her and those dangerous savages was Broken Wing, a man whom she hardly knew and whose friendship she had accepted only at his own word. Perhaps he had lured her in here so these wild men might sacrifice her to some heathen ritual.

But when she was presented to Black Kettle, he was notably civil with her. He was a man in his late fifties who radiated a sage and benevolent image, though not without a liberal mix of shrewd cunning in his intelligent eyes. She suddenly found herself thinking of the Texas Ranger, Sam Killion, and what he had once said about being "gentle as a dove and wise as a serpent." This certainly fit Black Kettle, peace-chief of the Cheyenne.

Speaking in the Cheyenne tongue with Broken Wing translating, he welcomed her and expressed his pleasure at her surviving her illness. Then Black Kettle sat in the circle of chiefs and warriors, motioning for her and Broken Wing to join them. There she sat, with Broken Wing quietly interpreting the proceedings.

The first order of business was the passing of the pipe. It traveled around to everyone present and when it came into Broken Wing's hands, Deborah began to worry. He inhaled deeply from the long wood pipe, blew out a stream of smoke then, much to Deborah's relief, passed the pipe to the next man. The smoky fumes filling the lodge were beginning to make her head reel as it was; what would actually smoking the thing do to her? She realized it was honor enough to be included in this predominantly male council and could not restrain an inward smile as she imagined Caleb's and Leonard's outrage over even that. But she was not the only woman in the place; two or three squaws were seated toward the back, one an elderly woman who must have been ninety years old. The women were silent throughout the meeting and Deborah had no problem with doing the same.

Soon the talk began. Broken Wing tried to translate, but it quickly exceeded his incomplete knowledge of English. He shrugged about halfway through, looking frustrated, and fell silent. Before he gave up, however, she caught the gist of the interchange between the chiefs and warriors.

Black Kettle spoke first. "One winter ago, before the snows came, I sat in council with white man chief, Evans. This is what I told him: 'We have come with our eyes shut, like coming through the fire. All we ask is that we may have peace with the whites; we want to hold you by the hand. I have not come here with a little wolf's bark; instead, I want to speak plainly with you. We must live near the buffalo or starve. When we came here we came free, with no worry, to see you; and when I go home and tell my people that I have taken your hand and the hands of all the chiefs here in Denver, they will be glad.' The white chief accused us of starting the war and did not take our hand of peace. The one truth he spoke was that soon the plains would be covered with white man soldiers as they now are covered with buffalo. He advised us to help the soldiers by controlling our young warriors. I said we were willing to do this. We were told we could camp on the big bend of the Sand Creek and our young men could hunt and be safe."

When Black Kettle paused a younger warrior spoke. "And the white man lied, as always!"

"It is true," Black Kettle continued. "The soldiers attacked our camp. I put my big flag of the stripes and stars in front of my lodge with a white flag of truce. But the soldiers did not heed it. Sixty warriors fell that day and more than that of our women and children. It was a black day, like traveling through a cloud."

Another warrior spoke. Broken Wing whispered to Deborah that he was one of the Dog Soldiers, who were like the military police of the tribe. The man had several scars on his face that, with his flaming

145

eyes, gave him a ferocious appearance. "And still you go again to make peace with the whites?" he said in a challenging tone. "What promises do they make now with their double hearts and forked tongues? The Dog Soldiers will not make peace. I have given my word to fight with the whites. To fight and kill the whites is the only way to make peace."

Seven Bulls replied, "The white chief admitted the Cheyenne were forced to make war because of what happened on the Sand Creek. They saw the nine wounds on the body of Black Kettle's wife, and gave him a good horse as recompense. They promised to restore our lost property and give us land."

"And you believed them?" spat the Dog Soldier.

Black Kettle answered: "I told the soldier chief that I did not think their young soldiers would listen to them, that when I come to get the white man's presents I am afraid they will strike me before I get away. I told them I could not speak for all my people. But our friend, William Bent, encouraged us to trust the white chief once more. Bent himself will winter in our camps to see that the white soldiers do not break the treaty. We must make peace with the white man, Bull Bear," Black Kettle said to the angry Dog Soldier. The peace-chief's tone was sad and sympathetic.

"My brother died making peace with the white man," retorted Bull Bear. "And I believe I will die also in this way." He folded his arms obdurately and said no more.

Several others voiced their agreement with the Dog Soldier. Others supported Black Kettle, and the debate around the council circle became a heated crossfire of reaction and opinion. Even though Broken Wing had not been able to translate the exchange, it didn't take a knowledge of Cheyenne for Deborah to discern that whatever peace Black Kettle and the other chiefs had just made with the U.S. Army, it was a tentative one at best.

As she returned to the lodge of Crooked Eye and Gray Antelope, Deborah wondered if she was going to end up in the middle of an Indian war. She wondered, too, if that were the case, which side she would take.

26

THE FOLLOWING WEEKS WENT unthreatened by imminent war, and Deborah dwelt in a tranquil security with the Cheyenne.

With the village at peace and the coming of inclement weather, many of the warriors remained near the camp. Thus, Broken Wing had more opportunity to spend his time with Deborah, who had asked him to teach her the language and Cheyenne culture.

By the end of November, she had learned enough of the language to communicate, though somewhat clumsily, with Gray Antelope Woman and others with whom she was becoming acquainted. She was able to learn so quickly because she had much idle time on her hands. Her ordeal in the wilderness had robbed her of more strength than she had at first realized. She tired easily and once, while helping to carry water from the creek, she fainted. After that, Gray Antelope refused to allow her to do any other work. Thus, quickly growing restless, Deborah began to monopolize Broken Wing's time.

During this time, one of the braves brought two captive white children to the camp. Deborah watched them with a sinking heart. She had come to trust her hosts, or at least believe in their good intentions. This incident stirred her earlier apprehensions. Agitated, she sought out Broken Wing.

He explained, "Red Feather bought the captives from the Kiowa."

"But why?"

"Red Feather's nephew is among Indian captives in the white man fort. He wishes to trade white captives for Indians. Very simple."

"Simple!" sputtered Deborah. "I thought Black Kettle wanted peace, yet here are Cheyenne bartering in innocent children. How can you hope to convince the United States officials of your sincerity by such inconsistency?"

Broken Wing was puzzled at her outburst, for, to him, it was all quite logical. "We do not hurt the children. In fact, though we are at peace with the Kiowa, it is known they are not good with captives. The Cheyenne take better care of captives. So, this is good for the children."

"And what of their families? What happened to them?"

"I do not know."

"May I speak with the children? It might comfort them to see a white woman."

"You are right. I will ask Red Feather."

About an hour later, Deborah was taken to Red Feather's lodge where the children were kept. She found them huddled closely together in a dim corner, fear etching their smudged, pathetic faces. One was a girl of about thirteen whose name Deborah learned was Mary; the other was her younger brother, Arthur, who was nine or ten. They were both shocked and relieved when they saw the yellow-haired white woman in Indian garb approach. The girl actually smiled.

"Are you being treated well?" asked Deborah, kneeling down beside them.

They nodded.

"We miss our mama, though," said the girl.

"What happened to her?" Deborah wasn't certain she wanted to know the answer. When she heard it, she was positive she didn't.

"She's dead," said Mary, tears welling up in her eyes.

"The Indians?"

"They attacked our farm and Papa was killed. They took us and Mama captive. Mama said . . ." The girl paused as a sob caught her voice. She swallowed and continued tremulously. "Mama said she couldn't stand being captured. She was afraid . . . that they'd force her to . . . to marry with them or something."

"Did they do anything to her . . . or you?"

"No . . . they beat us sometimes and made us work, but we were always together until—" Tears spilled freely from her eyes. "Mama hanged herself."

Deborah gasped. "Dear Lord, no! But she had no reason. . . ?" She wasn't certain if she meant her words as a question, a statement, or a wishful hope.

"But she was powerful afraid."

Deborah put her arms around the two children and drew them close. She knew of nothing else to say or do. It all seemed so senseless. She herself could have just as easily been in the same predicament, but when she found herself at the mercy of these Indians, she had been given no reason to fear. In all the weeks since her arrival,

148

she had received nothing but friendship and kindness from them. Were all the present troubles with the Indians based simply on gross misunderstanding? The Indians would no doubt be blamed for the woman's death, resulting in retaliations by the whites, followed by counter-retaliations by the Indians—back and forth until they exterminated each other. What would happen if other whites could have the opportunity to see the Indians from her present vantage? They had helped her, saved her. But they had also been directly responsible for orphaning these children. Of course, the Kiowa had done that, not the Cheyenne; but that distinction would not matter to most whites.

Deborah smoothed back the tangled strands of the girl's light brown hair. "I don't think you need fear these Cheyenne you are with now," she said soothingly.

"But they killed our pa!" blurted out the boy in a hard and bitter voice.

"It was other Indians, Arthur," Deborah replied, "but I know how you must feel. Yet, try to understand that the Indians believed they were protecting their own land, their own homes."

"How can you talk like that?" asked Mary. "Didn't they kill your family and capture you?"

"No, they didn't. They found me dying on the prairie, and they took me into their camp and cared for me." She sighed. "I know it must be complicated for you to understand. It is for me also."

At that moment, Broken Wing, who had been waiting outside, came into the lodge. The children instantly tensed and cowered fearfully against the lodge wall. This brought visible distress to Broken Wing. He stopped, coming no closer and seemed almost about to retreat when Deborah spoke again.

"This man," she said to the children, "is the man who saved me on the prairie."

The children looked up with disbelief at this tall, imposing, fierce Indian. To them he appeared one and the same with those that had attacked their farm and killed their father. Yet why should this kind white woman lie to them? It *was* confusing.

"The wife of Red Feather has food for them," said Broken Wing in Cheyenne. He obviously felt awkward, keeping his eyes averted from the children.

"Children," said Deborah, "I'm going to go while you eat, but I will come back soon. Don't be frightened, all right? And if you need me, I will be nearby." She thought about giving them her name, but if they did return to the army fort, there might be a slim possibility

149

the wrong people could hear of her presence. It was still too soon after her escape from Stoner's Crossing to be careless. She gave each child an embrace, then followed Broken Wing from the tepee.

"What will happen to them?" Deborah asked when they were outside. The cold air made her breath come out in a frosty mist. She hugged the buffalo robe Gray Antelope had given her close to her body.

"We will have council with white men and make trade," said Broken Wing. "They will return to their people." His voice was suddenly as cold as the winter air.

"What's wrong?" She had gotten to know him well enough to recognize this abrupt change in his usual warmth.

"I do not like being thought ill of," he answered.

"They are just children; they don't know any better." They conversed mostly in Cheyenne now, with an occasional smattering of English.

"I understand it is not their fault. They have been given these fears by others."

"What do you expect when your people perpetrate ugly rumors by taking captives, or even buying them from other tribes? Or, by attacking farms and wagon trains?"

"I heard what you said to those children," Broken Wing replied. "I give you the same answer. We are protecting our lives. The white man came and took our land, slaughtered our buffalo without even taking the meat. They did not ask, they just took. They make roads through our best hunting grounds. They do not care that we will die without the buffalo. Do you wonder that my people feel they must fight?"

"I am trying to understand," Deborah softly replied as they walked toward the stream, now mostly frozen.

"I feel bad for the children," he continued. "It is not good that they should suffer. I am glad you are here; it is a comfort for them."

Deborah had said she was trying to understand, but could she ever? Or, was it merely her own part in what was happening that confused her? Perhaps the problem was that both sides were right. She had heard some men say that the land was big enough for all of them, and she could see how such a defense made sense on the surface. But the white men were taking all the best land. They had pushed many Indians out of the east until the tribes were left with nothing but what most whites considered barren wastelands. As much as Deborah herself appreciated the peculiar beauty of the plains she had traveled on, in the end they had little to recommend them to

150

more profit-minded folks. Even the Indians had had to learn to adapt, changing from an agrarian people to a society of hunters, until, over the generations, they had become dependent on game and not crops. This was fine with the white man until he found a use for the plains. What were the Indians to do now? Learn to become desert dwellers? But then, sooner or later, the whites would find some use for the desert.

And there lay Deborah's present perplexity. She knew both were not right. The lines might be fuzzy at times, but she was seeing more and more clearly the justification for the Indian grievances. If sides were ever drawn, she might not find herself in the middle as she feared, but instead set against her own people.

The sight of the white children saddened her and sickened her, but even that she had been able to justify. Deborah shivered, only partly from the cold.

"You are cold," said Broken Wing. "We should go back."

"Not yet. I'm not quite ready." She didn't want to have to see the children again.

"I think I know this confusion you feel, Deborah."

She looked at him, a little surprised at his insight. He looked like an uncivilized, wild man, and this only reminded her again of the unjust misconceptions with which she had been indoctrinated.

"How could you, Broken Wing?" She sighed. "Your people have been good to me. Gray Antelope and Crooked Eye, and you have shown me more kindness than I have received from my own people in a long time. Yet those children are my people. How can I look at them, whose parents are dead because of the Indians, and say that their parents' deaths were justified? How can I once more be at odds with my people? Yet that seems my lot in life.

"No, Broken Wing, I don't think you can comprehend what I am feeling."

"Maybe so . . ." He looked out over the frosty landscape, dotted with bare trees. The winter breeze blew loose strands of his shining black hair across his face. He reached up a hand and brushed them aside, revealing eyes filled with a depth of wisdom that was far from savage and uncivilized. He continued speaking in a sad, faraway tone that made Deborah's throat tighten and tears well up in her eyes.

"I loved a white man once," he said. "Do you remember that I told you I lived some years with a mountain man? He married my mother in my third summer, and we lived with him in the hills many miles from any white or Indian camps. We were happy there. He was a good man. He and my mother had a daughter. But in my eighth

151

summer, my mother and sister got the smallpox when we went to a white settlement to trade. They died."

"I thought your mother was killed last year at Sand Creek," Deborah said.

"To the Cheyenne, aunts and uncles are the same as mothers and fathers, and nieces and nephews are as sons and daughters. So it *was* my mother who was killed then, but she was sister of my father, the blood mother of my brother, Stands-in-the-River. And it was she who took me into her lodge when I was left alone."

"What happened to your stepfather?"

"We lived together after my mother died for the passing of many moons. I was as a son to him and he was my father, for I never knew my true father. But in my ninth summer, we were hunting and he was bitten by a snake. I tried to take out the poison; he tried, also. But too much remained and he grew sick. When he knew he would die, he packed a few things for me and took me into the white man's fort. Ten miles he walked with the poison filling all his body, but he did not want me to be left alone."

"But you didn't stay there, did you?"

"My stepfather taught me the white man's tongue, but in every other way we lived more in the Indian way than the white. So, the white ways were strange to me, and I was strange to them. They put me and some other captive Indian children in a wagon and took us around to some big white man villages to show us to people who had never seen an Indian before. They looked at us and pointed with their fingers, and some white children cried from fear. I think if my stepfather had known this would happen, he would have left me alone in the hills.

"I did not belong with the whites, and I longed for my own people, so I escaped and returned to my Cheyenne father's camp. But I do not hate the white man, because when I look upon them I always see some of Abraham Johnston, my white stepfather, in them."

Deborah's eyes went unconsciously to the strand of light brown hair hanging from Broken Wing's braid. "But you fight them."

"When I must." He fingered the strand of hair. "I have fought white enemies and Indian alike. I have taken scalps; it is our way. But every time I take a white life in battle, I think of Abraham Johnston, and my heart breaks a little."

"I am so sorry, Broken Wing," Deborah whispered in a voice strained with emotion.

And as she lifted her eyes to meet those of the Cheyenne warrior, his head straight and proud, the muscles of his jaw twitching as they struggled against his own emotion, Deborah vaguely realized that she too would not finish with these, her new friends, without her own heart breaking.

27

NEAR THE END OF THE YEAR 1865, two other white visitors came to the Cheyenne camp. Edward Wynkoop, who had been the army commander at Fort Lyon and was now the Cheyenne and Arapahoe agent and friend to the Indians, came to the camp with several wagonloads of annuity supplies. With him was John Smith, another great friend of the Cheyenne, whose half-blood son, Jack, had been executed by Chivington's troops during the Sand Creek massacre.

Deborah watched from a crack in the lodge opening, careful not to make her presence known. The men held a council in Black Kettle's lodge and Deborah later learned, much to her pleasure, that arrangements were being made to return Mary and Arthur to the fort.

Two days later the children were taken away and when Deborah bid them goodbye in the privacy of their lodge, she smiled when Arthur said he might not mind staying with the Indians. He said he had no family anymore, and Red Feather and his family had been nice to him. Deborah encouraged him to go with his sister and that if he did so, perhaps one day he might better be able to help the Indians.

Deborah was glad to see them go—for their sakes, but also for hers, because they had been a constant reminder of her own private paradox. Soon, however, Deborah's mind was given a kind of respite from these tormented thoughts.

A blizzard blew in on the Cheyenne camp that last week of December. The fire in Crooked Eye's lodge burned constantly yet hardly took even the edge off the freezing cold. Everyone stayed indoors, huddled within the warmth of many buffalo robes. It was not an ideal time to have a baby. But then, Leonard Stoner's child had not been convenient from the moment of its conception.

Deborah's pains began in the middle of the night. She awoke Gray Antelope Woman, who in turn roused Crooked Eye. The shaman left the lodge, for though he was a medicine man of some repute, births were best left in the hands of women. He had prepared an elixir, *hituneisseeyo,* or bark medicine, that Gray Antelope had been faithfully administering to Deborah in the last several days in order to make her delivery easier. But now his presence was no longer needed.

Two other women joined Gray Antelope, one an elderly lady whom Gray Antelope assured Deborah was an experienced midwife. They had built a frame of stout poles in the lodge in preparation for this moment, and Gray Antelope had carefully explained the age-old birthing procedure to Deborah who, knowing of no other way, accepted it in good faith. The women tended her with great tenderness, and Deborah determined to show her gratitude by being brave. Somewhere she had heard that Indian women gave birth with extreme stoicism, and though Gray Antelope had laughed at that myth Deborah longed to earn their respect by her behavior. So, instead of screaming, she bit the inside of her mouth until it bled. When her labor was well advanced, the women looked at each other with wonder, for they, too, had heard stories of white women giving birth, and the old woman had even attended the delivery of a white woman captive who had married a warrior. What they had seen and heard was not especially complimentary toward Deborah's race. Yet, here was a contradiction, and it did indeed renew and strengthen their respect for their visitor.

When the labor had reached its last stages, Deborah was brought to kneel at the frame. She was instructed to grip a vertical pole while Gray Antelope embraced her from the front, offering many loving words of encouragement and wiping away the perspiration that dripped from Deborah's face in spite of the sub-zero cold outside.

Deborah cried out near the end; she couldn't help it. She had never experienced such pain in her life, and she found all her hatred for Leonard surfacing in her again. Even dead, he was bent on making her suffer! And now . . . now she would have his child. All her fears might at long last be realized. Was she about to give birth to a monster? Maybe it would be best to give the baby to Gray Antelope after all. The kind Indian woman would not hate it, would not be reminded every time she looked upon it of the nightmare out of which it had been spawned.

How could she have this child? How could she love it? Why did its coming have to hurt so much? For the pain only made her hate it more. Why couldn't it stop?

But she chewed her lip and, tasting blood, did not stop. She had no choice in the matter. She would have Leonard's baby. She would try not to hate it.

The pains came fast and hard; her hands ached and turned white as they gripped the pole.

Gray Antelope told her to bear down, and Deborah obeyed, finding great relief in those instructions. But she was too exhausted to feel much ecstasy when the climactic moment of her child's birth came. The old Cheyenne midwife, standing behind Deborah, took the baby, cut its umbilical cord, applied a healing salve to the wound, then wrapped the child in a soft, warm blanket. Deborah slumped against the frame and heard, as if from a distance, the small infant cries.

But those cries were heard distinctly outside the lodge where Broken Wing was holding anxious vigil, pacing back and forth across the frozen earth, hardly noticing the swirling wind and snow blowing all around him. Crooked Eye had called him from his lodge when Deborah's labor had begun, and he had come immediately. During the hours of early labor, he had come and gone between his and Crooked Eye's lodges, keeping himself apprised of Deborah's progress. In the last hour, however, when he knew the child could come at any moment, he was too restless to remain in his lodge. His feet were now frozen through his heavy winter moccasins, and his hands were numb, but for some reason he could not sit at ease and warmth while the white woman suffered so. Besides, he was concerned because he had heard that white women had poor constitutions and often died in childbirth. Thus his relief was only partial when he heard the infant cries. Not until Gray Antelope stepped outside and assured him of the patient's healthy condition did he feel free to relax.

"She is well," said the shaman's wife, her pride clearly evident, as much as if Deborah truly had been her daughter. "I have never known a white woman to be so strong and brave."

Broken Wing smiled, almost as if a compliment toward Deborah somehow reflected upon him. But then, he had been the one to find her, claiming she was from the Wise One Above. Perhaps now they would believe him.

"Come in before you freeze," said Gray Antelope Woman. "I have seen fathers worry less over the birth of their own children," she teased him good-naturedly.

So had Broken Wing, and he had no idea why he was behaving in this manner.

He ducked into the tepee just as the midwife was laying the wrapped bundle into Deborah's arms. She was lying down now on a soft bed of hides, her trembling body covered with several more. She took the baby in her arms but did not look at it. Broken Wing came close and knelt down beside her.

"Gray Antelope Woman is much impressed at your strong way of giving birth," he said.

"I didn't want to be a trouble to her." Deborah noticed with pleasure the high esteem in his tone.

"Do you have a son or a daughter?"

"A daughter."

"And does she look like you?"

"I—I don't know. . . ." Deborah closed her eyes in anguish. "I am afraid to look."

"But why should this be? Gray Antelope said she is healthy."

They think I am strong, maybe even brave, Deborah thought despairingly to herself. *If they only knew what a coward I am, that I cannot even look at my own baby.*

"Broken Wing, would you . . . would you look at her for me?"

The Cheyenne warrior nodded solemnly. He had no idea why this woman could not look upon her child, but he sensed this was a crucial, important moment and treated it as thus. His gentle hands, the same hands that did battle with his enemies, now moved with deep reverence. And the sleeping baby did not stir as he lifted her feet and ran a finger along her toes, then lifted each tiny hand, inspecting the fingers on each.

"She is whole," he announced.

"What . . . what does she look like?"

Here, Broken Wing's solemn expression softened. "She is . . . different," he said; then when he realized how his words might be interpreted by the distraught mother added quickly, "—but beautiful! I have never before seen a white baby. She is bald—no wait! She has hair, but very pale and soft like a chick's first feathers." Unable to restrain himself, he reached up and touched the fine fluff of hair on the very top of the baby's head. All at once the child's eyes opened. But she did not cry, she merely gazed up at Broken Wing who was hovering over her as if she were a sacred war bonnet. "Ah!" breathed Broken Wing.

"What is it?" Deborah's tone betrayed her concern.

"Her eyes are pale, like yours—maybe gray, maybe blue, I cannot

156

tell. But I see you in her face. She is very beautiful. You can be proud."

"Really?"

"Look for yourself."

Deborah hesitated, then slowly turned toward the child in her arms.

She *was* beautiful.

In fact, so absorbed was Deborah in this revelation that she forgot to note any similarities to Leonard. Her baby was healthy, her baby was no monster, and more than that, as the child turned to look at her mother, Deborah saw how delicate and helpless she was. This realization pushed all thought of hate and rejection from Deborah's mind and heart. This baby was not just Leonard Stoner's child, it was hers also; moreover, the child was her own person too, utterly independent of the disastrous union of her mother and father. For that reason alone, for her own individuality, she deserved acceptance.

Deborah smiled down at her baby. "She is lovely, isn't she?"

"Why would you think not?"

"I don't want to think about that now, Broken Wing. But thank you for helping me."

"I know it is the white custom to name children right at birth," said Broken Wing. "Do you have a name for your daughter?"

"I haven't even thought of that. But I will name her Carolyn, after my mother."

"That is good. It will bring happiness to your mother."

"My mother is dead."

"Then it will bring happiness to the child to be named for an honored grandparent."

"I hope so, Broken Wing." Deborah gazed at her daughter. "I do hope so...."

It was hard for Deborah to imagine happiness, real happiness as she had once known in Virginia, uncluttered by bitterness and confusion and empty loss. It was hard to think that she would ever be happy in that way again. Yet, might there not be a chance for Carolyn? Must she inherit all the sins of her parents?

Without thinking, Deborah began to pray for God to bestow such happiness upon her daughter. When she realized what she was doing, she stopped herself. She was in no position to ask favors of God. When she was strong, when she was independent, when she had something to offer in return, perhaps then she might do so. In the meantime, she considered it too dangerous to place herself at the mercy of anyone so powerful. It might become too easy, too necessary, and she could not afford that. She had to be strong on her own.

157

She had to be able to take care of herself, and her baby also, without leaning on others. At least here with the Indians she could accept their help because she knew that she would soon be able to give something in return, even if only her strong back.

So, Deborah did not ask God for her daughter's happiness. Somehow she would provide this for Carolyn, although she herself was empty and bitter. Thus, the Great Burden-bearer stood with outstretched hands before Deborah, waiting . . . patiently waiting.

28

SPRING CAME AT LAST TO THE PLAINS. The snows melted, the rivers swelled, the cottonwoods budded, and the rolling, grassy prairie was dotted with an array of wild flowers.

Deborah grew strong and healthy in this friendly environment, and as each week passed she became more and more an integral part of the life of the Cheyenne camp. She took to wearing moccasins with her buckskin shift, and laying her baby in a cradle board strapped to her back while she went about her chores. Using a dark, gooey concoction prepared by Gray Antelope, Deborah darkened her skin and hair so that, at least from a distance, any traders or soldiers or other "foreigners" venturing near the camp would not readily discern her race. Of course, as summer came, the rays of the sun greatly assisted the dye, giving her skin a healthy bronze tone. Her hair, however, would always betray her, and to wear a head covering, uncommon among Cheyenne women, would have marked her just as much. Except for the flecks of gold that inevitably escaped the effects of the dye, Deborah marveled at how quickly and easily she had taken to the Indian attire. The idea of sitting in a proper Virginia parlor came to appall her. She supposed she had come full circle from the tomboy days of her childhood.

In winter, the young braves had kept fairly active hunting and raiding, but with the coming of fair weather, they were far more at liberty to roam the countryside, especially as their horses grew strong after winter privations.

One night, the camp was awakened to a furor of excitement—dogs barking, people shouting, gunshots exploding in the air. Deborah clutched Carolyn to her and stared at Gray Antelope, who had her arms around both the frightened white woman and the baby. Deborah wanted to go outside to see what was happening, but she knew to do so was foolhardy. She would just have to wait to hear from Crooked Eye, who had gone to investigate.

"If we must go," assured Gray Antelope, "the men will tell us." A slight tremor in her voice betrayed her concern, for she had been at Sand Creek and knew that sometimes the warnings did not come soon enough.

"Do you think it's soldiers?" asked Deborah.

"Not enough gunshots. The bluecoats waste much precious ammunition when they raid."

At last Crooked Eye returned to the lodge out of breath with his haste, and wearing a grim expression.

"Pawnee," he said, speaking the name of the Cheyenne's perpetual enemy with revulsion. "They are many. We must go to the river, for it may be that our braves will not be able to hold them off."

Gray Antelope sprang immediately into action, grabbing a couple of hides, then quickly filling a leather bag with a small supply of meat. Deborah snatched up a blanket for Carolyn, and in less than a minute the three, with Crooked Eye in the lead, were exiting the lodge. Deborah glanced back once to see a battle raging between the Pawnee and Cheyenne warriors. Several lodges had been set on fire, and the Cheyenne warriors were gradually being pushed back toward the center of the village.

In the gray light of early dawn, Crooked Eye's party was joined by many other fleeing Cheyenne—mostly women and children, led by a few of the older men carrying rifles and bows. They were running in a near panic, toward the river, with children crying and dogs yelping and darting dangerously underfoot. Suddenly a handful of Pawnees broke through the Cheyenne defense, racing on horseback at the fleeing villagers. One of the Pawnee grabbed a Cheyenne woman, hauled her on his horse, gave a loud whoop, and turned away. The screaming of the women brought some of the Cheyenne braves to their defense, but the main body of warriors was still intent on holding back the larger force of the Pawnee war party.

Deborah could not quell the impulse to look back and did so just as a Pawnee caught an arrow in the throat. He lurched from his horse and as he hit the ground, the Cheyenne who had killed him raced up to his fallen body. Deborah shuddered as she thought the brave

159

was going to scalp the man, but the warrior merely thumped the body with a stick and then returned his concentration to the battle.

In the brief instant her head was turned, Deborah stumbled over an exposed root. She went down with a thud and only the soft, river-watered grass kept her and Carolyn from serious injury. But as she struggled to her feet, still clutching her daughter to her, she suddenly found herself alone, momentarily separated from Crooked Eye and the others.

Before she could fully gain her balance to make a sprint to cover, one of the Pawnee swooped down on her. She could tell by the gloating expression he wore that he believed he had found a prize, indeed, in this white captive. He grabbed Deborah with such force she lost hold of her baby and the precious bundle fell, squirming and crying, into the grass. The Pawnee, unaware of the lost bundle, cared only about the valuable white woman now grasped in his hands.

Deborah screamed as her captor's horse reared; it would certainly crush her baby. But suddenly, as if he had sprung from the grass itself, a figure on foot bodily charged the Pawnee, coming between the infant and the rearing horse. The animal's lethal hooves thundered down, missing the interceding warrior's head by mere inches, but a safe distance away from Carolyn.

In spite of the sudden attack, the Pawnee kept his head and man-aged to hold his mount under control, so that when its hooves struck the ground, he spurred it immediately into a gallop away from the battle, his prize still in tow.

But the Cheyenne warrior's objective had not only been to save the baby. He gave chase to the Pawnee on foot, and though he stood little chance of catching him, he did keep within shooting range. Thus, running to maintain this edge, he lifted his bow from where it was slung over his shoulder, whisked an arrow from his quiver and set it to the bowstring. He stopped running only when he was ready to take aim.

Twang!

Many a seasoned marksman could have failed at such a range, but it was a shot one desperate warrior dared not miss.

Deborah, lying nearly horizontal across the Pawnee horse, had no idea what was happening. Nevertheless, she was nearly in a swoon thinking her daughter was dead. Her first clue that something had changed in her fortunes came when her Pawnee captor slumped over, his weight nearly suffocating her. She struggled desperately to free herself. The galloping animal jogged her terribly, making movement awkward at best, but dangerous, too. At last she managed to push the dead Pawnee from the horse, but, as good a horsewoman as she was, from her present ungainly position, she had difficulty bringing the racing animal under control.

She fought tenaciously and finally caught hold of the reins, which she tugged at furiously until the horse slowed enough to allow Deborah to swing a leg over the saddle and wiggle into an upright position. Easing the mount to a manageable canter, she was at last able to turn him around.

Deborah was almost afraid to go back. Her baby was dead, and even if she may have wished her dead on occasion before her birth, she knew she had never really meant it. Still, those bitter wishes now heaped guilt upon her grief.

29

THE CHEYENNE RESCUER, NOW standing over the dead Pawnee, was Broken Wing. In the heat of danger, Deborah had not been able to discern such details. Now details were all too clear. In one of his hands he held a bloody knife which he wiped against his leggings before sheathing it. In the crook of his other arm, he held a small bundle; this he held out to Deborah as she rode up.

Deborah slipped from the Pawnee horse and, half-stumbling on shaky legs, ran to him.

"She is well," Broken Wing said with a relieved grin. "She bellows like a wolf. I think you should call her Singing Wolf."

Deborah grabbed her child as if the devil himself were holding her. All she saw at that moment was killing and wild Indians with the vicious cries of battle still rising from the village. On the ground lay the dead Pawnee, a bloody patch on his head indicating that even those she had thought her friends could be dangerous adversaries. Was she crazy to think she could make a home with them, bring her child up in this savage environment?

Yet the squirming bundle in Deborah's arms forced her thoughts away from her renewed confusion and horror. All attention focused on the noisy, wiggling child. The baby was indeed crying at full throat. Deborah loosened the blankets and carefully examined her daughter, finding, to her relief and astonishment, that Carolyn indeed seemed no worse for her recent ordeal. All at once she realized this miracle had occurred only because of Broken Wing. Both she and her daughter lived because of him.

"Come," Broken Wing said urgently, "you are still not safe."

Leading the Pawnee horse by its buckskin rein, he saw them safely back to the river. He then returned to the battle.

Another hour raged on before the Pawnee war party was finally repulsed. The victory carried with it heavy losses. A woman had been taken captive and two warriors killed, in addition to the loss of three lodges and about fifty horses stolen by the Pawnees. But, even as Crooked Eye made his gloomy report, his sinister face lit up in a heartening grin as he told the price the enemy had paid for their booty—five dead warriors and three lost horses.

"And the best Pawnee horse now belongs to you, Deborah!" he exclaimed. "You have counted your first coup!"

"But it is only a horse," said Deborah, perplexed. "I didn't kill anyone."

"The white man thinks killing is everything," said the old shaman. "But that is not so with the Cheyenne. The highest honor for a warrior is to count coup on a living enemy. Most white men do not understand that counting coup is to touch an enemy, so it takes more courage to touch a living one than a dead one. But living or dead, the warrior must touch the enemy to receive credit. Three coup may be counted upon a single enemy, but it is the warrior who counts the first coup that receives the greatest honor."

Deborah had observed this procedure when she had returned to the safe cover of the river: one or several warriors striking a fallen body. Now she knew what it meant. But there was something else she had seen that she did not understand.

"What about scalping?" she asked, still shuddering at the shocking introduction she had already received.

As she spoke, Broken Wing approached where the group was still seated on the banks of the creek, eating some meat and taking a short rest from the rigors of battle before returning to the labors that lay ahead in restoring order to the village.

Broken Wing stood silently by while Crooked Eye answered Deborah's inquiry. "Phsssh!" he said with a depreciating shrug. "Scalps are nothing—unless the one removed happens to be *your own* scalp!" He chuckled at his humor.

"What Crooked Eye means," added Broken Wing, "is that we do not fight for scalps because they are not an important coup."

"But you—"

"I am sorry if what I did in battle disturbs you. That Pawnee was an old enemy of mine. I have fought him before, and once he counted coup upon me. His hair is a great trophy to me, but now I wish I had not touched him."

He turned abruptly and strode away. Deborah remembered how it had disturbed him when the captive children had cowered away from him in fear. Of course no one would like such a thing, but could it be that to Broken Wing, it was also a matter of honor? Deborah wondered if she would ever comprehend the complexities of the Indian mind, especially the mind of this particular Indian. Surprisingly, understanding him was suddenly very important to Deborah. She jumped up and hurried after him.

"Broken Wing!" she called.

He stopped but did not turn. She had to walk around him to face him.

"Broken Wing, forgive my hasty judgments," she said. "The Cheyenne way is so foreign to me. Maybe I will never be able to understand it. What I saw today shocked me and it nearly made me forget something very important. You saved my life and the life of my baby. We are strangers and of the race of your enemies, yet you risked your own life for us. I may not understand your ways, but I know enough to realize you are a man of courage, and you deserve my thanks, which I have rudely withheld. Thank you, Broken Wing; I am again in your debt." She paused, remembering something Gray Antelope had recently told her of Cheyenne customs. "Wait here," she said and hurried off to the riverbank.

When she returned a few minutes later, she was leading the Pawnee horse.

"I wish to give you a gift to show my gratitude." She extended the reins to him.

"This is a very expensive gift," he replied with a clear note of humility in his tone. "A good horse with a blanket and a saddle."

"It is nothing to what I owe you."

"It is your own horse."

"Gray Antelope told me squaws don't own stallions."

"Not usually, but you won it fairly."

"Only because you shot its rider. But I'll tell you what, let's consider it an even trade if you allow me to ride him once in a while."

He smiled. "I saw that you ride well."

"Yes, I love to ride and I haven't been able to do so for a very long time. Though I was scared nearly to death when that Pawnee had me, I also felt a certain sense of exhilaration."

"Then ride now!" urged Broken Wing, his dark eyes flashing with enthusiasm.

"But the Pawnees?"

"They are far away and will not risk losing their stolen horses by returning." He handed back the reins.

Remembering the feel of the animal's mighty flanks beneath her and the sting of the wind on her face, Deborah could not refuse. After determining that the strange animal would cooperate with a new rider, and coaxing him with soft-spoken words and a gentle touch, Deborah mounted. The saddle, which she later learned was made of a folded strip of buffalo hide stuffed with grass, was soft and pliable, more comfortable than the English saddles she had used in Virginia or the western ones on the Stoner Ranch. This, Broken Wing told her, was a war saddle and thus was lightweight for speed and agility. She had already seen the other more cumbersome wood-frame saddles used by the Cheyenne for transport.

Broken Wing watched with folded arms and a slight smile on his face. "Indian horses do not usually take well to white riders. I think you are becoming more Indian than white already!"

Deborah pressed her heels gently into the animal's flanks.

The horse, a gray stallion with a charcoal mane, stepped out into an easy canter. He was a lively mount, no more than three years old and in the prime of life. Riding in a wide circle upon the same open grassy area where the ordeal with the Pawnee occurred, Deborah could sense the stallion holding back his great strength.

"So, you are a runner, are you?" she murmured to the gray.

She, too, was holding back. It had been so long since she had ridden, so long since she had really been so free. On the Stoner place, her rides had always been accompanied by a cautious fear lest her husband discover and punish her, and the flight with Griff had been far too dangerous to appreciate.

Did she dare now to give vent to the straining desire within her? Was there anything to prevent her?

Laughing aloud, she dug her heels deeper into the stallion's sides.

He needed little urging. His mighty legs stretched immediately in response and flew away in a fleet gallop. Deborah gave a whoop as unabandoned as any Indian war cry. The ground was level and offered no resistance to horse or rider, and they covered a mile in less than two minutes. The gray, for all its shabby coat, painted now

164

with war paint, would have been a prize to any thoroughbred stable in Virginia, perhaps in the entire South. Deborah spurred him into a wide turn, and he lost an incredibly small amount of time in the maneuver.

Deborah gave him full rein for the run back. She could tell he was hardly exerting himself. This indeed was a fine mount, and she was glad she had given him to Broken Wing. A man like that deserved an animal like this, and the gray deserved a master like the strong and courageous Cheyenne warrior.

He was watching her, laughing, too. Deborah would have been surprised to know that he was thinking the same thoughts about her.

Finally, she reined the gray to a stop, but the horse pranced and snorted, obviously unhappy with the brevity of its exercise. Just as reluctantly, Deborah dismounted. She gave him an affectionate pat. "I wish I had a lump of sugar for you," she told him, then turned to Broken Wing. "Thank you! I can't remember when I have enjoyed myself more."

"You have great joy upon the back of a horse, with the wind blowing through your hair as if you were an arrow shot from my best bow." He studied her for a long time, her glowing face, pink and windburned, her eyes shimmering with joy. He especially listened to her merry laughter, realizing it was the first time he had heard such music from the white woman's lips. It was a pleasant sound, indeed.

"It is time you had a Cheyenne name," he said suddenly. "I have wondered about this before, but until now I have seen none that fit." He paused, momentarily uncertain. "But it might be you don't wish to have such a name."

Deborah had been dismayed by the events of the day, the battle and the horrors accompanying it. Did she want to be identified with them to the extent of having a Cheyenne name? She had been disillusioned by Broken Wing's part in it. Yet, she could not deny the overwhelming sense of love and acceptance she had felt since her arrival here. She only subtly recognized the deep need these people were answering in her wounded heart. Their customs were wild, perhaps even savage, and it would take some time for her to accept that, if she ever could; but she knew without doubt that the hearts of these Cheyenne who had become her friends were good and noble, and to be associated with them could only be an honor.

"I would like a Cheyenne name," she said simply.

"I think you should be called 'Wind Rider.' " Deborah wrinkled her brow at this, and Broken Wing asked, "You do not like this name?"

"Well . . . it sounds a bit much, as if it should belong to a warrior.

Just because I like a fast horse doesn't mean a name like that fits. How about 'Horse Woman'?"

"Wind Rider fits you well, because I think that inside, you are a warrior." He again studied her with that intense, probing gaze that made her tingle all over.

But Deborah recovered quickly from her discomfiture. Even if Broken Wing had read her character incorrectly, she realized he saw, if not the reality of who she was, then at least who and what she desired to be.

"Broken Wing, I think I am too helpless and ignorant to be a warrior. But more than anything, I desire to be. Would you teach me?"

"You wish to join the braves on the warpath?"

"I just wish not to be helpless as I was when you found me on the prairie."

She remembered when she had made the same request of Griff. He hadn't had much of a chance to help her, and now he was probably dead. Would she fare better here with these Cheyenne, with Broken Wing? Would she at long last become a self-reliant woman, the kind of woman who would never again be at any man's mercy? She thought of that Pawnee warrior who had nearly taken her captive. What would have happened had he succeeded? Again she would have been a man's slave, powerless and impotent. She knew that as long as she remained ignorant of even the most elemental methods of self-defense, she would never be safe, never truly free.

She cast imploring eyes at Broken Wing. She could not degrade herself by actually begging him, but he did not give her reason to,

He answered quickly. "I will do it," he said without reluctance.

"Thank you," she replied with as much relief as gratitude.

30

IN JULY, BLACK KETTLE'S BAND moved north to take advantage of the excellent hunting in the rich region between the Smoky Hill and Arkansas Rivers. Deborah worked alongside Gray Antelope Woman to disassemble the lodge, an almost exclusively female task. Smaller lodges were comprised of perhaps eleven buffalo hides, but Crooked Eye was affluent, and his tepee used twenty-one. Packing the heavy hides was no small chore. Several horse-drawn travois were necessary to hold the hides and all the other household belongings. Then the stock had to be rounded up and driven behind the packhorses which, in the case of Crooked Eye's and Gray Antelope's combined wealth, amounted to a sizable herd.

A white visitor to the camp once commented on how Indian women worked like slaves while the strong warriors sat back like lazy overseers. A squaw corrected him, reminding him that it was the warrior who almost daily risked his life raiding enemy tribes to bring more horses and weapons home, and who labored, at no small danger also, to supply their families with meat and vital skins. The division of labor was equal enough, though even Deborah wondered as she whisked a stream of sweat from her brow.

Deborah was able to pack her gradually accumulating possessions, greatly increased since the birth of her daughter, on her own pony. The horse, a roan and white pinto mare, had been a gift from Crooked Eye. He had been tremendously impressed by her generosity in giving the fine gray stallion to Broken Wing, in the true Cheyenne spirit of giving. Moreover, he had begun to feel certain familial obligations toward the white woman who was becoming more and more a part of his family.

"It is customary," he told her, "for the child's father to give away gifts when a child is born, but you have no husband and no gifts to give, so I have given away horses for you. I also give you a pony, so that you might one day be a squaw of important standing in this camp."

Crooked Eye's words made Deborah ponder once more her place with the Cheyenne band. At first it had simply been based on survival, but now that her child had been born and her health was back to normal, she was free to leave. She even had her own horse to carry her away.

It was summer now, a year since Leonard's death, and nearly nine months since being separated from Griff McCulloch. It had been six months since Carolyn's birth. Yet she felt no urgent desire to move on.

Why should she?

Perhaps it was possible for her to one day become a "squaw of important standing" in this tribe. Thus far they had accepted her fully, as if she were one of them, a fact that never ceased to amaze her. She doubted an Indian would find such acceptance among the whites. She thought of poor Jacob and Laban who were only half-Mexican, not even as lowly as Indians were considered to be, and they had been treated like nothing, especially by Caleb and Leonard, but to a slightly lesser degree by others in the community also.

Had Deborah at last found her place in life, here among the wild Indians of the Plains?

She still harbored some ambivalent feelings regarding the disparity between the sometimes savage customs of the tribe and the kind-hearted, honorable character she encountered more often than not among the people. Yet, day by day, her confusion was gradually being overcome by her sense of security and belonging. Through Gray Antelope's patient guidance, she was learning how to tan animal hides, a major industry among the Cheyenne. They were not weavers of cloth, and thus, hides and other animal parts provided clothing, shelter and many of the necessities of life. She learned how to preserve meat, especially of the buffalo, the tribe's main food source. But root-digging was also important, and Deborah learned of the abundance the dry prairie soil provided. She had guessed correctly, when she had been stranded out there, that her helplessness had been due only to her ignorance.

What Deborah enjoyed most, of all her instruction, was when Broken Wing had time to take her aside to teach her the ways of the warriors. He taught her the use of the bow, and in short time, because of her persistence, she became quite a good shot. He even showed her how to make her own bow from a tree branch and how to shape crude arrows, though he said the best bows were made by a very elite circle of experts in the tribe, and it was to them the warriors usually went for this work. Broken Wing gave Deborah his second-best bow when she became consistently adept at striking the target.

Unfortunately, however, her instruction in the use of firearms was still limited because ammunition was too precious a commodity to be used frivolously. Yet, even if she could not often fire, she learned proficiency at handling, loading, and cleaning. Much to her delight, Broken Wing took her hunting one day, and she bagged two jackrabbits and a wild turkey.

She also helped both Broken Wing and Crooked Eye with the care of their stock. She learned the Indian way to break a horse by leading it into the middle of a stream before mounting. There, in the deep water, a horse had difficulty bucking, but even if the animal did manage to throw its rider, the fall was considerably softened by the water. Deborah and Broken Wing had many a riotous moment splashing into the water while attempting to tame a particularly obstinate pony.

For the present, then, Deborah was content to move with the flow of events, feeling no pressure to make any life-altering decisions. Settling into the new camp afforded her ample diversion from more probing thoughts.

No sooner were the lodges raised on the banks of a tributary of the Smoky Hill River than the Cheyennes began preparations for the celebration of the Medicine Lodge, or Sun Dance.

"It is a time of renewing for my people," Broken Wing explained, "like making over the whole world—everything is new once again."

"Do you worship the sun?" asked Deborah. She was able to converse almost entirely in Cheyenne now, lapsing only occasionally into English.

Broken Wing pondered her question a few moments before answering. "No, the sun is only a symbol for the Wise One Above. It is not the sun but *Heammawihio* whom we reverence, because he knows how to do things better than all others. He is the Great Spirit, over all others. *Aktunowihio* is the Wise One Below, who dwells in the earth, but he is not as great."

"So the purpose of the Medicine Lodge is to petition *Heammawihio* for special blessings?" asked Deborah.

"The Medicine Lodge came to us many summers ago during a time of famine among our people. Our great ancient warrior, Erect Horns, then called Standing-on-the-Ground, journeyed to a sacred mountain to seek favor from the Great Spirit. There, he was taught the Sun Dance and the Spirit gave him the sacred buffalo skin hat from which Erect Horns took his new name. The Great Spirit of the sacred mountain promised Erect Horns that if he followed all his instructions, he would have strong magic. The heavens would open and water the dry land, an abundance of food would spring from the land, and all the animals would follow him from the mountain to his home. And it was as the Great Spirit said; the land was reborn, the buffalo came to us, and our people survived." Broken Wing paused, perhaps to give Deborah a chance to respond, but she was content to listen to Broken Wing's fervent sincerity; the way his dark eyes danced as he spoke from his heart stirred her in a way she thought impossible.

Perhaps she had not become such a hardened cynic after all. But was that safe? Could she afford such a weakening in her protective walls?

Broken Wing continued, "The ceremony will last eight days. The first four days will be spent building the sacred lodge for the dance, then will follow the gathering of the people. It will include the entire tribe. You will be much impressed."

"I'm certain I will be."

"I must go now, there is much to do. We hunt buffalo at the next rising of the sun." He rose to go.

Deborah wanted to ask a hundred questions, to say anything that would induce him to tarry. But the moment the urge struck, she quelled it. Whatever this attraction she was feeling for Broken Wing, she must not encourage it. She wanted a friend, indeed needed a friend, but she absolutely wanted no more. She had been hurt enough and would be a fool to place herself in such a precarious position again. So, Deborah bid Broken Wing goodbye, and watched him go with a rather mixed sense of relief.

Later that day, Deborah learned yet another significance of the Medicine Lodge ceremony.

————

Deborah was in Crooked Eye's lodge, now her own home also, feeding Carolyn. Gray Antelope had been out assisting her husband with some preparations for the Medicine Lodge, but she returned to the lodge wearing a wide grin on her face.

Indian humor was not new to Deborah, for she had learned early that they were not the stoic, serious types the white man had always painted them. Nevertheless, there was something peculiar in Gray Antelope's expression that afternoon, especially when she erupted into a girlish giggle.

"What is it?" Deborah asked, curious, but not alarmed.

"You have not looked outside the lodge?"

"No. Why?"

Gray Antelope motioned for Deborah to come to the door. Laying Carolyn carefully on a buffalo robe, Deborah rose and obeyed. The older woman pushed the flap aside the barest crack and Deborah peered out. All she saw, besides the usual camp activity, was a young warrior pacing in front of the tepee. She had seen him before, even spoken to him occasionally. His name was Walking Wolf, which especially fit him now as he burned a rather agitated path in front of the lodge.

"What is he doing?" asked Deborah, realizing the warrior must be what Gray Antelope wanted her to notice.

The shaman's wife dropped the flap, closing off the crack, then led Deborah toward the back of the tepee where their voices would not be easily heard.

Then, without preamble, Gray Antelope answered, "Walking Wolf wishes to court you."

"What?" Deborah sputtered and it was a moment before she could form a further reply. Then, "That's ridiculous. I don't want to be courted. He hardly knows me. I—I . . ." Her voice broke off as her shock overcame her power of speech.

"You do not wish to marry, Wind Rider?"

"I was married once, Gray Antelope, and it was a disaster. I don't wish to make another mistake."

"But if you marry and are not happy with each other, you can just end the marriage."

Deborah gave a dry ironic laugh at the innocent statement. The Cheyenne held marriage and fidelity as very sacred, but, although it didn't happen often, the manner of ending a marriage was astonishingly simple.

"It is not that way with the white man," Deborah said. "Once you marry, it is considered to be for life. If I were ever to marry again, I could do it no other way—and for that reason, I doubt I will ever remarry."

"But if you are fond of a man, what will you do?"

An image of Broken Wing flashed across Deborah's mind, but she quickly shook it away. "I don't know. When my husband died, I did not think I could ever love a man again—not that I loved him, but it made me fearful of doing so. He made my life miserable, and I fear that might happen again."

"But if you loved a man perhaps it would be different," said Gray Antelope. "And if he truly loved you."

"Those are big 'ifs,' aren't they? I'm afraid I could never be sure."

"Ah, but who is sure of anything in this life? If you do not try things because of this fear, then you will miss much that is good in life. Sometimes the bee stings when I pick a pretty prairie flower, but oh, how sad if it keeps me from enjoying the others."

"I had more than a little bee sting, Gray Antelope."

"The time of the Sun Dance is a time of powerful medicine," said Gray Antelope. "Perhaps now is the best time for you to begin anew. I am sure that is why Walking Wolf chooses now to court, for it will insure that good spirits accompany the marriage."

"I appreciate all you have said, Gray Antelope, but I still can't encourage him. He will have better luck with another girl. I had best go talk to him immediately."

"Do not talk to him," said the older woman, "for that will make him think you accept him. Take the water skin and go to the river to get water. And when you leave the tepee, walk by him without saying a word."

"But that seems so hard, so cruel."

"He will feel bad, no matter what you do, but he will understand this way, and his disappointment will not last long. Then he will find another girl."

Deborah hesitated, not caring to be placed in such a distasteful position. Nevertheless, she absolutely did not want to encourage this man. Sighing, she rose and fetched the water skin.

"Will you watch Carolyn?"

Gray Antelope grinned. She never had to be asked twice to care for the baby she considered her granddaughter.

Deborah ducked outside. Walking Wolf paused in his active vigil. Deborah averted her eyes from him but not before she noted the spark of eager anticipation in the warrior's eyes. She took a few hesitant but determined steps as Walking Wolf looked on. She passed him, silent, feeling his gaze penetrate her back. She finally could stand it no longer. Pausing, she turned, saying in Cheyenne:

"I'm sorry."

Then she hurried on to the river.

31

DEBORAH CONTINUED TO WALK out to the river. She supposed that since she was here anyway, she would fill the skin.

The day was warm and sultry; only the slight breeze off the river gave any relief from the heat. Deborah did not go immediately to fulfill her intended task—instead she found a high grassy rise by the shore and sat there gazing out upon her surroundings.

Lately, this particular piece of land had become the focus of much controversy and hostility between the white man and the Indians. It had long been a favorite hunting ground for one tribe or another. Most recently it had been the Kaw and Otoe, semi-civilized tribes of Kansas. But about five years ago, a Cheyenne and Arapahoe war party claimed the land and a great battle had ensued with the more warlike Otoe. Though the battle had ended in a standoff, the Otoes, realizing hunting would no longer be possible that season, retreated. The wilder Plains tribes came to dominate the area.

Deborah could understand the peculiar draw of the place, with its verdant, timbered streams supporting an abundance of wild turkeys, antelope, and deer. But the most distinct and enchanting feature of the Smoky Hill region was the prominent ridge of rugged buttes pitched against the horizon on the north bank of the Smoky Hill River. Now resembling miniature mountains, they had once been high, imposing tablelands that over the years had been worn away by erosion. Even in ancient times, this place had been populated by the prehistoric ancestors of the present tribes, as evidenced by the remains of mounds and burial places and camps.

Peering through the perennial haze by which the hills and river had acquired their names, Deborah could just make out a herd of buffalo, numbering perhaps in the thousands, grazing in the distance. Over these poor, dumb beasts the present difficulty had arisen. Earlier in the year the whites had established a stage route from Leavenworth to Denver along the Smoky Hill River, right through the rich hunting ground. The Dog Soldiers, led by Bull Bear, had declared they would not surrender this area. They considered it a blatant breach of the treaty concluded the previous fall. Conducting raids, stealing horses, and generally harassing the white travelers, the Dog Soldiers were aggravating an already tenuous situation. No one doubted it was bound to erupt into bloodshed sooner or later. What made the situation even worse was that many of the other warriors were beginning to join the Dog Soldiers, abandoning the peace-chiefs like Black Kettle.

The timing of the Sun Dance ceremony could not have been more ideal. Hopefully it would draw the various bands of the tribe back together, healing the breaches caused by the militancy of the Dog Men and other soldier societies of the Cheyenne. Of course, it was possible it might only fire up already simmering emotions. That's what the nervous whites feared.

Deborah hoped for peace, if for no other reason than because she did not want to be caught in the middle of a war. Yet, on the other hand, she did not sympathize with the white traders who had so callously invaded the hunting ground. There were other routes where roads could be built, but of course, the white men were in too much of a hurry to consider anything but the most direct path, expecting all obstacles to yield to their manifest power.

Deborah, deep in thought, did not notice the approach of soft moccasined feet—not that she would have, for Broken Wing knew well the fabled art of Indian stealth. However, at that moment he was not so concerned with surprise as he was simply hesitant to intrude upon his white friend's solitude. But he forged ahead because he was not sure his concern could wait.

"Wind Rider," he said softly.

Oddly, the sound of Broken Wing's voice penetrating the deep silence did not startle Deborah; it seemed almost to blend naturally into the surrounding sounds of nature. Nevertheless, it did cause an electric thrill to course through Deborah's body. She had come to enjoy, even anticipate that voice.

She turned on her perch toward him. "Hello," she said, smiling a welcome.

"I hope I have not disturbed you."

"No, I was just taking in the beauty of this country. I was thinking how it was too bad a shadow of trouble has to darken it."

He nodded silently, seeming almost unwilling to broach the topic of the current dispute with the whites. This became further evidenced as he quickly changed the subject.

"There is a good herd of buffalo," he said. "We will have a good hunt, perhaps tomorrow."

"Maybe the stage route won't disrupt the hunting grounds, after all."

Again, Broken Wing seemed to avoid the subject of the dispute with the whites. "I have made a new lance. Being made during the Sun Dance will give it good medicine."

"Yes," said Deborah, "Gray Antelope Woman was telling me of the strong spirits prominent now."

"Is that so?"

"It seems a young warrior named Walking Wolf has seized this opportunity to pay court to me." Deborah tried to keep her tone light and conversational.

"I have heard this," said Broken Wing gravely. "And will you favor him?"

"I don't wish to marry Walking Wolf." Though the thought entered her mind, she did not add that she didn't want to marry anyone. Somehow, Broken Wing's presence made her unable to verbalize that particular thought.

Short of an outright sigh of relief, Broken Wing visibly relaxed.

Deborah continued, feeling tension growing within herself proportionate to the easing of her companion's tension. "He hardly knows me; I don't know what encouraged him to try in the first place. I suppose in ignorance of your customs, I must have unwittingly led him on."

"It is not so surprising," said Broken Wing. "I have heard Walking Wolf talk. He wants a white woman. He is much impressed with the blue of your eyes and the yellow of your hair. He has said you should be given the Cheyenne name of Golden Hair."

"I don't know what to think about that."

"Walking Wolf is looking for a trophy, not a wife. Be glad you did not favor him."

The similarity of Broken Wing's analogy to what she had often thought about Leonard was not lost on Deborah. She suddenly found herself wondering what a man like Broken Wing thought about such matters. How would he treat a woman, a wife? Did he speak, as the Indians said, with a double heart, saying one thing to lure a foolish girl, then practicing another? How could she ever be certain again?

"I am glad" was all she said.

"You are very beautiful, Wind Rider," said Broken Wing suddenly. Deborah gaped, speechless, as the warrior continued. "Your hair does shine like the gold the white man is so fond of, and your eyes are as blue as a winter stream." Deborah's heart pounded as his eyes roved over her with admiration. "But the Wise One Above gave the best gifts to the Indian—hair as black as the wing of a raven, eyes dark like flint, and skin brown with health." Deborah found herself gaping again, not knowing what to think. A slight smile softened Broken Wing's earnest expression. "You are upset at my words?"

"I—I don't know . . ."

"I am not good with words—not those spoken from the heart to a woman. Forgive me; I did not say what I meant." He paused, gazing along the stream as if he could find the right words there. When his eyes lifted once more to face her, the earnestness had returned. Deborah wondered how she could fail to trust a man who looked at her in that tender way.

He took a breath and began again with resolve. "It is not your hair, Wind Rider, nor your eyes that have won my love. It is what you have inside. You have a Cheyenne heart, a strong heart, and for that reason I love you—"

"Broken Wing—". Unexpected tears welled up in her eyes, and a lump in her throat made it impossible for her to say more.

"You do not talk much about your past," said Broken Wing. "But from the little you say, I think you have had much hurt. I do not wish to hurt you more. I know you are torn between your people and mine, and I would not make more trouble for you. But I believe you feel something for me also."

"I do, Broken Wing!" Deborah said through her emotion. "But I am afraid and confused also. You are right—it is because of the pain and hurt of my past. I don't know what to do about it."

"The Medicine Lodge is a time of renewal; maybe it will be so for you." The hope in his voice made Deborah's heart ache.

"If only it were possible," she said, half-musing to herself.

"I wish to be your husband, Wind Rider. I wish to make a lodge of my own with you. But I do not require an answer of you now. I know you must search yourself much for this decision.

"It is the Cheyenne custom," he went on, "for the suitor to stand in front of the girl's tent as Walking Wolf did today. Sometimes they also follow the custom of the more forward Sioux and wear a blanket over their bodies. When the girl comes out, they embrace each other in this blanket if the match is agreeable. But I will not do this with you. For you, Wind Rider, I will make a new custom." He paused, smiling gently, pleased with his solution to their problem. "You may come to my lodge if you wish to marry me. Then I will know you have searched yourself and found you have feeling for me and desire to be my wife. If you do not come to my lodge, I will understand."

Everything within Deborah wanted to shout, "I do love you and I want to marry you!" But the words could not break through her fear. All she could do was nod and watch him retreat back to the village.

32

DEBORAH DID NOT SLEEP THAT NIGHT. She lay awake on the soft buffalo hide bed, unable to get Broken Wing out of her mind.

How could she love him? He was a wild Indian, uncivilized, illiterate, foreign to everything she had always known. If she married him, she might as well forget ever returning to her own people, for she had heard how white women who had married Indians, even if it had been against their will, were shunned by civilized society. That was why many captives killed themselves rather than unite with Indians. Such an act somehow tainted a woman, made her lower even than a slave.

Could I willingly cut myself off like that? For a savage?

A smile forced its way across Deborah's lips, full of bitter irony. She knew Broken Wing was no more a savage than her own father had been. Perhaps the Cheyenne warrior couldn't read, or eat with a fork, or dance in a ballroom, or drive a carriage; but she knew with every fiber within her that he was more civilized than any man she had ever known, except perhaps for her father.

Yet she knew that wasn't the real reason for her reluctance. She had already more than halfway committed her future to these Cheyenne, repudiating her so-called civilized ways. That day a year ago, riding away from the shame of the gallows with Griff and his outlaws, she had crossed over the chasm between her past and future life, knowing she could never return. She did not want to return. The past was lost; all the joys of her childhood and the hope of recapturing the happiness of her youth had been shattered in Leonard Stoner's

177

bed. Perhaps the forming of that chasm had been for the best. The Sun Dance meant renewal, new life, as Broken Wing had wisely pointed out. Maybe she was ready to hope again, to reach out for a new kind of happiness. Perhaps the very contrasts Broken Wing presented made him the logical choice to begin that new life with.

Her reluctance, then, had little to do with the life Broken Wing offered. Rather, it had to do with Broken Wing himself—not his race, or his wildness—but more with whether she could trust herself to a man again. It was his gender, not his character, that troubled her.

The real harm from her marriage to Leonard had come not so much from his physical abuse, but because he had invaded her youthful innocence, attacking that part of her that had wanted to trust, to love, and to give herself to a man. He had twisted those needs, nearly severing them from her. But she was still young, only twenty-one, and those desires still needed fulfilling. Her wounds were deep, but not beyond the healing scope of time. Simple logic told her that to let one man so destroy her would be foolish. And being a year removed from the horrendous situation, lying in the safe security of an Indian lodge, helped Deborah to remember that Leonard and Caleb were not the only men in her life. She had known tenderness and love and friendship from her father and brother, and Jacob Stoner. Even Griff McCulloch had been a decent man.

But she hadn't been married to any of them. Could there be something about marriage?

Lodging with Gray Antelope and Crooked Eye over the last several months had given her the opportunity to observe a marriage close at hand. Perhaps Crooked Eye was not the most affectionate of men, but he treated his wife well, with respect. Many times at night, after they had all retired to their beds, Deborah would hear them talking quietly on the other side of the lodge. He not only respected her opinion, he sometimes even sought it! Occasionally they had disagreements. Then one or the other—never the same one over and over—apologized, and all was well.

Deborah had also observed the marriage of Stands-in-the-River and Stone Teeth Woman. Stands-in-the-River could be a bit of a tyrant at times, and Stone Teeth was perhaps the hardest working squaw in camp. But Deborah had never seen her wear a browbeaten, miserable expression. Though she was known to complain at times, she did not do so bitterly; and just as often she sang the praises of her husband, who was likely to become a chief soon.

So, again, the question arose in Deborah's mind: *What of Broken*

178

Wing? What kind of husband would he make?

Deborah closed her eyes, visualizing his strong, sensitive countenance—the eyes that could dance with merriment, flash with passion, even draw within himself with introspection; the lips that formed a smile to melt the hardest soul, that spoke kindness and wisdom. In the months she had known him, she had never once seen a cruel or vicious look upon that face. Even when he stood over the dead Pawnee, he had worn no look of evil triumph. And in the few times he had chanced to touch her or even to behold her with his eyes, she had never sensed anything but kindness. She recalled the day of Carolyn's birth, and how tenderly he had touched her baby and how compassionately he had led Deborah to an acceptance of the child. Could a man maintain such a performance for over six months? After all, she had known Leonard only a few days. If she hadn't been in such a hurry, she might not have been so easily deluded.

She had believed that after Leonard, she could never love a man, yet she could not deny her feelings for Broken Wing. Nor could she deny her need for him—not on a physical level, for she was certain she could survive on her own now—but rather her need for his love and his friendship. No amount of abuse could ever totally destroy this need in a young woman, in any woman. When she recalled the things Broken Wing said earlier that day about her, it stirred her deeply. She needed to be loved like that, she needed to know it was possible.

Oh, Broken Wing, I do love you! Is it possible that I might truly find happiness again? Perhaps it is time I try.

———

Deborah slept little more than an hour the whole night. Still, she awoke refreshed, and with a rare smile upon her face. She was ready to take another chance at happiness. With Leonard, she had been running away, but now she felt as if she were running *toward* something—perhaps a new life. A small, nagging fear still tried to tug at her heart because she had lost so many people that she loved. Yet an inner sense seemed to assure her that she had to take the risk sometime. This life, especially on these untamed plains, was hard and harsh. Survival was more a miracle than the norm. Even if she was doomed to lose Broken Wing, could she really live in her protective shell forever? Did she want to?

That morning, before leaving the lodge, Deborah fed Carolyn, then spoke to Gray Antelope who received Deborah's announcement with pleasure. The older woman found a good blanket, one given to the tribe last winter by the government, and gave it to Deborah.

Feeling just a little silly, Deborah wrapped the blanket, shawl-like, over her head and shoulders. It fell around her body, nearly to the ground.

As she approached the lodge of Stands-in-the-River, where Broken Wing lived, she wondered if he was even there. Today was supposed to have been the day of the buffalo hunt. Might he not have left hours ago? He never said he'd wait in his tepee until she came. Would she have to pace for hours, perhaps days, before seeing him? She was already causing quite a stir in the village with her unorthodox behavior. When did a proper Cheyenne girl ever court a man? The Cheyenne women were considered to be the most chaste women on all the plains, and she must now appear to them to be a brazen hussy. Already, some were casting her expressions of shock, although some were smiling and giggling.

They must think me crazy! They must—

Suddenly the lodge flap opened. Broken Wing ducked outside and quickly strode toward her.

Feeling just a little trepidation, faltering for a moment, Deborah finally took a breath and did what Gray Antelope had instructed. She opened wide her blanket and threw her arms, and the blanket, around him. Without hesitation, Broken Wing returned the embrace. He had passed up the hunt, waiting for her, hoping she would come, praying she felt for him even just a fraction of the love he felt toward her.

Later that day Broken Wing, adhering to accepted tradition, sent six horses, each laden with hides and many other trinkets, to Crooked Eye's lodge.

The shaman grinned and said to Deborah, "Well, daughter, a young brave wishes to wed you. Is this acceptable to you?"

Deborah nodded, unable to repress a joyous grin.

Crooked Eye continued. "Then I, as your father, accept his gifts."

He took Deborah to his remuda, where he kept his stock, and led in Broken Wing's animals. Then he picked out eight different horses. "These are for your husband-to-be to seal our bargain. And . . ." he paused, raising his hand in a sweeping motion toward the remuda, "because this is such a joyful moment and I am pleased with you, you may choose any horse for yourself."

There were twenty or thirty horses in the remuda, for Crooked Eye was a man of substance in the tribe. He no longer went on horse raids with the warriors, but his services as shaman garnered him a rich income.

Deborah concentrated on the mares, and she quickly saw the one she wanted. When she led out the chestnut with its silky coat and black mane and tail, Crooked Eye nodded his approval, despite the fact that she had chosen one of his best animals.

"You make yourself worthy of the name Broken Wing has given you," he said. "You do know horses. That is good. Maybe I should have married you myself."

"Gray Antelope would not have liked that," Deborah replied coyly.

"She is spoiled. I should have taken a second wife long ago. But she has no sister, and it is dangerous to have two wives who are not sisters."

Deborah was in a thoughtful mood later when she happened to see Broken Wing. They walked under the cottonwoods by the river. He talked to her about the tribal marriage rites and encouraged her to speak in detail to Gray Antelope Woman, who would act as her mother in the ceremony.

"We will not have a big lodge to start with," he said apologetically, "for I have only three horses left besides the new ones from Crooked Eye." Deborah realized he had given more than half his wealth to Crooked Eye as a marriage pledge, and though he had received more than that as a dowry, his generosity touched her. "I had more," Broken Wing continued, "but when the Pawnee raided before we moved the camp, I lost many. After the Medicine Lodge dance, we will take out a raiding party and replenish our stock."

Deborah wasn't thinking about horses just then. Rather, her earlier conversation with Crooked Eye had been disturbing her. She was again thinking about trust and hope and taking risks.

"Broken Wing," she blurted as a new panic caught her, "will you take other wives?"

"It is the Cheyenne custom . . . but it is not always done."

"Will *you?*"

"Would this displease you?"

"I want to be a good Cheyenne wife," she replied, "but . . . I don't think I could accept that. There are some white customs that are simply too deeply inbred to shake."

He smiled down at her. "It would not be fair for me to take another wife, Wind Rider, for I would always hold you in esteem over that one, and thus she would be too miserable."

Deborah sighed with relief, and laughed and threw her arms

181

around Broken Wing, kissing him enthusiastically on the lips.

"This is one white custom you may keep!" he laughed as he returned her passion eagerly, seeming to quickly master the foreign ritual.

Still breathless with emotion, Deborah asked as they fell reluctantly apart, "How long are Cheyenne engagements?"

"Very quick," assured Broken Wing. "We can be married tomorrow while the Medicine Lodge still stands to bless us with good magic." He paused, then said more solemnly, "If it is your wish. . . ?"

Because her last marriage had happened too quickly, Deborah should have felt nervous. But this time it was her choice, her decision; and whether it occurred tomorrow or in a year, she sensed intuitively that Broken Wing would always be the man he was this moment— the man she loved.

33

SO IT WAS, ON THE FOLLOWING morning, in accordance with tribal tradition, Deborah dressed in one of Gray Antelope's finest deerskin shifts and was placed on the back of the spritely chestnut mare. Twelve Beads Woman, one of Gray Antelope's close friends, led the chestnut, while Gray Antelope followed, leading Crooked Eye's gift horses. Like a small parade, they traveled the short distance to the lodge Broken Wing shared with his brother. There, while Gray Antelope took charge of Carolyn, several of Broken Wing's male friends and relatives took Deborah from the horse, placed her on a blanket and then, taking up the corners, carried her into the groom's lodge. She was given the place of honor in the rear of the lodge, and when the braves departed, her new female in-laws redressed her in a new buckskin outfit, this one of a soft hide so pale in color that Deborah thought it must have come from a white deer. This, and the intricate beading on the dress marked it as a rich gift, and Deborah wept as she received it. She realized that these women, some whom she barely knew, had spared nothing for Broken Wing's bride. Stone

Teeth Woman embraced her warmly.

When Deborah was dressed and her hair braided and wrapped in beaver skin and adorned with silver disks and beads, Broken Wing was summoned to receive his bride. He stopped abruptly in the tepee door as he first beheld his beloved Wind Rider, and tears rose in his eyes.

He still did not know how he could be so fortunate to have deserved such a gift as this white woman who now stood before him, a lovely Cheyenne squaw. She was his best dreams fulfilled. Ah, dreams . . . surely this must be their meaning!

He took her hand and together they sat in Stands-in-the-River's lodge, now quickly filling with wedding guests. Hours of feasting followed, and dancing by the men, both inside and outside in the cool summer evening. It was nearly as festive and enthusiastic as any of the Sun Dance ceremonies. Deborah hardly noticed that Gray Antelope and Stone Teeth had slipped out of the tepee until she saw them return sometime after dark. The noise of merry-making quieted as Gray Antelope Woman stepped forward and addressed Deborah.

"Daughter," she said, then swept her arm toward the open tepee door, "there is your lodge; it is your home; go and live in it." She tried to be solemn and grave as she spoke, but her eyes twinkled and her lips quivered with her joy.

Broken Wing took Deborah's hand and together they stepped outside. There, beside and somewhat behind Crooked Eye's spacious lodge, sat a smaller tepee that had not been there that morning. Deborah realized that during the wedding feast her new "mother" and "mother-in-law" had been busy erecting a home for the new-lyweds. Weeping, Deborah embraced and kissed the two women, who responded with pleased grins.

Amid an onrush of well-wishing from Crooked Eye and Stands-in-the-River—embraces for Deborah and slaps on the back for Broken Wing—the bride and groom walked arm-in-arm to their new home.

Deborah tried to focus on the generous household supplies the older women had given them. Two backrests, and a cradle for Carolyn, now unoccupied, since Gray Antelope had insisted on keeping her during the wedding rites; several cooking utensils, including a cast-iron kettle and large water skin, which were all displayed against a wall in the tepee. But then Deborah's eye rested on the thick winter buffalo hides spread out on the dirt floor, and the realization of what she was embarking upon finally struck her. Immediately she grew tense and fearful. A near-panic gripped her as the awful image of her first wedding night leaped into her mind.

What have I done? she silently screamed. *What makes me think it could ever be different?*

Broken Wing had already sat down on one of the hides and was holding a hand out, entreating her to join him. She stood stiff and tense in the middle of the tepee, feeling cold and sick. Gray Antelope had once told her love might make her change her attitude about the union of a man and a woman. But all at once, Deborah was afraid that not even love would be enough.

Broken Wing read her fear and reluctance. He spoke to her with patience, as if to a child. "You may sit, Wind Rider. I will not touch your cord until you are willing."

Gray Antelope had done her best to instruct Deborah in the intimate customs of the tribe. She had even given Deborah her own cord to wear, a kind of chastity belt worn by all Cheyenne women, similar to the breechcloth worn by the men. However, where the male article was a sign of manhood, its removal signifying the loss of one's virility, the female's stood for purity. A woman's cord was considered inviolable; for a man to violate it, it often meant he risked a death sentence. A husband, too, was expected to respect his wife's cord.

Deborah wondered if her reluctance had less to do with fear than it did with simply desiring to test her new husband. She had believed that in deciding to marry him she had also decided to trust him, yet now she realized how much more was involved. Would she ever be able to completely erase the deep injuries of the past?

But, whatever her reasons, Deborah could not so easily shed her fears.

"Sit," Broken Wing said again, softly, gently.

She hesitated only another moment. After all, to do otherwise would have seemed like a slap in the face of the man she claimed to love.

"You are trembling," said Broken Wing, and pulled the other buffalo robe up around Deborah's shoulders. Then he continued talking. "I have often wanted to ask you, Wind Rider, about the white man's world, but you had so much to learn of the Cheyenne way that I did not find time. Have you ever been to a big white man's village? Some of our chiefs have been to the village of your Great White Chief, but they could not find enough words to describe it to us. Have you been there? What is it like?"

Deborah could hardly believe her bridegroom could be interested in Washington, D.C., at a time like this, but she grasped eagerly at the offered reprieve and launched into a detailed speech, worthy of any tour guide, describing the city she had visited many times before the war. Before she realized it, she began to tell him about how the government operated, about the war, and about her home in Virginia, and her family. He asked many questions, her answers leading them even further afield to a discussion of the world in general. Nearly two hours passed in this manner.

Deborah's shivering eased, although she didn't know if it was because of the robe or from something within herself. When the conversation waned a bit, Broken Wing reclined on the hide bed; and Deborah tensed again. Almost babbling, she barraged him with a stream of trivial questions, which he answered patiently, unhurriedly. At one point, she was talking again, telling him something about the President she had forgotten to mention before. After ten minutes of this dissertation, she heard a quiet purring sound beside her. Broken Wing had fallen asleep.

For a brief moment she felt only mortification. He would hate and scorn her now for treating him thus on their wedding night. He would believe her dishonest and selfish. Why hadn't she at least explained the reason for her reluctance? But how? Ladies did not speak of the kinds of things that had hurt her in her marriage to Leonard, not even Cheyenne ladies. Moreover, a simple, honest man like Broken Wing doubtless would never have been able to fathom what she was talking about.

Instead, she had treated this man she loved cruelly and faithlessly, no better than Leonard had treated her. Then Deborah gazed at Broken Wing's sleeping face. There was no tension in it, no pent-up resentments. He seemed content. She suddenly believed that this man would indeed wait until she was willing; he loved her too much to do anything else.

And what of the love she claimed to have for him? Was it really love she felt if it was not coupled with trust?

Was it too late? Could he ever forgive her?

Studying his face once more, she knew that to believe otherwise of him would be her greatest disservice to him. She reached toward him to brush aside a strand of his long black hair that had fallen across his face. He sighed and stirred, but did not wake. Deborah found she was disappointed at this, but she still seemed to lack the courage to wake him outright.

In that moment, it occurred to her that lovemaking had nothing to do with the commitment she had made and was even then making to Broken Wing; her "savage" Indian husband had understood that subtle fact all along.

At last content, Deborah stretched out on the soft robe beside her sleeping husband, pulling the second robe over them both. For the first time, perhaps in her life, Deborah knew the peace of true love.

Broken Wing stirred again and rolled over on his side, facing her. He gave her a groggy, half-awake smile.

"You no longer tremble," he said.

"No."

"And you are no longer afraid?"

She gave a slight smile and shook her head.

"That is good." But he made no move toward her; in fact, he laid his head back as if he would sleep again.

Deborah reached beneath the buffalo robe and, loosening her cord, moved close to him. Broken Wing then took her in his tender embrace, full of love, full of honor.

PART 4

WIND RIDER

34

IF THE FOLLOWING MONTHS WERE of blissful joy for Deborah, they proved to be filled with fomenting turmoil for the tribe in general.

The Smoky Hill region continued to smolder with tension. A party of some forty Dog Soldiers, led by Bull Bear, attacked a stage station at Chalk Bluffs, killing two station keepers. The Dog Men denied the attack and were defended even by Black Kettle, who laid the blame on the Sioux. But the whites were not appeased, and the Cheyenne were soon the first to be blamed for all ensuing depravations in the area. Though Bull Bear was innocent in the Chalk Bluffs incident, he was certainly involved in other attacks.

Fortunately for Deborah, before the worst of the trouble erupted, Black Kettle's band had moved south of the Arkansas River to camp on the Cimarron River. But unsettling news of violence and misunderstanding still reached them, casting a shadow over Deborah's new and happy little home.

One of the most volatile incidents occurred in the fall of 1866 after Major General Winfield Scott Hancock arrived to take command of the Military Department of Missouri. A Civil War hero with presidential ambitions, he determined to grab the glory and promotions to be obtained in the Indian wars. With the newly reorganized Seventh Cavalry under the command of Lieutenant Colonel George Armstrong Custer, Hancock launched an unrelenting campaign against the unruly Indians of western Kansas, with decided emphasis on the Cheyenne. The Fetterman Massacre of eighty soldiers that December by a Cheyenne and Sioux war party in Wyoming Territory only aggravated white hostility.

Hancock called the Cheyenne chiefs in for a council and assaulted them with threats, warning that the bluecoat chiefs commanded more soldiers than the Indians could even imagine.

Stands-in-the-River, who had attended with the chiefs, reported the dismaying proceedings to Deborah and Broken Wing with bitter contempt.

"The white man chief, this Hancock, wanted only to frighten us! He cares nothing for peace. He spoke with double words, not from his heart—" Stands-in-the-River thumped his chest as if to verify that he, at least, knew what it meant to speak from one's heart. "These were his false words: 'I'll help the cooperative Indians who want peace, but any rebellious, bad chiefs, I'll crush.' Ha! We will see who crushes who!"

Then Stands-in-the-River went on to describe how Hancock had shocked and truly frightened the chiefs by telling them he intended to take his troops on an inspection of the Cheyenne villages. The memory of the betrayal at Sand Creek, when the Cheyenne were invited to make camp by the creek only to be attacked by the army, was still too raw for the chiefs to accept the presence of the bluecoats in their villages.

"But when Hancock arrived the next day with his troops," said Stands-in-the-River smugly, "he was met by a wall of three hundred warriors, ready for war. Only Major Wynkoop was able to keep disaster from falling on the bluecoats. He convinced the Indians to retreat, which we did reluctantly. Then the chiefs agreed to another council with Hancock." This last comment Stands-the-River said with some disdain, as if he would have surely done differently.

What followed caused horror and indignation even in Deborah, and this was multiplied many times in the Cheyenne listeners. While the chiefs met with the general that night in one of the villages, the rest of the villagers, fearing a repeat of Sand Creek, fled, leaving their lodges standing empty. Whatever Hancock's true designs, he did not like being outwitted by the Indians, and he dispatched Custer and his Seventh Cavalry in pursuit of the escaping Indians. But Custer, inexperienced in Indian tactics, managed to lose the Cheyenne, several hundred in number. Empty-handed and humiliated, Custer returned to his commander some days later. Stands-in-the-River gave a rare chuckle as he recounted this part of the story, but his expression returned to stone as he concluded.

"To revenge his shame, Hancock ordered the empty Indian village burned, destroying hundreds of valuable hides and possessions, making many Cheyenne homeless and destitute. They were caught in a snowstorm without homes or warm robes. We will see what happens the next time the whites call a council!"

Deborah and Broken Wing cast apprehensive frowns at each other. As much as they both desired peace, they had to empathize with Stands-in-the-River, for it could have just as easily been their village to burn, their loved ones made homeless through such a mindless act of vengeance.

It had been a particularly severe and long winter. In many places on the prairie, snow would still fall as late as April. Deliveries of the government annuity supplies had been irregular, if they came at all. The government blamed this on Indian hostility; the Indians took it as just another governmental breach of faith. Whatever the reason, the Cheyenne, especially those more disposed toward peace, knew that further disturbances could only heap more doom upon them—thus their chagrin when they learned that a party of Dog Soldiers had taken some white captives. Black Kettle, as he had been known to do in the past, used his own wealth to buy three of the captives, which he returned to Fort Dodge.

One captive, a woman, came too late to be part of this arrangement. Instead, she was sold to young Walking Wolf, the brave who had wished to court Deborah and who was so enamored with her fair white complexion. Since his rebuff by Deborah, he had married a Cheyenne girl, but he was still anxious to have his own white woman. He often looked enviously upon Broken Wing and had even on several occasions offered to buy Deborah from him, to which Broken Wing would only reply with a chuckle and a shake of the head. No warrior on earth had enough horses to equal the value of his beloved Wind Rider.

The moment the captive woman arrived in camp, she was a source of anxiety. Every day she cried in the most pitiful manner, which disintegrated into mournful sobs at night. The squaws in camp felt sorry for her, but when they tried to comfort her, she just wailed all the more. Once Deborah even risked her anonymity by trying to speak with the woman. But much to her dismay, the woman responded by shrinking back in horror, obviously seeing in Deborah the realization of her worst nightmares—being forced to become an Indian's wife. Deborah could say nothing to allay her fears and distress, and finally gave up.

After four days of this, the Cheyenne women began to prevail upon their husbands to talk Walking Wolf into taking the woman back to her people. Broken Wing, Crooked Eye, Stands-in-the-River, Red Feather, Yellow Shirt, and two or three others who had tepees near Walking Wolf and thus were most affected by the white woman's grief, all confronted Walking Wolf with the problem.

"I paid many horses for the woman," protested Walking Wolf.

"We all have agreed to make up the loss," said Crooked Eye, who

191

as the elder of the group was made the spokesman. In reality, he had not exactly agreed to part with his horses; his wife had pledged hers. Such was the case with several others of the committee also.

"It is too dangerous to have her in camp," said Stands-in-the-River.

"Broken Wing's woman is white," said Walking Wolf with a trace of bitterness.

"She is here willingly," countered Stands-in-the-River.

Walking Wolf knew his argument had been feeble, but he still thought it terribly unfair that he could not find a willing white woman. He shrugged and added somewhat lamely, "Who is to say it will not be just as dangerous to take her to the white man fort?"

"The other captives were returned safely," said Broken Wing.

Walking Wolf was silent several moments while he pondered his alternatives. In the end, however, he realized he had none except to return his prize or bring trouble upon the camp. He comforted himself with the thought that he, too, had begun to weary of the woman's carrying on and would be happy to have peace return to his own lodge.

"I will do as you ask," he finally replied. "But I will do it when the Indian agent comes to camp. I will not risk taking her to the white man's fort."

"But who can say when the agent will come?" said Broken Wing.

"And if we try to send him a message to come," added Red Feather, "it could take many moons. The woman is miserable, and it gives our women misery to see her. My wife keeps thinking how she would feel if she were taken from her lodge."

The situation seemed to be at a stalemate, with Walking Wolf refusing to risk going to the fort. Then Broken Wing came up with a solution.

"I will go with you," he said. "And we will carry a white flag so no harm will come to us."

But Yellow Shirt, a younger warrior and cousin of Broken Wing, and the only member of the party who was not married, interceded.

"Broken Wing, you are just married; it is not right for you to take such a risk. I have no wife; I will go."

Broken Wing protested—it was his idea, after all. "I hunt, I raid; this is no greater risk than that."

"I wish to see the fort," said Yellow Shirt. "Let me go."

"This is no war party," warned Broken Wing.

"I know. I will carry the flag."

In spite of his misgivings over sending the unwilling Walking Wolf and the cocky, over-zealous Yellow Shirt, Broken Wing agreed. The

192

next morning the two warriors, with the white woman between them, rode away from camp, a large white flag flying from Yellow Shirt's lance.

The camp settled back into a peaceful lull. But it was a deceptive peace, the kind that precedes a wild prairie tornado.

35

TWO AND A HALF DAYS AFTER THE three riders left camp, a lone rider returned. It was neither Walking Wolf nor Yellow Shirt, but rather an Arapahoe named Tall Tree. Across his saddle he carried a tattered and dirty white flag wrapped around the broken fragments of Yellow Shirt's best lance. Tall Tree told the crowd that gathered around him a grim tale.

He had been on his way to trade at the white man's fort when he came through a wooded area and saw the bodies hanging from a tree. He immediately identified them as Cheyenne, and on closer inspection found that he recognized one of the men as a worthy warrior he had hunted with many times.

Broken Wing, standing with the listeners, now stepped forward and asked tensely, "What was his name?"

The Arapahoe also knew Broken Wing and replied with sympathy. "It was your kinsman, Yellow Shirt." There could be no doubt that the other warrior was Walking Wolf.

Broken Wing and Stands-in-the-River exchanged looks of grief. Yellow Shirt was not only a relative, but was also a close friend with whom they had grown up, and hunted, and gone to battle. Stands-in-the-River let out an angry curse, his eyes flaming with immediate fury.

Broken Wing's sorrow was mingled also with guilt. It should have been *his* lance that had been shattered, and *his* neck broken by the white man's rope; and although Tall Tree had not yet finished his story, there could be no doubt who had caused the deaths of the two Cheyenne. Perhaps it was this sense of guilt that ignited the sudden rush of anger that mingled with all his other raging emotions at that moment.

Whatever the cause, it surprised him, for he had always thought himself above the rash outbursts of the militant warriors. But his blood was liberally infused with the ancient passions of his tribe. In spite of his guilt, reason told him he had no more caused the deaths of these men than had Black Kettle himself. Yet the same seething desire to retaliate that he had felt after Sand Creek assailed him again. But now he had more reason than ever to quell those passions.

Tall Tree continued. "I cut the warriors down and laid them under a tree and covered them with my best hide that I was taking to trade. I knew they would not mind lying on the ground where the wolves and coyotes and eagles could eat their flesh and thus scatter them all over the beautiful, wide prairie.

"I was afraid to go to the fort after what I had just seen, but Broken Wing and Stands-in-the-River, I knew you would want to know what had happened and how it came to be that your brother met with such a bad end. So, I went to the fort and there I saw some white man soldiers drinking whiskey in the trading post, and they were bragging about how they had strung up two kidnapping Indians. I listened and realized that the two Cheyenne had a white woman with them—"

Red Feather quickly informed the Arapahoe, "They were returning her to the fort because she did not want to stay here."

"It is what the soldiers said the Cheyenne claimed, but they did not believe the Cheyenne." He spoke this as if it were too incredible to believe anyone would doubt the word of an Indian. "They said they would make sure the thieving Indians got their punishment."

When Tall Tree stopped his recital, the small crowd erupted into a chorus of angry exclamations. Silence fell over them like a black shroud when Walking Wolf's wife, Buffalo Calf, approached. One of the village children had run to tell her the terrible news. As she came, she was shocked and stricken, looking all the more pitiful because she was pregnant with their first child.

Deborah, Gray Antelope, and some of the other women tried to comfort her, but her sorrow was inconsolable. Deborah was reminded of the tears of the white woman whom the Indians had been trying to help. It was all so senseless, so unfair. Walking Wolf and Yellow Shirt, good men trying honestly to right a wrong, had been caught in the middle of a war of hate and misunderstanding. Had the soldiers acted without official sanction? If so, would they be punished for their crime? She doubted it, if they had been free enough to boast publicly about their deed. Most likely the bigot, Hancock, and his henchman, Custer, would give the bluecoats a promotion for their actions!

All the Cheyenne had wanted to do was return the woman because they felt sorry for her! True, she should not have been in the camp in the first place; but then, neither should the white men be building their roads across Indian land. . . .

Suddenly Deborah closed her eyes and tried to shake the muddled dilemma from her distraught mind. It was a vicious circle—very, very vicious!

She wanted only to be with Broken Wing, to be assured that love and tenderness did still dwell in the world. But his countenance had begun to harden like stone; his sensitive, gentle eyes were darkening with grief and anger. She knew he must be thinking of revenge; it was the Cheyenne way. Wrongs must be avenged; and in the case of such a wrongful, depraved murder, Broken Wing's honor as a man, and the measure of his devotion to his friends, depended upon his eagerness to seek vengeance.

But first the sad and dark death customs must be observed. Within an hour of the delivery of the Arapahoe's message, a throng had gathered around Walking Wolf's lodge. All the relatives were weeping. Buffalo Calf's sisters had carried out all of her husband's property and were throwing it at the feet of various of the spectators who were not relatives. In this manner, all of the dead warrior's belongings were given away, culminating in the most grievous moment of all when the lodge itself was dismantled and the hides distributed. Walking Wolf's wife was left with nothing but the clothes she wore and a blanket to cover herself.

Since Yellow Shirt was not married, he had no lodge of his own to tear down; but his parents and other relatives were no less prostrate with their sudden bereavement. Making it even worse was the fact that there were no bodies to honor with proper ceremony, and thus, to allow the bereaved the comfort of a final goodbye.

Several hours after the mourning rites had been performed, Deborah saw Buffalo Calf. She had hacked off her long braids, her face and arms were gashed with deep, bleeding cuts. Instinctively, Deborah started to help her, but Gray Antelope laid a restraining hand on Deborah's arm.

"No, Wind Rider," said the older woman. "Let her grieve in peace. Her wounds show the greatness of her sorrow."

"Where will she go?" asked Deborah in a strangled voice.

"Wherever she will. It is her choice. When she is ready, she may go live in the lodge of her father. The lodge of her husband is no more."

The Cheyenne way . . .

Sometimes it was so hard to accept. When the poor woman needed her friends most, she was cut off from them. She had only the painful wounds on her body, now crusting over with dried blood, to give her comfort. Deborah recalled when her brother had died and how many tears she had shed each time she chanced to gaze upon some special reminder of him, that daguerreotype of him in his dashing gray uniform, or his favorite horse in the stable, or the fine saddle he had given her one birthday. Maybe there was something to this strange Cheyenne custom after all. Those awful memories had, in the end, driven her from Virginia into the arms of Leonard Stoner.

Yet, recalling her own grief and her desire to escape painful memories did not make her any less helpless and frustrated at not being able to reach out to her widowed friend. But what could she say even if she did speak to Walking Wolf's wife? What words of comfort did she have to offer? She thought of her father's ineffective speech about God's will. There had to be more to it than that, but Deborah could not guess what it might be.

So, Deborah did not protest when Gray Antelope nudged her back to her lodge. Maybe bleeding wounds *were* the only appropriate comfort.

36

THAT NIGHT DEBORAH COULD NOT get the heart-wrenching sight of Walking Wolf's widow out of her mind. As she lay next to Broken Wing, she turned to him, and suddenly her body began to tremble with the cold perspiration of panic. In that moment, she understood the depth of Buffalo Calf's love for her husband. She understood a grief so deep, even beyond what she had felt for her brother and father, that mere cuts in the flesh did not begin to match the open wound left in the heart.

"Broken Wing," she said in a tremulous voice, "I love you!"

He nodded silently as tears filled his eyes. She desperately wanted him to hold her, to assure her that his love would not ever be withdrawn from her. But she began to comprehend that he, too, needed her love and reassurance. For where her grief, at least that panic at her empathetic sorrow, had not been based on reality, Broken Wing's was very real. He had lost his friends, and she knew he blamed himself in part for their loss. Thus, Deborah ventured upon the truest expression of love by placing her own heartache beneath her husband's, and reaching out unselfishly to him. But when she wrapped her arms around him, his body was stiff and tense in her embrace.

She hadn't thought about it before, but all at once she wondered if his response to the tragedy was directed at her personally. She shuddered with renewed panic at this revelation, but she had to admit that her own people had wantonly killed his friends. And even if logic tried to tell her Broken Wing could never turn on her in this way, that irrational part of her which had been hurt so many times before was afraid.

"Broken Wing, I am sorry about what happened. I am ashamed."

"You did not do it."

"But my people—"

He broke in, his voice uncharacteristically harsh with its intensity. "You are Cheyenne!"

Was it that simple? How she wished she could convince her belabored mind of that.

"You haven't spoken to me all day; you haven't even looked at me. I was afraid..." She could not verbalize the awful words that would have completed her sentence.

"It is not because of you," he answered in a gentler voice. "It is because now I fear I must fight the white man again. I tried to believe in peace like Black Kettle, but it seems to be impossible."

"One isolated incident," said Deborah. "It might be that the officers at the fort are already on their way out here to apologize and make restitution."

"Do you think a horse or a load of food will heal this wound?"

"No," Deborah said honestly. "And if I could, I'd find the soldiers who did it and kill them myself. It is right that you go after them. Yet, I am afraid for you. I don't want to lose you as Buffalo Calf lost her husband."

"It is a warrior's duty to fight. A Cheyenne man learns little else. We hunt, we fight our enemies, we count coup; it is what makes us what we are. And Wind Rider, my love, it is for this very reason that I will eventually have to fight the white man soldiers. I have been feeling this for a long time, even before you came.

"When I met you, I fought against it more. I want peace with the whites, yet I fear they will only accept peace on their terms. I love Black Kettle and I honor him, but I think in the end he will give in to the white man's way. Do you know what that means, Wind Rider? They will not be satisfied until all our hunting grounds have the fences of their farms around them, until the buffalo have no more grass, until . . ." He closed his eyes, and even in the darkness of the lodge, Deborah could see the lines of torment etched across his brow. "Until they have fenced my people into their *reservations*." He spat that final word out with revulsion.

Deborah shuddered. He had never before spoken of these things in such a dismal, hopeless way. She understood now that he feared to give rein to these virulent emotions. His entire body trembled with rage. He had once loved a white man, and now he loved a white woman; his very soul was being torn apart by the conflicting hatred that had been unleashed that afternoon. He had once told her that he judged men individually, that he could love some men, whether they be white or Indian, and some he could not. It had been simple. But Deborah could see a change in him. His Indian enemies, the Pawnee or the Crow, might steal horses and occasionally women and children, they might kill Cheyenne warriors in battle, but they were not trying to destroy the very core of who they were as human beings, as *Tsistsistas*. He could still love Abraham Johnston, and he could love his wife, Wind Rider, but perhaps that was largely because he saw them as more Cheyenne than white. Intellectually, he knew there were good whites, men like Wynkoop, and John Smith, and William Bent, who had defended the Cheyenne and worked to gain fair treatment for them from the United States government. But Broken Wing was also coming to realize that when the final battle came, he might not have the luxury of segregating the good from the bad.

Deborah understood his dilemma; she had suffered from similar confusion. He feared being caught in the middle as much as she did. She continued to hope no battle lines would ever be drawn, but she knew, especially now as she studied her husband, that it was a futile hope.

"Broken Wing," she said, trying somehow to instill hope in him where she had none, "it may be that the government agents will still listen to reason when they realize how determined the Plains Indians are. You are different than the tribes they encountered in the East— you are stronger, more formidable. Many whites are terrified of the Plains tribes, and that alone may stop them. Perhaps all the tribes

198

could unite—not just little alliances here and there like you have with the Sioux and the Arapahoe, or with the Comanche and Kiowa, but all together, even the Pawnee, the Crow, the Ute. As it is, the whites pit one warring tribe against another, use renegades as scouts and traitors—why, all they have to do is sit back and let you do their destructive work for them. But together! Imagine what fear a united tribal front would place in the hearts of the bluecoats."

"What you say is impossible. No Cheyenne would trust a Pawnee any more than a white man."

"Are you saying, then, that your cause is lost? That there is no hope?"

"I used to believe there was a way to peace. I used to pray to the Wise One Above to place the white man's hand in ours as brothers." He stopped abruptly, shook his head and fell silent.

They both lay still and quiet. In a near corner of the lodge, little Carolyn stirred in her bed, but she did not cry, for she was a good Cheyenne baby. Gray Antelope had early shown Deborah how to teach her baby not to cry by taking her out of the lodge and away from the camp when she did so. A crying baby could endanger the entire camp by indicating to an enemy where they were located. Deborah slipped from her own bed and went to her daughter.

Carolyn was now over a year old, and in the daytime she toddled about on shaky legs. She was a good child, full of energy, but already showing signs of a decided stubborn streak. Deborah could not tell if it came from her or Leonard.

When Deborah bent over the child's bed, which consisted of a small hide spread on the floor with a wool government blanket for a cover, Carolyn looked up at her with wide, brown eyes.

"Mama, play?" she said in a sleepy voice that belied her desire for activity.

"It's still night," Deborah replied patiently. They both spoke Cheyenne. "It is time to sleep."

"You and Papa no sleep," Carolyn said petulantly.

Deborah could hardly be angry at her daughter's impertinence, not when she so naturally referred to Broken Wing as "Papa." She had never tried to teach Carolyn this; it had come about almost on its own, though it had been Broken Wing himself who had first used the term.

When Carolyn began to talk, it was Cheyenne she learned, and though her vocabulary was small, it still contained no English. It was *nahkoa* she learned first, the Cheyenne word for mother. When she indicated her keen mind by picking up the word so readily, Broken Wing immediately followed up with its counterpart.

"Singing Wolf," he had said to Carolyn, using as they habitually did, the Cheyenne name he had given her that day of the Pawnee raid, "I am *Nehuo.*" He thumped his chest and repeated the word. Deborah noted joyfully that he had used the term for father without hesitation. But why shouldn't he? In every way, he treated Carolyn like a daughter. Sometimes when he held her and the contrast of her pale white skin against his dark brown was most pronounced, Deborah marveled that neither seemed to notice.

If only this small miracle could be repeated on a larger scale. But Deborah realized that at least part of the problems between the whites and Indians stemmed from the belief on the part of the whites that the Indians were inferior, and thus they were justified in taking the best land and herding the savages into reservations like animals. She wanted to take comfort in the hope that her marriage to Broken Wing might somehow be a step toward a larger union between the two races, yet she could not help a nagging fear that instead of her love bringing together the divergent factions, it would be buried by them.

Quietly, Deborah soothed Carolyn back to sleep. She gently pulled the blanket up about the child's shoulders and bent over to kiss the soft fluff of pale hair on her head. Then she returned to her own bed.

37

BROKEN WING WAS STILL AWAKE, still tense. Deborah sensed that in the time that had lapsed since she left to tend Carolyn, he had come to some difficult decision.

"Broken Wing," she said somewhat fearfully, "do you wish to talk more?"

He was silent for so long that she began to think he was afraid even to tell her what was on his mind. At last he did speak, but it almost seemed as if he were avoiding the topic most heavy on their hearts.

"Wind Rider, what does your name mean?"

"You know, you gave it to me yourself."

"I mean your white man's name."

"I don't know. I think I had a great-grandmother or someone named Deborah. It's from the Bible."

"I have heard of this book. It is the book of the white man's God?"

"Yes," said Deborah.

"Then your name must have strong medicine."

"I don't know. I guess the whites don't give as much significance to names as do the Cheyenne. If a name is pretty, they use it, or sometimes they name a child after a loved one, as in my case and also Singing Wolf's."

"It is the same with us, but when a Cheyenne comes of age, when a girl marries, or a boy goes on his first hunt, we may change our names to signify some special meaning. Would you like to hear how I came by my name?"

"Very much."

"When I was a child I had my grandfather's name, Buffalo Robe. I was eleven when I returned to my tribe. My brother, Stands-in-the-River, who was my father's nephew, took me to him and taught me the ways of a warrior. I killed my first buffalo when I was fourteen. I counted my first coup in battle when I was fifteen and was accepted as a warrior in my tribe. But I knew that my time with the white man had changed me, made me a little different from my Cheyenne brothers. I was fully accepted by them, but within myself I knew I needed something more to remake my bonds with the tribe. For this reason, I decided to make the sacrifice of self-torture so that the Wise One Above might speak to me.

"With Crooked Eye as my elder, I went to a lonely place and there we found a sturdy pole that we planted in the ground. Then, as you saw warriors do in the Sun Dance ceremony, Crooked Eye pushed pins through the skin of my chest and a rope was attached to these and to the top of the pole."

Deborah recalled this part of the Sun Dance indeed, for it was not a sight easily forgotten. She had thought the warriors hanging from the pole by their impaled skin were trying to prove their manhood, but Broken Wing had explained they were instead seeking the favor of the Great Spirit, not only for themselves, but often for the tribe in general. Deborah had also seen the scars on Broken Wing's chest, but when she had asked him about them he had always been vague in his response.

Broken Wing continued. "I hung from the pole all that day with the hot sun burning down on me. I had no food and no drink and sometimes I think I was not always conscious. The purpose is to break the skin from the pins, but that does not often happen. At sunset, Crooked Eye came and cut the skin away from the pins and told me to sleep on the lonely hilltop. This I did, and in the night, I had a dream. It was this:

"I was standing in a clearing in a beautiful green wood. I knew it was a place filled with good spirits and I was glad to be there. Then a large white bird swooped down into the clearing. When it landed on the ground before me, I saw it was an eagle, but of the purest white, with not a single colored feather on its magnificent body. It was truly a great bird, but when it spread out its wings, a span that was longer than a tall man, I saw that one of its wings was injured, and the bird's proud face was weary with pain and fatigue.

" 'You are hurt,' I said.

" 'I am,' the bird replied, and I knew when he spoke I had come upon a medicine bird, perhaps a messenger from *Heammawihio* himself.

" 'Can I help you?' I asked.

" 'That is why I have come, for only you have the medicine that can heal my wound.'

" 'What medicine is that?'

" 'It is the medicine of love in your heart.'

"I gladly helped the eagle, and somehow—I am not certain how it came about—I fixed the mighty wing, and the white eagle flew away.

"When I awoke, I knew the Spirit had spoken to me. The eagle had stood for the white man. I might some way be used to bring healing and brotherhood between the people of my blood and the people of my heart. Since then I have always carried a white feather from an eagle in my medicine bundle. And I have sought to be faithful to the magic white eagle. It was at that time that I took the name Broken Wing as a reminder of the hope given me by the white eagle."

When he paused, Deborah wanted to ask what had happened, why he seemed now to have changed, but she couldn't form the words. But she knew she wouldn't have to ask, for the look on Broken Wing's face told her he had more to say, and it was not going to be a pleasant speech.

"I was first shaken from this conviction," Broken Wing said, "following the massacre at Sand Creek. It was then that I killed my first white man, during the defense of our village. We who survived this battle, hot with the hunger for revenge, went on the warpath against

202

the white man soldiers. Even Black Kettle did not stand in our way. We attacked the army fort, we plundered their supplies, we raided the roads and the farms. But when the fires of my vengeance began to die out, I was troubled by what I had done and soon wanted no more of this path. Black Kettle, too, was of this mind, and gathered to him about eighty lodges of Cheyenne who had their fill of revenge. We left the main force of warriors and moved south of the Arkansas River, where we wanted to live in peace.

"But I knew little peace within myself. In the next fall, we were hunting buffalo and something terrible happened. I was racing on my horse next to a large bull when my mount stumbled into a hole in the ground and both he and I went down. I was unharmed, but my horse had a broken leg and had to be killed. I had my medicine bundle with me because we needed to have a good hunt, and when I removed my saddle from the dead horse, I found my bundle had been crushed. My white eagle feather had also been broken. I was much distressed by this and sought council from Crooked Eye, who told me to go into the hills to fast and seek a vision from the Great Spirit. This I did.

"It is our custom in these cases to fast for four days, lying on the top of a hill the whole time, not eating or drinking. After three days, I had another dream." Broken Wing's voice grew very grim and taut. He did not like to think of that dream or talk of it, but he forced himself to continue. "I dreamed again of the white eagle. This time he came to me in a place like where I lay, a very common place with no particular magic to it. The eagle bore no injuries and was healthy and strong. He swooped down at me and, picking me up in his long, lethal talons, carried me far away to a land such as I had once or twice seen south of what the white man calls the Cimarron River. It was very flat and dry and dusty—a land of no great beauty. But its real ugliness came not from the land itself but from the fence that circled much of the land. It was a tall fence that seemed to go up as high as the heavens. Within that fence I saw many of my people. They were sad and sick and weak. They did not have the strength to try to scale that fence. They had not the courage even to try.

"I asked the white eagle why it brought me here, but it did not answer. In silence, it dropped me in the middle of the terrible fenced place. As the eagle flew away, to my horror, I heard the bird I thought was my friend laughing in a most evil way.

"My first thought was to escape that place. I spent hours trying, until my hands were raw, but it was impossible, even for a strong warrior such as I believed myself to be. But while climbing that fence,

I saw that there was only one way out of the prison . . . the only escape was the Hanging Road." Broken Wing stopped, his voice clogged with emotion. He could not speak again for some time, and Deborah, herself choked with emotion, lay in utter silence also.

But Broken Wing was determined, now that he had begun, to complete his grim tale. "You know as well as I, Wind Rider, the meaning of my dream. I saw the fate of my people. I saw what the final treaty with the white man will bring us. There can be no other way, not for them."

"You . . . you have never said anything about this to me," said Deborah, stricken.

"When my dream was over and I awoke, I ceased my fasting, for when bad dreams come to a man, it is best to give up the fasting and leave. This I did, and on my return journey to my camp I found you. I believed you were a sign from *Heammawihio,* a way to comfort me and counter the bad dream."

Deborah asked in a tormented voice, "How did you know I was not just an extension of your dream?"

He replied with soft assurance, the pain in his tone momentarily replaced with the intensity of his feeling for her. "Because you were another helpless white bird in need of the healing of my love."

Deborah closed her eyes as tears coursed down her cheeks. Broken Wing leaned toward her, kissing her tear-streaked face.

"My love for you, Wind Rider," he said, "has erased the torment of the fenced place from my mind."

"Until now. . . ?" she whispered.

"I have had the dream again. The sun has come and gone ten times since the dream last came to me."

"Ten days ago!"

"I could not tell you. I have tried to forget. But I can't. Do you know what I thought when I learned of Walking Wolf's and Yellow Shirt's deaths? I said to myself, 'They are fortunate, for they will never see the fenced place.' "

"Broken Wing—!"

He laid a finger across her lips to silence her. "I have not told you the whole dream. I have not told you its end."

"I don't want to know!" she exclaimed with such force she nearly woke Carolyn again. "It isn't good to know the end of things." She paused, knowing full well that her attempt to shield herself from the truth was useless. "Broken Wing," she said in a faint, reluctant whisper, "I already know the ending of your dream." She swallowed hard. "You took the Hanging Road, didn't you?"

He nodded, then said, "I will die like a warrior, not in a white man's reservation. But I still try to believe that there are two white eagles, and that if I can find the good eagle again, peace may still be, and the Cheyenne will keep their hunting grounds and the freedom to follow the buffalo. But, Wind Rider, it may be that I will have to fight the white man again."

"I can accept your fighting the soldiers," said Deborah, "but only if I know you are fighting to win, not to die."

"I do not wish to die."

"All right." She had to be content with that. She should have realized from the beginning that she had married a warrior, and a warrior's wife must live every day with the threat of death in battle. Had she considered this, would her decision have been different? She could not have stopped loving him, and the happiness she had known with Broken Wing surely must outweigh her anxieties. She thought of her brother, who had also been a warrior. It had been difficult to let him go off to war, but at the same time she had also been proud of him.

She was proud of Broken Wing, too—as long as she could be certain he had not given up.

"Broken Wing," she added, "you have much to live for."

"I know that, my wife." He gazed lovingly at her.

"More than that." She smiled, and if it was forced and frayed, at least it was sincere. "You will soon be a father."

He responded with a sudden, wide grin. All the previous pain, the confusion, the haunted torment disappeared in a joyous instant and, for a time at least, all thoughts of dreary fenced-in prisons faded away.

38

IN THE FALL OF THE YEAR 1867, Deborah gave birth to a son. She could not remember the last time she had felt such pure and uncluttered joy. She had not the least reluctance to look upon this child and felt only gladness when she saw how he resembled his father.

"Except for his blue eyes," said Broken Wing proudly.

"You don't mind. . . ?"

"Why should I? They are your eyes."

"You once said that the black hair and dark eyes and brown skin were the best gifts of the Wise One Above."

He smiled sheepishly. "I think I was wrong. It might be that in a time before memory, a drop of white blood found its way into me also. Nevertheless, here is a Cheyenne son, as perfect as I have ever seen, and his eyes are blue like the sky where *Heammawihio* dwells. So it must be that the Wise One has other perfect gifts I know nothing about." He paused, then added with satisfaction, "I will call him Blue Sky."

That night Broken Wing went out alone and raided a Crow camp, returning home with a dozen horses, which, in joyous celebration of his son's birth, he gave away to all his friends.

About two weeks later, runners were sent from the bluecoat fort requesting the various tribes to come in for a council.

In the preceding months, Broken Wing had committed himself to defending his tribe's rights to the Smoky Hill region by participating in raids on the stage line and the encroaching Kansas-Pacific railroad. But he considered his actions to be of a purely defensive nature, so when the whites began to make overtures toward peace, he believed himself honor bound to follow the path of peace whenever it was possible.

The Dog Soldiers, still furious over Hancock's burning of their village, wanted no part of it and even tried to physically bar any warriors from attending. But Black Kettle managed to evade the Dog Soldiers, and by October 14, he had moved his village south of Fort Larned to the Medicine Lodge Creek where the council would be held. Decked out in a robe of fine blue cloth, a tall dragoon hat upon his head, Black Kettle made an impressive sight as he rode up to meet the white chiefs. Broken Wing rode proudly with him, hopeful that this might be the council that would finally bring a true peace between the white and red men. Unfortunately, from the beginning, it was beset by misunderstanding, confusion, and intrigue.

Black Kettle told the United States commissioners that the Dog Soldiers were still on the warpath and he warned the officials that he could not guarantee that they wouldn't attack the camp. He also wanted eight more days to gather in the rest of the tribe. The commissioners were not happy about this delay; after all, the Kiowa, Comanche, and Arapahoe were already represented. They did not comprehend that in the Cheyenne power structure, a chief was not a supreme authority. He made no major decisions without the approval of the tribe in general. To foster good relations, the commissioners finally agreed. That night, however, another serious and startling delay occurred.

A party of Dog Soldiers, heavily armed, appeared in the council camp demanding a conference with Black Kettle. Broken Wing watched in shocked silence as they threatened and railed at the great peace-chief. The main point of their visit was to inform the chief that one of their number had pledged an Arrow Renewal ceremony, and if Black Kettle did not attend, they would kill his horses.

The sacred Medicine Arrows were the most revered possessions of the tribe, given them by their ancient hero, Sweet Medicine himself. Two of the four arrows gave the Cheyenne power over the buffalo, and the other two, power over human beings. They were customarily renewed in the presence of the entire tribe before most great undertakings, such as a great tribal hunt ... or a war. The significant timing of this particular ceremony was not lost on Broken Wing, nor on any who had an understanding of the Cheyennes.

Black Kettle requested of the commissioners an additional four days for the completion of the ceremony. He was obviously distraught and very likely feared for his own safety if he did not comply. Permission was granted and the council was delayed once more, much to the consternation of the commissioners.

Broken Wing rode out with the party, and when they paused for a rest on the way, he sought out Stands-in-the-River, who had begun more and more to associate himself with the Dog Soldiers and had joined them in approaching Black Kettle.

"Why are they treating Black Kettle in this way?" Broken Wing asked. "He is a chief, a man of honor."

"Black Kettle walks too close to the white man," replied Stands-in-the-River. "You know we cannot make peace with the bluecoats."

"We must try."

"They ask us to give up too much."

"Some of them are reasonable," argued Broken Wing. "We should hear their words, at least. If they ask too much, then we can fight."

"We have listened too many times and we have lost much. The Dog Men will listen no more!" Then he leveled a narrow, accusing stare at Broken Wing. "You are becoming two-hearted like the whites. Does your white woman make you into a white man?"

Broken Wing bristled at this, but he replied evenly, "You know that is not true. But if you treat a great man like Black Kettle with contempt, if you attack the innocent, if you deal deceptively, then it is you, not I, who becomes like our enemies."

Stands-in-the-River spat on the ground. "We do what we must do."

"And so do I," said Broken Wing.

"Do not forget, Broken Wing," Stands-in-the-River said, altering his tone slightly so that he sounded more like mentor and friend than adversary, "that a Cheyenne man is a warrior above all else, and it is a good thing not to live to be an old man."

Broken Wing responded with a halfhearted nod and walked away. He could not bear a falling out with his brother over this. Yet Stands-in-the-River had hit upon the truth, the central dilemma of Broken Wing's life—a life continually torn between two worlds, two philosophies. He desired peace with the whites, if for no other reason than because he saw the futility of any other path. But he also knew he would rather die in battle than live to be a toothless old man in the white man's world.

In spite of his ambivalence, however, he participated in the renewal ceremony. And, as was certainly the Dog Soldiers' intent, it instilled in him a renewed sense of who he was as a man and as a Cheyenne. It confirmed the importance of maintaining their way of life, the way he loved.

This sense of tribal and individual pride was heightened in Broken Wing, and no doubt in every member of the tribe, on the fourth and final day of the ceremony. While all the females were securely out of sight within the walls of their lodges, the sacred Medicine Arrows, ritually attached to a pole, were brought out into the sunlight in open view of all the Cheyenne males. Then every male, regardless of age, passed solemnly by the arrows. Broken Wing, carrying Blue Sky in his arms, joined the procession, and gazing upon the arrows saw in them the soul of the tribe. In them lay the very survival of his people, the assurance of ultimate prosperity. And Broken Wing knew it was no accident that this was represented by arrows and not some other more passive objects.

He looked down into his son's blue eyes. "You are *Tsistsistas*," he murmured, although the child was too young to understand his words. "Be proud. Your way of life is worth fighting for. But I hope, for your sake, victory will come by peace and not war."

At the council camp, the commissioners and the retinue of soldiers and journalists and other white spectators grew more and more concerned at the delayed return of the Cheyenne. Several days beyond those requested by Black Kettle had already passed, and the whites were becoming decidedly nervous.

A treaty was concluded with the Comanche and Kiowa and Apache. The Arapahoe asked to be dealt with separately from the Cheyenne, obviously fearing that if the Cheyenne were about to make war on the camp, their close association with the Cheyenne would go ill for the Arapahoe. But the commissioners ignored the Arapahoe.

Tensions mounted when the Cheyenne chief, Little Robe, rode into camp to tell the commissioners the Cheyenne would be there soon and not to be alarmed if they heard gunfire because the warriors would be firing into the air.

The next day came the cry, "Cheyenne!"

Broken Wing rode the gray stallion, a robe of crimson silk around his shoulders and white feathers and brass disks ornamenting his long, flowing hair. His solemn, proud face was painted with bold geometric designs, as were the flanks of the stallion. And he was not alone.

With Broken Wing was a column of Cheyenne warriors, five abreast and five hundred strong, led by the fierce and determined Dog Soldiers. All were ornamented similarly to Broken Wing, the sun glinting off the thick array of silver and brass the men wore. But more striking than that was the obvious presence of weapons, accompanied by the deafening explosions of the firearms.

No white man could look upon the ensuing scene without some trepidation. Most felt utter panic.

Stands-in-the-River, riding next to Broken Wing, grinned at his brother. "Look at them!" he shouted above the din of gunfire and the hoots of the Indians. "The whites will think twice about their dealings with us now!"

Broken Wing thought about what Deborah had once suggested about a united Indian front. Was it truly that simple? But Broken Wing had heard there were thousands upon thousands of bluecoats—even after the war they had had between themselves, there were still thousands. Deborah herself could not deny this. A mere five hundred Cheyenne would appear as nothing to such a mighty force.

But, for the time being at least, they made a sight to be reckoned with, and as the vanguard of the Cheyenne splashed and clamored across the stream, every white soldier and spectator braced for a charge. But the galloping Cheyenne ponies pulled up to an abrupt stop before the line of waiting commissioners. Then a group of chiefs, led by Black Kettle, dismounted and strode up to meet the white chiefs. An almost audible sigh of relief rose up from the camp.

But the tensions quickly returned during the negotiations.

Oddly, it was not Black Kettle who was chosen by the Cheyenne nation to be spokesman—an indication not only of his eroding prestige among his people but also of the growing discontent of the warriors with their treatment by the whites. Instead of the old peace-chief, a chief named Buffalo Chief spoke for his people, making clear the position of the Cheyenne, if not of all the Plains Indians.

"The land north of the river you call Arkansas is the land claimed by my people. The bones of our ancestors are buried there. You give us many presents, but all we want is to have our lives as they have always been. You give us presents and take our land; that is why there is war."

Broken Wing braced himself for a stalemate, because the Cheyenne wanted the very thing the commission was determined to take from them. The Indians desired peace and were willing to sign the white man's paper, but only if they could keep their hunting ground between the Arkansas and the Platte Rivers.

The delay was making the commissioners and other whites nervous, especially with the unpredictable Dog Soldiers still providing an ominous presence over the proceedings. A breakthrough finally came when Senator Henderson, one of the commissioners, drew aside the chiefs and gave them a verbal promise that if the Indians kept away from white settlements, they could continue to hunt in the disputed area as long as the buffalo remained. To the chiefs, this was as good as a guarantee of Indian rights to the land for many years to come, since the buffalo would remain plentiful for a long while.

Most neutral white observers of the day, however, were convinced that the Indians had no idea at all of what was happening. The treaty was never read to them, and it stated clearly that the Indians were to

210

give up the Smoky Hill lands in exchange for a reserve in Indian Territory. Even as the chiefs affixed their marks to the document, they stated that they intended on keeping the Smoky Hill region. To them the verbal agreement of the "White Chief" Henderson was incontestable. They had little or no concept of the grinding wheels of American politics, congressional debates and ratification, where the words of a single U.S. senator are easily lost in the rising dust.

Even Broken Wing, with his knowledge of English, could understand little beyond the surface implications of the entire flimsy affair. He could not read, and many of the large, fancy spoken words were lost on him. He, thus, went away from the Medicine Lodge Creek council feeling content. He had known all along that the white men would listen to reason, even if it had taken the chilling presence of five hundred war-ready braves to get their attention.

39

A QUIET WINTER PASSED, BOTH whites and Indians basking in the security, however false, of the new treaty.

Deborah watched her son grow strong and healthy, in spite of the fact that annuity supplies promised in the treaty never arrived. But Broken Wing was a good hunter and kept his family supplied with meat, taking pride in the fact that he did not have to rely on government "generosity."

Carolyn, now two years old, was also growing into a lovely little girl, but where her half brother was round and chubby and good-natured, she was wiry and angular, with her stubborn, energetic nature growing more and more pronounced. Her resemblance to her father was also becoming more striking right down to an identical birthmark on her upper arm. Oddly, while her Indian brother had soft blue eyes, hers, which had started out pale, were becoming a dark, rich brown. Her hair was also growing darker, but still Deborah had to be exceedingly cautious when strangers came to the camp for fear the child would be mistaken for a captive.

As spring approached, two other ominous events occurred. First, parties of surveyors were seen in the region, even south of the Arkansas River. The Indians were well aware of what this meant—railroads, and thus, more whites; and less land and buffalo for the Indians. This did nothing to soothe the continuing anger and distrust of the younger warriors, which was even further deteriorated by the second event—the arrival of whiskey peddlers from Fort Dodge who began making their rounds among the villages.

Broken Wing watched grimly as even Stands-in-the-River succumbed to the enticement of the "firewater." The older brother had traded off some good hides for the stuff and had gone with a party of Dog Soldiers to drink and, no doubt, malign their white enemies.

Broken Wing was rebuffed soundly when he tried to stop him.

"You are becoming an old woman," Stands-in-the-River taunted, already having had too many swallows of the alcohol. "Go with the women and sew moccasins! I prefer the company of warriors."

Disheartened and fearful of what was sure to come of his brother's behavior, Broken Wing departed. But when he was with Deborah in their lodge, he vented his frustrations.

"We used to be the strongest tribe on the plains, Wind Rider!" he exclaimed. "Feared by all were the *Tsistsistas*! Now, our enemies come boldly into our lands stealing our horses and women. We were a mighty tribe before the white man's drink came among us. We could fight the Crow and any of our enemies without help, but now we must have allies. The Crow don't drink whiskey. They trade their hides for guns and ammunition to make them strong. We trade our hides for more whiskey. The white man doesn't need to fight us—all he has to do is send his peddlers of firewater among us. We will destroy ourselves!"

"Do you think there will be trouble?"

"The whiskey always brings trouble; it makes my people crazy."

Later that afternoon, Broken Wing found an unexpected and surprising ally in his crusade against alcohol. John Smith, who again had been assigned by the treaty commission to live among the Cheyenne, became quite alarmed by the increasing drunkenness among the braves. But only a few paid his warnings any attention, and one of these was not associated with the government at all. He was an itinerant preacher, an ex-Texas Ranger named Sam Killion.

Deborah was outside, busy scraping a new hide Broken Wing had just brought in, when she heard the commotion of barking dogs and clamoring children that usually signaled the arrival of visitors to the village. Her children were safely in the lodge, so she did not immediately panic. She glanced up, wiping a strand of her dyed black hair from her eyes. Recognizing the newcomer immediately, her first impulse was to flee; but reason forced her to stifle this impractical notion, since any sudden move was even more likely to draw attention to herself. However, before she had a chance to jerk her eyes away from the familiar face, Sam Killion glanced in her direction. For a fleeting, fearful moment their eyes met, and if Killion did not at first recognize her, the puzzled crease in his brow indicated that he knew he should, and no doubt would, soon figure out why she appeared so familiar.

The moment his attention was diverted elsewhere, Deborah dropped her tools and hurried into her lodge, and there she stayed for almost an hour, like a frightened rabbit cringing in its hole. It had been so long—over two years—since her sojourn with Griff McCulloch and her first meeting with Killion. She had begun to think her past life was forever buried. She had at last found happiness and contentment. Would it once more all be shattered? What would Killion do? He had betrayed her once and she saw no reason why he would not do so again. Under normal circumstances, no one could make her give up her life with the Cheyenne, but Killion knew she was an escaped fugitive, no doubt still wanted in Texas for the murder of her husband. Killion had been a lawman, and no one had ever proved conclusively that he was not still a Ranger. They only had his word on the matter, and obviously his word was not to be trusted. If he had recognized her, he could notify the authorities at one of the forts and they could come after her within days.

Or, he could simply arrest her himself. That idea brought a thin smile to her lips. Let him try! She had no doubt Broken Wing and half the braves in camp would defend her. Killion wouldn't be that stupid, though. He'd leave and come back with a company of bluecoats to support him. The chiefs might then be constrained to give her up in the interests of peace.

Thus, Deborah mulled her fate over and over in her mind, alternately considering running away or fighting it out. Mostly, however, she just wanted to remain where she was in peace. She tried to distract herself by playing with the children; and as time dragged slowly by, she began to believe she had become alarmed over nothing.

The sudden voice outside her lodge quickly dispelled that illusion.

"Ma'am, if you're home, I'd be right pleased to talk with you," said Killion in a very neighborly tone.

213

Deborah sat deathly still, and when Blue Sky began to coo happily, she shushed him and held him close to muffle his sounds. She felt rather silly sitting in her own lodge like an errant child, but besides her fear of arrest, she simply did not want to see the man she had helped and who had betrayed her for thanks.

Carolyn thought her mother's behavior extremely peculiar because she had never seen her act so inhospitably to a visitor.

"Nahkoa," said the child in her high-pitched voice, "someone there."

"Hush, Singing Wolf!"

Now Deborah felt even more ridiculous, for it would be quite apparent to Killion that she was inside "playing possum." This finally ignited her pride. She would not cower in her own home, especially before a low human being like that Texas Ranger, or preacher, or whoever he claimed to be!

She jumped up, laid Blue Sky in his cradle, and resolutely strode to the door. Pulling aside the flap, she presented a countenance full of challenge, full of antagonism.

"Yes," she said in an icy tone.

"Well, it is you! I wasn't sure. I mean, you look a mite different—" He stopped abruptly, apparently over what he had been about to say. He paused, perhaps to give her a chance to speak, but when she returned only a chilly gaze, he continued. "Maybe you don't remember me . . . the cabin on the Red River . . . it's been a good—let me see—nearly three years, I reckon."

"I remember, Mr. Killion."

"I wondered what ever became of you. I never would have expected any of this. When I asked the chief about you, he said you was married to a warrior now. I guess a lot of water's gone under the bridge, as they say. How'd you ever get away from McCulloch?"

"I was never his prisoner."

"That's a fact, but you were mighty set on staying with him."

"And you have no idea what happened?"

"I don't know how I could."

"Did you have some particular reason for seeking me out, Mr. Killion?" she replied evasively.

He was clearly perplexed. "Well, no, ma'am. I just saw a familiar face and wanted to be friendly."

"Really? And I suppose you'd like me to invite you in for tea?"

"You have tea here?"

"You know what I mean," she replied caustically.

"I'm not sure I do, but I'd be right glad to come in anyhow and pass the time with you a spell. Would that be all right?"

She wanted to drop the flap in his face and be rid of him, but there was something so earnest in his tone, so plainly confused by her reception of him, that she could not bring herself to be so harsh and rude. She stepped aside, motioning for him to enter.

In the Cheyenne custom, she directed him to the honored place for guests at the back of the tepee where a thick hide was spread. He sat down facing the front of the tepee, and Deborah sat adjacent to him. Carolyn, boldly curious about the odd stranger with skin as white as hers, marched up to him.

"Who are you?" she asked in Cheyenne.

Deborah scolded the child for standing between the fire and their guest, considered rude behavior in a Cheyenne lodge. But Deborah regretted her harsh words, realizing they came from her own tension more than the child's behavior, and she gently took Carolyn's hand and eased her into her lap.

"It sure has been a long time," said Killion, "especially if that's the baby you was . . ." He paused again, flustered once more over an awkward topic.

Deborah, beginning to lose some of her hostility in her role as hostess, tried to ease the tension. "Yes, this is the child."

"She speaks mighty good Cheyenne."

"It is all she speaks."

"That so. . . ?"

Another pause. Deborah thought that perhaps she should offer him some refreshment. If Broken Wing were here, no doubt the men would smoke the pipe. But before she made a decision about what to do next, Killion spoke again.

"Ma'am, I can't help but feel that you are not at all pleased to see me—not that you have any reason to be glad, like we are long-lost friends or something; but it seems you're downright adverse to seeing me. I don't recall doing nothing to make an enemy of you, but if I did—"

"Come now, Mr. Killion, it wasn't that long ago; but then perhaps you are too accustomed to lying to remember it."

"Lying? I don't know what you're getting at."

Deborah studied him for a long moment. Was he really as innocent as he appeared? She remembered how two years ago his earnest assurances of his trustworthiness had convinced her to believe him. Was he really the man he appeared to be, or was he such a consummate liar he had all but perfected his ruse? Did he deserve another chance? She realized, if for no other reason, she had no choice but

215

to find out. His presence might be a danger to the entire camp if he were a spy for the army. Moreover, she was now placed in the awkward position of having to protect her own safety. How could she let him go if it turned out he was a liar? Yet, what could she do about it if he was?

Caught in this dilemma, Deborah was constrained to hear him out, hoping he was able to prove himself.

She said, "Do you mean to tell me, Mr. Killion, that you had nothing to do with the law discovering Griff McCulloch's whereabouts?"

"Nothing to my knowledge." He paused. "What happened after I escaped?" His question indicated a real ignorance coupled with concern.

"Griff was understandably upset—"

"They do anything to you?" he cut in sharply.

"They might have, but Griff protected me." This information seemed to genuinely surprise Killion. "He stood up for me even though he himself doubted your trustworthiness. He decided we had to abandon the hideout, and we left the next morning. We were on the trail less than two days when we encountered pursuers—only three days after your escape. We eluded our followers for three days, and I might add, it was three days of hard riding with little rest. But they eventually caught up with us, and we were convinced they had to be Texas Rangers to do that. One of Griff's men was killed in the gunfight that followed—perhaps others also, I am not sure. I was wounded in the gun battle and separated from them. I fell unconscious on the prairie and was apparently forgotten in the chaos." She paused, leveling a hard stare at him. "Do you dare say it was coincidence that we were pursued by Texas Rangers so soon after your escape?"

Killion rubbed his red beard a moment, then shook his head. "No, ma'am, I don't rightly believe in coincidence. I figure that everything is somehow ordained by God, but I never had anything to do with what happened to you. Though I suppose it does look mighty suspicious."

"Are you trying to tell me," Deborah said scornfully, "that God sent the law after us, perhaps as some kind of righteous avenger?"

"Not hardly, ma'am. But I ain't got no doubt there must have been some greater purpose in what happened. Maybe it was so you could come to be where you are today. Maybe it was God's way to get McCulloch's attention."

"Or perhaps to get him killed?"

216

"Did he get killed?"

"I have no idea what happened to him or any of the others. They may have been captured and hanged by now, or maybe they are rotting in some territorial prison."

"It's in God's hands, ma'am, and that's not a bad place to be."

"And you deny that you had any part in helping 'God's will' along?"

"I ain't saying that at all. I am happy to be an instrument of God's will. But I never said what happened was God's will. Either way, though, I never had anything to do with it. I lit out from the hideout, heading north, and saw nary a soul, 'cepting a couple parties of friendly Indians, until I reached Fort Dodge in Kansas. I never said anything to anybody about you folks, though I don't have no way to prove that. You got to take my word, ma'am, but I can see how that'd be hard for you under the circumstances."

Silence descended over the lodge. Deborah was momentarily distracted from responding to Killion's earnest tale when Blue Sky whimperd in his cradle. Setting Carolyn aside, she went to her son and lifted him in her arms. She couldn't help a covert glance toward her guest. What would he think of her tending another infant, an Indian child that was undoubtedly hers? Would she be met with the recriminations she automatically expected from this man?

It surprised her a little to find he was apparently not interested in her at all, but was facing the fire in the middle of the tepee. His eyes were closed and deep furrows lined his brow. Had she misjudged him? How could she be certain?

Before she could solve this dilemma, a sudden ray of bright sunlight shot through the tepee as the flap was abruptly pulled aside and Broken Wing stood framed in the doorway.

217

40

EVEN A SEASONED TEXAS RANGER had cause to be daunted by the sudden appearance of the imposing Cheyenne warrior who assessed the scene in his tepee with a none-too-friendly countenance.

Sam Killion's eyes shot open and his head jerked up. His ruddy complexion lost a good deal of its color. Deborah felt a little sorry for him to be startled so, yet she took an unmistakable pleasure in his discomfiture. If Killion did have nefarious designs, he would surely think twice about them now.

Broken Wing strode into his lodge, glaring momentarily at the stranger, but directing his words, in Cheyenne, at his wife. "You are safe," he said with relief. "I feared when I heard that a white man came to my lodge. Is this one from your past, who means you harm?"

Deborah did not quite know how to answer since she hadn't fully decided herself. "I don't know, Broken Wing. He is an acquaintance from my past, but not really part of it. He says he comes in friendship. I just don't know."

"Do you wish him to leave?"

"I don't think that would be wise until we learn his true intentions."

"You have welcomed him in peace?"

"Yes."

Constrained by the strict code of hospitality among his people, Broken Wing was bound to welcome the guest also. But he remained on his guard. He had run all the way to the lodge when he had learned of the intrusion of the white man. He had lifted the flap prepared to do battle. Deborah had told him few details of her past, but he did know that white men thought her guilty of a crime she did not commit and might yet be seeking her. He knew how cautious she was when strangers came to the camp, and he was ready to preserve her freedom—with his life, if necessary.

He studied the stranger in silence for a long time. At last Broken Wing spoke in English. "I am Broken Wing, husband to Wind Rider, who is also known by the white man's name, Deborah."

"Pleased to make your acquaintance," said Killion, standing. "I am Sam Killion, friend—I hope—of the Cheyenne."

"You will smoke?" asked Broken Wing.

"Yes, I'd be honored."

Broken Wing took down his pipe from where it hung on a lodge pole. He filled it with tobacco, lit it with a faggot from the fire, and sat down beside his guest. He lifted the pipe into the air toward the east from where the sun rises, then presented it to the four cardinal points: south, west, north, and east. This ritual completed, he took a long, deliberate puff from the pipe, finally handing it to his guest.

Killion took Broken Wing's pipe with an air of reverence. He fully understood the significance of being invited to smoke in a Cheyenne lodge. It was an indication of peaceful intentions on the part of the host; it was also the way by which a bargain was sealed. But most important for Killion, smoking the pipe was considered a way by which the truth was discerned. No Cheyenne could lie to a man with whom he had smoked. It was yet to be seen if the same could be said of this white man.

When Killion brought the pipe to his lips, Deborah saw that he did not do so casually. He was aware of the profound meaning in the ritual, and there was no patronizing mockery in him as he puffed from the long stem. He gave the pipe back to his host and their eyes met for an instant and held in mutual scrutiny.

Apparently satisfied, or at least temporarily mollified, Broken Wing took the pipe and laid it aside.

"Why do you come to our village?" Broken Wing asked.

"I came with your friend, John Smith. He is my friend also, and I asked him if I could visit some of the camps and maybe do something about the whiskey peddlers."

"You are with the government?"

"No, I'm just a preacher—"

"What is this *preacher?*"

"I am a minister of the Gospel of Jesus Christ."

"The white man's God."

Killion ran a thoughtful hand across his beard. "I guess that's a matter for debate—to some folks, that is. I believe He is every man's God; leastways, He died for all men, not just white folks."

"Why did He do this? Was He a warrior in a great battle?"

"He is a very great warrior, and He was in a big battle with the

219

devil . . . the prince of evil spirits." Broken Wing nodded at this explanation, understanding all about evil spirits. Killion continued. "You see, the devil wanted everyone to burn in hell for their sins, which we all fully deserved. But Jesus wanted to save folks because He loved them. So, He decided to die in their—that is, in our place."

"And He did this for the *Tsistsistas,* too?"

"Yes, Broken Wing, He did it for you, me, everyone."

"Sometime you must tell me more about this, for it is hard to understand, but it is interesting. Now, I would like to know what you can do about the whiskey peddlers."

"I figure if we can find out who exactly they are, we can run them out of the territory."

This statement both surprised and worried Deborah because it sounded more like the claim of a lawman, not a preacher.

"You could do this?" asked Broken Wing.

"I reckon I could, but I have given up violence in the service of my Lord. However, I've sometimes been known to be pretty convincing without resorting to violence. I realize that the few braves that oppose the whiskey have their hands tied with mixed loyalties, so maybe a stranger can take a few more chances. I'm willing to give it a try, anyway. Those varmints are the lowest snakes around. They don't care who gets hurt as long as they make some money, and I'm afraid their evil work is going to end up hurting a lot of innocent folks, Indian and white alike."

"You are right, Killion. The whiskey among the Cheyenne is worse than any weapon. I will help you. But first I must know if you intend to bring trouble to my wife."

"I have smoked with you, Broken Wing, and I swear by your sacred pipe, and by my own God, that I speak the truth with you when I say I do not mean any harm to your wife, nor—" and he glanced at Deborah as he added this, "—have I ever intentionally brought harm to her. I don't have no desire to take her back to the whites if she is content and happy to be here."

"Wind Rider," said Broken Wing, "do you take this man's word?"

Deborah glanced between the two men. They were so different from each other, but each wore such a similar demeanor of innate guilelessness that she knew she must believe Killion or never trust another man again. She nodded toward her husband.

"Good," said Broken Wing, relieved, for he was beginning to like this white man. "Then bring us some food, wife; Killion and I will talk."

Dusk had tinged the outside sky before the men finished with their talk. Deborah had busied herself with preparing a meal and tending the children, but she had listened attentively to the interchange between the men. In the time since she had married Broken Wing, she found that she never became angry at the subordinate position she, as a Cheyenne woman, was expected to take. Unlike Leonard Stoner, Broken Wing never demanded it of her. She submitted willingly to him out of respect for who he was and a growing trust that he had her best interests in mind. She was secure in his love, and when she did exercise her will, he received her with a mutual respect. Cheyenne and white women alike might be considered subordinate to men, though Deborah secretly doubted it, but a man did not have to crush and destroy to maintain his superior position. What Leonard Stoner could have learned from a savage Cheyenne brave!

Broken Wing and Killion smoked the pipe once more to seal their agreement to do something about the whiskey; then they both rose and left the lodge. Deborah watched them depart with a sense of both pride and concern. She was no longer worried about Killion's honesty. If Broken Wing trusted him enough to ally himself to the white man, then Deborah had no more qualms about him either, for she trusted her husband's judgment implicitly. What concerned her was that the whiskey peddlers were a rough and dangerous lot and would not take kindly to anyone trying to interfere with their brisk business.

41

BROKEN WING KNEW of a secluded place downriver where he had once or twice seen Stands-in-the-River go, and where he assumed some of the trading for firewater occurred. He had never gone there himself, wanting no part of the whiskey trade. He had also feared that if he made too much of an issue of his objection, it might weaken his standing among the braves regarding decisions on other matters. However, whiskey was becoming too entangled in the life of the tribe for Broken Wing to ignore it any longer.

The arrival of Killion provided Broken Wing with the ideal opportunity to strike a blow against the evil that had invaded his tribe. Killion could make the actual confrontation while Broken Wing remained in the shadows as backup, should resistance be encountered. Thus, avoiding direct participation, he hoped further rifts within the tribe would also be avoided. This plan met with the approval of Killion, who didn't seem to mind being at the forefront.

"If God is for me, then who can be against me!" Killion told his new Cheyenne friend. He was assured of the righteous calling of his task. When Broken Wing asked him where his weapons were, the preacher replied with a grin, "The weapons of our warfare are not carnal! But they are mighty through God to the pulling down of strongholds!"

This was a concept beyond Broken Wing's ken. He carried with him his bow and quiver strapped around his shoulder, and a rifle in his hand.

Killion didn't protest the presence of the weapons, but he did insist most emphatically that bloodshed be avoided at all costs.

Thus, the two mismatched partners ventured into what they both were certain was the stronghold of Satan himself. They quietly crept up to the trader's camp, nestled in a grove of cottonwoods. Though it was still early spring, the brush had grown out enough to provide sufficient cover under darkness, with only a quarter moon dimly illuminating the proceedings. In the center of a small clearing was an old covered wagon around which were milling three or four Indians and one white man.

"He's pretty sure of himself to be out here all alone," whispered Killion to his companion.

"What does he have to fear?" replied Broken Wing bitterly. "He is friend to the Cheyenne."

"Well, let's see how friendly he is to me."

"Wait for the Indians to go."

Killion nodded. He wanted this to be as peaceable as possible, and it was a sure bet the Indians would not take kindly to his interference. He might be able to intimidate the trader, but he doubted even he could smooth-talk four Indians who were likely to be half drunk.

The Indians had laid several hides at the trader's feet, and he was in the process of distributing two jugs of liquor to each. A couple of Indians immediately put a jug to their lips and took a swallow, grinning their approval. The deal was settled and the braves, who had by the look of their unsteady gait already sampled the trader's wares, staggered away. The path of their exit took them within a yard of Killion and Broken Wing's hiding place, and the two crouched low and held their breath for several tense moments until the voices of the retreating Indians faded into the distance.

The trader gathered up his booty, tossed the hides into the back of the wagon, then sat down before his campfire and poured himself a cup of coffee. As he leaned over the fire, the reflection of the flames illuminated the face of the trader.

"Well, I'll be!" Killion murmured. "That's Willie Burns."

"You know him?"

"He used to rustle cattle down in Texas. Never could get the goods on him, but not for want of trying."

"You arrest him now?"

"I don't have any real authority to make arrests; but even if I tried, I think I'd get some resistance from his 'customers.' I probably wouldn't be able to transport him unmolested even part of the way to the fort. Best if I can make him leave of his own accord."

"How will you do that?"

"The old silver tongue." Broken Wing took on a puzzled expression, then Killion added, "You just wait here and cover me in case he don't get convinced. And pray if you're of a mind—I figure your Great Spirit don't want no whiskey peddlers here any more than the Lord God does."

With that, Killion stood up and walked boldly into the trader's camp. He was greeted with a suspicious scowl from Burns, who no doubt feared competitors more than the law.

"What do you want?" said Burns most inhospitably. He was a stout, grizzled man whose creased, unshaven visage had seen much action on the western plains.

"Smelled your coffee," said Killion congenially. "I'd be mighty glad for a cup."

"Ain't givin' away no handouts, and I don't want no company, so you best be on your way."

"You didn't seem so unfriendly to them Indians—"

"What do you know about that?" Though he still did not stand, Burns drew up straight, his eyes suddenly sharp and narrow.

"Only that you should of stuck to cattle rustling," said Killion.

"Who are you?" demanded Burns.

"Name's Killion. We met a time or two in Texas—"

"The Ranger?" Burns immediately made a more careful examination of his unwanted visitor. "You ain't even carryin' a gun."

"No. I don't hold with gun-toting since I got religion."

223

As Killion spoke, Burns moved his hand slowly to his right to where his rifle lay. Just as his fingers curled around the butt of the weapon, Killion's foot shot forward, pinning the outlaw's hand against the rifle. Killion bent over, pulled the rifle free, and tossed it into the bushes.

"Why you—" blustered Burns.

"I just want to have a peaceable conversation, that's all," Killion said. He didn't remove his foot from the outlaw's hand, however. "I'd like to suggest that you pack up your wagon and vacate these parts. Your kind ain't needed around here. All you're doing is bringing trouble, so I recommend—friendly like—that you get moving."

As if to prove his sincerity, he lifted his foot, releasing the outlaw's hand, now sore and red, but no worse for the experience. Killion stepped aside.

"Yeah, and how are you gonna make me?"

Killion had anticipated this question. "I'm hoping you'll listen to reason. I could drag you up before the Cheyenne chiefs, who don't want whiskey peddlers 'round here any more than I do. But they might not be as friendly toward you as I'm being. And your loyal customers ain't going to stand up for you over something like this—they'll figure they can get their whiskey elsewhere. So, like I said, Burns, the chiefs ain't going to take kindly to you, and that might be too messy for my peace-loving nature. I'd prefer you to just start walking and to keep on walking until you're long gone out of Indian Territory. You'd prefer that, too, if you were partial to keeping your hair."

Burns shifted nervously. "Well, I happen to be ready to go anyway," he said contemptuously. "But I'll be back."

"I doubt that, Burns. I know who you are, and before the night is out so will the chiefs. Before the week is out, so will Wynkoop. You ain't got a future here anymore."

Burns chewed on his lip for a moment. He glanced longingly toward the bushes where his rifle lay somewhere out of reach. He seemed to consider his options, then shrugged. "Like I said, I was leavin' anyway." His tone was somewhat more contrite.

"Glad to hear that, Burns! I figured you were a reasonable man."

"You still want that coffee?" Somehow the peddler's voice still lacked hospitality.

"Thank you kindly, but I best be on my way; I don't want to hold up your departure. Adios, Burns."

"Yeah, same to you . . . amigo."

The tone of Burns' parting words was hardly friendly, and in his

224

days as a Texas Ranger, Killion would never have turned his back to such a man. But as a preacher, he tried to live less by the hard mottos of the West and more by the basic Christian virtues. His back, as well as every part of his life, was in God's hands. So, he turned and strode away.

And, as God had protected him so many times before during his travels around the West, He did so now, this time making use of the keen eye and quick reflexes of a Cheyenne warrior.

Broken Wing had quietly crept as close as possible to the trader's campsite and had witnessed, with some awe, Killion's bold confrontation with the outlaw. He saw Burns actually back down from the unarmed Killion. Then, most astonishing of all, Killion turned his back on the man and walked casually away!

When Burns reached his hand around to the back of his belt, Broken Wing needed no explanations of what the trader was up to. The Cheyenne instantly brought up his bow and set an arrow to the string, which he drew back and released just as Burns was aiming and about to discharge the small pistol he had hidden behind him.

The pistol fired almost simultaneously with the thud of Broken Wing's arrow as it struck its mark.

Burns shrieked, grabbing his shoulder where the arrow had imbedded itself. The derringer flew from his useless hand, but not before a wild shot was fired. Killion spun around an instant later, grasping a bloody spot on his own arm. He saw the arrow in Burns' shoulder; he saw Broken Wing step out into the open, and he knew the Indian had saved his life.

Broken Wing strode up to his victim and, with the intention of counting coup on him, raised his hand over the man. Burns yelled even more, covering his head with his hands. Broken Wing thumped Burns on the head and stepped back.

"Don't worry, Burns," said Killion, "I don't figure he thinks your hair's worth taking, no more'n he thinks your life is. If he thought it was, that arrow would have gone through your heart, not your shoulder."

"And you call yourself a Christian!" spat Burns.

"If it weren't for the love of Christ, Burns, you'd be dead now," said Killion.

Then Killion, accompanied by more curses and yells from Burns, pulled the arrow out of the peddler's shoulder. It had gone through only the fleshy part and had done little damage. Killion appreciated Broken Wing's restraint, for he knew that no Cheyenne warrior could have missed such a target unless it was his intent. Killion stuffed his handkerchief into the wound.

"You'll live," he said. "And I figure you can still drive a wagon."

"You don't expect me to—"

"I do," cut in Killion. "And the quicker the better. Who knows? This here fella may have some more tee-totaling friends out in them bushes."

"Why you—!"

"Don't thank me, Burns. It's my pleasure to do the bidding of the Lord."

Broken Wing took the derringer and all other weapons belonging to the trader, including the rifle in the bushes. In the meantime, Killion doused the fire and loaded the camp equipment into the wagon. He was about to hoist Burns into the driver's seat when Broken Wing held up his hand for Killion to wait.

Broken Wing jumped into the back of the wagon and began dumping out jugs and kegs of liquor. Burns protested noisily at the destruction of his merchandise.

Killion laughed. "I should have thought of that!"

Finally Broken Wing was satisfied that at least one enemy of his tribe was soundly defeated, and he leaped from the wagon. Killion hitched up the horses, prodded Burns into the wagon and gave the animals a firm slap to urge them into motion. And thus, none too graciously, the disgruntled whiskey peddler made his departure.

Broken Wing and Killion watched the wagon until it disappeared into the darkness.

"Well, that was a night's work," said Killion, a satisfied gleam in his eyes.

"It is but one peddler," said Broken Wing; "there will be others."

"That may be, but they'll think twice before coming, and that's something."

"I hope so. Now you must come to my lodge, and my wife will fix your wound."

"It ain't much, but I'd be glad to join you anyway." Killion stopped suddenly and faced the Indian squarely with a solemn expression. "You saved my life back there, Broken Wing, and I won't soon forget it. I am in your debt."

"There are no debts among friends," said Broken Wing.

"Maybe so, but if I can ever do anything for you, I will!"

"Come. There are no needs now but to celebrate our victory."

Broken Wing gathered up his booty—two rifles, a pistol, and the derringer—and the two comrades set off for the village.

Deborah greeted them with relief followed by pride. She gladly tended Killion's wound, then prepared for them a meal of their best

226

provisions. Black Kettle, having heard of their heroic exploit, came to offer his appreciation, and before long the lodge was filled with other chiefs and braves who hated the whiskey trade. The pipe was passed, songs were sung, and stories were exchanged until the early hours of the morning.

Deborah watched the proceedings with wonder. A few hours ago she had distrusted Killion almost to the point of hatred; now he was suddenly a hero of the tribe, and she could not believe that she had been such a poor judge of character. She was still a bit put off by his preaching, which he lost no opportunity to do during the evening. But his Cheyenne listeners heard with great interest his story of the Son of the Wise One Above who had sacrificed His life for all men to redeem them from the consequences of their evil ways. Broken Wing interpreted Killion's words to the others with almost as much zeal as the preacher himself. When Black Kettle invited him back to tell more about this wondrous warrior called Jesus, Deborah began to wonder if she had been too hard on the preacher.

Broken Wing had no doubts at all about this white man, who was steady and courageous in battle and merciful to his enemies. Between Broken Wing and Killion, Deborah could not tell who was singing whose praises more. Each man had gained a deep admiration for the other.

When Killion left in the morning, Deborah was able to apologize for her harsh misconception of him. Killion just shrugged good-naturedly. "Don't think nothing of it, ma'am. You had good reason. And I ain't forgetting what you did for me back at Griff's camp, nor what Broken Wing did for me. If you ever need anything, I'll do for you if it's within my power to do it. And, you may or may not like it, but I'll be keeping you in my prayers, too."

Deborah smiled and said, coyly, "I guess I will just have to live with that, Mr. Killion."

42

UNABLE OR UNWILLING TO FOLLOW the path of brotherhood Broken Wing and Killion had begun, the majority of whites and Indians stumbled upon a deteriorating and rocky trail.

In April the shipment of annuity goods promised in the treaty finally arrived. But Deborah wasn't surprised by the disenchanted Cheyennes' reception of the delivery.

As the women gathered at the riverbank to do laundry, Stone Teeth Woman scoffed, "Who needs their paltry goods now that winter is over and the worst days of starvation have passed?"

Deborah had never sensed that anyone in the camp had come all that close to starvation, especially Stone Teeth, whose husband was a successful hunter. But she understood her sister-in-law's sentiment and knew many others shared it.

"My husband is furious that no guns or ammunition came with the shipment," put in Yellow Beads Woman.

"Again we have been cheated by the white man," said Buffalo Calf, who had ended her mourning and rejoined the village, but who carried with her a bitter hatred for the whites. She cast a suspicious scowl at Deborah.

But Deborah pretended not to notice, focusing all her attention upon her wash. Most of the time, even during the most heated debates, no one seemed to regard her white skin. Deborah was accepted as Cheyenne; she could forgive Buffalo Calf, who was still grieving the loss of her husband.

Deborah had a harder time forgiving the United States government. Because the whites had so limited the Indians' hunting grounds, they needed—more than ever—means to hunt more efficiently. Guns were becoming necessary for their survival—for food and shelter, not war.

Thus, the Indians began to range more and more north of the Arkansas; and the whites, unaware of Senator Henderson's verbal agreement with the Cheyenne, became alarmed.

Several hostile incidents were reported, though where truth ended and exaggeration began Deborah could not judge. A man was killed and scalped near Fort Wallace, a wagon train was attacked, and there was even a report that William F. Cody had been chased by a Sioux war party. The settlers responded strongly to these reports, well out of proportion to the severity of the incidents, and Washington heeded the outcry. The Cheyenne and Arapahoe were flatly refused any shipment of weapons, and when the next load of annuities arrived devoid of guns, the Cheyenne, specifically the Dog Soldiers, refused the goods. The chiefs tried to be more reasonable, promising they would never use the weapons against whites. Wynkoop pleaded with the government to release the guns, convinced this would be the only way to insure a peaceful year.

Unfortunately, the government ignored the situation too long. In August, even while Wynkoop was pleading for the Cheyenne, a war party, primarily of Cheyenne and some Arapahoe and Sioux, began to vent their anger and frustration upon the settlers along the Saline and Solomon rivers. The Indians claimed they had been fired upon first—not entirely unlikely, considering the near-panic among many of the settlers. But what followed had the effect of destroying any credibility Black Kettle had worked so hard to achieve for his people.

Not less than a dozen whites were killed in these attacks, including women. Several women were raped, and an infant was reported murdered. At least one woman and two children were taken captive; though, while the war party was being pursued by a troop of cavalry, the children were released so the party could move faster. Reports varied depending upon the purveyor of the information, but even the Cheyenne chiefs agreed it was a wanton and unprovoked attack. Chief Little Rock of the Cheyenne was willing to deliver up to Wynkoop the leaders of the war party, but it was growing more and more obvious that the peace-chiefs were losing control of their fiery young warriors. In the end, the more peaceable chiefs like Little Rock and Black Kettle decided to take their bands and flee back to the sanctuary of Indian Territory, where they hoped to avoid the inevitable war.

Broken Wing followed Black Kettle with his family. He was sick about the Saline and Solomon raids and had little qualms about not associating with such braves as were responsible. Yet his heart remained divided because he was certain Stands-in-the-River had been part of that war party. Stands-in-the-River had in fact been there, but he had been among those who had tried to prevent the outrages. Thus, he, too, resolved to move with his family and his band to safety.

Once the camp was settled on the Cimarron River and the winter meat supply gathered, Stands-in-the-River became restive once more. He and two or three other braves got drunk one night on some stolen whiskey and talked each other into rejoining the Dog Soldiers, who had continued to range in the regions north of the Arkansas.

The drunken group left camp secretly in the middle of the night. Stone Teeth Woman wanted to believe her husband had gone hunting; and, fearing the bluecoats would try to capture him, she kept her true fears to herself for three days. Then, overwrought with anxiety, she finally went to Broken Wing.

"You must find him and bring him back," she pleaded.

"He has chosen his path," Broken Wing replied with less conviction than pain.

"He goes to his death!" she cried.

"He is a warrior."

"Then why don't you go?"

"Perhaps because I have not as much hope as he . . . or perhaps I have more."

Stone Teeth Woman wept bitterly, almost as if she were already mourning her husband. Deborah's heart went out to her, but she could not bring herself to come to her defense, thereby encouraging her own husband to place himself in danger. However, Broken Wing's own sense of honor prevented him from remaining in safety while the brother he loved was traveling, no matter how foolishly, into certain disaster.

He packed a leather sack with dried meat, and took a thick winter robe, for the warm summer days were already growing shorter and cooler. He saddled one of his horses to ride, choosing his favorite war pony, the gray stallion. Deborah saw that he was preparing as if going to war, but she did not know if he planned to fight his brother or the white soldiers. She almost did not care as long as he returned unharmed to her. She threw her arms around him and kissed him.

"I could not live without you, Broken Wing!" she said, trying to hold back her tears.

"Remember, you are a warrior, Wind Rider. You would live. You are strong." He kissed her in the white man's fashion and held her tightly for a long while.

"Be careful," she said.

"It is not the way of a warrior to be careful. But I am not seeking a battle; perhaps it will be that none will find me."

He embraced his children, including without hesitation his daughter by adoption whom he loved no less than the son of his

230

body. Deborah could not help feeling unsettled at how long he lingered over Blue Sky, almost as if he believed he were looking at him for the last time. Then he handed the child back to Deborah, swung up on his horse, and rode away.

Carolyn tugged at her mother's buckskin shift. "When Nehuo come back?" she asked sadly.

"Soon, Singing Wolf. Very Soon."

But even as Deborah spoke, the image of her brother riding off to war intruded into her mind. She had never imagined that day that she would never see him again, thinking so naively that their happy companionship would go on forever. Was it possible that nothing lasts forever? Could it be that she might never see Broken Wing again? He had left her before, to hunt buffalo, to raid his enemies, and always he had returned. Why shouldn't he now? Why had she suddenly thought of Graham?

All at once Deborah seemed to jerk alive. Hastily she set Blue Sky on the ground and ran after her retreating husband.

"Broken Wing!" she called.

He stopped and turned in his saddle.

"What is it?" he asked.

"I love you . . . that's all. I love you!" She no longer cared about the tears that spilled down her face.

"I love you also, my Wind Rider Woman!"

He leaped from his horse and raced up to her, embracing her passionately one final time before departing.

43

BROKEN WING STEALTHILY MADE his way north. Twice he barely avoided army patrols. Only his intimate knowledge of the land and his experienced trail skill kept him hidden from the disquieting presence of the bluecoats. He could think of no reason for battle-ready soldiers to be south of the Arkansas River, the supposed sanctuary of the Cheyenne, except for the purpose of making war.

The preacher man, Killion, had come to Broken Wing's lodge shortly before his departure and told them of changes among the white chiefs, changes that could only mean ill for the Indians. Hancock had been disciplined for burning the Dog Soldier village and had been sent away, but his replacement was no improvement. General Phil Sheridan, according to both Killion and Deborah, was an ornery, hard-nosed sort. Quick-tempered and irascible, he was not out to make friends.

"And he especially don't want to make friends with the Indians," said Killion. "He has as good as declared war on the Cheyenne nation. And believe me, he's got the ability to do it, too."

"And the government is behind him, no doubt," added Deborah.

"How will he do this?" asked Broken Wing. "Except for a few bands of Dog Men and those who must hunt, the Cheyenne are in the Indian Territory."

"Sheridan don't give a hang about Indian Territory. He thinks all the Cheyenne should pay for what was done by the few, and he ain't gonna let a little thing like a treaty protect those he thinks are guilty. There ain't no way the army can catch the Dog Soldiers; they've been trying for months and come up empty every time. Sheridan figures the only way he can get to the offenders is to strike at the villages, which are easier to find and a long sight more vulnerable."

"But the villages are south of the Arkansas River."

Killion had nodded grimly. "Cheyenne are Cheyenne to Sheridan. The friendlies are just as guilty as the guilty. I don't like to spread rumors, but I reckon you got a right to hear 'em and make your own conclusions. The Seventh Cavalry has been dispatched—and I quote what I heard directly from an officer—'Locate and make war upon the families and stock of the Cheyenne.'"

Broken Wing had come away from this encounter shaking his head in disbelief. The preacher was a man of honor, yet his words could not possibly be true. Perhaps Killion had heard wrong. If he were right, then nothing—nothing!—could be trusted again.

Yet now, with his own eyes, Broken Wing saw the truth of Killion's words. It sickened him to think that the treaty he had placed so much hope in was nothing more than a lodge of straw blown down in a slight prairie breeze.

It took Broken Wing over a week to locate Stands-in-the-River, so effectively were the Cheyenne warriors evading the bluecoat invaders. When he finally reached his brother, he was torn in his heart and had no ready answer to Stands-in-the-River's greeting:

"So you have decided to join us!"

232

"Don't you realize you are bringing danger on the whole tribe!" said Broken Wing somewhat lamely.

Crow Killer, a Dog Soldier, answered, "When have our people ever been free of the danger from the whites? And now because they cannot find warriors to fight, they will attack our families."

"And what of the white families that were attacked in the north?"

"Only a few Cheyenne were responsible for that," argued Stands-in-the-River. "But the white man soldiers had already killed our women and children. We will not forget Sand Creek. My mother died there, as did yours, Broken Wing."

"When will it end?" sighed Broken Wing in despair.

"It will not end!" exclaimed Crow Killer. "Not until the whites are forced from our land."

"Do you fight with us?" Stands-in-the-River asked again with a hard edge to his voice. "Will you protect your family from the soldiers? You know they will have no mercy. They will not say, 'This Indian was our friend; we will spare his wife.' To them all Indians are the same, all Cheyenne are enemies. Black Kettle was their best friend, yet the agent at Fort Cobb has refused to give him sanctuary. He says he doesn't want to be responsible for another Sand Creek. But what kind of friend looks out for his own security when his friend is in danger? Either we fight now or watch our lodges, our lives, destroyed."

Broken Wing realized in that dark moment that their lives would be destroyed no matter what happened. More than anything, he had wanted to believe such an impasse could be averted, but his first sighting of heavily armed soldiers in Indian Territory had prepared him for this inevitable moment. He had tried to keep to the way of peace; he had deplored the Saline raids. But now none of that mattered. It had become a simple case of survival—not cultural or aesthetic, but plain life or death. And not his own life, for he had known for some time that he would not live to be an old man; rather, his struggle was for the protection of his wife, his children, his people. He had no argument against that. The soldiers would find and do battle with any Indians they encountered. Wind Rider, Singing Wolf, and Blue Sky were at serious risk, and it was doubtful their white blood would protect them. Besides, Wind Rider considered herself Cheyenne, and he knew she would sooner fight and die with her people than claim the shield of her skin color.

Broken Wing had avoided this moment for years, but he now knew he had no other choice—as a man or as a Cheyenne warrior.

———

233

Through the fall of that year Broken Wing rode with the band of Cheyenne braves, succeeding in thoroughly frustrating a very beleaguered Seventh Cavalry. In a way, it was exhilarating for Broken Wing; he was a born warrior. He found pleasure in the camaraderie of his brother braves and a sense of accomplishment in their success against the army.

The white warriors were such an inept lot that Broken Wing became almost drunk with a confident sense that the Cheyenne really would be able to drive the whites from their land.

Once, in a somewhat laughable episode, the Cheyenne had led the soldiers on a fine chase by making a false trail of travois marks so the bluecoats would think they had at last stumbled upon a village. Eager for the anticipated slaughter, the soldiers bore down relentlessly upon the tracks only to end up trapped in a series of sand hills. With their heavy wagon wheels spinning uselessly, the whites made an easy target for the furtive Cheyenne snipers. When the soldiers tried to give chase, the Cheyennes taunted them by leading them from hill to hill, always staying out of firing range, and mysteriously disappearing just when the soldiers thought they had them.

In camp that night, the warriors had a good laugh at the expense of the Seventh Cavalry who, with only one casualty, lost more in dignity than manpower.

But all was not a merry game. The Cheyenne may have had the upper hand, but they, too, were destined to pay a price for their small victories.

In November, a small party of warriors, led by Stands-in-the-River with Broken Wing riding at his side, took a brief respite from fighting the whites in order to hunt provisions to get them through the coming winter. Stands-in-the-River spied three white army scouts riding alone and recognized immediately the importance of such a coup.

Broken Wing tried to discourage him. Scouts were not bluecoats—they were seasoned frontiersmen and no easy prey, even to Cheyenne warriors. Moreover, their presence could mean only one thing.

"More soldiers cannot be far behind," Broken Wing reasoned.

"They will be truly lost without their scouts!" returned Stands-in-the-River.

The others agreed that taking the scouts would indeed be a hard blow to the soldiers. Before Broken Wing could protest further, they had spurred their mounts into a charge. The scouts were momentarily shocked by the sudden appearance of charging Indians over the rise of a hill, but their canny experience stood them in good

234

stead, and they quickly gathered their wits about them and returned fire almost immediately. However, the Indians had cut them off from the larger force, and the scouts knew they had little chance of holding out for long. They had no idea that the vanguard of the force had drawn up within earshot of the melee.

Alerted by the gunfire, the main force speedily dispatched a troop to the rescue. When the troopers burst in on the scene, the warriors were suddenly not only outnumbered but also facing a two-front battle. They returned several rounds of fire, inflicting little damage to their enemies, and were soon forced to retreat to a more tenable position. There was a sparsely wooded area some three hundred yards away, but an open, grassy meadow had to be traversed in order to reach it. The Cheyenne were now as exposed and vulnerable as the three scouts had been fifteen minutes before.

A hundred yards from the trees, Little Left Hand's horse was shot out from under him and he was trapped beneath its crushing weight. Broken Wing and Stands-in-the-River reined their mounts to an abrupt stop, both men leaping to the ground even as the horses were still in motion.

With bullets crisscrossing over their heads from several different directions, the brothers dragged their comrade free. Then Broken Wing, using the fallen horse as a shield, provided a cover of rifle fire as Stands-in-the-River lifted the injured Little Left Hand onto his own mount.

"Come!" Stands-in-the-River shouted to his brother, turning to make sure Broken Wing would make good his escape.

Broken Wing fired his last shot and spun around to make the sprint to his waiting horse. He reached the gray stallion, but as he leaped into its saddle one of the soldier's bullets hit its mark. The searing pain was so explosive, so unexpected that Broken Wing lurched forward and nearly lost his grip on the stallion, and would have if the stallion had not bravely held its ground. His hands clutched around the Pawnee war pony's neck, Broken Wing maintained his own footing and swung successfully into the saddle. The gray covered the rest of the distance to the trees in a lightning sprint that left the soldiers amazed.

But Broken Wing was hardly aware of the speeding powerhouse under him. To the wounded warrior, it seemed an inordinately long time before the sounds of gunfire and the noisy pursuit of the soldiers faded into the distance. Crushed beneath the weight of his wound, Broken Wing kept pace with the other warriors only by the tenacity of his fine gray stallion. When the party, having evaded their pursuers, finally halted in a secluded gulch, Broken Wing was bent over his pony's neck barely able to hang on.

This was the first indication to Stands-in-the-River that his brother had been hurt. He rushed up to him and helped ease him from the horse onto the soft ground, grimly aware of the widening splotch of red on the back of Broken Wing's buckskin shirt.

"Oh, my brother!" groaned Stands-in-the-River. "This is my fault. I have led you to your death by my foolishness."

"You did—*we* did what was necessary."

"Wind Rider will never forgive me!"

"I fear it is the whites she will not forgive—" Broken Wing paused as a spasm of pain shot through his body. Then urgently he gripped his brother's hand. "Stands-in-the-River, go to her . . . help her understand. . . ."

"I will bury you here and then keep on fighting the white man soldiers," said Stands-in-the-River, anguish and bitter gall nearly choking his speech.

"Go to your lodge, my brother. There is no other way. . . ."

"Broken Wing!" Only the warrior's stoic reserve kept his overwhelming emotion at bay. "This must be avenged!"

Broken Wing shook his head. "I want no hate spent on me. . . . Remember, nothing lives long, only the mountains and the earth. Tell this to Wind Rider. And tell her to remember only the happiness we had, and the love. It was good—"

But Broken Wing said no more. He closed his eyes and began the journey upon the Hanging Road to the happy place where he could hunt and ride in peace and freedom with his long-departed friends and ancestors—perhaps even with his white stepfather, Abraham Johnston.

44

TRUDGING UP FROM THE RIVER, carrying two heavy skins of water, Deborah glanced toward the village where riders were approaching. Half a dozen warriors were returning to camp, and as she always did since Broken Wing's departure, she studied the group closely, hoping one would be her husband returning. She hurried back toward the village and as she came closer she recognized Stands-in-the-River clearly. Then she saw the gray stallion—riderless, with a load laid across its back.

"Broken Wing!" she cried, and, dropping the skins, ran to the stallion.

After that, everything passed in a dark haze for Deborah. She stood by silently, numbly, and watched as several of the women began the awful ritual of dismantling Broken Wing's lodge. They gave away all his possessions, his shield he had made during the last Sun Dance, his favorite bow, his hides, his horses, even the cooking utensils. When they finished, nothing remained, not even the lodge poles. She knew she must have wept during the whole ordeal because she felt inside that hollow, raw sensation of one who has cried for hours and hours. She knew Gray Antelope must have held her through it all because she saw her friend next to her, but she could not feel the woman's comforting arm around her shoulders. She could feel nothing, only emptiness.

When it was done, when there was only flat, bare earth where once her happy lodge had been, Deborah was left with only two possessions—a buffalo robe and a knife. Leaving her children in the care of Gray Antelope, Deborah went off alone to complete her expression of grief.

The grass by the bank of the river was cold as she fell to her knees in it, a reminder that winter was not far away. But Deborah's winter had begun the moment she had laid eyes on the riderless stallion. Deborah took the knife firmly in her hands. She had seen other

Cheyenne widows do this, but until now had not fully understood the extremity of grief, the magnitude of loss that could give a woman the courage to honor her dead mate in such a way. She brought the knife to her hair and sliced away the long, dyed braids. She slashed the sharp blade across her arms and legs and, as she watched her blood drip into the grass, she did so with the knowledge that with each wound she inflicted upon herself, she was elevating her husband in honor and respect. In this way the others would know what a great man he was and that he was loved beyond the mere expression of words. It was the Cheyenne way, and it was no longer hard for Deborah.

When she had finished, she stood, somewhat unsteadily, and went to the scaffold where they had laid Broken Wing. There she placed the blood-stained knife.

More than anything she wanted to join him on that scaffold. She wanted to die also. What reason was there to go on? Life was filled with too much loss, too much pain. What good was a little happiness if it was only going to end in heartache? Why did God taunt her so?

"Oh, Broken Wing, why didn't you take me with you on the Hanging Road? You were never selfish with me before—why now?"

The knife caught her eye. She thought of the times she had faced the possibility of death before in her life—when Leonard had driven her to the brink of suicide; when she stood on the gallows with a rope around her neck; when she struggled, hopeless and alone, on the prairie. Each time she had chosen life, chosen to fight to live. She might have been weak and helpless, but she had always been a fighter. Broken Wing had seen that; he had called her a warrior.

Did that mean she must now find the strength within herself to fight once more? But she had none left.

How could she possibly go on if she chose not to take the knife and finish the work the ritual wounds had begun? The steel that had kept her back straight and proud as she walked up the gallows steps now suddenly seemed bent and useless. The stamina that had forced her to crawl on hands and knees, hungry and tired, grasping at the prairie grass as if for life, had all melted away. The sheer stubbornness that had once prevented her from pulling that derringer trigger was gone.

"I am no longer able to fight!" she silently cried into the prairie wind.

And out of the far distant past, her father's voice responded to her anguish.

"My flesh and my heart faileth; but God is the strength of my heart, and my portion forever."

238

Deborah had scoffed at those words as a seventeen-year-old girl grieving the loss of her brother. She had believed that her father, at a loss to comfort her, was merely placating her. But what if he had been right? What if God truly was the only source of strength?

Yet, how could He cause all this pain and misery and still be the same God who brings comfort and strength?

She wished she could forget all about God. Why did He have to be part of the equation, anyway? She managed without Him quite well—until a crisis struck her. Then, for some reason, He would leap back into her thoughts as if He were trying to haunt her. All the teachings of her childhood would spring into her mind. She did not want to be the kind of weak, ineffectual person that turned to God only in time of need. She wanted to be independent, self-sufficient.

But if God were truly the only source of strength. . . ?

She seemingly had only two choices then: give up and take that knife and end her suffering, or turn to the One who was ready to give her the strength to go on.

"I don't know . . . I don't know . . ."

Falling to her knees beneath her husband's scaffold, she began sobbing once again in agony and confusion.

"If I had a reason to live . . . just *one* reason!"

Several minutes later, Deborah struggled to her feet. Her emotional stamina was gone, and her physical reserves were drained as well by the loss of blood and pain from her wounds. She might have stayed longer at the foot of the scaffold, but the coming of evening brought a biting cold wind that penetrated even her numb senses. She remembered the robe she had left by the bank of the river. She thought she would fetch it and return to her husband and there wait until she knew what to do.

She had taken no more than a few steps when a little figure burst through the bushes that surrounded the burial site. It was Carolyn, her face damp with tears, her little voice broken with emotion.

"Nahkoa!" she screamed. "You go away, too?" Weeping, she threw her arms around her mother's neck.

In a moment, Gray Antelope came huffing and puffing into sight. She held Blue Sky in her arms. "I'm sorry," she said, "the little one got away before I knew. She was afraid you would go away, too, like—" Gray Antelope broke off, for it was not right to speak the name of the dead. "I could not stop her."

Kneeling by her daughter, Deborah brushed away her tears. "Oh, my dear Singing Wolf! I won't go away from you, don't worry. But I must be alone for a while because . . . because . . ." How did one

239

explain such a thing as mourning to a child? How did other Cheyenne children accept the temporary absence of their mothers during the mourning time? Maybe it was wrong of her, selfish, to follow the traditions if it meant causing pain for her child. At a loss for the proper words, Deborah looked up to Gray Antelope for help.

The older woman faced the child and spoke with the assurance of one who had lived her life with these traditions, who understood them and knew they somehow brought order and cohesiveness to her people.

"Singing Wolf," she said with pride and confidence, "your mother must mourn; it is the way of our people. In this way she brings honor to the dead. You must be a brave Cheyenne child and allow this to be."

"Then I want to mourn too!" said Carolyn, her previous fear turning into stubborn determination.

"Mourning is not for children." The finality in Gray Antelope's voice did not invite argument even from a petulant child like Carolyn.

"You come back," Carolyn said to her mother. It was not a question but a demand.

"I will, my dear . . . I will."

Gray Antelope Woman looked at Deborah as if to affirm the truth of Deborah's statement, for she had been nearly as fearful as the child—with perhaps more reason, since she had a better understanding of the depth of Deborah's grief.

Deborah responded to her old friend's questioning look. "I know now I have a reason to come back."

Deborah kissed her children and hugged Gray Antelope, then watched them go. She wasn't ready to go with them yet, and she did not know when she would be, but at least now she knew she would return to them. It was not yet her time to travel the Hanging Road.

She had asked for a reason to live and she had, in her children, been given two reasons. It almost seemed as if Carolyn's arrival, timed so perfectly, had indeed been an answer to her outcry. Was that answer from God? Had He interpreted her cry as a prayer and then answered it faithfully, as her father would surely have believed?

"I wonder," she said softly into the wind. "I wonder . . ."

45

BLACK KETTLE'S BAND MOVED TO A winter camp in the broad basin of the Washita River in Indian Territory. It was a fine place for a camp, with thick stands of cottonwoods lining the sandy banks, while precipitous red bluffs looked over the scene like a domineering father. Some six thousand Indians, including bands of Arapahoes, Comanches, Kiowas and Apaches, had taken advantage of it, spreading out along a fifteen-mile stretch of the river as it curved back and forth through the valley.

The peace-chief's village was at the most western point of the line of encampments, somewhat isolated. But the chiefs considered that as soon as they did some hunting and obtained a small supply of food, they would move closer to the other camps for added protection.

A thick layer of high clouds overshadowed the valley, portending an early snow. Deborah pulled the buffalo robe tightly around her shoulders. She had walked on the fringes of the camp for several weeks, eating meager handouts from Gray Antelope and other sympathetic women, and sleeping out in the open wrapped like a cocoon in the robe.

She had lost weight, grown weak, and in the last day or so had developed a mild fever. She didn't know how she managed to go on, if it was hope or despair that drove her. She missed her children terribly, and she still cried often, especially at night when she'd unconsciously reach out for Broken Wing's loving warmth only to find a cold, empty place at her side. She wept even more when she realized it was not only a husband she had lost but a friend. A terrible void had been left in her life.

Yet something had begun to happen inside Deborah that day when Carolyn had come running to her in apparent answer to her anguished cry. She couldn't quite explain it. She wouldn't say, in the words of Sam Killion, that she had found religion. But she had found hope, or at least she had come to see that hope was possible, that it might truly be found by a diligent seeker. Unfortunately, in the days that followed, she had become too absorbed in her struggle against the physical elements to give this search for hope much attention.

The little hope she had appropriated, however, sustained her, until one day Gray Antelope Woman came out to the place where Deborah had made her destitute camp. She gave Deborah some pemmican and a cup of water, and squatted down beside her while she ate.

"Crooked Eye sends me," she said. "He wants me to tell you it is time for you to cease your mourning."

"I will never quit mourning," said Deborah.

"I know, Wind Rider," said Gray Antelope with compassion, taking Deborah's hand in hers. "The wounds on your heart will take much longer to heal than those on your skin, but if you do not come back, you will die. The snow will fall soon, perhaps tonight; the earth will freeze, and I fear you will also. Besides, your little ones need you. As much as I would like to be, I am not their 'nahkoa.' It is you they want."

"You are right, my friend. There are others I must consider now."

With Gray Antelope's help, Deborah stood, and together they returned to the village.

"You will live again in the lodge of Crooked Eye," said Gray Antelope.

"Thank you. I would be honored to live with my dear friends."

That night an early snow fell upon the Washita valley. Deborah was kept warm by the nearness of her children and, though they could not replace the friend and companion she had lost, she knew they were a gift of inestimable value.

As winter closed in with certainty upon the prairie, General Sheridan was faced with the repeated failure of his troops to make contact with the hostile Cheyenne. He finally was convinced his only hope of success was to mount a winter campaign by which he might catch the Indians at their weakest, and thus most vulnerable. For this task, he called upon Lt. Colonel George Armstrong Custer, who had not long before been relieved of his command of the Seventh Cavalry because of desertion, for which he had faced a court-martial. Sheridan believed that only the daring Civil War hero, the youngest general of the war, could pull off the risky campaign. Eager to take back the reins of the Seventh, Custer returned to Fort Hays immediately.

While Custer was refitting the Seventh Cavalry, Black Kettle was convinced by Ten Bears, of the Comanche, to make another attempt at peace with the whites. Thus, he traveled to Fort Cobb to meet with its commander, General Hazen.

"I am not afraid to come among the white men," Black Kettle told him, "because I believe they are my friends. My people want peace, and for that reason we have stayed south of the Arkansas as the treaty on the Medicine Lodge Creek said we should. But I have not been able to keep all my young warriors home. Some became angry when they were fired upon by the white settlers, and now they want to keep on fighting. I cannot speak for the Cheyenne north of the Arkansas; I cannot control them."

Hazen, who had already taken in some bands of Kiowa and Comanche under the protective custody of the fort, regretfully told Black Kettle that he had no authority to do so with the Cheyenne. He told the peace-chief that only Sheridan could make peace with the Cheyenne, but he was quick to warn Black Kettle that there were already troops in the field and he could not guarantee their intentions. He believed Black Kettle truly wanted peace and promised he would make this known to the authorities. But in the meantime, he could do nothing to stop the war.

On the twenty-third of November, as Black Kettle was returning to his camp on the Washita, a heavy snowstorm blanketed the land. The Cheyenne felt relatively safe as the wind and snow beat down upon their secluded and well-hidden village. No army would venture out to make war in such weather. But they had not taken Custer into their reckoning.

On that very day, in freezing wind and knee-deep snow, all eleven companies of the Seventh Cavalry, with a complement of white and Indian scouts, set out from the newly constructed Camp Supply to make war upon the Cheyenne. Custer pushed his troops relentlessly, especially after the third day out when one of his Osage scouts reported signs of a village nearby. First came the smell of fire, then the bark of a dog, and finally, the definite confirmation of the cry of a baby.

Thus, in the late hours of the night, still undetected by the unsuspecting Cheyenne village, Custer deployed his troops, effectively surrounding Black Kettle's village. More than seven hundred well-armed and mounted soldiers stood against fifty-one lodges, some three hundred Cheyenne men, women, and children.

Under a strict order of silence, not even permitted to light fires to stave off the frigid winter night, the troops waited for the first light of morning to signal the commencement of battle.

Dawn had only begun to lighten the sky when Stone Teeth Woman, carrying two empty water skins, plodded through the snow to the river. The morning was quiet, but not unusually so, for snow always seemed to have that effect on the landscape. The sound of a whinnying horse did not at first disturb the Indian squaw and she continued unconcerned through the wood. But when the sound came again she stopped. Something was wrong. What was it. . . ?

Then it came to her. The horses were grazing at the opposite end of the camp. Even the sound of Black Kettle's horse, which was tethered next to his lodge, could not have come from the direction where she had heard the horse. She peered toward the hills where the noise had originated. The light was still dim and could have deceived her, but she thought she saw movement—

There it was! It flickered above the ridge of the hill for only an instant, but it was unmistakable in its contrast to the surrounding snow and shrubbery.

A blue soldier hat!

Stone Teeth Woman dropped the water skins, spun around, and raced back toward camp.

"Soldiers!" she cried. "Soldiers in the hills!"

The sleeping camp, nestled so peacefully in the pleasant, white-blanketed valley, seemed slow to respond. It was inconceivable that soldiers would have fought the snowstorm and still been able to track the Indian trail, obliterated by the snow.

Only when she roused Black Kettle and he grabbed his rifle, firing warning shots into the air, did it truly seem possible.

But the shots that warned the camp also, unwittingly, were a signal for Custer to commence his attack if he wanted to retain the element of surprise. He ordered the bugler to sound the charge, and Custer himself, grandly mounted on his black stallion, led the attack down the bluff banking the Washita River.

Within moments the quiet morning was shattered by a barrage of rifle fire mingled with the war cries of the bluecoated Seventh Cavalry.

46

DEBORAH AWOKE WITH A jarring start at the sound of Black Kettle's first warning shot. In another instant, the entire lodge was astir.

Crooked Eye grabbed two rifles and a belt of ammunition while Deborah and Gray Antelope grabbed the children. There was no time to think of food or protection from the cold, for already the sound of heavy gunfire was penetrating the lodge. Deborah did pause to take her own weapon, a bow and quiver of arrows made for her by Broken Wing and spared by Gray Antelope when Broken Wing's belongings had been distributed after his death. It was not sentimentality, however, that prompted Deborah to take the bow. She knew how to use it, for Broken Wing had taught her well; and she had no qualms about doing just that.

As she exited the tepee with Blue Sky in her arms, she was only a few paces behind Gray Antelope, who was holding Carolyn, and Crooked Eye who led the way. She saw many others racing through the village seeking the protective covering of the riverbank. She was reminded of the Pawnee attack two years ago; only now the enemy had white skin and wore the dark blue of the United States Army. They swept through the village like a blue avalanche, shooting and hacking at anything even remotely resembling an Indian, shooting first, and asking no questions at all.

The warriors tried to mount a defense with their bows and rifles, but they were far outnumbered; their only chance was to run into the woods and surrounding hills and take up sniping positions. The responsibility of herding their families to safety fell largely to the older men. But men like Crooked Eye, who had weapons, paused as often as possible to get in a shot or two as they fled to the cover of the river grasses. Women and children plunged into the icy water to hide from the barrage of bullets; as many succumbed from the cold as from the battle itself.

Deborah, holding a screaming Blue Sky, kept her eyes fastened on Crooked Eye—and especially on Gray Antelope and Carolyn. She wanted desperately to turn and assess what was happening behind her, but she still recalled what had happened during the Pawnee raid when she had looked back. It was awful to hear the shots and the cries both of the soldiers and the wounded Indians, and not know how close they were to her.

Then she lost sight of Gray Antelope. The woman seemed to have dropped suddenly out of view, almost as if she had been . . . cut down by a bullet.

Before Deborah could fully incorporate her panic over this, she saw Crooked Eye stumble and fall. She raced to the old shaman's side and touched his arm, but he did not respond.

"Oh, Crooked Eye!" she murmured, but there was no time to weep over his death or to think how he had once saved her life and had cared for her like a dear father.

From her kneeling position she was now able to gain a view of the battle, if such could be called this dreadful slaughter. She was immediately surprised at the number of soldiers and horrified at the growing number of bodies, Cheyenne bodies, littering the muddy ground. Only the cries of her son prevented her from stopping right then and doing battle against the bluecoats. Feeling cheated again by the terrible obstacle of being a woman, Deborah lurched to her feet and began her flight once more.

Several yards from the river, her eyes frantically swept the tall grass, but still there was no sign of Gray Antelope or Carolyn. But in the midst of the fleeing Indians, a mounted warrior with a woman seated behind him galloped toward the river. Deborah thought of the Cheyenne fables of their ancient hero, Sweet Medicine, and could easily have believed that he had come to life to rescue his people. However, this was a flesh-and-blood hero and she recognized him too well to mistake him for a phantasm, even if he looked like one.

It was Black Kettle.

Never before had she seen him look so regal, although he wore none of the finery of his station as chief. His proud visage, even in the surrounding chaos of battle, still maintained that wise benevolence that had so marked his tenure as peace-chief. Deborah thought that even then, with soldiers murdering his people, he would hold out his hand to the white man, if only they might take it.

All at once, a volley of bullets exploded in the air around him. The force of the shots knocked his wife, who was seated behind him, off the horse into the river. Black Kettle had only a moment to absorb

246

this loss, perhaps thinking of how they had been miraculously spared at Sand Creek. He turned in his saddle, then suddenly slumped over, taking at least one shot in his stomach and two more in his arm and chest before he, too, slipped from his horse into the water next to his wife. Thus died the greatest peace-chief of the Cheyenne, the friend of the white man.

Deborah watched, transfixed, momentarily forgetting her own pressing danger, until a mounted soldier galloped past, nearly knocking her to the ground. She caught herself in time and, forcing her concentration back to her present peril, started running once more for cover. Reaching the tall grass at last, she paused for breath.

"Wind Rider!"

Deborah had to look in several directions before she saw her friend hidden in the grass.

"Gray Antelope—I was afraid—" Then the emotion of the last few terrifying minutes all at once assailed Deborah and her voice caught on a sudden sob.

"Nahkoa!"

Deborah threw an arm around her daughter, covering both her children with tears of relief and fear. Singing Wolf and Blue Sky clung, sobbing and weeping, to their mother.

"I have not seen Crooked Eye," said Gray Antelope, peering over the top of the grass, hoping he might soon come to her.

Deborah closed her eyes and shook her head. She could not speak.

Gray Antelope was silent for several long moments, but Deborah saw the pain of grief and loss distort and twist her gentle features. Deborah widened her embrace to include her Cheyenne friend and mother.

"It is good he died in battle," said Gray Antelope at last, "as a great Cheyenne warrior should."

The pressures of imminent danger allowed time for no more mourning than that. No sooner had Gray Antelope spoken but they looked up to see another friend running for her life. Stone Teeth Woman, who had been the first to detect the soldiers, had been among the last to vacate the village. She had three children to tend and her husband had gone to join the warriors in the hills. The younger children had responded quickly to her urgent commands, but the eldest child, an eleven-year-old son, was determined to join his father. This was the first time he had ever flatly disobeyed her, and she watched him run away only to be cut down by a soldier's saber. She had barely escaped with her two younger children.

247

But as she neared the river, a soldier rode hard toward her—as if he did not know she was a woman, or did not care. He fired his rifle once and Deborah saw Stone Teeth jerk violently with the impact of the shot. Stone Teeth fell to her knees, losing her balance because of the baby she held in her arms. Deborah watched, horrified, as the soldier took aim again. Before she knew what she was doing, Deborah shook her own children from her arms, snatched up her bow, and set an arrow to the string. The soldier fired but the shot went wide. While he reloaded, Deborah fired her arrow.

It hit its mark and the soldier fell back into the snow-covered grass. Deborah did not have time to think, to debate the consequences of her actions, to even feel any elation or revulsion over counting her first coup upon an enemy. All that mattered was saving her friend who was, especially now that she was wounded, still easy prey for the on-coming soldiers. Slinging her bow over her shoulder, Deborah sprang from the cover of the grass and sprinted to Stone Teeth Woman. Placing an arm around her, she helped her to her feet, laid the baby securely back in her arms and was about to scoop up the six-year-old when a familiar voice called out.

"Nahkoa!"

Carolyn, afraid to be separated from her mother again, had wiggled from Gray Antelope's hold and run into the middle of the insane battle scene.

"Singing Wolf!" Deborah screamed.

"Go to her," said Stone Teeth. "I will be well."

Deborah did not hesitate. But barely had she gone two paces when the unthinkable happened. A soldier, whose horse had been shot out from under him and was thus afoot, saw Carolyn and grabbed her.

"Lookee here!" he shouted to one of his comrades. "I got me a white captive."

Again, Deborah did not think before she swung her bow into position, firing an arrow. All she could see was that the terrible enemies who had killed her husband and her friends now were about to take her daughter.

The arrow struck the soldier and he fell, not fatally wounded, but hurt enough to lose his grip on Carolyn. The child stood screaming, still in the middle of the battlefield.

Another soldier, on horseback, saw who had fired the arrow and wasted no time in aiming his rifle at Deborah's head. But as he pulled back the trigger, the mechanism jammed. In that fortunate instant, Deborah sprang toward her child.

Lowering his useless rifle, the soldier dug his heels into his mount's flanks, galloping forward, and reaching Carolyn just as Deborah was about to take her into her arms.

"Why, you dirty Injun tramp!" he bellowed, raising his bayonet to finish off this kidnapping Indian who had also shot his friend.

Another shout pierced the air.

"Hey stop! That's a white woman!" This newcomer was a lieutenant and, fortunately for Deborah, the other man was only a private who knew the lieutenant's voice well, and knew he had better obey.

Deborah did not pause to thank her rescuer. She enveloped Carolyn into her arms and dashed away.

"Lady, we're here to help you," the officer called after her.

"She killed Rogers," said the private.

"She's probably gone insane living with these savages."

Deborah heard the exchange. Perhaps one day she would think about it, grimace at its irony, weep at its truth; but at the moment she could only think of survival. Besides, she was more than convinced she and her children had as good a chance with the Indians as with the soldiers.

The main thrust of the attack lasted ten minutes. It took only that long for the bluecoats to gain control of the village. But many of the warriors who had taken to the hills and woods continued to maintain a defense, sniping or ambushing troops who had taken to the field to capture escapees. By then, several of the other villages in the area had heard the sounds of battle and had sent warriors to the aid of the beleaguered Cheyenne village. One troop of about fifteen soldiers was surrounded and wiped out by an Arapahoe war party, but this was to be the greatest Indian victory that day. Including these fifteen, the Seventh Cavalry lost only twenty-two men. The final toll of Indian casualties was never ascertained with complete accuracy. Custer exaggerated the count at one hundred and three warriors, leaving unclear the number of women and children. More reliable estimates noted fifty warriors killed, along with seventy-five women and children. Almost as devastating as the loss of life was the loss of all the lodges in the village and the entire winter supply of food and hides. Custer kept one lodge as a souvenir; the rest he put to the torch.

Many of the warriors escaped, along with a number of women and children who had found refuge in the other Indian encampments. Deborah might also have been able to escape downriver had she not gone back after Stone Teeth Woman. As it was, both women, along with Gray Antelope and the children, were cut off from retreat by a troop of soldiers.

Thus, at gunpoint, they were herded with about fifty other women and children into a roped-off area, and Deborah once more found herself a prisoner of the white man.

PART 5

SQUAW LADY

47

CUSTER LEARNED AN INTERESTING lesson at the Washita River. And, if it was not one that would curb his lust for glory, at least it had the effect of benefiting Deborah.

After herding together more than eight hundred of the Indian horses, the famed commander discovered that Indian mounts appeared to have an instinctive hostility toward white men. When roped, the animals fought wildly to escape, and the soldiers who tried to mount them were thrown unglamorously to the hard, cold ground. The troopers had even been forced to press some of the Indian female prisoners into service to herd the horses.

Deborah joined these women at the makeshift corral into which the soldiers had herded the horses. Pausing by the gate, she observed a corporal trying to mount Broken Wing's gray stallion. Had she any humor in her at that moment, she would have laughed at the spectacle. The gray shied away with every approaching step the corporal took, so that they were backing step-by-step around the corral, with the soldier looking most foolish. He threw a rope around the gray's neck but the horse reared, whipping its neck so violently back and forth that the rope was finally wrenched from the soldier's hand. Many of the troops, now idle with the main thrust of the battle over, stood by the corral both cheering their tenacious comrade on and hurling taunts at him.

"I seen prettier dancing partners, Collier!" shouted one.

"That Injun horse don't like your smell."

"I'll bet a month's pay he gets you afore you get him!"

Deborah loved the gray, as she did all horses, and at that moment she felt a particular thrill upon seeing Broken Wing's favorite war pony take command of the situation. She almost smiled when the hapless Corporal Collier, desperate to redeem himself, threw his arms around the gray's neck and attempted to swing his leg over its bare back. The gray reared mightily and jerked its neck in one swift motion, throwing the man to the icy ground—all to the riotous guf-faws of his comrades. When the animal's front hooves came crashing to the ground, they missed the soldier by a fraction of an inch.

The corporal, furious now, jumped to his feet and drew his pistol.

"You worthless, no-good monster!" he shouted.

Deborah's amusement abruptly turned to horror. She had seen too much death that day, and this final outrage against the only thing that still existed to remind her of her husband was more than she could take. Without thinking, she raced to the scene, thrusting her body between the drawn pistol and Broken Wing's horse. She did not stop to think that the death of one more supposed Indian prob-ably wouldn't matter to this soldier, who had killed more than his share that day.

"Get outta my way!" he raged, cocking his gun.

Deborah did not budge. She was just as willing to take a bullet to save the horse as she would have to save one of her children.

"All right, Corporal Collier! Holster that weapon. Don't you see this is a white woman?" The words were spoken as if it might not have mattered as much had she been an Indian.

Glancing around, Deborah saw that the new speaker was the same lieutenant who had interceded on her behalf once before. He was a young man, probably younger than she. He had blond hair and peach fuzz for a beard, but he spoke with a deep authoritative voice and wore a commanding visage. Deborah didn't have to guess why his men obeyed him so quickly.

The corporal was not happy about it, but he jammed his gun into its holster and, with a surly smirk, saluted the lieutenant.

Again, Deborah felt no overwhelming urge to thank this soldier who, in spite of his benevolent lapses, had killed her people and destroyed her home. Instead, she turned her attention to the gray, rubbing his twitching flanks and soothing his agitation. The gray, hearing a familiar voice and perhaps smelling a familiar smell, swung his head around and gave Deborah an affectionate nudge.

"It's all right, boy," she murmured in Cheyenne. "I won't let them hurt you."

"You are the white woman who took the child," said the lieutenant in a friendly tone. When Deborah did not answer, he continued. "I wondered what had happened to you. Do you speak any English?"

Deborah nodded. She had by no means forgotten her native tongue, but just then she was reticent to use it, almost feeling it would have amounted to betrayal of her people—her Cheyenne people.

"You can rest assured, ma'am," said the lieutenant, "that you will be cared for now. My name is Lt. Godfrey. Feel free to call upon me if you need anything." He paused, then, suddenly inspired, added, "You seem to know this horse, and since you'll need a mount when we move on, you may as well take him."

Deborah gaped, astonished at this unexpected act of generosity. But before she could respond, Lt. Colonel Custer strode up to the corral.

Though he was normally a man who paid meticulous attention to his physical appearance, even his impressive image was now slightly marred by the dust of battle. His pale hair, still long, though cut much shorter than he was reputed to have worn it as a daring Civil War general, clung in dank strands against his sweaty brow, and his face was smudged with dirt and gunpowder. Yet, he was no less an imposing personage, making Lt. Godfrey seem pale by comparison.

"What's going on here, Lieutenant?" asked Custer.

"We're having some trouble with the horses, General." The soldiers persisted in referring to Custer by his Civil War rank.

"Cursed Indian ponies." Scowling, Custer examined the scene in the corral. "Well, there's no time to tame these animals. The scouts tell me there are five or six thousand Indians in the encampments downriver. We are already having trouble with the escaped warriors and others who have regrouped and are causing some havoc on our perimeter."

"Some of the women are having luck bringing them—the horses, that is—under control."

"We could never trust them," said Custer. "Regardless, herding all those horses along with us would only be a greater temptation for the free warriors to attack us."

"Should we let them loose?"

"What? And let those murdering savages have mounts to attack us on? No, Lieutenant. I want all the horses killed. Cut out enough for the prisoners to ride and let the officers have their pick of the better ones, then kill the rest."

"All of them, sir?"

"You heard me, Godfrey. And make it as speedy as possible. It won't be safe to linger around here much longer." He paused and for the first time noticed the gray stallion. "This is a fine specimen. I wouldn't mind including him with my personal stock."

"This one, sir?"

"Is there some problem with this animal?"

"No, sir . . . but . . . well, I just told this woman she could have it."

255

Godfrey spoke hesitantly, somewhat surprised at his own boldness in the presence of his august commander.

Now Custer took note of Deborah. He quickly saw through the buckskin clothing, the bronzed skin, and the clumsily dyed hair.

"A white woman," said Custer. "Good Lord! What have they done to her? And, Godfrey, how come she wasn't reported immediately?"

"I was about to do that, General."

"Who are you, madam?" General Custer asked.

Deborah could not speak because of the seething anger that had begun to well up in her the moment Custer arrived on the scene. In her eyes, this man was nothing more than a cold-blooded killer. The other soldiers were merely following orders, but this was the man who had given them. Stories of Custer's war exploits had reached Texas, and Deborah had heard them even in her isolated life. Some called him fearless, daring, brave—"the finest example of military prowess around," as one reporter wrote. But his critics were more apt to define his actions as reckless, even foolhardy. A dozen horses were shot out from under him during the war, and his regiment had suffered more casualties than any other northern unit. The Cheyenne had already heard of the man and knew him as one to be wary of. Thus, Deborah could barely endure his conciliatory tone toward her.

"Lieutenant, does she speak English?" asked the general.

"I believe so."

"Have those savages frightened the speech out of her?" Custer addressed himself again to Deborah, "Madam, you have no need to be afraid any longer. If you tell us who you are, we will be able to take you home."

"You have destroyed my home!" Deborah blurted in English, unable to restrain her hatred.

"Madam, you don't seem to understand—"

"I understand clearly. You are the savage, and if there is any justice in this world, you will meet with the same end you have brought upon my people!"

"I see they have turned your mind," Custer replied, unruffled by Deborah's harsh words. "How long have you been held captive?"

"I was never a captive!" Deborah retorted with all the pride she had learned from her adopted people.

"Then how did you come to be with them?"

Deborah considered ignoring the question. She had already said more to these people, her enemies, and spent more time in their company than she wished. But she also realized that they might just keep interrogating her until they got some answer from her, in which case she'd be forced to be with them even longer. She already missed the nearness of her children and Gray Antelope and Stone Teeth and her other friends who remained alive. Deciding that she must come up with some plausible response that could explain her presence with the Cheyenne, she quickly formed a reply that, believably, she hoped, combined fact and fiction.

"My wagon train was attacked by Pawnee," she answered, cool and distant. "They left me for dead on the prairie, and a Cheyenne warrior found me and doctored me."

"What warrior?"

"We do not speak of the dead."

"How long ago was this?"

"Several years."

"And you were free to go at any time?"

"Yes."

Custer shook his head, somewhat bemused. It wasn't the kind of report a man liked to hear of a people he had just effectively massacred. Nevertheless, he showed no remorse. He was content to convince himself that this woman's mind had obviously been harmed by her years with savages, and that nothing she said could be reliable.

"What is your name?" he asked after a short pause.

"Wind Rider," Deborah answered without hesitation, her white name such a distant memory that it did not come as easily to her lips as did her Cheyenne name.

"Your *Christian* name," Custer said with pointed emphasis.

Deborah knew that to hesitate too long might arouse suspicions, but it had been a long time since she had given thought to this present dilemma. Even after three years, she knew that caution must still be exercised, for at any time someone might turn up who knew of those events in Texas. It was not every day a woman was sentenced for execution, and so the news of events at Stoner's Crossing must surely have spread around.

When she looked at General Custer, she considered sticking to her Cheyenne name, but that no doubt would only aggravate her captors and perhaps make things that much more difficult for her. So, she responded evenly, a name coming to mind with surprising ease.

"I am Deborah Graham."

"Where are you from, Miss Graham?" asked Custer.

"Virginia."

"A southerner."

Deborah responded to this with icy silence, realizing Custer's

257

Union service was but one more mark against the man.

"We will be moving on soon," said the general. "I will see to it that special quarters are prepared for you."

"I will remain with my people."

Custer shrugged, clearly indicating his ire at having his courtesy rebuffed. "As you wish." His tone was short and irritable.

"I may go, then?"

"I don't care."

"And the horse. . . ?" She hated lowering her pride to make such a request, but she could not leave the gray to the fate Custer had ordered.

"Keep the cursed horse!" he retorted; then he turned away from her as if he could be rid of the nuisance of her presence so easily. To Godfrey he said sharply, "Get on with carrying out my orders, Lieutenant! I want to get on the move as soon as possible." Then General Custer stalked away.

Deborah waited until he was well away before she prepared to go. She picked up the corporal's rope from where it had fallen on the ground, and looped an end around the gray's neck. The animal offered no resistance.

But she paused suddenly and turned back toward Godfrey. "Thank you," she said quickly.

Then she led the gray away, holding her head as high as that of the Cheyenne war pony.

48

DEBORAH WAS SEVERAL PACES away when Godfrey gave the order for the extermination of the horses. The shocked dismay of the soldiers who had so recently wiped out an Indian village was unsettling. But to many of the soldiers, the horses were of far more value than a bunch of Indians.

About seventy-five ponies were cut out of the herd for the prisoners and the officers. Then the shooting began. Custer himself, an avid hunter, shot a few of the horses. And, in spite of the initial dismay at the task, many of the soldiers joined in on the shooting spree with some relish, making wagers on the various feats of skill they might achieve.

It was no small task, killing eight hundred horses, especially when the incessant gunfire was driving them crazy with fear. Deborah winced with every shot and only once did she glance toward the macabre spectacle. The sight sickened her and brought tears to her eyes. It would remain imprinted upon her memory for the rest of her life.

Gray Antelope, weeping also, chanced to look toward the hills, and when Deborah followed her line of vision, she saw two or three braves watching. What must they be thinking as they observed their wealth so wantonly destroyed by the soldiers? Deborah was enough acquainted with her Cheyenne brothers to know this would be yet another wrong that must be avenged. She did not envy the bluecoats, for, though she knew the final victory would be theirs, they would yet pay a stiff price for that triumph.

Deborah took her children onto her lap and tried to ignore the insane scene in the corral, but the stench of blood and death was already permeating the chilly air; and the screams of the doomed animals pierced her ears with an unrelenting agony. Her children's cries, as if instinctively aware that ominous events were transpiring, mingled with those of the horses and echoed in Deborah's head until she, too, wanted to scream.

Would there ever be an end to all the hatred and contention? Would she know peace again in her life? Those idyllic years with Broken Wing seemed so far away, as if only a dream. All she could remember was Leonard Stoner's spiteful face, a hangman's gallows, and a coarse, ugly bluecoated soldier aiming a bayonet at her heart.

Suddenly it occurred to Deborah that her life had again been miraculously saved. But why? Wouldn't it have been better for that soldier's weapon to have done its work? What good was her heart to her now? It felt so heavy within her chest that she knew it must certainly be turning to stone. She had taken a great chance in loving Broken Wing, making herself vulnerable to the pain that seemed so persistent in stalking her. She had allowed herself to love and had been terribly hurt when that love had been wrenched from her. Even then she had been able to cling to her children and her love for them and their need for her. She had found comfort also in her friendship with her Cheyenne friends, with Gray Antelope and Crooked Eye and the others. Now that, too, was taken from her—they were all dead, or prisoners, or fugitives. The future seemed to hold no hope for Deborah. She felt as desolate as she had when Broken Wing died; only now she could not even find comfort in her children. She was almost afraid to love them for fear it might bring doom upon them also. Would she ever be able to love again?

As the last gunshot faded away, Deborah's sorrow remained. Gray Antelope Woman knelt down beside Deborah and, placing an arm around her, drew her close. Deborah laid her head against the older woman's shoulder, trying not to think of how much she loved this Cheyenne woman.

"Wind Rider," Gray Antelope murmured gently, "nothing lives long, only the earth and the mountains."

Tearfully, Deborah answered, "If only it didn't hurt so much."

"I have mended a torn hide," said Gray Antelope, "and when I am done, that place where my stitches are becomes the strongest part of the hide. It is so in nature, also. I think it is the Wise One's reward for not giving up, for not throwing away a valuable hide or burning down an injured tree. The hurts we feel now will make us stronger if we let them, Wind Rider."

"How can I do that?"

"By not giving up."

"It is so risky."

Gray Antelope sighed, knowing well that what she suggested wasn't an easy thing. "That white man who has visited our village, the one called Killion, told of a God who carried a person's burdens, who even went so far as to die in a man's place."

"I didn't think anyone was listening to that preacher."

"I listened because he spoke from his heart," said Gray Antelope. "The words he said seemed true, and hearing them made me glad. I thought that with such a one as this Christ helping with the burden, I could face a life on the white man's reservation. I was not so afraid."

"I know a lot about this white God," said Deborah. "Sometimes I think what you say is true, yet at other times I'm confused. I wonder, if He is a god who wants to bear our burdens, why does He give the burdens at all?"

"I do not know the answer to this; that preacher might, but I do not. Are burdens a bad thing if they make us stronger?"

Deborah took a deep, ragged breath. Her tears were spent for the moment, but her grief had fatigued her. "I've been so confused about these things for so long, I cannot guess at what the answers are. If I ever see that preacher again, maybe I will ask him instead of being as critical toward him as I have been."

"It can hurt nothing to ask," said Gray Antelope Woman.

"I wonder . . ." Deborah mused and fell silent.

All these years she had been apathetic, perhaps even cynical, toward religion. She had turned her back on her father's God because she had felt wronged. Wouldn't it be ironic if it now turned out that this very God was in fact her only refuge? How would one right such a miscalculation? Did she even want to? Wouldn't she still be in danger of surrendering the independence she so desperately wanted? But what good was independence if it caused her to be crushed beneath the weight of her sorrow and pain? Did anyone truly have the strength to survive alone?

Deborah shivered and pulled an army blanket snugly around her shoulders, tucking the folds around her children also. It seemed ironic that winter was closing in upon her again when she was at her most helpless. Was it wrong to desire to be strong and independent? Did a woman have to be helpless and frail, a slave to a man's whims? Is that how God really intended it to be? Was it possible that Leonard Stoner had been right all along? She hated to consider the possibility. If it were so, then the things he said about her being a rebellious, strong-willed vixen, and his even worse references to her tainted moral fiber, might well be true.

Broken Wing had treated her with love and respect, but he had been a godless heathen. Or had he?

It was all so confusing. Maybe Sam Killion would have the answers, though why she thought of him, she did not know. Broken Wing had respected him; maybe that was enough. Somewhere there had to be answers, and comfort for her pain . . . and peace.

49

AFTER DEPARTING THE RAVAGED village on the Washita, the army, with their prisoners, moved back to Camp Supply where the Indian prisoners wintered. The Seventh Cavalry, reinforced by the Nineteenth Kansas and several companies of the Third and Fifth Infantry, continued their winter campaign against the Indians.

Heartened by the success of the Washita campaign, the first solid military triumph over the Plains Indians, Sheridan intended to make a clean sweep of the unruly Indians, including the previously peaceful Arapahoe, Kiowa, and Comanche. Sheridan was especially encouraged over the death of Black Kettle, whom he believed was nothing but a liar and a troublemaker. He blamed the peace-chief for the worst of the Indian depravations, and for villainy too cruel for words. His final estimation of the great Cheyenne chief indicated a typical ignorance of the military establishment: "Black Kettle was no more than a worthless and worn-out old cipher."

"If we can get in a few more good blows," Sheridan said, "there will be an end of Indian problems."

Thus, harried relentlessly by the army, the Indians began to consider more seriously the inevitability of surrender. Stands-in-the-River was among the Cheyenne fugitives hiding out in the hills, making raids when possible, somehow surviving. But he missed his wife and children and feared for them when he heard they were captives of the bluecoats. Sometimes, when he was weary of the cold and hunger and loneliness, he thought of turning himself in at the fort. But these were only momentary lapses. He would never stop fighting; he had sacrificed too much to fall back now. The only thing he could do was move forward, even if it was toward his inevitable journey on the Hanging Road.

"It is not a good thing for a Cheyenne warrior to grow to be a toothless old man," he said both to himself and to his comrades.

But Little Robe and a delegation of Cheyenne and Arapahoe chiefs, still hopeful—or at least at the point of desperation—came in for a council with Sheridan, who made it clear that he would not release the Washita prisoners until the Indians still at large showed beyond doubt their honest intentions by bringing in their people. The chiefs continued to fear treachery and were slow in coming in.

Stands-in-the-River, now riding with the Dog Soldier Chief, Medicine Arrows, would never feel secure enough to go to the whites, but they did allow Custer to enter their village. And their mistrust was only cemented by Custer's double-dealing.

Unknown to the Cheyenne, Custer, despite his peaceful overtures, had ordered his troops to surround the village and to await his signal in case of trouble.

The Cheyenne were suspicious all along. Stands-in-the-River eyed the bluecoat chief and his men warily, feeling more naked than ever without the comforting nearness of his rifle. But this was supposedly a peaceful council where weapons should not be necessary. Medicine Arrows also was wary. At one point he told Custer, "If you are planning to betray us, then you and all your soldiers will be killed."

Stands-in-the-River watched with grim satisfaction as they passed the pipe around the circle of Indians and bluecoats. Medicine Arrows further indicated his contempt for the general by spilling the pipe ashes over the toes of Custer's boots to bring him bad luck.

The famed "Custer's luck," however, was to hold—for that night at least. When Custer learned the village held two captive white women, he ordered his troops, hidden in the woods, to draw their weapons on the village. He seized Medicine Arrows and three other chiefs, holding them hostage in order to effect an exchange for the white women. But when the Indians finally sent the two women to Custer's camp, the general refused to release the chiefs. Instead, he burned an evacuated village, leaving the Cheyennes even more destitute.

Stands-in-the-River, who escaped with others of the Dog Soldiers, watched all this with bitter hatred. As Medicine Arrows and the other captured chiefs were herded back to Camp Supply, he swore to have his revenge.

News of these and other actions against the Indians were received with dismay by the Washita prisoners. Hope of release dwindled. One woman and a child died of wounds received in the Washita massacre. Others of the younger women were used to service the troopers. Supplies were scanty; cold and hunger constantly hounded the Cheyenne women and children.

Lt. Godfrey made several attempts to win Deborah away from her Cheyenne comrades. He nearly succeeded during one particularly miserable week when Carolyn took a chill and was ill for several days with a fever and earache. Deborah debated painfully with herself, questioning the nobility of her staunch loyalty to her Indian friends if it endangered the welfare of her children. Godfrey assured her there were at least two families, one of settlers, one of the military, who were willing to take her in. But how could she go live in comfort while her friends and their children suffered?

When Carolyn's fever broke and her health gradually returned, Deborah's inner turmoil temporarily eased. She traveled with the prisoners when they were moved that spring to Fort Dodge and continued to live in the meager quarters provided for the Indians.

Lt. Godfrey pressed his argument once more. "Mrs. Graham, it won't be long before the southern Plains tribes surrender and are placed on reservations. Surely you don't plan to follow them into such a life. You are white! You are a southern lady. If not for yourself, think of your daughter. Will she grow up among savages, marry—" But he stopped suddenly, the rising glint in Deborah's eyes warning him he was treading upon tender ground.

"I am a Cheyenne in my heart," Deborah said with an evenness that belied the ire in her eyes. "Only my skin is white. My daughter does not even speak English. My son is Cheyenne. I am where I belong."

Godfrey threw his hands up in frustration and left. But later that evening he returned with reinforcements. When Deborah saw who it was with the lieutenant, she began to wonder if fate, or God, or perhaps even the devil, was conspiring against her.

By the lieutenant's side walked none other than Sam Killion, whom the frustrated army officer had sought to convince this wayward white woman of the error of her ways. Godfrey had heard the ex-Texas Ranger preach, and his fire and vigor had changed the lieutenant's life in many ways. He thought it might help if the man plied Deborah with his rigorous rhetoric.

Killion wasn't surprised to find that the "Mrs. Graham" of whom Lt. Godfrey had spoken was the same Mrs. Stoner he had known before. He had heard all about the Washita massacre, even though Killion had been farther north at the time, at Fort Hays. He had been concerned when he learned Black Kettle's village had been the target of the attack and had made several anxious inquiries. He learned that a white woman with a white child and a half-breed had been found in the village, and that despite conciliatory efforts made by General Custer, she had refused to leave the company of the Indian prisoners. The trader who had given Killion this information said he thought the woman's name was Graham, but Killion instinctively believed it could only be Deborah Stoner. The distance, however, combined with harsh weather and the imminent danger of Indian attack, prevented him from going immediately to Camp Supply to see for himself. Moreover, a certain unrelated reticence, uncharacteristic to his bold and gregarious nature, also held him in check. Deborah Stoner was a proud and stubborn woman who might well recoil at efforts to help her. After all, she had rejected General George Armstrong Custer; why should she concede to a mere itinerant preacher whom she had already proven to have little use for? He sensed that she had finally accepted him on their last meeting only because her Cheyenne husband had accepted him. Things were vastly different now. Obviously, Broken Wing was no longer with her, being either a fugitive or dead. In either case, she would not be too kindly disposed toward any white man, including Killion.

Yet he could not refuse Godfrey's plea on his first night in Fort Dodge. Besides, learning of her close proximity, he could not have stayed away long. There was something about her that intrigued him. Or maybe she simply challenged him. Whatever her particular draw upon him, in the last three years he had never been able to get her completely out of his mind. More often than he cared to admit to himself, his thoughts wandered toward her. What was she doing? Was she safe? Was she free? Was that hard protective shell still enclosing her heart? And Sam Killion prayed for Deborah as often as he thought about her.

So, when he found out she was at Fort Dodge, where he had traveled when weather permitted, and where he was scheduled to commence an evangelistic crusade, he did not hesitate to go to her, even if it meant incurring her rejection and wrath.

He stepped into the barracks where the prisoners were being kept and, finding her distracted in the care of the children, had a brief moment to assess the changes in her since their last meeting a year ago. She was more spare and lean than he remembered, most likely due to the poor winter provisions in camp. Her skin was pale, in spite of the bronze it had acquired during her years with the Cheyenne. Her hair, all the dye gone, was cropped to shoulder length, but its color was now more golden than ever and it seemed to form a misty halo around her fine features. Dark circles ringed her vivid blue eyes, and an aura of hardship clung around the edges of her visage. But still her beauty caught Killion's breath. In that brief instant he realized what it was that so intrigued him about her, that made his heart ache with both joy and sadness. It was not so much her beauty, but rather a peculiar blending in her appearance of fragile delicacy and intrepid steel. She was like the wild flowers that each spring dot the tough prairie grass—so exquisite, but with a sturdy tenacity that makes them able to survive the stiff winds and dry heat and bloom again and again one spring after another.

Killion did not realize he was staring until Godfrey gave him a nudge.

"There she is, Reverend Killion," said the lieutenant, unaware that she was already the object of Killion's intense interest.

Killion swallowed, experiencing a rare moment of embarrassment. "Yes, I see," said the ex-Texas Ranger in a hoarse whisper as he regained his composure.

At that moment, hearing the male voices, Deborah looked up. She immediately noted Killion's presence and, to his relief, gave him a not unfriendly nod.

"Ma'am," Killion said, tipping his wide-brimmed hat and stepping forward, his customary boldness returning.

"Mr. Killion, this is a surprise." She rose and politely offered her hand.

Much to Killion's surprise when he took Deborah's hand in his, he found it was rough and work-worn—the hand of a Cheyenne squaw, not a delicate southern belle.

"You two know each other?" said Godfrey, a bit bemused as he began to sense a peculiar energy to the exchange.

"We have met before," answered Killion. As her hand lingered briefly in his, he noted the scars on her arms and frowned slightly.

Those scars had not been there a year ago; neither had her eyes been so taut with pain. When he last saw her, she had seemed content, at ease, and even happy. He had hoped that the strained, haunted woman who had helped him at the outlaws' hideout had at last found some peace, though he knew she'd never know true peace until she surrendered herself to God. Now, however, he had to wonder what had happened to her in the last months to cause her to slip back to her previous self. Of course, there was the obvious, the massacre of her adopted people, but Killion sensed there was more to it than that. He breathed a silent prayer as he let her hand slide from his.

"We do meet in the oddest places, Mr. Killion," said Deborah, her attempt at lightness seriously undermined by the grim set of her face.

"I reckon there ain't no *normal* places out here in the West," Killion replied. "I'm just glad to see you're ... well. And the young'uns, too. God's been looking over you, that's for sure."

"Is that what you call it?" Deborah's tone contained a sharp edge. "What about my friends ... my husband? Who was looking over them?"

Killion removed his hat and scratched his head. "I guess I don't pretend to understand the ways of God, ma'am. I do know He watches over everyone, even those who don't care. But why troubles come to some and not others...? That's one of those mysteries I suppose no one will ever know the answer to."

"Then what good is religion if it offers no answers when you need them most?"

"Mrs. ... uh, Mrs. Graham," said Killion, "I'd really like to talk more about this with you. Can we go someplace? Maybe walk outside a mite?" He paused and turned to Godfrey. "You don't mind, Lieutenant, if we leave for a while?"

"No, Reverend, not at all," said Godfrey. "But you won't forget to mention what we talked about?"

Deborah responded first to the lieutenant's question. "Is that why you've come here, Mr. Killion—to talk me into leaving my people, to get me to 'come to my senses'?"

"That's why Lt. Godfrey fetched me, Mrs. Graham, but it ain't entirely why I came. You see, when I learned you were here, I thought I wouldn't be much of a friend if I didn't come see you."

"A friend, Mr. Killion?" Deborah's voice held more hope than suspicion. She did not know what it was about this man, this preacher, but she couldn't help believing him, and thinking he might indeed be a friend if she would only let him.

"Yes, ma'am." He adjusted his gaze until it focused squarely on her. "Would you walk with me, Mrs. Graham?"

"Yes."

She asked Gray Antelope Woman to watch the children; then she and Killion took their leave of Godfrey and headed across the main compound of the fort.

50

SET ON THE NORTH BANK OF THE Arkansas River, Fort Dodge had, since its founding four years earlier, grown into a substantial plains outpost. The original sod huts, or "soddies," as the soldiers called them, had been abandoned soon after their construction because of frequent flooding, and had been replaced by sturdy buildings of limestone, hewn from a quarry several miles north of the fort. There were barracks housing a hundred soldiers, officers' quarters, a headquarters, and a hospital where many of the Washita prisoners had received their first substantial medical treatment since the fight. In addition to this, there were other wooden buildings for a blacksmith's forge, a carpenter's shop, and a recreation parlor that served as a gaming room with billiard and card tables. There was also a small school and a chapel. But perhaps the most important building of all was the Sutler's store, where the Indians came to trade, and where the soldiers could buy whiskey to dull the boredom of post life between Indian wars.

Dominating the center of the fort was a parade ground that stretched over a space of a hundred square yards. Deborah and Killion crossed the open field as several troops of infantry were drilling, kicking up a cloud of dust into the chilly afternoon wind.

"Ma'am," Killion began, speaking what was at the moment most on his heart, "I don't mean to pry, nor to cause you any upset, but I've been concerned about what has happened to your husband."

"It is not right to speak ... of the dead. ..." A lump rose in Deborah's throat and tears suddenly welled up in her eyes.

"Oh, ma'am. . . !" Killion, too, seemed to suddenly choke up. "I am sorry. He was a fine man. Was it at Washita?"

She shook her head, almost unable to speak. But, even though Cheyenne custom discouraged speaking of the dead, even for a wife to utter her dead husband's name, Deborah felt an undeniable need to tell this white man of her husband's bravery and his honor. So, taking a determined breath, she forged ahead.

"He was killed last fall . . . in a skirmish with soldiers," she said. "He had gone intending to convince his brother to give up fighting the soldiers, but then he discovered Sheridan was ignoring the treaty by sending troops into Indian Territory. My husband believed, as did Black Kettle, that his family would be safe there, for we were not at war with the whites. Not long after your final visit to our village, my husband went in search of his brother. As you had warned, there were battle-ready soldiers in the field south of the river. He needed no further proof of General Sheridan's intent to strike the villages. Only then was my husband able to believe it. "

"That's when he entered the fight?" asked Killion.

"He did so only to protect his family. He would never have fought otherwise."

"I know that." Killion shook his head mournfully. "It's a sorry pass when a good man like that has to be sacrificed in such a way. He had so much to offer both the whites and the Indians."

"Nothing lives long, Mr. Killion, only the earth and the mountains." She spoke the Cheyenne death song without a firm conviction of its truth.

"Ma'am, in my time dealing with Indians, both lately and in my rangering days, I heard much wisdom from them, and I think the Cheyenne ability to accept death as the natural flow of things is commendable. They mourn bitterly over their dead, but not without the hope that the Hanging Road provides. I figure it's about as close to eternal life as they know about, and I only wish they could hear the whole story. I've often wondered what happens to an Indian's soul when he dies. Does God have some special dispensation for them? I like to think so. I like to think when God comes across a fellow who has never had the chance to hear the gospel, that He looks on that man's heart and judges him by his response to the truth that *has* been revealed to him. I don't know if this sort of thing worries you, Mrs. Graham, but it helps me to know that Broken Wing—forgive me for speaking his name, but I do so only to honor him—is standing absolved before the throne of God, at last fully basking in God's love. It's a comfort to me, and I hope it is to you also."

"Do you mean to say a savage Indian has gone to heaven?" She could not hide a touch of cynicism in her tone.

"I believe so, because if given half a chance, I think your husband would have come to embrace his true Savior."

"That is quite a statement," Deborah said, truly amazed. "I grew up with Christianity, and at this moment I feel further from God than the most remote savage."

"That's the way it is sometimes, ma'am. We whites get almost overexposed to Christianity, which would be just fine if most of it wasn't a cockeyed version of it. Unfortunately, a large part of what we hear is about religion and nothing else."

"But it's not just *religion* to you, is it, Mr. Killion?"

"Not at all," said Killion enthusiastically. "It is about personally knowing Someone who loves me more'n I can ever imagine, more'n my own ma—" His voice caught suddenly and he quickly swiped a sleeve across his eyes. "Pardon me, ma'am, I can't rightly talk about it without getting a mite emotional."

"I think my father had such a faith," said Deborah quietly.

"Did he?"

"It doesn't surprise me that you'd wonder how I could have back-slidden so far with such a parent. Well, I'll tell you frankly, Mr. Killion, I came to a place in my life where his faith simply failed me. It left me with more questions than answers, at a time when I desperately needed answers, not vague words of comfort like, 'Your brother is in a better place, Deborah.' And, to tell the truth, I wondered at times if his faith was even able to comfort him when my brother died. What good is a faith if it is powerless when you need it most?"

Killion did not respond immediately. Deborah might have thought that, quite unintentionally, her question had stumped the preacher. But as she glanced at him she saw not confusion on his face, but rather a thoughtful serenity. It was almost as if he were praying, though his eyes were wide open and he walked at her side quite normally. They had long since exited the gates of the fort and were now walking along the north bank of the river. Killion gazed toward the sparkling water, then back at Deborah.

"Ma'am, would you like to hear something that may surprise you? In fact, it may even shock you."

"I doubt there is anything left in this world that can shock me, Mr. Killion."

"This ain't exactly 'of this world.'"

"Now I'm curious. Do go on."

"Well, you said something a minute ago that I hear a lot. I guess it is one of those cockeyed notions I mentioned before. You spoke of your father's faith and how it wasn't enough for you."

"Yes . . ."

"Here's what you might find surprising: your father's faith is just that—his faith. I expect a parent's faith covers a child while he is young, but there comes a time when that just ain't enough, when a man—or woman—has to blaze her own spiritual path, acquire her own faith and relationship with Jesus Christ. You take my ma, for instance. She is about the most saintly, godly woman I know. But that didn't keep me from having to test the waters myself, though I know now her prayers protected me in some pretty dangerous situations. But I had to go under many times before I finally struck the true path to God. And I had to do that alone, just between me and God. It was only then that I began to change and grow, and that I began to see the answers to my need. Oh, believe me, I've still got plenty of questions and there's still a passel of things I don't understand, but now that I know God personally, I can better trust Him to eventually come through for me, even when times get dark and the questions start to outdistance the answers.

"My mother's faith is a beautiful thing, but it was no better to me than a valuable china bowl on a shelf. Faith ain't no delicate china. It's a good sturdy tin plate you can pack in your saddlebag and take along and use every day on the trail. But even a tin plate is useless unless you got it right along with you and it's yours. I wouldn't want to trust borrowing someone else's, especially in a pinch." Killion paused, took a breath and smiled rather sheepishly. "Once I get started, Mrs. Graham," he said, "I can go on forever."

"You need not apologize, Mr. Killion. What you said makes a lot of sense. It does rather surprise me, for I have never considered it in quite that way before."

"Most folks haven't."

"I always thought of myself as a good Christian girl. Maybe that's why I became so bitter when it seemed to me I had been deserted."

"God never deserts, ma'am. It's always us who do the deserting."

Killion paused as a large cloud of dust in the distance caught his attention. Riders were approaching, but they were still too far to discern who they were and if they were friendly.

"Mrs. Graham," Killion said, a bit concerned, "I think we ought to head back to the fort."

Deborah felt more hope than fear at the sight, though she knew it could not possibly be a war party. The Indian horses, that early in spring, would be too weak and hungry to ride at such a hurried pace. It was not a war party come to rescue her and the others. Yet she returned to the fort with Killion just the same. She did not like to be gone so long from her children. Besides, she had begun to feel strange emotions within at the direction of her conversation with Killion, and she was somewhat fearful of it continuing. So, she accepted this interruption as a rescue of sorts. She needed time to absorb all Killion had said—time alone, not in the company of this convincing and charismatic man.

As they stepped inside the protective gates of the fort, she politely, perhaps coolly, thanked him for taking time to visit her. She gave him no reason to doubt that the conversation was over.

Before they parted, however, Killion spoke once more. "I'd like to invite you to my meeting this Sunday, over in the chapel—well, I'd like to think of it as a chapel in spite of the heavy presence of stale tobacco smoke and whiskey in the place. It's really the recreation hall because the chapel is too small. Anyway, I'd be pleased if you could come."

"Thank you, Mr. Killion. I will try to attend."

He wasn't sure by her tone if she truly intended to try or if she was just patronizing him, but, undaunted, he continued. "Also, before I take your leave, I best speak for Lt. Godfrey as I promised."

"Please, don't waste your breath, Mr. Killion," she said without rancor. "I know what he wants, and I cannot comply."

"Just as long as you know he is a good man and has only your best welfare, as he sees it, in mind. They ain't all bad, you know, Mrs. Graham."

"I know." Then suddenly she smiled and added, "Neither are all preachers, Mr. Killion." Her tone warmed as she spoke. "I am grateful for your concern."

"I hope to see you Sunday."

Deborah nodded vaguely and continued on her way toward the prisoners' quarters. Killion watched her until she had disappeared inside. She was quite a woman. In many ways she was a mystery, but she was the kind of mystery that you didn't mind devoting a lot of time to solving. She was so vulnerable, yet Killion had the distinct impression that once she got her life in order and once she realized who ought to be first in that life, she would be a woman of tremendous substance.

"Lord," Sam Killion prayed silently, "bring Deborah face-to-face with you. Let her see your majesty and your unrestrained love."

Killion nodded to himself, satisfied that his prayer would reach up to attentive, loving ears, and that his God would not forget Deborah Stoner.

51

ON THAT SUNDAY IN SPRING of 1869, Deborah felt oddly compelled to attend Sam Killion's church service. She tried to tell herself it was from politeness—after all, he had showed interest in her and so it was the least she could do to return the gesture.

She bathed herself and the children, scrubbing them as clean as was possible in the small basin provided by the quartermaster. She dressed the children in clean clothes that had been provided by some benevolent army wife. They were white man's clothes and it irked her to use them, but since she had no other clothes for the children, she was forced to swallow her pride in this instance. She continued to wear her same buckskin shift. When it needed to be washed, as she had made a point of doing before the service, she wrapped herself in a blanket while Gray Antelope Woman did the washing. Gray Antelope and many of the women had eagerly taken to wearing the clothing provided. To them, the calicos and the full skirts were an unequaled luxury. There were even a couple of corsets in the box of castoffs that both perplexed and amused the Indian women. The shoes, however, were a torture none could bear; they remained untouched except by some of the children for their make-believe games.

Deborah supposed she had more to prove than her Cheyenne sisters, whose skin and hair color was the only badge of honor they needed. Thus her Indian garb offset her pale skin and hair and marked her, for good or ill, as one of the prisoners.

Gray Antelope surprised Deborah by agreeing to accompany her to the service. Deborah had forgotten her friend's comments some time ago about the white preacher. She was just glad to have the older woman's company, even more so as they approached the recreation hall and fell in with the other residents of the fort who were making their way to the service.

The presence of bluecoated soldiers made her nervous, as did the two or three frontier scouts in the crowd to whom this was probably a rare opportunity to attend a real church service. But far more than these, it was the white women in the gathering that most disturbed Deborah. Isolated as she had been with the prisoners, she had had little cause to mix with the handful of white women in the fort. One or two had paid goodwill visits to the prisoners' quarters, but Deborah had always made a point of being absent at those times. Even on the Stoner Ranch she had been given little opportunity to interact with the other women in the area. Now, for the first time in years she was mingling with women of her own race. She felt odd, out of place, awkward. These women with their fine calico frocks, bonnets tied primly around neatly groomed hair, skin as soft and smooth and white as alabaster, were of a world as far removed as any make-believe fairyland a child might imagine. Deborah's bronzed skin, so pale compared to her Cheyenne friends' skin, all at once stood out like a glaring flaw. She had never felt shame before about her place among the Indians, and was certain she did not feel so now; but suddenly she found herself thinking of what she might have become had she stayed in Virginia, the pampered daughter of gentry, a southern lady.

But would she also have looked with disdain upon outsiders, as several of these women were now doing? Would she have whispered carelessly behind their backs, convinced that savages, and those who consented to live with savages, had no feelings?

Deborah caught snatches of the whispers as she passed, but she held her head high, set her chin defiantly, and walked resolutely.

"White squaw woman . . ."

"Half-breed son . . ."

"Did so *willingly!*"

"Of all things!"

Any doubts Deborah might have had about her loyalty to the Cheyenne prisoners were dispelled. She knew she was better off as she was now than as she might have been. She would never fit into that world of genteel white women.

These thoughts did not leave her in the best frame of mind to accept words about the "white" God. These women were Christian, God-fearing scions of civilization, yet where was their love and simple compassion? Did they believe in a different god than the one her father and Sam Killion spoke of? By whom was she expected to judge God? If not by His followers, then by whom, or what?

Deborah's reverie was momentarily interrupted as she entered the hall and found seats on the rough wooden benches procured for the occasion. She and Gray Antelope sat toward the back, not so much because of the children, who were too well-trained to disturb the meeting, but rather because she felt little welcome from the occupants of the front rows, mostly officers and their wives.

Killion was seated at the front of the room facing the congregation. His head was bowed as they entered but when the audience began to settle down and quiet, he lifted his head and stood.

"Mrs. Travis," he said to a woman seated at a piano, "would you begin with 'Rock of Ages'?"

Killion began the hymn with robust enthusiasm and soon even the most grizzled soldier in the crowd was joining in. Deborah found herself singing the familiar old hymn, too. The words escaped her lips easily, as if it had been only a week, not many years, since she had heard the song, or even been to church.

The next hymn Killion seemed to take special relish in, as evidenced by his broad grin and the lively swinging of his arms. And, because of its aptness to this particular gathering, the audience took up the rousing tune eagerly.

"Onward Christian soldiers, marching as to war, with the cross of Jesus going on before. . . ."

When everyone was adequately warmed up, Killion motioned for Mrs. Travis to end her piano-playing; then he turned to the crowd, eyes blazing with anticipation of what was to come.

"Whew!" he said with a laugh, "that makes my blood run hot! I'm ready for war, folks. I'm ready to fight the good fight! How about you?"

From the crowd, a man yelled in response, "There's plenty of Injuns to go 'round, Preacher!"

Without a moment's hesitation, Killion replied, "Don't you know, brother, our battle ain't against Indians. No sir! The Word of God itself declares, 'For we wrestle not against flesh and blood, but against principalities, against powers, against the rulers of the darkness of this world, against spiritual wickedness in high places.' The apostle Paul surely wasn't referring to no Indians when he said that, my friend! He'd never laid an eye on one of our Indians. I'll tell you who Paul was talking about: someone more cunning, more deceptive, more evil than anyone you'd ever find on the Plains—none other than the devil himself. Satan! That's who our battle is against, and if he wins, you don't risk just losing your scalp, or even just your life. You're gonna lose your very soul!

"And I'll tell you plainly, it's gonna take a lot better commander than Phil Sheridan or George Custer—no offense, boys!—to win the fight against such a foe. In fact, there ain't no man around, not even

Ulysses S. Grant himself, who can fight that fight!

"But don't give up hope. We ain't doomed. We ain't alone! We ain't surrounded and out of ammo. We have, but a prayer away, more power than a hundred Gatling guns, a thousand cannons, and all the generals ever to take the field. You all know who I'm talking about, don't you?"

Killion paused, looked around the audience, lingering upon several faces, catching their eyes with such a personal interest they felt as if he were speaking directly to them. When his gaze fell upon Deborah, her eyes held his for a moment; then, flustered, she looked away. But she continued to listen raptly to every word. It wasn't easy to ignore the intense fervor of Killion's voice, especially when he answered his own question with a tone that trembled with awe and reverence.

"The Lord Jesus Christ!" The name of his Lord tumbled over his emotion. Tears stood in his eyes as he raised his voice and quoted as if he were gazing directly at the throne of God: " 'Lift up your heads, O ye gates; and be ye lifted up, ye everlasting doors; and the King of glory shall come in. Who is this King of glory? The Lord strong and mighty, the Lord mighty in battle.' What a general we have in Jesus! What a warrior we have! If God is for us, then who can be against us?"

Several hearty "Amens" from the audience accompanied his statement.

Then for several minutes, Killion spoke about how to have this mighty warrior on a man's side and what kept Him at bay, elaborating on the folly of sin and the fate of those who persist in sin. He minced no words, observed no polite decorum. He laid out in clear, terrible terms just what it meant to be separated from God by sin. Sweat trickled down his face with the exertion of his emotion, and the skin beneath his red beard flamed crimson with his passion. He emanated a very real distress over the prospect that any should be caught in that terrible place. Many of his listeners began to squirm beneath the reality of such zealous concern.

Deborah listened to his words, but her mind wandered—not from boredom, for no matter what a person's reaction to Killion's preaching might be, boredom certainly had no part in it. What captured Deborah's attention, almost mesmerizing her, were Killion's expressions and the captivating tone of his voice. His was not a polished, intellectual bearing. If he had ever received any formal training in the ministry, it had not robbed the quintessential element of personal involvement from what he preached. Then Deborah recalled

276

what Gray Antelope had once observed about Killion. *He spoke from his heart.* He *felt* every statement, *believed* every word, and the sorrow he experienced over those who rejected these things sprang from a fountain of love.

It surprised Deborah when she realized thirty minutes had passed. Hardly anyone had moved or even breathed. Blue Sky had fallen asleep in Deborah's arms, and even Carolyn was sitting quietly, sucking her thumb.

Then Killion's tone abruptly changed, lightening with a hope that reflected brightly in his eyes.

"But don't despair!" he said. "All is not lost. You are hanging over a fiery pit, by a rope that is slowly but surely unraveling. It looks bad; you ain't got much time left. But the hand of God is ready at a moment's notice to save you. Don't be mistaken, though, He ain't gonna be impressed by your goodness or your virtue. No sir! There is only one thing that is going to make Him able to look upon you and pluck you from Satan's lair.

"Only the blood of Jesus! The pure, clean, wonderful blood of our Lord. The blood He shed in order to bring salvation to this rotten, despicable world. Are you covered by the blood, folks?"

Again Killion's eyes swept the audience, probing, searching, beseeching.

"Are you *sure?* You don't want to take any chances; this is too important. Your eternal soul lies in the balance.

"God wants to reach out to you. He wants to save you from Satan's pit. He loves you—each and every one of you. That's the really good news! God loves you! He loves you enough to have sacrificed His Son for you. Jesus spilled His blood for you. He doesn't want anyone to fall into that pit. But it's up to you. God is waiting patiently . . . patiently." Killion lowered his voice to a fervent whisper, "Patiently."

His eyes closed and, tilting his head back as if his inner eyes were focused fully on the heavenlies, he began to sing in a stirring tenor:

There is a fountain filled with blood
Drawn from Emmanuel's veins;
And sinners, plunged beneath that flood,
Lose all their guilty stains:
Lose all their guilty stains,
Lose all their guilty stains,
And sinners, plunged beneath that flood,
Lose all their guilty stains.

The audience listened in rapt silence. Killion's voice floated over the gathering with such subdued power, such reverent love, that Deborah found tears welling up in her eyes. Words she had heard all her life suddenly seemed to come alive, and it was obvious they were not mere words to him.

> E'er since by faith I saw the stream
> Thy flowing wounds supply,
> Redeeming love has been my theme,
> And shall be till I die. . . .

As he began the next verse of the hymn, his voice trembled over the words and tears seeped from the corners of his closed eyes:

> When this poor lisping, stammering tongue
> Lies silent in the grave,
> Then in a nobler, sweeter song
> I'll sing Thy power to save. . . .

Killion's voice trailed away, and complete silence filled the room. His eyes remained closed, and though Deborah noted that many others also had closed eyes, she could not shut hers even if she did feel somewhat like a Peeping Tom spying on the audience. But for the most part, she was watching only Killion, fascinated by his animation as he communed with the One whom he had so eloquently extolled. Tears continued to trickle from his closed eyes, but an enraptured smile slipped across his lips.

When he spoke again, Deborah was a little disappointed that he had stopped singing, but she continued to be compelled to listen, especially since his voice had become soft with gentle entreaty.

"Father God in heaven, I know you are working on the hearts of every man and woman in this room. I know you love us and will never give up on us." He paused, then, still with eyes closed, directed his next words at his listeners. "My friends, will you join me in singing a final verse to this precious hymn, and as we sing, search your hearts, and don't put off for another minute entering into the glorious life Christ has waiting for you. Come forward and publicly proclaim your repentant heart and desire to follow Jesus!"

Mrs. Travis played the introduction to the hymn, and it was lovely playing, but Deborah knew she would never again hear music as sweet as Killion's simple a cappella rendition. Several in the audience joined Killion in singing.

The first movement in the quiet room came from a section of

278

benches occupied by common soldiers. A young man, tears welling up in his eyes, rose to his feet and stumbled forward. He fell on his knees before Killion.

"I can't live no more with what I done," the young private wept, "with the things I done in battle. God, forgive me!"

"He will, son." Killion knelt down with the man and laid a comforting hand on his shoulder. "The blood of Jesus covers even the blood of battle."

Seemingly heartened by this, another soldier, a corporal this time, lumbered forward. And a moment later, a captain joined him. Killion prayed with each man, and before he finished, two civilians joined the group at the makeshift altar.

"Folks," Killion said, "we're gonna be praying and praising God here for a spell, so if you like, come on down and join us. If you can't stay, feel free to be on your way. Thanks for coming, and God be with you all!"

Deborah was ready to leave—not that she hadn't been touched, but she felt no further reason to remain since she would have felt terribly out of place there at the front. She turned to let Gray Antelope know her intentions when, to her astonishment, she first noticed that her friend's place on the bench was empty!

Deborah looked hastily around, first toward the back door, thinking Gray Antelope might have left already. Then a small hand tugged at her dress.

"Nahkoa, what is *nishki*, grandmother, doing?" said Carolyn.

Deborah swung her gaze toward where her daughter's little finger was pointing. Gray Antelope Woman had made her way to the front and was at that very moment praying with Killion. Deborah could not help gaping, stunned, at the unexpected sight. Whatever had come over this woman, the medicine man's widow? Though Gray Antelope had been learning English from Deborah, Deborah never would have guessed the woman had learned enough to have followed the sermon, or, even if she could understand the words, had grasped their meaning. Yet, there she was, kneeling at the altar, clearly there by design, not by error.

At a loss over what to do next, Deborah soon found herself moving into the file of people leaving the hall. Part of her, of course, did not want to leave her friend. Yet she had absolutely no idea what she might do for her if she stayed. But it was more than awkwardness that prevented her from going to the front. Things were happening up there that were both wondrous and fearful. She could easily get caught up in it all, and that scared her. Instinctively, she fought any situation where she might lose control. Her innate desire to be self-sufficient, independent, in control of her life, had not changed, though circumstances over the years had varied. And now that she was alone again, and once more at the mercy of others, she was even more determined to take charge of her life. Yes, everything Killion had said sounded appealing. To be loved, to be clean again, to feel safe . . . of course, it was desirable. But Killion never spoke of the sacrifice it all involved. She remembered other preachers speaking of the "free gift" of salvation—but it wasn't free, not really. It involved giving yourself up to God, and she simply was not ready to do that.

So, Deborah gathered up her children and stepped outside alone. And, oddly, as the spring sunshine blazed over her, she felt more alone just then than she had even in the lowest moments of her life.

52

DEBORAH AVOIDED THE SUBJECT of the Sunday meeting when she saw Gray Antelope later. She was intensely curious, but not enough to risk her already wavering spirit. And Gray Antelope's reserved and private nature prevented her from sharing such a personal experience openly. One day, however, toward the middle of the next week, Deborah did inadvertently catch a glimpse of what was transpiring in her friend's heart.

Since Sunday, Gray Antelope had been slipping off alone—or at least away from the prisoners' quarters—every day, for about an hour each time. Deborah questioned her once about her mysterious absences and Gray Antelope vaguely replied, "I have been studying."

That particular day, after Gray Antelope returned from her outing, she was playing with the children when Carolyn clamored for a story. Gray Antelope always had a fine Indian legend at hand to tell, often a different one; but many times the children asked her to repeat old favorite ones. This time she had a new one.

"I will tell you a story I just heard about a young man named Beloved One. He would one day become a great warrior, but when he was a boy, the youngest of seven sons, he only tended the herds while his brothers went off to fight great battles."

As she spoke, several other children in the barracks migrated toward her and formed an attentive circle around her. Deborah pretended to be busy sewing moccasins, but her ears were also tuned to the older woman's compelling voice.

"This boy's village," Gray Antelope continued, "was at war with a mighty tribe, worse even than the Pawnee or Crow. Beloved One tended the horses while the warriors fought, but he longed to join the battle. His father asked him to take food to his brothers, for it was a long battle and the warriors could not leave to hunt buffalo. So, Beloved One did so, and when he approached his brothers he saw that they, and all the warriors of the village, were very dismayed. The enemy tribe had produced a warrior who was nine feet tall! His spear was the size of a lodge pole and its iron tip was as heavy as a large rock. He was fearsome to behold, and Beloved One's people were trembling at the sight. The giant warrior taunted them and challenged them to choose their best warrior to fight him. He told them that if they defeated him, his people would be their slaves; but if he won, then they must serve his people. No one was brave enough to count coup against this warrior giant.

"Beloved One saw this and was distressed, not about the warrior's taunts, but because his people were so afraid. He said, 'This man does not mock us but the Great Spirit in whom we believe. Who does he think he is?'

"The boy's brothers told him to be quiet, that he was only a boy who tended herds, and he had never been proven in battle and never even had counted a single coup. But Beloved One said that the Wise One Above, who had protected him against wild animals that had tried to attack his herds, could protect him against a giant! His brothers and the others laughed at him, but Beloved One ignored them, took his slingshot that he sometimes used to frighten off wild animals, and went out into the valley to face the giant.

"The giant laughed, too. 'Do you make sport of me, to send a mere boy against me?' he shouted to the frightened army.

"Beloved One did not flinch. 'You face me with a bow and a spear and a sharp tomahawk, but I come against you in the name of the Lord God Almighty, who you think to defy. Today, I will strike you down and take your scalp, and then all those here will know what a powerful God we worship.'

"And that is exactly what Beloved One did. When the giant raised his spear to attack the boy, Beloved One took a smooth stone, placed it in his sling, and hurled it at the giant. It struck him in the forehead, and the giant fell down dead. After that, Beloved One became so greatly esteemed by his people that they made him a chief. All because he trusted his God and did not let a thing like size make him afraid."

Deborah had certainly never heard such a charming version of "David and Goliath." Besides her creative interpretation and captivating style, Gray Antelope lent an earnest joy to the story that gave it life beyond the telling. She seemed to be sharing her own newly acquired concept of God, and the meaning He had in her life. She understood well the Goliaths of life, and had at last found the way to defeat them. This was most noticeable in the glow of hope that had lately replaced her defeat. The Cheyenne people were facing their Goliath, but at last Gray Antelope had found the strength to accept the inevitable. If only the same could be said for the others, many of whom were still on the warpath.

These new discoveries would hold Gray Antelope in good stead in the days that followed when more upheaval came.

———————

Word reached Fort Dodge that Little Robe and Yellow Bear, the Cheyenne and Arapahoe chiefs, had surrendered at Fort Sill, in the southwest corner of Indian Territory. But Sheridan steadfastly refused to talk peace until all the bands came in. John Smith, however, warned the Cheyenne that Fort Sill and Fort Cobb were traps—not an entirely unfounded assumption considering the heavy concentration of troops around these forts. Thus, many of the Cheyenne continued to be reluctant to surrender and moved far to the south, to the *Llano Estacado,* or "Staked Plains," of Texas.

In May, the Cheyenne held council. The chiefs sensed a desire for peace among the people. The Dog Soldiers, however, stubbornly held out for war, declaring they would go north and join the Sioux. They would never accept a peace that would rob them of their freedom.

In the meantime, the status of the Washita prisoners remained doubtful. It was finally decided to move them to the more secure environs of Fort Hays, some seventy miles north of Fort Dodge. This prompted another sad and difficult change in Deborah's life.

When news of the move reached the prisoners' quarters, Gray Antelope drew Deborah aside.

"It is time for you to rejoin the white men," she said sadly but resolutely.

"What?" exclaimed Deborah, completely unprepared for this suggestion. "I don't belong with them. I am Cheyenne. I belong with you."

"You will always be one of us, Wind Rider; forgive me if I have made it sound otherwise. But it is only a matter of time before all the Southern Cheyenne, indeed, all Indians, are put in the white man's reservations."

"I know, and I am ready to go."

Gray Antelope shook her head. "The rest of us have no choice, but you do have a choice. It is not right for you to choose a life that will not be a happy one—"

"But—"

"Listen to me, Wind Rider," said the shaman's widow sternly. "It is not for yourself that you must choose, but for your children. It would not be right of you to deprive them of their freedom."

"You sound as if a reservation is just another prison."

"In a way, it will be, especially for the braves who are not used to having their movement regulated, and who have learned that the way to manhood is upon the warpath. Think of what the white man's ways will take from them. And think of your beloved Blue Sky growing up in these surroundings. He deserves the freedom his white blood entitles him to. Do not rob him of it."

The logic of Gray Antelope's words was irrefutable, but it was no less difficult for Deborah to accept. "If you are strong enough to face such a life, if even Little Robe is able, then we can also."

"Who knows now if we are strong enough. Because we have no choice, maybe we will find the strength."

"Then I will too!"

Gray Antelope barely restrained a smile, for at that moment Deborah took on a rare likeness to her daughter during one of the child's temper tantrums.

"I can force you to heed my words no more than Little Robe can force the Dog Men to surrender. I hope that if there is wisdom in my words, then you will listen."

Deborah looked away, her face taut as she tried to cover her rising emotion. She well knew what reservation life could mean for a people accustomed to the freedom of the open ranges. The drunkenness of the warriors, the privations caused by governmental ineptitude, the disease that often went with adjustment to a new environment. She had already been frightened once by Carolyn's illness. What if

283

one of her children died because of her stubbornness? What if Broken Wing's son grew to be a drunken, unhappy, bitter man? She could never bear to be the cause of the demise of the dear legacy of the man she loved.

But how could she turn her back on these Cheyenne who had become her people? How could she leave Gray Antelope, whom she loved as both mother and sister?

"Would you come with me?" Deborah said to her friend.

And much to her disappointment, Gray Antelope slowly shook her head. "As you must choose for the benefit of your children, I must choose for my people. In these last days, Wind Rider, I have learned to have hope. I have learned that I am not alone, that One who is greater than all the spirits, will always travel with me. Like the boy in the story about the giant that I have told the children, I know a way to defeat hopelessness and despair. Perhaps I can show my people this way, and they can find happiness no matter where the white man takes them."

"Oh, Gray Antelope! What will I do without you?" Weeping, Deborah threw her arms around her friend and they held each other, both shedding unrestrained tears.

Gray Antelope said, "Maybe you will find this Jesus, so you will not be alone when we part."

"I—I don't know. Maybe . . ." Deborah sobbed and could say no more for some time.

After a while, Gray Antelope took a cloth and lovingly wiped away both hers and Deborah's tears; then she smoothed several strands of Deborah's yellow hair from her face and smiled at the woman whom she considered a daughter.

"I know you will find a good life for yourself and your children, Wind Rider Woman," she said. "I do not fear for you. Your husband called you a warrior, and I believe it is true. Only I pray that you make sure of your battles. Use love, not bitterness, as your weapon. As for me, don't worry. I am content that I am where I am meant to be."

Three days later Deborah watched as the caravan of Washita prisoners and a retinue of army guards departed the fort. Her heart wrenched with sorrow as she beheld another chapter of her life clamp shut, with only the yawning emptiness of uncertainty looming before her. But she remembered her friend's words: *Use love, not bitterness, as your weapon.* Yet, how could she follow this wise advice when all she loved was now disappearing through the wooden fortress gates? How could she risk loving again when the sacrifice it involved was so painful?

Still, Deborah could not forget her parting embrace with her friend, Gray Antelope, nor could she forget the sublime mark of peace in the woman's eyes. Though Gray Antelope faced many more months' imprisonment, and after that a future relegated to the confines of a reservation, yet she wore no despair on her countenance. Somehow she had found a way not only to accept her lot but to triumph over it.

Somehow. . . ?

Deborah knew better than that. It was more than some vague happenstance that had helped Gray Antelope. Deborah was certain it had something to do with Sam Killion.

53

AS STUDIOUSLY AS DEBORAH had avoided the subject of the Sunday church service with Gray Antelope, she had avoided the preacher.

Now, however, she suddenly knew she must seek him out.

She had to know what had happened that Sunday. She had to know about her friend's mysterious absences, which Deborah suspected had something to do with Killion. And, more than anything, she had to find out about this peace and contentment Gray Antelope had begun to exhibit.

With Blue Sky in her arms and Carolyn toddling behind, Deborah set off for the recreation hall. It was the only place she knew to look for the preacher, having no idea where Killion lived.

Not finding him there, she began to ask around, learning, much to her dismay, that he might have ridden east to see some settlers.

"Don't recall when he left," said one man. "Maybe he's back. You can try the Sutler's."

Killion was nowhere to be found in the store. The storekeeper, a man from Tennessee named Hardee Smith, knew Killion well and assured Deborah that the preacher was gone and wouldn't be back for a couple days.

Deflated, disappointed, and discouraged, Deborah nearly crumbled right there in the middle of the store. With one dismaying circumstance after another seeming to pile upon her, the loss of Gray Antelope, and then finding the only other friend she had to be gone, Deborah was suddenly overwhelmed. In spite of all her experience in closely guarding her emotions, tears rose to her eyes.

She was helpless and alone again. Was this to always be her lot?

She turned away from the storekeeper, but not in time for him to miss the anguish in her eyes.

"Ma'am!" he called after her quickly retreating form.

She stopped but, ashamed of her weakness, did not turn.

"Ma'am," Smith went on, seeming to be making conversation for its own sake, "ain't you that white squaw that wouldn't leave the Injuns? Sure 'nough, you gotta be, but why ain't you left with the others? You sticking 'round these parts, then? Well, you must be if you're here. Killion'll be right glad to hear that."

With those words, Deborah turned and faced the storekeeper, and for the first time took careful appraisal of him. Her first impression was that he was the ugliest man she had ever seen. Not just homely but downright ugly. His eyes fairly bulged from his head, giving him a great resemblance to a frog, although his large ears made her think of an entirely different species. His mouth, with lips as thick as ropes, was too big to offset his other features, and any appeal it might have had was quickly negated when he opened it and revealed two rows of the most crooked and rotten teeth she had ever seen. His thinning black hair, tangled, matted, and curled in long strands around his ears, had not a trace of gray in it, lending some mystery as to his age, especially since his stubbly beard was liberally peppered with gray. He talked with a distinctive Tennessee twang, made nearly undecipherable by the thick plug of chewing tobacco lodged between his cheek and yellow teeth.

"Killion has spoken to you of me?" Deborah asked, unsure whether to be upset or pleased.

"Once or twice, you know. As a matter of fact, I asked him, and he seemed to know you. Weren't nothin' for you to take no offense at, ma'am. He spoke with what I reckon you'd call discretion—and respect, too. Is it true you lived with the Injuns?"

"*Indians,*" Deborah corrected, but not harshly. "Cheyennes. And it is true."

"I didn't mean no offense, ma'am. I got nothin' but high regard for them Inj—I mean, Indians, ma'am. Big part of my business is tradin' with 'em, and it's a cryin' shame what's become of 'em. Not to mention how this trouble's played the dickens with business. When I took over the place last fall, it were thrivin'. I thought I had me a gold mine."

"It will pick up again now that the weather is clearing," offered Deborah, politely trying to keep up her end of the conversation.

"I reckon so. Winter's never good for much of anything 'cepting cold and hunger. I've sold a lot of whiskey, but I'd prefer trade of a different nature." He paused, seeming for the moment to have run out of conversation.

Deborah took the pause as a sign that she should leave. "I had best let you get back to work, Mr. Smith. Thank you for your time."

"Not a bit of trouble." He smiled and the warmth of that small gesture more than made up for his alarming features. "As you can see—" he swept a hand in the air to indicate the empty store, "I got loads of time."

She smiled in return, then turned to go. But as she reached the door, she realized she had no idea at all of where she would go. She was not only alone, but penniless, as well. Of course, the army would have been more than willing to put her up in one of those homes Lt. Godfrey had often mentioned, but she had no desire for this kind of charity. Instead, she turned back to the friendly storekeeper.

"Mr. Smith—"

But the fellow interrupted her with a loud but good-natured snort. "Oh, ma'am! I don't know what to do when someone calls me *Mister* Smith—sounds like one of them fancy Nashville lawyers. I'm just Hardee to ever'one."

"Well . . . Hardee, I was wondering if you knew where I might find lodgings in these parts?"

"Humm . . ." He ruminated as he rubbed his salt-and-pepper stubble. "There ain't no such thing as a hotel here at the fort. But shouldn't the army be obligated to look out for you?"

"I have been their prisoner for several months. I hardly relish the thought of now becoming their houseguest."

"That do make sense, I reckon."

"You wouldn't perhaps have something," said Deborah boldly, "that I could take in exchange for work . . . since I also have no money."

"You'd be wantin' to work for me?"

"I am a good worker."

"I wouldn't doubt it . . . wouldn't doubt it a'tall. But it ain't exactly genteel work here. Wouldn't you prefer gettin' back to the life you had before?"

287

"Never, Hardee."

"Well, if'n you're serious ... I got a little room in back—nothin' fancy, mind you, just big enough for you and the young'uns to be snug. I might could use help 'round here once the trappers start coming 'round, and the settlers, too, lookin' for seed and what all."

"Then I'll take it, if you are willing."

"I sure am." He paused for a moment as another idea came to him. "I'd be even more willing if you could do somethin' else for me. I reckon after all them years with the Cheyenne, you can speak the lingo right well."

"Yes, I can, and Arapahoe as well, and some Sioux. I even know some rudimentary Pawnee."

"Could you teach me the talk? I figger it could double my business."

"I'd love to teach you."

"Then it's a deal."

They shook hands on it, and Deborah found that she once again had a new home. And Hardee Smith never made her feel as if she were taking charity—in fact, he gave the distinct impression that he needed her as much as she needed him. Still, as he helped her turn the back room into living quarters, dragging in a straw mattress someone had traded him a while back, gathering blankets, and even locating a small storage chest, Deborah was acutely aware of the fact that she was again dependent on another—a man, to boot.

Would she ever be on her own, have her own place, her own home, be in control of her own destiny?

PART 6

SURRENDER

54

KILLION WAS DELIGHTED WHEN he heard of the turn in Deborah's fortunes. However, knowing how difficult it must have been for her to break from her Cheyenne family, he made a concerted effort to subdue his enthusiasm.

He had sensed for some time that her path would eventually lead back to the white man's world, though he had never voiced this feeling to her. Gray Antelope had shared her concerns with him regarding this, and he had encouraged her to talk to Deborah. Apparently she had, and had convinced Deborah not to follow the Indians onto the reservation. He regretted that he had been called away to officiate at a funeral and had not been there to lend support and encouragement to Deborah when the move took place, but, as he should have known, God had made provision for Deborah. He still could hardly believe she had cast her lot with good old Hardee Smith. A more mismatched pair he could not imagine, but Hardee was a kind, well-intentioned, if gruff and coarse, man; and Deborah could not have found a better situation for her and the children.

Over the next weeks Killion watched with satisfaction as Deborah settled in. Even while caring for her children, she earned her keep well in excess, and Hardee insisted on paying her a small salary as well as room and board. She not only kept the store clean beyond all the unkempt storekeeper's dreams, but she proved to be a natural teacher and had Hardee speaking many full Cheyenne sentences before her first month was over. In addition, she cooked for Smith—better food than he had enjoyed in years—and helped him with the bookkeeping, a task that had always been difficult for him with his negligible education. A side-benefit to all this for Deborah was that daily exposure to Hardee was encouraging the children to pick up English.

But what delighted Killion more than all this was Deborah's growing willingness to talk with him about the gospel. He didn't even have to bring up the subject on their first meeting after his return to the fort. *She* accosted him!

"Mr. Killion, I'd like to talk with you about my friend, Gray Antelope." She had sounded so formal; he at first thought she was going to take him to task for haranguing a poor, helpless Indian.

"I'd be pleased. Do you want to go somewhere more private?" They were standing in the store with several customers milling about.

"Shall we walk?"

"Let's."

The days were growing definitely fairer, more than hinting at the approach of that summer of 1869. A flock of geese winged overhead, and the gentle breeze carried the fragrant scent of prairie grass. The feel of newness and vitality pervaded the air. Killion knew that the land still suffered because of the Indian wars, the raids on settlers continuing, while the army maintained its unfair superiority. Misunderstanding and deceit seemed to reign over the affairs of men. But, nevertheless, Killion felt a lightness of heart as he stepped out into the balmy spring afternoon. Was it entirely because of the woman at his side, that she at long last seemed open to him, and perhaps even to his God? He had never ceased praying for her, although at times he had wondered if she would ever surrender. If all the trials and hardships she had encountered hadn't turned her heart toward God, what would it take?

In Deborah's case, it seemed her troubles had turned her *from* God instead of toward Him. Killion had puzzled over this, and though it wasn't uncommon, he found himself often beseeching God about just how to minister to such a person. Once, while in prayer, the scripture in 1 Kings had come to his mind: *And, behold, the Lord passed by, and a great and strong wind rent the mountains, and brake in pieces the rocks before the Lord; but the Lord was not in the wind: and after the wind an earthquake; but the Lord was not in the earthquake: and after the earthquake a fire; but the Lord was not in the fire: and after the fire a still small voice. And it was so, when Elijah heard it, that he wrapped his face in his mantle, and went out.*

All the big, dangerous things weren't getting Deborah's attention. For her, perhaps it must be on the scale of that "still small voice." And perhaps it would, after all, be better that way, for Killion was always uncomfortable with the convert who did so under the stress of adverse circumstances. He preached his share of "hellfire and damnation" sermons—most of his listeners would have been downright disappointed if he didn't—and he earnestly believed in the ultimate penalty for sin; but he always stressed that above all, God drew His people in love, not fear. That's how he hoped Deborah would come to her God, through a deep stirring of love in her heart and a yearning after the true Lover of her soul.

He gazed covertly at her for a brief moment—still in her buckskin, still with her pale hair, grown somewhat longer since the death of her husband, and braided and wrapped Indian style . . . still lovely. Yet all the pain of her past was etched deeper into her countenance than the scars of mourning on her forearms. It was in the hollow, lost aspect of her eyes. But he sensed intuitively that her pain had not yet reached the point of complete despair. Though she might have experienced occasional moments of despair, he was certain he saw an unquenchable hope within her. Or was it simply wishful thinking on his part?

"So, Mrs. Graham, you're concerned about Gray Antelope?" he asked casually enough to mask his anxious anticipation of this opportunity he felt God had provided.

"I don't know if that is exactly how I would have put it, Mr. Killion. Of course, I am concerned about her well-being, now that we are separated. But my purpose in approaching you was due more to my curiosity."

"Curiosity?"

"She had begun to act somewhat . . . peculiarly after the Sunday meeting we attended. She went up after the service to speak with you, and though I know that what transpired there is none of my business, I cannot help but wonder if her later actions had something to do with that incident."

"She never spoke to you about what happened?"

"No, not really. But I never asked her."

"Really? Weren't you close friends?"

She stopped abruptly in their casual stroll and turned sharply to face him. One look into her stormy eyes told Killion he had spoken amiss.

"No, I didn't ask," she retorted. "It was none of my business! I don't make a habit of interfering into other people's lives."

Killion made no response, his expression of benevolent concern did not alter. He had dealt with people enough to know when anger was directed inwardly and not at him personally. Deborah was struggling with herself, and that was good, but Killion felt a sympathetic distress for her nonetheless.

Deborah began walking again, and Killion strode quietly at her side. She could have walked off and left him at any moment. She could have asked him to leave her. But she said nothing about his continued presence. They walked for several minutes thus, Killion praying silently, Deborah staring straight ahead, the stony stillness of her face a poor mask for all the turmoil of emotions swirling about in her head. When she at last did speak, her features had begun to soften, and a smile even tried to infiltrate her earnestness.

"Thank you, Mr. Killion, for your patience with me," she said. "I don't know why I was suddenly so touchy."

He smiled in return, a broad, easygoing smile. He knew exactly why she had behaved so, but he showed the good sense to keep this insight to himself. "No harm done, Mrs. Graham. I've met folks touchier than that. Why, just a couple of months ago a fellow in Wichita even challenged me to a gunfight after one of my services."

"Really?"

"He said he'd become a believer if I was faster than him. Well, I told him I knew some about shooting and for his sake he oughta make his peace with God *before* the gunfight. Someone in the crowd shouted I was Killion the Texas Ranger, and that fellow dropped right then and there on his knees and accepted Christ as his Savior. But when he was done, he said he was still ready to fight me."

"After all that, he still wanted to fight?" said Deborah, incredulous.

"That's sort of the code of the West, ma'am. He called me out, and he felt honor-bound to give me satisfaction. Well, I looked at him and said, 'I forgot to mention one thing. I don't draw my gun on human beings anymore.' He seemed relieved to hear this. I said, 'If you want to change your mind about your conversion, I'll understand.' He shook his head and said, 'I reckon if this here Jesus Christ is good enough for a Texas Ranger, he's good enough for me!'"

"You must have many interesting experiences in your profession," said Deborah, relaxing.

"Indeed I do."

"How many Indian converts have you had?"

"Gray Antelope Woman was my very first one."

"Would it be a breach of confidentiality for you to tell me what happened to her? Or, perhaps I should tell you what I observed. I could tell you about the great peace I saw in her those days after Sunday. And her serenity in spite of the fact that her world was obviously crumbling around her. She'd found something to sustain her, and she found it at your meeting. You know, she was a medicine man's wife, deeply steeped in the spiritual traditions of the tribe. Thus, I find it incredible to think that she actually found Christianity."

"She didn't find Christianity, Mrs. Graham," Killion replied matter-of-factly. "Not in the sense that you mean it. She didn't find a religion.

She found a *Person*. She told me that she thought that in these difficult times her people could use what I spoke about. I told her, I knew they could, but that Jesus Christ didn't usually save nations; rather, He saved individuals like her. I explained that it was like each member of the tribe having his own personal Sun Dance, only in this case it was more like a Son Dance—the Son of God renewing each of His people. She said this was a dance she wished to join. I spoke with her on several occasions after this to make sure she had it all straight, and she really seemed to. That is one intelligent lady!"

"Yes, I have never known one wiser."

"Wise enough to know a good thing when she sees it."

"Would that I were so wise," mused Deborah half to herself.

"You saw it in Gray Antelope, Mrs. Graham; that's half the journey."

"I've seen it also in my father, and in you, Mr. Killion. And I have admired it, yet at the same time, I must frankly admit that it has frightened me also, especially lately."

" 'It is a fearful thing to fall into the hands of the Living God.' "

"Exactly!"

"What scares you most?"

Deborah could have given him the answer in a single word without even pausing to consider. She could have said, "I fear surrender, giving up control, remaining helpless." But Sam Killion was a man. How could he possibly understand a woman who yearned for her independence? And, in order to make her case, she would have to talk about the last five years, especially the horrible time with Leonard Stoner. Not only was it all too painful to recount, it was too personal, too intimate, especially to tell a man. She hadn't even been able to tell Broken Wing; and Killion, a nice enough man, was practically a stranger.

So, she buried this essential, fundamental fear deeper in her heart, and instead verbalized another, albeit valid, concern.

"How can I truly trust God, Mr. Killion?" she said. "How can I place myself in His hands when it seems He has brought so much difficulty to my life? Just when I think I might be able to, another crisis occurs. You talk about God loving and caring for people, but I wonder. Or, maybe it is just me He despises."

"I'm sure it ain't that, Mrs. Graham." Killion scratched his red beard thoughtfully. "You know, it always amazes me how quick we are to blame God for all the bad things that happen. From hurricanes to heartburn, He seems to be the ready scapegoat. Maybe folks think that because He is all-powerful, and can do anything, that if He doesn't stop the bad things, then that makes Him to blame for 'em. Just because He doesn't *prevent* hardships, it doesn't mean He *causes* them. Supposing He did prevent all disasters from happening? What would life be like then? Could we grow and learn; would we ever learn compassion or patience? It seems to me God has His reasons for not stepping in. If He did, we'd be like some china doll in a child's playhouse. We'd be empty and hollow, helpless, useless almost. God don't want no playthings; He wants real people who can think for themselves and make choices."

Killion paused briefly, and when he continued, his eyes were glinting with enthusiasm. "But I'll tell you what really bothers me about blaming God for the bad things—" but he stopped abruptly with an apologetic grin when he realized he was starting to preach. "I'm sorry, ma'am. I guess this is one of my pet peeves. I didn't mean to light into you."

"Don't stop now, Mr. Killion. If you have an answer to this, I want to hear it," encouraged Deborah.

"I don't know if it's an answer. It's more like an insight, and it's just that we seldom think to 'blame' any of the good things on God. The flood that wiped out the farm is God's fault, but the sunshine that brought the bumper crop of wheat . . . it just was. Mrs. Graham, you feel hurt and even betrayed by the awful things that have happened to you—and you've had a heap of them, I won't deny. I don't know why your brother was killed, or why things didn't go better for you in Texas, or why Broken Wing had to die. I just don't know! But try to look at it from a different angle. You could have been hanged in Texas, but Griff McCulloch came out of nowhere and rescued you. You could have died out there on the prairie when you got separated from him; you could have been found by a rattlesnake, but instead, it was Broken Wing who found you. And with him you knew real happiness, didn't you? Did God give you that time of happiness, or did He take it away? I guess that's what it boils down to—what kind of God is He? I can tell you what I believe, what I know in my heart, but it won't mean nothing to you until you figure it out for yourself."

"How do I do that?"

"Ask *Him,* Deborah!"

She smiled slightly at his use of her given name. It was obvious from the earnest tenderness, the true concern in his countenance, that they had suddenly progressed leagues in their budding friendship. He was no longer a preacher trying to win a convert, but rather he was a friend who was willing to open his heart and soul to her.

"Sam, is it really that simple?"

He smiled, too. He liked hearing his name from her lips. He said,

"If you really want to know, then it's simple."
"I want to know."

SAM DIDN'T PRAY WITH DEBORAH. He sensed this was something she would have to do alone. He also sensed that there was more to her reluctance in accepting God, but he hoped that as she sincerely confronted God and as He revealed His true nature to her, her other inhibitions would melt away.

Deborah went to the post livery stable where Lt. Godfrey had generously granted her permission to board the gray stallion. She had no saddle for the animal, its Indian saddle having been lost at Washita, and the gray did not take well to the army saddles. But Deborah was proficient enough to ride bareback. The Indian bridle that Broken Wing had made and that the gray had worn since Deborah had won him from the Pawnee brave was all the apparatus she needed. She led him from the stable, mounted under the afternoon sun, and rode to the fort gates where the sergeant in charge appeared most reluctant to let her leave the fort unattended.

"There's still hostiles out there, ma'am."

"I will not be going far. And, besides, I am armed." She patted the bow and quiver of arrows slung at her back, which she had traded for from an Arapahoe at the store.

"You know how to use 'em?"

"I can manage."

He raised an eyebrow, gave her another intense glance and, sensing no reason to disbelieve her, gave the order to open the gate.

Deborah rode about a mile from the fort, confident that from this distance the gray could outrun any adversary who tried to molest her. There were plenty of grassy knolls, now dotted with colorful wild flowers, where she could have dismounted and basked in the warmth of the sun, but she felt far too relaxed and content on the back of the gray to desire to stop even for the inviting surroundings.

Besides, she had always been able to think better, with a clearer head, on the back of a horse. Maybe that was half her problem; she had ridden too seldom since leaving Virginia.

No, there was much more to it than that; she could not deny it. From the beginning, when her brother was killed, she had challenged God, dared Him to prove himself worthy of her faith. She had chosen to be His adversary. Probably because of her background, her father's faith, and her religious upbringing, she could not simply ignore the spiritual realm altogether. She could not deny God's existence without, in essence, declaring her father a fool. But in her pain, grief, and even anger, at her brother's death, she could not placidly say it was God's will and leave it at that. Her emotional upheaval demanded a target.

It had seemed so natural at the time to blame God, yet would she have done so had she been acquainted with His true nature? If she had really *known* God? That's what Sam had tried to tell her once when he pointed out how she had depended on her father's faith to carry her along, never getting to know God personally. How many times had she heard her father talk of God's love, His tender mercy, His caring nature, yet she had not once asked God to show these things to her. Could it possibly be so easy?

"Ask Him, Deborah!" Sam had said.

But how could she be sure He'd hear her? Sam, of course, would say God hears everything. So would her father. But Deborah no longer wanted to take another's advice on this matter. She had to know for herself, and there truly was only one way to do that.

Ask.

If He wasn't listening, if He wasn't even there, then she'd know. But if He was...! If there really was a God out there with the kind of character extolled by men like Josiah Martin and Sam Killion, then she'd be a fool to ignore Him. She didn't care so much about having all her troubles erased; she knew they were just a part of life. What drew her longing heart most was the peace of mind and spirit she had observed in her father, in Sam, but especially in Gray Antelope. The transformation in the Cheyenne squaw had been simply too compelling to ignore. Something had given Gray Antelope the strength not only to go on but also to do so with hope, even though the future before her was at best uncertain ... at worst, bleak. If this something was a relationship with the Jesus Christ preached by Sam Killion, then she could not rest until she found out all she could about Him.

As Deborah guided the gray stallion down a steep gorge and

splashed across a little stream, a tributary of the Arkansas, she thought of that new strength she had noted in her Cheyenne friend. Strength and independence was the goal Deborah had been seeking all along. Her complete helplessness in the face of Leonard's abuse had scarred her deeply, had made her a woman almost obsessed with grasping control of her life. Since escaping his tyranny, she had continued to find herself helpless and at the mercy of others. That had been the case even during her time with the Cheyenne. She loved Broken Wing and cherished her life with him; she would have been content to spend her whole life with him, but as soon as he was taken from her, she was helpless again. And now she was dependent on old Hardee Smith.

Was it possible that she was looking for strength in the wrong places? Could it be that with a relationship with Christ she could have been strong even in the terrible presence of her first husband? Was Gray Antelope's example telling her that strength came not from independence but from inner peace?

Deborah gasped audibly at the novel idea. "Is that true?" she murmured into the wind. "Have I been so wrong?"

She rode on a little farther, her head spinning with this new insight.

She had heard the phrase *surrendering to God,* and it had always left a sour taste in her heart. But if surrendering meant peace, and peace meant strength—did *surrender,* then, mean strength?

Deborah smiled. This ride had been intended to answer her questions, not create new ones. But perhaps she was getting ahead of herself. Maybe all the other questions would fall into line if she returned to the original.

Who is God?

Is He a god of retribution or love, of troubles or peace, of neglect or caring?

Deborah knew she had no choice except to speak directly with God. The prospect frightened her, for if she received no answer, she must face the emptiness, the hopelessness of her life alone, and that would be much harder now that she had seen other possibilities.

She reined in the gray, stopping atop a low rise on the opposite side of the stream. From that vantage point she could see the sparkling shore of the Arkansas to the south, but the fort was farther west on the river, and several intervening hills blocked it from view. Looking all around at that height and seeing no other sign of civilization intensified her sense of solitude. There seemed no better time to find out if she were truly alone. She must speak—either to the wind or to a listening, caring God. Deborah hesitated, feeling awkward, even silly. She was alone. What did she expect to happen, anyway? Killion didn't say if he thought God would actually answer her question. That sort of thing only happened to biblical prophets, not an ordinary person, a woman to boot. She wished she had asked Sam if God spoke to him. She at least should have asked how to be sure if He was speaking or not. Deborah's father had sometimes spoken of a "still small voice."

If only I knew more! Deborah thought.

She took a determined breath. There was only one way to know. *Ask.*

"God," she said aloud, her voice hoarse and unsure, "I must know who you are. I see now I will never experience peace until I find out, though I am afraid I will never know peace at all if none of what I have heard from my friends is true. But I am willing to take the risk. I have nothing right now, no hope, no joy, no strength. If it's all a lie, I will be no worse off. . . . No! Now that I think of it, I will be worse off, for now I am only desperate; then I would be desolate. But I've come too far to worry about that. I must know the truth, even if it means accepting hopelessness.

"Show me!" Deborah cried into the wind.

And she was suddenly surprised to feel tears fall down her cheeks. She realized that with the simple utterance of those words, she had come to a turning point in her life. She would never be the same after this moment. No going back . . . for good or ill, she must face what lay ahead, her only comfort the knowledge that she had asked for it, demanded it. She could have continued as before, in ignorance, living with the occasional confusion and the constant emptiness in her heart. But she had chosen, fully cognizant of the risks, to step off the precipice.

Would someone—God, perhaps—catch her? Or, would she keep on falling for eternity?

Deborah closed her eyes and waited. The gray snorted and stomped his hoof, craving to be on the move. But Deborah had come too far to be so impatient. Yet little doubts, like pebbles cast against her resolve, assailed her. *How long should she wait? How would she know? How . . .*

Be still, and I will come.

It was no voice she heard, no audible words, yet the impression upon her mind of having been spoken to was no less real. And with that silent thought, *Be still, and I will come,* she felt assurance wash over her like a cool stream on a hot, sticky day. She recalled the hauntingly beautiful song Sam had sung at his Sunday service.

There is a fountain filled with blood drawn from Emmanuel's veins; and sinners, plunged beneath that flood, lose all their guilty stains. ...

Was this what it was like to stand beneath that fountain? Clean, yes, but refreshed also ... and renewed. For Deborah, the mere promise of fulfillment was almost as profound as the total experience. And for the present, it was enough to know that answers were there, that she need no longer hang suspended, or fall forever with none to care or save her.

I will come.

She needed no more profound revelation. The growing sense of peace in her heart told her that God had indeed spoken to her, and that He would continue to do so until her questions were answered and her confusion satisfied. There *were* still questions and there was still some confusion, but it no longer frightened her. She need not fear a desolate future. And if God cared enough to assure her of this, then she had confidence that this was the kind of God who was blameless. There might be pain and grief, but it was not from this God.

Deborah bent over and rubbed the gray's neck. "It's going to be okay, boy. I can't wait to tell Sam!"

She dug her heels into the animal's broad, strong flanks and the stallion eagerly wheeled into motion, leaping almost immediately into a full gallop.

56

SAM WAS IN THE SUTLER'S STORE, and Deborah, fairly glowing with the combined effects of her newfound assurance and the stimulating ride, burst upon him with a rather uncharacteristically effusive greeting.

"Sam, I'm so glad you are here. You won't believe what a time I've had—"

But she stopped suddenly when she saw he wasn't alone. Three men were lounging around a table, half-filled glasses in front of each man and a bottle of whiskey in the middle of the table. Sam had been standing nearby with a foot propped up on a vacant chair conversing with the men. This, however, was not what brought her excited speech to such an abrupt end. She knew those men, though she had long ago given them up for dead.

"Griff McCulloch!" she exclaimed. "Slim! Longjim! I can't believe you are alive!"

Sam had somewhat prepared Griff for Deborah, but no words could have fully primed him for what his eyes now beheld. This woman *looked* like the girl he had rescued from the gallows four years ago, but he saw now that the pretty, taciturn, sorrowful girl had been a mere shadow of what had flowered over the years. If she had been lovely then, she was beautiful now in a way that only depth of experience could produce. What he didn't realize was that much of that glowing beauty had lighted her countenance only in the last couple hours. Nevertheless, his mouth went dry, and as he stood with Slim and Longjim to welcome her, he felt wooden and awkward. He was suddenly painfully aware of the days of traveling dust clinging to his clothes, and the several days' growth of beard on his face. But he held out a hand to her and managed a grin, though he felt he must look completely repugnant to this exquisite frontier woman.

"Howdy, ma'am," Griff said, and his companions added similar greetings. Griff continued, "I reckon I'm as alive as I'll ever be. And I'm glad to see the same of you. I've hated myself for years 'cause I couldn't get back to you that day."

"Everything worked out for the best, Griff," Deborah answered with a depth of sincerity that made Sam take a closer look at her. She'd left a couple hours ago confused and fearful, but she definitely looked different now. Sam was suddenly anxious to talk with her. He knew something wonderful had happened out there on the prairie, but the arrival of McCulloch was going to delay a private conversation.

Deborah spoke again. "I have so many questions. Let me check on the children and then we can talk."

Carolyn and Sky, as everyone had come to call Blue Sky, were happily occupied "helping" Hardee stock the shelves with some new merchandise. The minute Sky saw his mother, he lost interest and wanted to be held. But Carolyn only gave her mother a nod, returning immediately to the absorbing task. Deborah scooped Sky up in her arms, took a biscuit from one of the cracker barrels for him to nibble on, and returned to the unexpected reunion in the Sutler's store.

As Deborah approached the table, she took a closer look at the three outlaws. They had changed little over the years. Griff, beneath all the dust, was still the rugged man of authority, with a humorous glint in his steely eyes. Longjim had a few strands of gray in his black hair and beard, but his compact, muscular figure gave no less the impression of the tough frontiersman. Slim's long, angular face had a few more wrinkles, but he had not added an ounce to his lean, lanky frame.

"Them's fine-looking kids," said Slim, reaching out a finger to tweak Sky's chubby cheek. "Seem's like a coon's age since I been around young'uns. Mind if I hold him a spell, ma'am?"

Deborah looked at Sky. "Would you like to sit with Nahkoa's friend?" she asked in Cheyenne. The boy, not yet two, gave the stranger a suspicious glance and clung tighter to Deborah.

"He's a bit shy of strangers," Deborah apologized.

"Oh, I understand," said Slim. "My young'uns were like that, too." At this Griff and Longjim swung their heads around with surprised stares at their partner. Slim muttered in response, "Well, you don't know everything!"

Deborah smiled. "I'm sure he will warm up to you."

And so Slim spent the remainder of the conversation entertaining Sky; making comical faces at him, wiggling his large ears or twisting his lips, rolling a ball back and forth across the table or playing "peek-a-boo." Thus, the interchange between the others was punctuated at increasing intervals with giggles from Sky and coarse laughter from the outlaw. Deborah recalled when she had held a gun on Slim while Sam tied him up. She was glad he seemed to hold no grudges.

"Aside from all my other surprises today, Griff," said Deborah, "I am surprised to see you come into the fort so boldly."

"We been laying low for a spell, ma'am—"

Deborah interrupted, "Why don't you fellows just call me Deborah. I feel like we're old friends."

"Be proud to do so, ma'am—that is, Deborah," said Griff. "Well, anyway, with the war over and what with bein' gone for so long, the law don't seem much interested in a few 'has beens' like us."

"So, you've been staying out of trouble all these years?" asked Deborah.

"More or less."

" 'Cept for that time in California—" began Longjim.

"Nothin' no one does in California counts," cut in Griff. "Mostly we been drifting. Even spent a year scouting for Sheridan up north— imagine us Rebel reprobates actually working for Yankees. We're okay long as no one looks too closely, and believe me no one looks close out West, 'cause half the fellows here, including lawmen, would have to be hauled into jail if they did. We hightailed it to Mexico when we was scattered four years ago."

"I hope Sam explained that he had nothing to do with that unfortunate incident," Deborah quickly interjected.

"We knew that years ago," Griff replied. "Weren't the law at all that was chasin' us. See, when we were at the hideout we had been planning to hold up a Wells Fargo shipment. That's why we had to keep Killion out of the way. Well, when we got there we found it had already been robbed. We was pretty put out about that till we chanced upon them other robbers. They was so sure of themselves, they hadn't even set a lookout. Me and the boys lifted the loot from them and got away clean—"

"Or, so we thought," said Longjim.

"Yeah," concurred Griff. "Turns out they had a Crow Indian with 'em, and it was only a matter of time before they caught up with us. They dogged us all the way to the Staked Plains after the gunfight on the Cimarron. We hoped to slow 'em down with the miserable heat and lack of water; though, of course, it didn't do us no good either. I guess it was the Apaches that finally saved our necks."

"Apaches?" said Sam with a raised eyebrow. He had fought enough of that fierce tribe to know they seldom *saved* any enemy's neck, especially that of a white man.

"Durned near massacred us," said Griff. "But it was the other outlaw gang that took the brunt of it. By then it was just Slim and me and Tom Carver, since we had separated from the rest of the boys back there in Indian Territory. Well, the Apaches killed Tom, and the other gang held off the Indians while Slim and I got away—that wasn't their intention, of course, but that's how it worked out. I felt a mite bad getting away at their expense, but since it was them or us, I figured I made the right choice."

"They woulda killed you, anyway, if the Apaches didn't," added Longjim.

"And where were you during all this, Longjim?" asked Deborah.

"I lit out north at the Cimarron and ended up in California. It was there I met up with Griff and Slim 'bout a year later. I figured I was ready for the reformed life, too."

"Reformed?"

"Well," put in Slim, momentarily distracted from his play with Sky, "after that run-in with the Apaches, Griff and I decided to try going straight. Don't take too many close calls with the Apaches to get a man to rethinking his life."

" 'Rethinking,' you say?" said Sam, a glint in his eye.

"Whoa, Preacher!" said Slim, quickly regretting joining the conversation. "I didn't mean *that.*"

"Well, if a near Apache massacre ain't enough to bring a man to God, I don't know what will," said Sam.

"We're too far gone for that, Killion," said Griff, "so you may as well not waste your preaching on us."

"It's never a waste, McCulloch." But for the time being Sam contented himself with listening instead of participating.

And he was especially satisfied to remain quiet since the really interesting part of the conversation was about to unfold as Griff asked Deborah to tell her story. Sam had never heard all of Deborah's tale, and most of what he had heard had been delivered in bits and pieces, so he was eager to hear her now. But even if he had heard it many times, he would not have missed this rare opportunity to listen to her speak at length in her quiet, intense voice. Nor would he have missed studying the various moods and expressions on her lovely face.

And, from that perspective, her discourse was much too short. She recounted facts—names, places, dates—with little or no emphasis on feelings and emotions. She summed up all the pain and heartache of the death of Broken Wing with the simple words, "My Cheyenne husband died last fall shortly before the Washita massacre."

But even Griff, not the most sensitive of men, could see from the tautness of her eyes and mouth that she had suffered much with that loss.

He said, "I'm sorry to admit that we was fightin' Indians while you was one of 'em."

"It's a complicated situation," answered Deborah without ire.

"We were hopin' to get hooked up with Sheridan's scouts again, but they want to put us with the Seventh Cavalry."

"We don't fancy riding with Custer," said Longjim distastefully.

"He's one Yankee I still ain't able to stomach," said Griff.

"So, what are your plans?" asked Deborah, wondering even as she spoke what *hers* were. She remembered that she had just had a wonderful experience that she had not even had a chance to share with Sam. How would that affect her future?

Griff scratched his grimy, unshaven face. "First off, I'd give a pound of gold for a bath."

Deborah laughed. "I think that can be arranged much cheaper."

"Afterward..." Griff continued, "I don't know. There's always something. Riding shotgun for a stage, or a freight shipment, or sign-ing up with one of them cattle drives they been running since the war. And I hear the railroads are looking for guns, what with the Indian troubles—though I'd rather rob a train than try to protect it from Indians."

"I'm sure something suitable will turn up," said Deborah. "In the meantime . . . well, I'm afraid I can't offer you the same hospitality you once gave me, but—"

Hardee Smith had been half aware of the conversation on the other side of the room, but now his ears really perked up. Hoisting little Carolyn easily up on his thick shoulders, he ambled over to the table.

"You got guests, Deborah," he said, "and don't you turn 'em away on my account." He looked at the men. "Why, this here girl can have anything she wants 'cause I don't know what I'd do here without her."

Deborah smiled at her employer. "Thank you, Hardee. In that case, then, you fellows can at least stay for dinner. I owe you that much."

"You bet, ma'am," said Slim eagerly, obviously glad to have his blossoming friendship with Sky prolonged.

"You ain't gonna find three drifters like us ever turn down a home-cooked meal, Deborah," said Griff.

57

THREE DAYS PASSED BEFORE Deborah had a chance to talk with Sam. Griff, Slim, and Longjim, seemingly reformed outlaws, had a pleasant dinner with Deborah and Hardee and the children, but she saw little of them after that. They bunked with some of the scouts they knew and were away from the fort most of the time—on what business, Deborah never knew. She had been relieved on first seeing them to find they were still alive, especially Griff. But she was nevertheless glad they weren't planning to remain constantly at the fort. They reminded her too sharply of her past helplessness, and in spite of her recent experience with God, she still coveted her independence.

That, in fact, was one matter she wanted to discuss with Sam, though he had been busy over the last few days "ministering," as he called it, to some of the enclaves of settlers located around the fort.

Sam came into the store full of his usual exuberance, spirits not in the least dampened by the late spring rainstorm that had followed him into town.

"Whew! It's really coming down," Sam said as he shook off his hat and coat before hanging them on a hook near the door.

There were several customers milling around the store and others seated at the three tables, obviously, at that hour in the morning, more interested in getting in out of the rain than in Hardee's inferior whiskey. A warm fire blazed in the potbellied stove situated in the center of the store.

"Howdy, Preacher," said one of the men at a table. "You figure you can put a fix in with the Man Upstairs to get this here rain over with? Haven't been able to get a blessed thing done for two days."

"I'll see what I can do, Jasper," replied Sam, "but you'll be appreciating this weather come July when the sun is scorching your back and the dust is choking your throat."

"It's a long way till July."

"A perfect chance to learn patience!"

"I'm doing that, Preacher, but it ain't easy."

"Never is, Jasper." Sam turned his attention to his reason for coming to the store. "Anyone seen Hardee or Mrs. Graham?"

"I'm back here," called Hardee from behind a stack of tin goods he was trying to inventory.

Sam sidled over to the storekeeper. "Is Deborah around, Hardee?"

"In back with the young'uns. Sewin', I think."

"Be okay if I go back?"

"Sure. I reckon you can be trusted, Sam." Hardee gave the preacher a meaningful wink.

Sam shrugged and strode to the doorway leading to the back rooms, ducking under the low lintel to enter the cramped, musty quarters. As he approached the room that he guessed, from the sound of familiar voices, to be Deborah's, he pondered Hardee's comment and the fact that he could indeed be trusted with Deborah. He cared too much for her to risk their growing friendship by venturing into territory where his heart might want to lead him, but where common sense told him Deborah would not soon be able to tread. But Sam was willing to be content with the situation as it now stood. Though he was thirty-three years old, he had only recently begun to consider the possibilities of the more settled life of a family man. There had hardly been a place for a family in his past life of wandering and danger, and now, though the element of danger was somewhat reduced, he was still almost continually on the move. He had to admit he had always rather liked that life. Only lately, perhaps especially since Deborah had returned to his life, were his thoughts turning more and more to a home and a woman to love.

Sam raised his hand and knocked on the door, feeling a little hesitant and sheepish because of the direction of his thoughts, but also excited because he knew something special had happened to Deborah the other day and he had been anxious to talk to her about it.

"Come in," she said, and Sam obeyed, his hesitancy, as always, overruled by his ebullient, zealous nature.

"Hello, Deborah," he said. "I hope you don't mind me barging in on you."

"Not at all." She laid aside the shirt she was mending for Sky. "Only I don't even have a chair to offer you." Deborah herself was seated on the bed, a straw mattress laid on the floor and covered with hides. It was far more luxurious than anything she'd had with the Cheyenne, but it was hardly suitable for entertaining guests. A highboy chest was the only other furnishing in the room. Sky was on the bed with Deborah, playing with some tin cups Hardee had provided for that very purpose. Carolyn was seated on a braid rug on the floor playing with a hide Indian doll—not her favorite doll, which had been lost at Washita, but another one Hardee had obtained in trade from a Pawnee.

Sam looked around at the Spartan surroundings. He tried not to feel sorry for Deborah because he knew that would be the last thing she'd want from others. Yet he wondered if God might have a better life in His plan for her. Or, perhaps, He would teach her contentment no matter what her surroundings. That was the best way, but he hoped for something better for her also.

He smiled cheerfully. "If it's all right with you, I'll just pull up a rug and sit on the floor."

Sam hunkered down on another rug, larger than Carolyn's and arranged adjacent to the bed. Carolyn glanced up at him and smiled as if she were glad to see a man sit in what was to her a normal fashion, as the Indians did, and not in those hard and uncomfortable chairs.

"The kids are looking real good, Deborah," said Sam. "You can be proud of them."

"I am. They're all I have, but they make me feel rich. I read this morning that children are a heritage from the Lord and His reward. Sky and Carolyn give me no reason to think otherwise."

"You read. . . ?"

"Yes, Sam. I have been reading the Bible. Hardee had three of them stashed away in a corner of the store." She paused and, reaching beneath the folds of the covers on the bed, produced a brand new volume, bound in black cloth boards. "My father used to read to me often from the Psalms, though I recall that his favorite book was the gospel of John. So, that's where I have begun; since I last saw you, I have read both books."

"Great!" Sam replied enthusiastically, then paused before adding, "So, what happened to you the day you took that ride?"

"It was wonderful, Sam!"

"I could tell."

"Really?"

"Oh yes. The minute you walked in that day, I saw a difference in you. You can't imagine how frustrated I was not to be able to talk to you right then."

"I was also, but perhaps it was for the best. It gave me a chance to read this Bible on my own and find out that God does want to show me who He is. I suppose nothing really dramatic happened. It was more of a quiet assurance that I was heading in the right direction.

"I'll tell you what's truly exciting!" Deborah smiled, and Sam could not remember when he had seen one of her smiles invade her eyes so charmingly. "My father often read the Bible to my brother and me. I've heard it many times, though usually I listened out of politeness and respect for my father. Since yesterday, though, it's been entirely different. I am seeing it all in a completely new light. I can hardly put it down! The Twenty-third Psalm, for example. How many times did my father read that to me! I even memorized it once in Sunday school. But I never truly *read* it until yesterday. 'The Lord is my shepherd, I shall not want . . . Yea, though I walk through the valley of the shadow of death—' " Deborah stopped suddenly as unexpected emotion choked her throat. "Forgive me, Sam," she said, almost apologetically as she dabbed her moist eyes. "Every time I think of it, I become emotional. For so many years I was in that valley, and He was there all along, but I refused to let His rod and staff comfort me. Have you ever known anyone so dense and foolish?"

Sam grinned, though his own eyes were filling with tears as well. "Nope," he said teasingly, "except for this here dense and foolish fellow sitting in front of you!"

They chuckled together over this, then Deborah said in a more solemn tone, "Sam, I really do believe all these things, and I know my heart has been changed in a way I will never forget. I don't mean to be stubborn, though some have said I am too much so for my own good, but I still have many questions. One in particular troubles me."

"Everyone has questions, Deborah, even itinerant preachers. But at least when you've got the peace of God in your heart, you can rest assured that God will either answer those questions or make you content without the answers."

"I see that now, but . . ." Deborah looked down into her lap as if that were the only way she could find courage to express what lay most heavily upon her mind. "Sam, I don't want to be helpless any-more; I don't want to depend on anyone again. I am afraid I will not be able to give up everything to God. I know it sounds silly, especially as I learn what a loving God He is; yet I can't help myself. Surely you must understand, Sam. Wasn't it hard to give up who you were when you became a Christian? All the freedom and adventure of being a Ranger, all the skills you knew. I've heard the saying about Texas Rangers, that they 'ride like a Mexican, shoot like a Tennessean, trail like an Indian, and—' " Deborah stopped short and blushed slightly as she suddenly recalled the last part of the old ditty.

" 'And fight like the devil,' " Sam finished for her. "I've heard that, too, and I guess I used to be proud of it."

"Didn't it bother you giving all that up?"

"Bother me . . . ?" Sam chewed his moustache thoughtfully. "Deb-orah, why don't I explain to you what I gave up, and then maybe you can answer your own question. But it might take a while."

"I'd like to hear, Sam. I've got time. The children seem to be content." Sky had crawled into Deborah's lap and was sucking his thumb, half asleep. Carolyn was rocking her own "baby" to sleep, but seemed also tuned in to the grown-ups' conversation.

"Like I said, Deborah, I was proud of the Rangers' reputation," Sam began. "In fact, all my life I didn't want to be nothing else but a Ranger. My uncle was a Ranger, among the first recruited right after Texas got its independence from Mexico. Since he practically raised me, I suppose I wanted to be just like him. I refused to learn from his mistakes or see the struggles within his own heart about his rangering days. All I saw was the glory and the chance to avenge my father's death. I made my uncle teach me everything he knew—and he did, 'cause I guess he figured I was going to learn it anyway, and he wanted to be sure I learned right. When he taught me all he could, I asked anyone I could find to teach me to be better. By the time I was thirteen, I could handle myself pretty well and I was off fighting Indians—Apache and Comanche, mostly. I joined the Rangers when I was fourteen, lying about my age to get in. I'll risk sounding boastful to make my point, but I was as good with a gun as Rangers twice my age. All I wanted to do was fight. I was partial to fighting Mexicans because of what happened to my pa at the Alamo. But I had so much hate in me that I wasn't too choosy. I'd fight Indians or white outlaws, too, if they was around. The other Rangers jokingly made sport of the name Killion by changing it to killer. 'Killer Sam' they'd call me. And, believe it or not, I took it as a compliment.

"Well, just before the war between the states, me and three other Rangers were down in the Pecos area tracking a bunch of Mexican rustlers. They'd been wreaking havoc among all the ranches from the Rio Grande to the Pecos, and we were determined to get them. The four of us decided to split up into pairs in order to cover more ground. My partner, Doug, and I caught up with the banditos' trail and the next day sighted them. There were half a dozen of 'em, all heavily armed, and they were herding some recently rustled cattle. We followed them all day, 'cause there wasn't enough cover to mount a successful attack on them. By sunset they led us right to their hide-out, an abandoned ranch house nestled in between some scrub-covered hills. We wouldn't have minded being outnumbered if there had been some decent cover around. But as it was, we decided to go for reinforcements instead of risking the odds. Doug went and I stayed to keep an eye on the desperados.

"I didn't do a very good job of it, 'cause toward morning I dozed off to sleep. When I opened my eyes again I was looking up the barrel of a shotgun. They dragged me down to the barn, tied me up, and threw me in. I could hear 'em outside debating about what to do with me, and I speak Spanish well enough to know the majority wanted to kill me right off. They figured to make some sport of me first, though, 'cause they didn't often get a chance to kill a Texas Ranger. I remember how filled with hate I was, daring them to untie me and let me defend myself properly. I cursed them and called them cowards, lumping their present cowardice with what they did at the Alamo, even though most of them had only been babies in '36, if they had been born at all.

"They hauled me outside, and I realized I was a dead man and didn't have nothing to lose by making a bold escape attempt. I waited till they were distracted in arguing who'd have the first crack at me; then I dove at the one I estimated as the easiest mark. I knocked him down and grabbed his six-gun in my tied-up hands; then I rolled back into the barn under a heavy barrage of gunfire. I got off one shot on my way to the barn and killed one bandit. That left five.

"Inside the barn, I locked the door and discovered I had taken a fully loaded gun and had five shots left. Next, I got the rope off my hands with an axe blade I found. By then, the banditos had the barn surrounded. If they had been smart they would have hightailed it out of there right then, but they were so mad I got the better of 'em there was no way they was gonna leave without killing me first. They were firing like crazy, but I knew I couldn't waste a single shot. Though I figured I'd never make it out of there alive, I thought at least I could lower the odds for when the other Rangers arrived. Every time I fired my gun I thought of my pa so hopelessly outnumbered, and Santa Anna vowing to take no prisoners—a vow, I might add, that would later become one of the Texas Rangers' own mottos. Maybe it was my hatred that made my bullets fly so true—my own private vengeance, I guess, for the Alamo. When I walked out of the barn, I couldn't believe what I'd done. Four of them was dead. One was gut shot and would die pretty quick. The sixth one was shot in the leg, and when I cautiously eased my way out of the barn he fired at me and missed; then he slipped down into a gully and knocked himself unconscious on a rock. We hanged him later.

"I should've felt relief that I had escaped alive, but as I stood there among all those bodies, I was suddenly sick—really physically sick, and also sick in my heart. That wasn't the first time I'd killed anyone, and it wasn't the sight of death that bothered me. But in that moment, I'm sure God opened my eyes. He made me see with such awful clarity what I was capable of. It scared me that anyone should be that good with a gun and be considered a 'peace' officer and a hero. And believe me, all of my comrades did indeed cheer me as a hero, as did all the local ranchers. Back in Laredo, they gave me a commendation. But despite the glory, God always kept that sight of them dead bodies, killed by my own hand, before me. I was kept awake for weeks with nightmares of it. My hand trembled every time I picked up my gun. Finally, my captain saw I was a wreck, though he didn't know why, and he sent me home on leave.

"Everything kind of broke when I walked up to my house and my ma opened the door for me. Seeing her, the godliest woman I know, just did me in. I ran up to her, fell on my knees and wept. All I could say was, 'Ma, I'm a killer!' " Sam paused in his recounting of his experience as the remembered emotion caught hold of him again. Tears welled up in his eyes, but he dashed them away and looked steadily at Deborah.

"Tell me, Deborah," he said finally, his tone husky and taut, "what did I give up? Sometimes I still have nightmares about that day and about all the men I killed in the name of justice. At least now when I wake up I can give it all to Jesus and He makes me clean all over again. I shudder at what would have become of me if I had been able to shrug off that experience and continue on my same path. I believe I would have become a truly cold-blooded killer. As it says in the Scriptures, 'What is a man profited, if he shall gain the whole world and lose his own soul?' I think that's where I was headed, Deborah. But I guess I ain't giving you a chance to say what you think."

Deborah sighed. "When you talk about it, Sam, it sounds so plain and simple. And as I learn about God I see it can't possibly be any other way. He offers so much, He gives so much . . . what He asks in return seems so small by comparison."

"It wouldn't be fair if I misrepresented things here, Deborah. God asks us to surrender *everything* to Him. In the epistle to the Romans it says that we should present our bodies as a 'living sacrifice' to God."

Deborah raised an eyebrow and half her mouth curved up into an ironic smile. "You are not going to make this easy for me, are you, Sam?"

"Somehow, I don't take you for the kind of person who wants the easy, superficial road. I think you'd rather have the whole truth even if it hurts you a little."

"You are right, I suppose."

"Then the truth is, Deborah, that God isn't satisfied with just a corner of your heart, or even half of it. He wants it all. Complete and total surrender, and absolute control over your life. It's hard for me to say this because I know after all you've been through, you are afraid to trust that much to another. But it's better to know this now than later."

"Absolute control . . ." It was difficult, almost impossible, for Deborah to force out the words. It was the last thing she wanted to hear. She had spent the last few days learning to know a God of love, a God of mercy, a Comforter. That was the God she could easily accept. But a Controller? Wasn't that what she had escaped when she fled Texas four years ago? The interim years with Broken Wing had begun to show her life could be different, that love and freedom were not always mutually exclusive. Could she now risk being thrust backward into a situation, the very thought of which sickened her?

Sam seemed to understand her hesitation, and when he spoke again it was with gentle entreaty. "Deborah, God does want complete control, but at the same time He doesn't expect you to be a helpless weakling. Surely you have noticed in the Psalms the many references to strength—how He gives strength to His people. He wants us strong! But He is the only source of true strength. You spoke of independence, Deborah. Well, the book of John says the truth will make us free! I guess that's the paradox of Christianity: strength through being made weak before Christ; freedom through surrender. And it only makes sense when you know, truly know, the God who makes such requirements of us."

"The kind of God who leads us beside still waters . . ." mused Deborah.

Sam nodded, but suddenly he couldn't speak as a well of emotion rose in his heart at the thought of this God whom he loved and to whom he had committed his life.

"I am beginning to understand now, Sam," said Deborah.

Deborah was not finished with her struggle with these truths, but she was able to see clearly that it was a path worth following. And that day she chose to do so regardless of the risks. Once God had begun revealing His true nature to her, she could do nothing else.

God was no Leonard Stoner, whose purpose was to grind her down for the sheer sake of exercising his own power. God's demands had only the result of growth and joy and contentment. Deborah understood now what had happened to Gray Antelope. And she understood that in giving everything to God, she would receive everything in return.

58

THAT SUMMER TWO BITS OF good news came to Deborah's ears and greatly heartened her as to the future of her Cheyenne people. In June, after the Indians began to show their good intentions by surrendering in greater numbers, Sheridan released the Washita prisoners. As the women and children rejoined their bands and began to migrate south to the reservation, Deborah was overjoyed to receive a visit from her dear friend, Gray Antelope. They had a wonderful day of sharing their new faith with each other as they had never done before. Deborah verbally translated some of her favorite scriptures into Cheyenne for her friend, who was thrilled to hear these things in her own tongue. It was a sad but hopeful parting, each at last assured they had chosen the right path.

Gray Antelope also brought greetings from Stone Teeth Woman who, upon release from Fort Hays, had been secretly met by her husband. Stands-in-the-River had joined the Dog Soldiers and had only been waiting for the release of his family before accompanying the other renegades in continuing to wage war against the whites. Deborah was not surprised to hear this, and though she wanted all the fighting to end, she held a secret hope that this last stand of the Southern Cheyenne might not be entirely in vain. Perhaps through it, they might somehow win a fairer settlement from the government.

The next positive news came from Washington a few weeks later. President Grant signed a bill that made the "Society of Friends" the official overseers of the southern Plains Indians. Deborah knew something of these Quakers and their fine Christian principles and hoped that at last the Indians would be cared for with compassion and justice.

But the summer drew to a close on a note of tragedy with the Battle of Summit Springs, the culmination of a campaign designed to halt the flight of the Dog Soldiers north. The great Dog Soldier chief, Tall Bull, was killed; and though some Cheyenne managed to escape, the battle did effectively end the Cheyenne occupation of the region between the Platte and the Arkansas Rivers. Stands-in-the-River and his family apparently survived the battle and took up residence with other renegade bands, but Deborah would not hear from them again for many years.

Besides the far-reaching political changes touching Deborah's world, a change of a more personal nature was about to enter her life. It appeared in the person of a Tennessee migrant named Calvin Farley who, one scorching hot day in late August, bounded noisily into the Sutler's store.

"I've had it!" he declared to any who cared to listen. "Heat and wind, a belly full of dust, Comanche raids, the stink of them cursed—"

"Whoa, feller!" interjected Hardee quickly. "Watch your tongue; we got a lady present."

Farley swung his head around till he spotted Deborah talking with a pair of Arapahoe traders. "Pardon me, ma'am," he said, tipping his grimy, sweat-soaked hat toward her. "But if you knew what I been through lately, maybe you'd forgive a couple slips of the tongue."

"We can be very forgiving here," Deborah replied with a smile. Then, turning to Hardee, she added, "Hardee, this man looks as if he can use a cold drink."

"Beer, if'n it's all the same to you," said Farley with an appreciative grin toward Deborah.

Deborah shrugged noncommittally, deeming this an inappropriate time to harangue the poor man about the evils of liquor.

Farley gulped down half the glass with relish before speaking again. "Oh, ma'am, that's the best thing that's happened to me all week!"

"It must have been a pretty bad week, then," offered Deborah, sensing the man wanted to spill out his woes.

"Been driving my herd north—"

"You're a mite off'n the track for that, ain't you?" asked one of the other customers milling about the store. "It's Abilene you oughta to be heading for."

"I know that," said Farley, "and that's where I was, and where my cattle still are, and no doubt losing money for me with every passing day. My wife is the one that got herself mixed up. She sent me a letter here, which I didn't find out about till I got to Abilene and an army fella said there was a letter for me at Fort Dodge. It was just a coincidence he bumped into me a'tall. Of course, he didn't have the letter with him, and I had to ride all the way here to get it. But my spell of bad luck began long afore that. I lost half my herd on the way to

Abilene in a stampede when some cursed redskins spooked 'em with their yelling and carrying on. But before that, before I even left my place in Texas, we was raided by Comanche and lost more'n fifty head of cattle. At top dollar, that's twenty-five hundred dollars! I was willing to take my losses and plug away 'cause there's money to be made in cattle. Even when one calamity and another held us up on the trail and we got to Abilene behind the other drives, and found out we'd missed getting top dollar, I still wasn't inclined to give it up."

"You mean you have now decided to give up?" asked Deborah.

"I ain't no quitter, ma'am, but a man can take only so much. The letter in Dodge finally decided me."

"From your wife?"

"That's right. But if I don't do something quick, she ain't gonna be my wife for long. She's done left our place in Texas and gone back to Tennessee. Said she couldn't take another minute of that—and these is her words, ma'am—'living hell.' Seems the Comanche attacked again. Killed two of our hands and mighta got her and the young'uns 'cepting there was a couple of ex-Rangers living in the area that came and scared off the Injuns. Well, while the Rangers were still there, she packed up and had them escort her to Fort Richardson, where she wrote me this here letter—" He paused and waved a crumpled sheet in the air. "Then she joined an army convoy to Fort Worth, and then home."

"I'm sorry for you, Mr.—" Deborah paused, realizing she now knew nearly everything about this stranger but his name.

"Name's Calvin Farley, from Decaturville, Tennessee, and bound directly back there soon as I can unload the shackles of Texas from 'round my neck!"

"I suppose you are quite justified in doing so."

"Justified or not, I got me a pretty little wife and three fine young'uns to think of, and my wife said I got to choose between her and Texas. Well, it ain't no contest, far as I can see." Calvin Farley gave the room a quick survey, noting two soldiers, three or four settlers, two Indians besides the white woman dressed like an Indian, and a smelly, hairy mountain man. "I don't reckon anyone here is interested in a piece of land down Texas way?"

"You ain't givin' it much of a sales pitch," said one of the soldiers.

"Well, 'cepting for the Injuns, it's a right tolerable tract of land, purely for grazing, mind you. Can't grow nothin' on it. It's in the Brazos valley, near Fort Griffin."

"You got water?" asked one of the settlers.

317

"The Brazos runs right through it. I grazed me four hundred head of cattle on it. Bought most of them cows in Texas for four dollars a head. But I got me a goodly number of longhorns that was just wild, roaming free and all I had to do was round 'em up. Coulda had horses, too, if I'd a had a mind to round 'em up and herd 'em. Well, what with them cattle the Injuns stole and what we lost on the trail, I still brung three hundred head to Abilene. In dollars and cents, that's a profit of seventy-five hundred dollars."

Someone in the store gave a low whistle.

"For that kind of money, I'd get me another wife!" said the mountain man.

"I don't care if it was seventy-five thousand dollars!" said Farley emphatically. "I'm for Tennessee!"

"What'd you want for the land?" asked Hardee.

"I got me five thousand acres I bought for five cents an acre, but I'd let it go for four cents. You interested?"

"Naw, just curious."

"Well, if any of you are interested, I'm only stickin' around here for a few days. I can sell it just as well back East."

"Yeah," observed Hardee, "where they think Texas is the same as freedom and adventure and you can't convince 'em about the heat and the dust and the 'skeeters."

"And the Injuns!" added a settler who was relieved that the pesky Indians near his Kansas home had finally been subdued.

The lively conversation waned. Farley made a few purchases and left the store, while those who remained turned their attention to other topics. Only Deborah continued to ruminate over the preceding interchange. And her pondering thoughts jumped from the Tennessean's hardships directly to his statement about selling his land. It made her think of how she longed for a home of her own—not merely a roof over her head but her own place where she might earn a living for her children so they wouldn't always have to depend on others. She didn't think this conflicted with her commitment to God. Sam said God wanted her to be strong as long as she acknowledged exactly where that strength came from. She couldn't see anything wrong with wanting a home of her own. But it suddenly occurred to her that she ought to pray about it just the same.

Thus, that night, after the children were asleep beside her on the big straw mattress, Deborah closed her eyes and turned this desire over to God.

"Dear Lord, I want my own home. I want to be settled so my children will feel secure. I know you are our security, but I guess you have provided homes and such things for a reason. So, if it is your will for me, could you provide a way for this? I have no money, no possible way on my own, even if I wanted to buy Mr. Farley's land. It's only two hundred dollars, but I barely have ten dollars saved from what Hardee pays me.

"But, Lord, it doesn't have to be Mr. Farley's land, or even land at all, though how I would love a place where I could raise horses, with acres of pasture to ride them on!

"If you truly want me to spend my life here with Hardee at the store, I will try to be content with that. But if you want something else for me, show me like you showed me your nature when I asked. Could it be that for this very reason you brought Mr. Farley into the store? Oh, how I wish Sam were here to help me discern better what you might be saying!"

Deborah lay awake for some time, her mind as skittish as a newly broken stallion. She fantasized about herself as a Texas rancher. It seemed the most outlandish possibility, yet she never would have guessed she'd be a Cheyenne squaw either, or a storekeeper's assistant on an army post. But perhaps all those years since leaving Virginia had been preparing her for this very thing. She could still close her eyes and recall vividly the broad, grassy prairies she had traversed on the Stoner Ranch. The memory still gave her a peculiar thrill, totally detached from the horrors of life with Leonard himself. Deborah remembered also the time she had been stranded and lost on the prairies of Indian Territory. Never once during that time had she feared the land itself, for it had always seemed to offer a kind of security.

Life with the Cheyenne only deepened her appreciation for the plains. She doubted now that she'd ever be stranded there again, for she had learned how to survive by becoming a partner with the land, not its enemy—a skill unfortunately lost to most whites.

A Texas rancher. . . ?

It seemed farfetched, but not impossible. What did it say in the Bible? "With God nothing shall be impossible."

"Whatever you wish, Lord," Deborah finally sighed as her eyes grew heavy and sleep seemed not far distant. "Anyway, it's silly of me to even think of buying land since I have no money and no prospects."

"With God, nothing is impossible. . . ."

Deborah's eyes grew heavier, the colliding thoughts growing sluggish, marching like foot-heavy soldiers through her sleep-benumbed brain until the landscape of her mind was no longer real but rather the images of dreams.

A broad, golden plain, broken only by an occasional grassy hill with the bright stalks of bluebonnets bending in the wind . . . the inevitable dust risng, floating in the warm air as a splendid horse traverses the expansive scene . . . not one horse, but many . . . a herd of mustangs . . . like none ever seen in Virginia . . . all riderless, save for one, a mighty gray . . . its rider, with golden hair flowing behind her, does not even need a bridle; she is one with the gray. . . .

"What a fine dream," murmured Deborah groggily as she rolled over to sleep.

But with a sudden jar, sleep instantly fell away from her. Deborah's eyes flew open.

Virginia!

No . . . no . . . that *was* impossible! But why should she think of it now when it had not entered her mind for four years?

She still had no desire to return to Virginia. She was a frontierswoman now and wished her children to grow up here in this lovely land. Especially did she want Sky to be close to the land his father had so loved. But the estate in Virginia still belonged to her. At least it had before the trouble in Stoner's Crossing. Her able, and she believed honest, manager and lawyer, Raymond Stillwell, had kept her apprised of the standing of the property during the marriage to Leonard. She remembered Leonard once saying, "I should get a nice price for that land after the war." His use of the possessive "I" had angered her but not surprised her. He said little about selling when the war turned against the South. And when the war ended, Leonard's death had happened too quickly upon the heels of Appomattox for Deborah to have a chance to learn how her Virginia home had survived the war, or if it had at all. Reports of devastated plantations and estates had begun to reach Texas and it had not appeared hopeful. Moreover, she knew that for many southerners, reconstruction had finished off what little the war itself had left intact.

How had the Martin estate fared?

Perhaps it was about time she found out. It could do no harm to inquire, but she must do so discreetly because it would never do if Caleb Stoner heard of her inquiries and through them traced her whereabouts.

Seven years ago, though her grief had forced her from her home, she had been loathe to sell her father's beloved land. Now, so far removed both physically and emotionally, she felt no such compunctions. If the estate still belonged to her, and if she could sell it . . .

Suddenly Farley's land in Texas did not seem such an impossible dream.

"Dear God, could this be what you'd want for me? Did you nudge the memory of Virginia just for this purpose?"

Deborah hardly slept the rest of the night. She couldn't wait until the first light of day so she could go to the post telegraph and contact Mr. Raymond Stillwell.

59

IMMEDIATELY AFTER BREAKFAST the next morning, Deborah went to the fort telegraph office. She would have gone sooner, but she wanted to draw as little attention to herself as possible. As it was, she caused enough of a stir—the white squaw woman, who until recently had so stubbornly dwelt with the Indian prisoners, now wishing to send a telegram. But her request was granted.

She had spent over an hour constructing the wording of her message so that it would be clear to Stillwell, but shrouded to anyone else who handled the message:

> DEAR MR STILLWELL STOP AM INQUIRING AS TO THE HEALTH OF MY DEAR FRIENDS THE MARTINS WHOM I HAVE RECENTLY LEARNED MIGHT BE IN ILL HEALTH STOP MY NAME IS DEBORAH GRAHAM AND I SPENT MANY HAPPY TIMES RIDING UPON THEIR FINE ESTATE STOP I ESPECIALLY RECALL HOW JOSIAH MARTINS DAUGHTER WHEN SHE WAS BARELY ABLE TO TALK CALLED YOU UNCLE SILLY BECAUSE SHE COULD NOT PRONOUNCE YOUR NAME CORRECTLY STOP I WOULD GREATLY APPRECIATE ANY NEWS YOU MIGHT FORWARD ME OF THESE FINE AND DEAR FRIENDS STOP I CAN BE REACHED AT FORT DODGE IN KANSAS STOP THANK YOU MOST KINDLY END

It was pretty cryptic, perhaps too cryptic even for Stillwell, but Deborah hoped the reference to "Uncle Silly," which no one but she ever called him, along with the use of her first name and her brother's name as a surname, might clue him in on the truth. He had always been a kind, genteel man who had never married and, having no children of his own, had taken a partiality to his friend Josiah's children, especially Deborah. But Deborah recalled her father often saying of Stillwell: "That man is a saint, to be sure, but the shrewdest saint there ever was." She hoped now that particular trait of shrewdness would come to the surface. She feared the risk of saying anything else more specific in the telegram, and she only hoped that if he replied he would understand by her covert style that discretion was vital. She saw no way to avoid risk entirely.

After leaving the telegraph office, Deborah found Mr. Farley in the mess hall finishing his breakfast. Not wanting to go into the place herself, she asked a passing soldier to deliver a message.

Farley was surprised to hear that the pretty white woman from the Sutler's was asking for him.

"What can I do for you, Mrs. Graham?" he asked, wiping a sleeve across his mouth as he stepped outside to greet her.

"May I speak with you privately, Mr. Farley?"

"Well, I ain't got no place—"

"We could walk about the parade ground."

They walked around the perimeter of the vacant parade ground. The day was already warm and muggy.

Farley opened the conversation. "We got the prettiest, coolest little stream running by my pa's place back in Decaturville. I reckon it gets hot there in summer, but never like this—and never, ever like in Texas!"

"I've been in Texas," said Deborah. "It certainly had its faults, but I thought it had many redeeming qualities as well."

"Far as I'm concerned, you can have it! I don't want no more part of it."

"That's what I wanted to talk to you about, Mr. Farley," said Deborah evenly, despite the anxious thudding of her heart. "Is your land still for sale?"

"Sure is. You know someone interested?"

"I am interested."

"Ma'am?" His forehead creased with perplexity.

"I am interested in purchasing your land."

"Ma'am, I don't think you understand what I been saying. It's good land, and there's money in cattle these days, but it's a wilderness out there, on the frontier of Texas. It ain't fit for families, especially for women alone—and I take it you're a widow with no man to protect you?"

"I am alone, but isn't my safety my concern?"

"I'd feel responsible, like I was taking advantage of a poor widow and her fatherless children."

Even though Deborah realized this man's statement indicated only the best intentions, it rankled her nonetheless. The part of her that wanted to be self-reliant and independent reared its prideful head. She caught it in time to utter a silent prayer for God to help her keep this part of her in harmony with her commitment to Him.

"Mr. Farley, I appreciate your concern and your honesty," she said calmly. "Believe me, I don't want to do anything foolish, but in this country, it's a risk for anyone to strike out alone, as your own situation proves. I do not plan to marry simply for protection, and thus I may be alone for a long while. Yet, I nevertheless desire my own home. I doubt I can afford a place in a settled area, but even if I could, I prefer these plains and the challenge and isolation they provide." She made no mention of the anonymity they also would give her. "As far as protection goes, I will have to hire men to help with the ranch. I believe they would offer adequate protection."

Farley just stared in response. In a moment he rubbed his scrubby chin and shook his head, still silent.

"I believe," Deborah went on, sensing even as she spoke how right this decision was for her, "with God's help, I can do this, Mr. Farley. My one drawback is I don't have any ready cash."

Now Farley quickly found his voice, for he could understand money far more than this feisty woman's compelling argument. "No cash, ma'am? How do you per-pose—?"

"No *ready* cash," Deborah corrected with emphasis. "I have an inheritance, but it may take some time to sort out all the remaining assets."

"Time, you say?"

"A few weeks."

"Ma'am, this is pure craziness. Here you are alone, with two young'uns, and no money to speak of, and you want to buy a ranch. But that ain't even the craziest part! What's really loony is you almost got me plumb convinced to sell it to you!"

"Then you will consider it?"

"I don't know why I should—"

"But you will?"

"Tell you what, I got to get to Abilene to sell my cattle. I'll be there a spell. If you can get there with the money before I leave, I'll consider it . . . long as no better offer comes along. I won't be able to pass up someone with a fistful of cash."

Farley wasn't the only one to think Deborah had gone crazy. Hardee sputtered and clicked his tongue over it all afternoon, but when

Griff happened into the Sutler's he was far more effusive with his opinion.

"You've gone loco, Deborah! Plumb touched in the head!" he said as they sat alone in a far corner of the store. "I ain't saying you couldn't run a ranch if you put your mind to it; lots of women did during the war. But you're talking about one of the most unsettled parts of Texas. Your closest neighbors might be fifty or even seventy-five miles away. And the Comanche are a durn sight closer!"

"That's one thing that appeals to me, Griff," said Deborah with calm reason. "Not the Comanche, of course, but the isolation. I don't need a bunch of neighbors around asking questions about my past."

"And speaking of that," Griff put in hurriedly, "why Texas at all? Wouldn't you be better off and safer farther away—California, maybe, or even Virginia? I'd think you'd never want to go back to Texas."

"I know it doesn't make sense, but despite everything that happened there, I liked Texas. And maybe if I went back, I might someday be able to clear my name."

"Not while Caleb Stoner is alive."

"He can't live forever."

Just then the front door of the store creaked open and Sam Killion strode in. Squinting momentarily at the change in light from the bright sun to the dim interior of the store, he didn't immediately notice Deborah and Griff seated alone together at a table farthest to the rear of the store. When his gaze finally adjusted and turned in that direction, he seemed to hesitate, reticent to intrude upon what seemed a private conversation. But Deborah saw him before he had a chance to retreat and waved to him.

"Sam, I'd like your opinion about something," she said.

"I'll bet it's about that land deal you want to make." Only his twinkling eyes hinted at his suppressed grin.

"So you've heard."

"It's all over the fort. That Farley's been telling everyone about that crazy woman in buckskin who wants to be a rancher."

"I should have told him I wanted it confidential."

"Doubt that would have mattered."

"Well, now that it's out, what do you think? Am I crazy?"

"Tell her, Preacher!" put in Griff. "She's slipped over the edge on this one."

"Why?" said Sam. "Because she wants her own place? Who can blame her?"

"But in that country? You been there Killion; it ain't no place for a lone woman—"

324

"I won't be alone," said Deborah, growing defensive and sorry she had brought up the subject at all. Why was she asking anyone's advice, anyway? Maybe it was time she made her own decision. She'd pray about it, of course, but no need for it to go beyond her and God.

"Yeah," said Griff cynically, "a bunch of cowboys who can't be trusted no more'n the Comanche."

"Have you prayed about it, Deborah?" asked Sam.

"I have and I plan to again. I haven't made a final decision yet."

"Well, if it's what God wants—"

"Come on!" exclaimed Griff. "God don't want her to get butchered by Indians—and I'll tell you, Comanche and Apache are a different breed from Cheyenne, and don't you forget it. They don't take prisoners—except maybe women and children who'd be better off dead, anyway."

"That is said about all Indians," said Deborah.

"But it's true 'bout them two tribes."

Deborah shook her head with disgust and, not wishing to discuss that sensitive topic, turned her attention back to Sam.

"Sam, how will I know if it is God's will?"

"Pray about it and read your Bible; maybe He will show you something in His Word. Maybe He'll show you by making all the pieces fall together. Maybe He'll show you through good counsel—"

"That's it right there!" broke in Griff smugly. "Half the fort will counsel her against it."

"Could be . . ." said Sam, drawing out the words thoughtfully. He looked directly at Deborah. "In the end, though, the decision will rest entirely with you. You'll have to step out in the way you feel is best, the way your heart is leading you. Maybe a little verse I always have liked will help you a mite. In the Psalms it says, 'The steps of a good man are ordered by the Lord.' I think that includes women, too—" He added that last remark with a slight smirk at Griff. "If you ask God and you trust Him, I don't figure you can go too wrong."

"I want to trust God, Sam. I really do."

"I can see that, Deborah."

"Oh my!" groaned Griff sarcastically. "Ain't this the sweetest thing I ever seen. You're *both* loony!"

"I'm touched by your concern, Griff," said Deborah sincerely. "But there's no sense wasting your worry now, because it may turn out to be all for nothing. I still have no idea about the status of my family estate, and perhaps no way of finding out. Even if I do find out, the chances are pretty slim that I will get to Abilene in time to catch Mr. Farley."

"It's in impossible situations just like this," offered Sam, "that God can truly show His hand."

"I can't think of a better way to have it, then," Deborah replied. And she meant it, for as much as she wanted her own place, she desired even more to please the God to whom she had so recently committed her life.

60

FOUR QUIET DAYS PASSED. Deborah fell back into her usual routine and all but forgot the prospective Texas land deal. She'd decided the timing was all wrong—for Farley's land, at least. However, it all had one positive consequence because it had prompted her to contact Stillwell about her inheritance. She might never have thought of it, or had the motivation to pursue it otherwise. Of course, that might become as much a pipe dream as the land. Seven years was a long time, especially with a war intervening. Also, she wondered if word of her trouble with the law had reached Virginia and Mr. Stillwell. If it had and he thought she was dead, he might have already sold the estate and pocketed the profits as his reward for all his trouble over the years. Who could blame him.

Thus, when an enlisted man came to the store after breakfast on the fifth day, no one was more surprised than Deborah. As he handed her the envelope, she hardly had the courage to take it. Its contents could have the power to make or break all her dreams.

Hardee watched with a grimace as Deborah took the envelope with a wooden hand.

"Bad news, I shouldn't wonder," he muttered. "No one ever pays money to send good news."

"Thank you," Deborah said to the soldier, who tipped his hat in reply before leaving the store.

Deborah lifted the flap and slid out a sheet of paper inside. "Here goes, I guess." As her eyes scanned the single sheet they began to widen with excitement.

HOW KIND OF YOU TO INQUIRE OF THE MARTIN FAMILY STOP
YOU MAY NOT REMEMBER ME MRS GRAHAM BUT I KNOW WHO
YOU ARE STOP I AM SORRY TO SAY JOSIAH MARTIN AND HIS
SON WERE KILLED IN THE WAR AND THE DAUGHTER IS AWAY
HOWEVER I HOPE TO SEE HER AGAIN IN THIS LIFE STOP I
REMAIN THE MANAGER OF THE FAMILY ESTATE UNTIL HER
RETURN STOP THE LAND IS FINALLY BEGINNING TO TURN A
PROFIT SINCE THE DEVASTATION OF THE WAR THOUGH I
HAVE HAD TO SELL OFF SOME TO PAY TAXES AND SUCH STOP
I HOPE OVER THE YEARS I HAVE CONTINUED THE MARTINS
FAITHFUL SERVANT AND AS THEIR FRIEND YOU MAY CON-
SIDER THE SAME OF ME SHOULD YOU VISIT HERE IN FUTURE
STOP REGARDS R STILLWELL END

Smiling, Deborah refolded the paper. Old "Uncle Silly" was a cagey one indeed! *I know who you are.* That simple phrase said it all. Not only that he knew it was Deborah Martin writing him, but that he knew of the trouble in Texas and understood the need for discretion, also apparent in the covert wording of the telegram. And the faithful family friend and lawyer had remained so all these years, loyally holding on to the land in hopes of her return. Deborah decided then and there that if she could sell the estate, she'd give a substantial portion of the proceeds to Stillwell. He had earned it.

Hardee had stopped work and was waiting impatiently for some clue about the contents of the telegram. Finally he could stand it no longer and ventured, "Ain't bad news, is it, Deborah?"

Deborah looked up. "I don't think so."

"You gonna get that land?"

"It may take time to come up with the money."

"You know, Deborah, I got me a little stash—"

"Thank you, Hardee, for the thought, but I won't borrow money. If I do that, how will I ever know if it's God's will that I have it?"

"Hearin' that would sure make Sam happy," said the storekeeper, his own pride obvious. "An' I admire you, too, for stickin' to your principles. But it's there if you want it."

"Thanks, Hardee. You are a true friend." Deborah paused, tapping the telegram thoughtfully against her chin. "Hardee, how far is it to Abilene?"

"Oh, a good four days' hard ride."

"Do you mind watching the children while I see Sam?"

"No problem." But Hardee paused, then added hesitantly, "You ain't thinkin' of riding to Abilene, are you, Deborah?"

"Not right away."

"That's a wild an' lawless place there, Deborah. Don't you think 'bout goin' alone."

"I won't."

She left the store and went in search of Sam, whom she located in the mess hall talking with two recently converted soldiers. She entered the place rather timidly. Not only was she reticent about being a female invader of male territory, but, despite her months at the fort, she continued to hold resentment in her heart toward the bluecoats who had killed her husband and destroyed the life she had come to love. With no one at hand to go in for her, she had no choice but to venture in alone. She paused at the open door, taking no farther step inside, and cleared her throat to get someone's attention. Luckily, there were only a handful of men remaining from breakfast, but even her timid entrance roused their immediate attention. Sam also saw her and greeted her.

"Howdy, Deborah!" he said in his usual buoyant tone.

"Good morning, Sam. Would it be possible for me to speak with you . . . in private?"

"Sure." He turned to his companions. "You fellas don't mind, do you?"

Since they had to return to their duties, they did not protest. As Sam rose from his seat, however, he was met with several good-natured winks and meaningful chuckles. Deborah reddened slightly but Sam took it in his stride.

With mock ire he said, "You blue-bellies better get about your own business before you end up on report!"

General laughter followed Deborah and Sam out of the mess hall. Once outside Sam turned to Deborah apologetically.

"I'm sorry 'bout that, but you know how soldiers are."

"Yes, I suppose." She paused with a wrinkled brow. "Are you sure that's all it is, Sam? I mean, they don't really think—"

"Maybe some do," he replied frankly. "Would it bother you if they did?"

"It shouldn't, I suppose, seeing that I've been the brunt of so many other rumors and gossip. But, Sam, you have a certain respectability that I am certain you must uphold—"

His laughter cut her off. "Deborah, you ain't concerned for my reputation, are you?" When she nodded, he went on emphatically.

"Why, you couldn't do anything but enhance whatever respect I have here!"

"I doubt that, Sam. There are many who believe I am tainted because I married an Indian and have a half-breed child. I see their looks of disdain and hear their whispers."

"You know better than to pay heed to the talk of fools!" Sam exclaimed, all previous amusement fading. "I don't think those things—you know that, don't you?" But before she had a chance to reply, he rushed on. "Why, I'd consider it nothing less than an honor to ... to—" Suddenly he stopped, stumbling over his words as he did so. He blushed, not so much at what he had said, but at what he had been about to say. He would take it as an honor to have her for his wife, but he had never meant to reveal this to her, nor to reveal that he had considered it before this moment. He tried to recover himself, but not too successfully. "It's just that any man in his right mind would ... well, Deborah, you are a fine woman, that's all, and don't you let them gossipmongers make you believe otherwise."

"That is kind of you to say," she replied. "And, Sam, if I were ever to think of marriage again, I would think the same of a man like you. But I have lost so many people I love that I believe I will not soon take the risk of loving another."

As they walked, Sam slowed to a stop. When Deborah drew up beside him, he gazed deeply into her eyes. His voice as he spoke was solemn, conveying far more meaning than his simple words. "I understand, Deborah, I truly do."

Deborah felt that he wanted to say more, but he did not. In a moment, after a final poignant glance at her, he started walking again. They continued in silence, neither feeling uncomfortable or awkward, but each with a need to allow stirred emotions to settle before venturing to speak again.

Sam, always willing to forge ahead, to take risks, broke the silence. "You wanted to see me about something in particular, didn't you?"

"Yes ... but to tell the truth, I wonder if it would be appropriate now."

"Ain't no way to know except to lay it out to me."

"Sam, today I received a reply to my telegram to my family lawyer, Raymond Stillwell." She handed him the paper and he quickly scanned the sheet. "I know it's cryptic," she continued, "but I believe he understands my situation. And, more importantly, I still have the property in Virginia. So, now it is time to send something more specific."

"Deborah, I'm curious about something. Maybe I already know

the answer, but I suppose I'd like to hear it from you. Now that you know you got a home in Virginia, wouldn't you rather go back there?"

She replied without hesitation, "I would no more fit in back there than you would with your old Texas Ranger company. This is where I belong. I love this country, and I want my son to grow up in the land his father loved and died for. I let grief and despair force me from my home once before, and it was a mistake. I won't do that again. This is my home now. Virginia is a million miles away and at least that many lifetimes removed. Besides, if I took up residence again in Virginia, there is no way Caleb Stoner would not hear of it. I can never forget that I am still a fugitive."

"Do you plan on being a fugitive forever?"

"I see no way around it."

Sam opened his mouth as if to speak, then clamped it shut again, remaining silent but thoughtful.

Deborah gave him a slight smile. "Thank you, Sam."

"For what?"

"Ever since we first met in Griff's hideout, you have never asked me if I killed Leonard."

"I never had to ask. You're no killer."

"It's all so complicated," she replied with some of her old pain creeping into her voice. "Sometimes I'm not even certain what happened that awful day."

"Do you want to talk about it, Deborah?"

She shook her head. "Perhaps I'm just afraid to get to the truth."

"If you ain't ready to talk about it, Deborah, I ain't gonna force you. Whenever you feel of a mind too, though, I just want you to know I'm here for you. And you know, if you'd like I could always ride on down there and poke around a mite and see what I can uncover—"

"Please, Sam," she put in quickly, a hint of panic in her eyes, "don't do that. If anyone tries to stir it up now, I don't want to even think of what Caleb might do. He could trace you to me; then he would have me executed before anyone could uncover the truth. Then he'd take Carolyn and . . . I hate to even think what he would do with Sky. I would rather be a fugitive than risk that. And what if . . . what if—" She stopped, visibly shaken as visions of her dreams and nightmares of that terrible time flashed through her distraught mind.

She began again with a heavy sigh. "I just don't think I could handle stirring everything back up, Sam. All I want right now is some peace. I know I have the peace of God, but I want to feel settled. I want some security for my children. Maybe later, but for now I'd like to forget all about that time."

"Whatever you say, but I am available if you need me."

"Thank you. And I do need a favor from you now, Sam."

"Anything."

"I must send a telegram to Mr. Stillwell, but it can't be from here, where it seems all my affairs are common knowledge. I can no longer speak in cryptic phrases to him. I had hoped that you could take a message to Fort Larned and send it from there. It would also involve awaiting a reply. And then—" She stopped suddenly and sighed. "Oh, Sam, who am I kidding? By the time I do all that, Mr. Farley will be long gone."

"There will be other land," said Sam. "And next time, you'll be ready. But even if it doesn't work out this time, it don't mean you shouldn't give it a try. You never know what God'll do unless you give Him a chance."

Deborah smiled at his encouraging words. She could hardly believe there had once been a time when she did not trust Sam Killion.

"I'll tell you what," Sam went on with growing enthusiasm, "when I get that reply, if it's favorable, I can head right up to Abilene and try to catch Farley and see if he's still looking for a buyer."

"It seems impossible," said Deborah. "There must be hundreds of cattlemen in Abilene looking for land. And even if you do find Farley and he is still selling his land, you still won't have the money. It would take months for Stillwell to sell my property and forward the money to me."

"There just ain't no telling what God can do, Deborah. I'm game to try."

"Oh, Sam! What would I do without you?"

"I think you'd do just fine." And there was a tinge of regret in his tone, for part of him dearly wanted her to need him.

61

IN 1867, ABILENE HAD BEEN A sleepy, dirty village consisting of a dozen dirt-roofed log huts and a saloonkeeper so bored and broke that he sold prairie dogs, present in greater abundance than people, to eastern tourists. But in the summer of that year an enterprising fellow named Joseph G. McCoy chose the town as the rail connection between the Texas cattle range and growing eastern markets.

Thus, by the fall of 1869, a far different town greeted Sam Killion as he rode through the narrow streets clogged with billowing clouds of dust and traffic and knots of unruly, loud, and troublesome cowboys. Over a hundred fifty thousand head of cattle would pass through town that season leaving more of a mark than mere hoofprints.

On every hand were saloons and dance halls, with the brassy strains of lurid music pouring from their doors, punctuated by stray gunfire and verbal obscenities. Several women with painted faces and revealing dresses called out to Sam as he passed, thinking him a cowboy in search of a good time after too many lonely, dangerous months on the trail. Sam politely declined their various offers, instead inviting them to a meeting he planned to have the following day. He had come to Abilene on business for Deborah, but he saw no reason not to kill two birds with one stone, as it were. Here was a place crying out to be evangelized, and he was not a man to pass up such an opportunity.

A week and a half ago, Sam had gone to Fort Larned and sent Deborah's telegram. He waited three days before a reply came, but when it did arrive, he headed directly for Abilene. Despite his solid, unflinching faith in God, even he was astonished by the surprising response. Upon receipt of Deborah's first telegram, Stillwell had prepared for the possibility of selling the estate. He not only already had a buyer for the property, but the papers were drawn up and signed, needing only Deborah's signature to finalize the deal. He had sent out the papers that day in care of Deborah Graham at Fort Dodge, just in case. He explained the speed with which a buyer had been found; Stillwell himself wished to purchase the land if it was Deborah's intent to sell. Having worked so hard to maintain it over the years, he had developed a fondness for it. He was offering five thousand dollars to buy Deborah out; and, though he admitted the land was worth more, so much of it had been mortgaged to pay for restoration after the war, and to pay exorbitant taxes levied by greedy carpetbaggers, that Stillwell would end up taking a loss if he gave more. From what Deborah had told him about what she expected to get out of the estate, Sam thought she would be most agreeable to Stillwell's offer. Sam was beginning to sense, without a doubt, God's hand in the entire matter.

The only obstacle now to be overcome was finding Farley and convincing him to sell his own land on faith.

Sam rode directly to the Drover's Cottage, the main hotel in town patronized by cattlemen from both the West and East. It was packed that time of year, and dominating the milieu of bustling noise and activity was the sound of deals being concluded and fortunes made. As he walked through the door, Sam said a quick prayer that somehow in that impossibly chaotic mass, a Tennessean cattleman named Farley could be found.

Sam's patience was sorely tried that day and the next, for he could locate Farley nowhere. Several had heard of him, one eastern businessman had purchased half his herd, but none knew where Farley was or if he was still in town. The next evening Sam went ahead with his church service, held in a saloon belonging to an acquaintance of Sam's who was willing to suspend the sale of whiskey for an hour for the sake of friendship and a debt he owed Sam.

As Killion preached, he scanned his audience for the face of the scruffy Tennessean Deborah had described in detail, but to no avail. The next day he was prevailed upon to officiate at three marriages and four funerals. He could have stayed busy for days at this work; it had been months since a cleric had last been through town. Not until the final wedding ceremony, four days after his arrival in Abilene, did Sam finally spot Farley. Apparently the ex-cattle rancher had been pining away after his own wife, and wandered into the hotel where the wedding ceremony was being held, seeking consolation in the marital bliss of others.

Moments after Sam pronounced the couple man and wife, he pounced upon Farley.

333

"Hey!" said Sam. "Ain't you Calvin Farley from Tennessee?"

"That's right. Do I know you?"

"No, but I heard all about you in Fort Dodge. You had some land for sale, didn't you?"

"Yup."

"Is it still for sale?"

"I'm gonna meet with a fella in an hour to close the deal. He's offering me half what it's worth, but I can't wait no longer."

"I'm surprised you ain't sold it by now."

"I been laid up for days with this here head of mine." For the first time, Sam noticed a bandage under Farley's hat.

"What happened?"

"Got robbed a week or so ago in an alley here in town. Luckily I weren't carrying anything valuable, but they laid me on my back for days. If'n I don't get to Tennessee soon, I ain't ever gonna make it."

"Did the law catch the robbers?"

"Naw, not with my luck the way it's been. And now I'm still gonna lose my shirt with my land."

"Maybe it'll work to your advantage that you were forced to stick around here, 'cause I'd like to make you an offer."

"I'm listening."

"I'm speaking on behalf of an interested party in Fort Dodge."

"Oh yeah? When I was there, there wasn't no one even close to interested, except that white squaw woman." When Sam nodded, Farley's eyes widened. "You mean you're speakin' for her?"

"Yep, and she is prepared to pay you three hundred dollars."

"That's a hundred dollars more'n I even asked." Farley's eyes narrowed as he searched Sam's face for some larcenous motives. "You being a preacher an' all, you wouldn't be thinkin' of pulling something on me, now would you?"

"No, but there is a catch to the deal."

"I figgered as much. What is it?"

"Mrs. Graham has no ready cash. But she'll soon come into some money. For an extra hundred dollars all you have to do is trust her for the money. I think it can be very simply arranged for you to pick up the money from her lawyer in Virginia, which ain't far from Tennessee, if I recall my geography correctly."

"She's a mighty determined woman, ain't she?" said Farley.

Sam smiled and nodded.

"Well," Farley continued, "I know'd this was craziness right from the beginning, but I couldn't help admirin' that there woman. Even though she lived with Injuns, you just couldn't keep from liking her.

And I 'spect it's been pretty rough for her and all, and I'd like to do her a good turn—"

"But. . . ?" prompted Killion.

"I'd not only have to trust her, but I got to trust you, too. I mean you're a preacher, leastways it appears that way, but I don't know you from Adam—"

"Where you been, fella?" put in a man from a nearby table in the still-crowded hotel who had caught a bit of the conversation. "Why, this here's Sam Killion, Texas Ranger turned preacher! Fastest, surest shot in all of Texas."

"That true?" said Farley with renewed interest. "You're a Texas Ranger?"

"Used to be," answered Sam.

"You know, it was Rangers that saved my family from Indians a few months back."

"I'm glad to hear that, but I wasn't a Ranger then."

"Still, I owe the Rangers a lot and would feel it a matter of honor to trust 'em."

Sam smiled inwardly at the irony that this man felt safer trusting a Texas Ranger than a preacher. But since he saw no use in debating the matter, Sam made no further comment. He sensed intuitively God's hand in this, for only God could use for good that time in Sam's life that he himself had renounced as violent and godless.

"Does that mean you're willing to strike a deal?" asked Sam cautiously.

"Like I told that squaw woman, I'm just as loony as her. But I'll be switched if I ain't gonna do it!"

An arrangement was made whereby Deborah would send a letter to Raymond Stillwell instructing him to send the money to Farley in Tennessee at an address he gave Sam. Upon receipt of the money, Farley would send the property title to Deborah. Sam and Farley shook hands on the deal, and the look in each man's face indicated clearly that they both fully comprehended the solemnity of the gesture. Farley was so pleased afterward that he ordered drinks for everyone. Sam had coffee, but was no less pleased with how everything had turned out.

62

DEBORAH HAD HER LAND. Though it would take weeks, maybe months, before all the transactions were completed and that all-important deed arrived, it was still something to rejoice over. A self-satisfied grin spread across Sam's face as he leaned back in his chair in the Drover's Cottage sipping his coffee.

By Christmas Deborah could very well be in her own home, on her own land—five thousand acres, no less! She'd be free to ride to her heart's content, traversing miles before she came to the end of it.

By Christmas . . . three short months . . .

But all at once Sam realized what this would mean for him! Deborah would be leaving Fort Dodge, leaving Kansas, going several hundred miles away. Away from him! He had been so intent on encouraging her to do what would make her happy and what would be God's will, he had forgotten to take into account his own happiness. He tried to console himself with the fact that God surely had not forgotten about him. It might well be that this separation had somehow been orchestrated to benefit them both. Only last week, she told him she would not marry again. Perhaps God was going to use this move to spare him the torture of being around her, knowing their relationship could never progress beyond friendship. Maybe—

But a voice interrupted Sam's thoughts.

"Seems to me that land was selling for two hundred dollars a few weeks back," it said in a none-too-friendly tone.

Sam jerked around to find Griff McCulloch standing over him. He was looking bleary-eyed and meaner than usual, having visited one too many of Abilene's saloons.

"I don't see where that's your concern, McCulloch," said Sam, taken aback by the outlaw's menacing tone.

"I figger *someone* better look out for Deborah's interests."

"Are you implying I ain't?"

"I ain't implyin' nothin'. Seems she's gettin' cheated if she has to pay three hundred for land that's worth two."

"Maybe if you'd eavesdropped on the entire transaction, you'd know why."

"Yeah? Well, maybe you better just tell me!"

"I don't see why I should. Deborah never gave me leave to discuss her personal affairs with everybody." Sam realized he was antagonizing Griff, but the man's belligerent, surly attitude was irritating. Moreover, he believed it risky to discuss Deborah in public with the drunken outlaw.

"Well, I ain't just anybody! I saved her neck—"

"Shut up, Griff!" Sam cut him off.

"What? Why you—" But instead of completing his sentence verbally, Griff lunged toward Sam with a clenched fist.

Sam's reflexes were too quick for him. He easily caught Griff's fist, twisting it to the side, forcing him to the ground. As soon as Griff hit the plank floor, he scrambled to his feet, cursing and sputtering, and sprang at Sam again.

The preacher jumped up from his chair, causing Griff to lunge at empty air, sprawling once more on the floor, this time on top of the chair, splintering it into pieces with his weight. Still not discouraged, Griff lurched once more to his feet, obscenities pouring from his mouth.

"You no good rattlesnake!" he yelled. "You ain't nothin' but a yellow-bellied coward, spoutin' all your religious jargon. I don't know what she sees in you!"

"You ain't yourself, Griff. Go somewhere and cool off; then we'll talk."

"You think yer a mighty cool number, don'tcha? Let's just see how cool you are, big, tough Texas Ranger! I'm callin' you out!" Griff's hand went for his gun.

"I ain't armed!" said Sam quickly.

"You ain't gonna hide behind your Bible this time, Preacher! You got to the count of five to get a gun!"

"Be reasonable, Griff. You ain't got no quarrel with me—it's the drink talking."

But Griff responded only with, "One, two, three . . ."

"Hey, Preacher!" someone called from the crowd of onlookers. "Here you go!"

A Colt .44 came sailing through the air. Griff counted, "Four . . . five!"

By pure reflex, Sam's hand flew up and caught the pistol an instant before Griff drew his own gun. Sam fired a split second after Griff discharged his first shot. The entire scene was over before any of the crowd had even a chance to blink. Griff was standing, very bewildered, rubbing a painful right hand, while Sam, in silent shock, watched. Sam's shot had blown Griff's gun from his hand.

Someone in the crowd whistled. "Now, that's shootin'!"

But another was less impressed. "Whatcha mean? Ain't no one dead, is there?"

The brief interchange brought Sam to himself. He dropped the gun on the floor as if it were a poisonous snake; then he strode over to Griff.

"You okay?" he asked with real concern.

Griff shrugged away from him. "Leave me alone!" he growled.

At that moment, Slim hurried forward. "Can't leave you alone for a minute, you fool!" he yelled to Griff, then turning toward Sam, "Thanks, Preacher. You coulda killed him."

"He *shoulda* killed me!" blustered Griff. " 'Cause soon as my hand's better, I'm comin' after him!"

"Aw, pipe down, Griff!" said Slim. "You ain't going after nobody."

"Leave me alone!" Griff stalked away toward a table in the corner of the saloon. "Gimme a chair!" he demanded of the occupants of the table, who responded by immediately vacating their places. None of them was as good with a gun as the preacher and dared not antagonize this fellow's hair-trigger. "Hey you, barkeep!" Griff shouted toward the bar. "Gimme a bottle of whiskey!"

Slim and Sam headed toward the table, Sam pausing at the bar to get a pot of coffee instead of the whiskey. When he came up to the table and slid into a chair, Griff, his head slumped over the table nearly unconscious, made no comment.

"What's his problem?" asked Sam of Slim as he poured out three cups of strong coffee.

"Griff never could hold his liquor. Always gets crazier than a March hare when he's drunk."

"Then maybe he shouldn't drink."

"He don't usually."

"Does he have some special reason for doing it now?"

"Woman trouble."

Sam raised an eyebrow, recalling Griff's remarks about Deborah. "Really?"

"Got himself a gal at the Longhorn Saloon. They been sparking each other for a couple of months. Well, he walked in on her with another fella."

"That's too bad." Sam restrained his inner relief that the "woman trouble" apparently had nothing to do with Deborah.

"Yeah. It woulda been better if he had killed the man right then, but instead, Griff went out and got himself drunk."

338

"And nearly killed me!"

"I don't think it was anything personal-like."

"It sure woulda been if I had ended up on Boot Hill."

"You was taking a big risk aiming for his hand like that," observed Slim. "First rule of gunfighting is always shoot to kill, 'cause that's what the other fella is doing."

"I learned that rule, too, and I used to live by it, but now I've got a higher rule to follow. It goes something like this, 'Do unto others as you would have them do unto you.' "

"Seems like a mighty shame wasting a gun hand like yours on Bible beating."

"Do you really believe that, Slim?" asked Sam pointedly.

Slim thought for a moment, then said, "Naw, I don't reckon I do. I suppose there's a lot of fellas alive today 'cause you gave up gunfighting."

Sam nodded gravely, but he was thinking more of those poor souls who *weren't* alive because of him. He sent up a brief silent prayer for the grace to look at it from Slim's viewpoint, and to remember that if the altercation in the Drover's Cottage had happened ten years ago, Griff McCulloch would also be dead now. There was always something to be thankful for.

As if Griff had been reading Sam's thoughts, he raised his head from its drugged stupor and peered hazily at him. "You still here?" he slurred.

"Have some coffee," said Sam.

Griff shook his head but raised his hand anyway to take the offered cup. The moment he tried to grasp it, he winced. His hand was red and black with powder burns. Sam jumped up, fetched a basin of water from the bar, and washed Griff's hand, and then bandaged it with his handkerchief.

Griff accepted all this attention passively, but at one point he stared at Sam and mumbled, "You're crazy!" Then his head slumped over, missing the basin by an inch. He was out cold.

Slim and Sam carried him upstairs to a room in the hotel where he slept soundly for the rest of the night. When he awoke in the morning, his head throbbing more painfully than his injured hand, he went downstairs and didn't know whether to be dismayed or relieved when Slim told him the preacher was gone.

63

AS GRIFF APPROACHED FORT DODGE about a week later, he noticed a cloud of dust rising in the air a few miles west of the fort. Curious, and half expecting to find soldiers in a fray with renegade Indians, he rode past the fort to have a look.

With his rifle lying across his saddle at the ready, he was relieved to find no Indians at all, but surveyors and workmen tramping over the dusty sod along the river.

"What's going on?" Griff called to one of the workers.

"We're building a town," the fellow replied, wiping a sleeve across his sweaty brow.

"Here, in the middle of nowhere?"

"Won't be for long. Railhead's coming through here. It's going to be a cow town."

"What's wrong with Abilene?"

"This'll cut miles off a trail drive."

"Yeah, but another cow town. . . ? Don't make no sense. That many folks want beef?"

"They'll take as much as can be shipped east. Cattle-raising is the way to wealth, man!"

Griff shrugged, not fully convinced. Of course, he'd already heard this kind of talk in Abilene, but he had dismissed it as the boasts of Texas cattlemen, always eager to promote anything from their state as bigger and better. Yet, seeing with his own eyes a town being built for that express purpose could not help but make an impact on him.

"They got a name for this here town, yet?" asked Griff.

"Dodge City."

"How creative," said Griff with a smirk.

He spurred his horse around and rode back to the fort, sensing only peripherally what an impact this little encounter was to have on his future. The monetary potential of the cattle business was only part of it; far more weighty was the realization that civilization was slowly encroaching upon him. He well remembered the days when

340

a man could ride these plains for days on end and never see another white man, and sometimes not even Indians. He remembered when the buffalo blackened the prairie. And now he knew that the railhead coming in was as much to ship the hides of slaughtered buffalo as it was for cattle. No one hunted buffalo anymore; they simply exterminated them. Griff had always been a man who loved a challenge. That's why robbing a train had appealed to him far more than owning one. Yet as he saw the changes creeping in on him, he began to feel as near extinction as the bison.

He was getting old—too old to have to always wonder where the next bullet was coming from. And the truth was that even if he was pretty much in the clear with the law, he still had made plenty of enemies in other arenas. After he had quit robbing banks and stagecoaches, he had made a living hiring out his gun when he could—a fact that he had never mentioned to Deborah. He had been wondering more and more of late about when a man ought to know the right time to stop tempting fate.

He had started out from Abilene a week ago with the vague idea that he was ready to take it easier. How much the incident with Killion had colored his thinking he didn't want to know. He still wasn't sure why he had flown off the handle like that. Killion wasn't a bad sort, despite all his religious prattle. And Griff didn't think it had anything to do with jealousy. If he wanted Deborah, he had no doubt he could win her from the likes of Killion.

Not being the analytical sort, Griff gave no further thought to the unfortunate incident. It happened and was over; it didn't matter why.

He didn't think his present decision had anything to do with it. He vaguely thought he would tell Deborah that he wanted to hire on as one of her hands in Texas. She was going to need help, and he was looking for a little stability in his life. There'd still be plenty of challenge with hostile Indians roaming loose, but it was a step in the right direction.

Now, as he left the new town site of Dodge City in the rising dust, he was more certain than ever of his decision.

At the fort, a company of infantry was drilling on the parade ground, making dust clouds of their own. Griff wondered when was the last time any of them had fought Indians. They looked bored and slovenly. Griff knew the Texas forts were having a hard time clearing out hostile Comanche and Apache, and the northern army units still had a ways to go before subduing the Sioux and the Northern Cheyenne. These boys at Fort Dodge might any day be sent off to fight other Indian wars, but for the time being they seemed representative of the waning frontier.

"Won't be long," Griff muttered to himself, "before we'll all be a bunch of old fossils."

He rode up to the Sutler's store, dismounted, tied his horse to a rail, and strode into the store. Deborah was standing in front of the counter trading with a couple of Arapahoe braves. They were speaking Cheyenne, and it still amazed Griff at how easily the Indian lingo flowed from Deborah's lips. But on this particular day, he was impressed even more by her appearance than by her speech.

She no longer wore the Indian buckskin shift. Instead, she was dressed somewhat after the white woman's fashion, although not in the calico frocks Griff was accustomed to seeing the settlers' wives and army wives wear, with their full skirts and ruffles. Deborah wore a simple dark blue cotton skirt and a pale blue chambray shirt, belted at the waist with a brown leather belt. The blue of her shirt brought out the color in her eyes, making them appear as dazzling as a river in spring. On her feet were deerskin boots—Indian made, as far as he could tell. Her hair, grown long again, was done in the Indian fashion, braided with beaver strips woven into the silky yellow strands.

His surprise at seeing her in this new garb lay not so much in its contrast to her previous attire, but in how very appropriate it all looked. He was immediately struck with the thought that she finally looked as she was meant to look. She was a woman of the plains who could ride and no doubt shoot and hunt as well as most men. He suddenly realized that her decision to buy that ranch in Texas might not have been so crazy after all. He also realized that his magnanimous offer to help her out on the ranch now seemed pretty lame. Yet even a seasoned frontiersman couldn't run a ranch that size all by himself. She was going to have to hire help, so he might as well be the one.

And Griff was beginning to see that he needed her as much as he thought she needed him.

The two Indians completed their transaction and turned around, both grinning and apparently pleased by the deal made with the white squaw woman. Griff stepped forward as Deborah busied herself with moving the animal pelts left by the Indians.

"Howdy, Deborah," he said.

She glanced up and a ready smile formed on her lips. "Griff! Hello. It's been a long time."

"Yeah, I guess so."

"Are you just passing through, or do you have time for a visit?"

"I reckon I can stay a spell."

"Well, let me take care of these skins; then we can talk." She began sorting the pelts, adding them to the stacks behind her. She talked as she worked. "What have you been up to all these weeks?"

"Nothing much," he answered laconically. "Drifting here and there. Nothing exciting."

"At least you are staying out of trouble," she said innocuously.

"Some might disagree there, but I'm trying."

"Sam said he saw you in Abilene."

"Did he?" She nodded, showing no opinion over what had happened. Could it be that she didn't know what he had tried to do to the preacher? Griff asked casually, "So, what did he have to say about that?"

"Nothing much, really." She glanced up from her work. "So, what do you think about me becoming a landowner?"

"I guess I was pretty clear about that before."

"You thought I was crazy."

"More about where you was buying land than about owning it." He paused, scratching his unshaven face. "But the more I think on it, Deborah, the more I can understand how you feel. There comes a point in a person's life when settling down starts to look mighty good."

"Not for you, Griff!" she said in mock surprise.

"Maybe so . . . that's kinda why I stopped in to see you."

Deborah put away the last pelt and brushed her hands together to shake off the dust and fur. "Let's have a seat, Griff. Hardee's got a fresh pot of coffee brewing; would you like some?"

"Don't mind if I do."

Deborah filled two cups and carried them to the table where Griff had already plopped down in a chair, stretching his long legs out in front of him. Deborah set the cups down and sat in the chair adjacent to him. She didn't seem to notice or mind that Griff made no move to stand for her or help her into her chair. He seemed to receive her as an equal, not as a helpless, ineffectual woman.

"Now, Griff, what is this wild talk about settling down? I can see it for me with two children to think of, but I never thought I'd hear such things from you."

"I ain't exactly thinking of settling down in the sense that I'm looking for a wife and family and all that—" He suddenly realized how she might have misinterpreted his words. "You understand that, don't you, Deborah?"

She chuckled softly. "Of course I do! I didn't think you were proposing to me, Griff."

He let out a relieved sigh. Then, flustered, added, "Not that I wouldn't be right pleased with you, Deborah. You're about the most

343

beautiful woman I know. It's just that marriage and all that ain't for me. I may think of settling down, but there's still certain freedoms I could never give up no matter how long I stayed in one place. I guess I been thinking that I'm getting too old to be drifting around eating jerky and hardtack all the time, dodging bullets and the law, never knowing from one day to the next where I'll be or if I'll be anywhere at all."

"So, what do you plan to do about it?" asked Deborah. "Are you thinking of buying land also?"

"I can't hold on to my money long enough for that." He paused to form just the right words. "Well, I been thinking, Deborah, that you're going to need some help on that ranch of yours—some cowpunchers, you know."

At first Deborah rankled at this, thinking it patronizing and gratuitous. Her stubborn self immediately hardened against the thought of being protected by others all her life. Now Griff was going to make the supreme sacrifice by going with her to Texas to shield her from Indians and rustlers and whatever other hardships running a ranch entailed. Yet her growing humble self, the one that desired more than anything to respond to the voice of God, quickly interceded, telling her to look more deeply at Griff's suggestion. She *would* need to hire help, and wouldn't it be better to have someone she knew and could trust? Perhaps God had placed this idea in Griff's mind just for this purpose. She would need help and protection. Even Farley, a man, had needed help. Besides, she would be paying Griff. It would be entirely a business arrangement. Yet, could she handle the implications of his presence? The fact that he was a friend helping her rather than someone she went out and hired?

But her proud self got the better of her. "Griff, are you suggesting this because you don't think I can make it on my own. Are you trying to protect me?"

"Well, I'll admit it may have started out that way. I guess when a feller saves a woman's neck once, he begins to feel a mite responsible for her. But shucks, Deborah, it's mighty obvious that you don't need more than the average amount of protection. I taught you to shoot, and that Indian husband of yours taught you a heap more besides that. So, I guess what it boils down to is that I need a steady job and you need a ranch hand. I figure we ought to be able to work out something congenial between us."

Deborah smiled sheepishly, inwardly embarrassed at her overreaction to the whole matter. As she relaxed and began to surrender her emotions to God, a twinge of enthusiasm began to build inside her, telling her this was just what she was looking for. Actually, she hadn't been looking for it at all, but as usual God knew her need even before she did. She wondered what Griff would think if she told him she believed the Lord had sent him to her. He might decide to look elsewhere for work!

"I think so, too, Griff," she answered. Then, feeling suddenly bold, she added, "How can I turn you away when it appears as if God himself has sent you!"

"Imagine that!" laughed Griff. "Let's just hope He don't ever regret it."

"I am certain He won't!" She grinned, satisfied, then continued. "What do you think of being foreman of the place?"

"I don't think you coulda chosen a better man!"

"Good. And I was also thinking, do you suppose Slim and Longjim might also be looking for work?"

"It can't hurt to ask 'em."

"All right, Griff, then it's settled. We'll get started as soon as I hear from my lawyer."

They shook hands enthusiastically, and Griff made his departure. He wasn't sure just what he had gotten into, but he felt good about it, certain he was headed down the right trail.

64

AFTER EXITING THE STORE, GRIFF crossed the parade ground, now vacated of drilling soldiers. The sudden appearance of Sam Killion at the end of the street took him by surprise, and he thought fleetingly about heading in the opposite direction, pretending he hadn't seen him. But in a moment it was too late. Sam spotted him, waved, and hastened toward him.

"Mornin', Killion," Griff said none too brightly.

"Good to see you, McCulloch."

"I'm surprised to hear you say that."

"I don't hold nothing against you."

"Well, it wasn't nothing personal, anyway. Just the liquor. Never could hold the stuff."

"Good reason to stay away from it."

"I reckon so."

They paused for an awkward moment before the silence was broken.

Griff spoke first. "I just saw Deborah. It might interest you to know I'm gonna be foreman of her outfit in Texas."

This was obviously news to Sam, who took another long, awkward moment to respond. "That so?" he finally said tightly.

"Yeah."

Sam gathered his momentarily lost composure. "I reckon I ought to be glad she'll have someone like you along."

"Ought to be, but ain't, right?" said Griff rather defensively.

"I'll be frank with you, McCulloch, it worries me a little. Deborah's had her full share of troubles in her life, and I don't want to see no more come her way if it can be helped."

"You think I'll bring her trouble?"

"You ain't exactly been an angel all your life—not that any of us have been. But I'm not fully convinced you are completely cleared with the law—"

"Set your mind at ease, Preacher," cut in Griff, though not harshly. "I don't want to bring no trouble to Deborah, either. I know this here lawman up in Wichita by the name of Earp. He says there ain't no papers out on me because no one ever clearly identified me. Without that, there ain't no proof against me. I'm cleared as long as I keep clean in the future."

"That's actually the question, isn't it?" said Sam warily.

"Ain't you preachers supposed to trust folks?"

"Gentle as doves, wise as serpents."

"Seems I recall hearing that before. Well, I'm through with that life. But if you're worried, why don't you go to Texas with her?"

That idea had occurred to Sam more than once in the past several days, but the answer was always the same. "I've got responsibilities here. This is where I must be for now."

"Well, you're a durn fool, Killion, letting her get away like that."

"What does that mean?"

"I think what is really worrying you is knowing her and me is going off together. But it's your fault if anything happens."

Sam bristled. He knew McCulloch was dead right. But he also knew he couldn't go running off to Texas after an illusion. Deborah wasn't ready for marriage, and he wasn't ready to accept anything else.

"Listen here, McCulloch," challenged Sam, sounding for the moment more like an angry Texas Ranger than a benevolent preacher, "I can't stop you from going, but if I ever hear that you hurt her—"

"Hold on, Preacher!" broke in Griff, half-mocking. "They'll defrock you for what you're about to say. I ain't never gonna hurt Deborah . . . and I doubt I'd ever marry her, even if she'd have me. I ain't the marrying kind—and Deborah ain't the kind to have it any other way. So set your mind at ease, unless one or the other of us makes a drastic change. But you're still a durn fool. I'll bet you ain't even *asked* her to marry you."

"Well, for one thing," defended Sam, "it wouldn't be proper since she ain't been widowed a full year."

"This is the West, Killion. None of that eastern propriety is worth spit here."

Sam tried to think of all the other valid excuses; suddenly they all seemed rather lame. But the outlaw Griff McCulloch suddenly made a great deal of sense. Sam should have realized right then there was something wrong with a conclusion that placed the ex-outlaw in the right. But in the heat of the moment, he decided he had been foolish to simply assume what might be and conclude what Deborah might be thinking without even asking her. Moreover, he had been so certain of her response that he hadn't even prayed about it.

Thus, when he left Griff that day, he knew exactly what he had to do.

———

Sam prayed about Deborah for several days after the conversation with Griff. He even went off for three days to a deserted cabin in the hills to be alone.

When he finished praying he still found himself reticent to approach her, a completely uncharacteristic sensation for him. He was so confused that he did not know if his hesitancy was a warning from God or his own cowardice. After all, asking a woman to marry was no small thing under even the best of circumstances. But in Deborah's case, considering her past experiences, this was greatly magnified. If he asked and was turned down, that was it; all his hopes would be ended in one quick blow. Still, wouldn't that be the best way? Get it over with quick, like pulling a knife out of a wound.

But he couldn't bear the thought of losing her friendship, as was sure to happen, along with his hopes. Yet, if she went to Texas without him, he would lose her anyway.

In the end he put off speaking to her about this for over a month, and it might well have been longer had not the arrival of a special mail pouch in October prompted him into action.

65

SAM DELIVERED THE POUCH TO Deborah personally, only guessing about what he held in his hand and how it would affect his future.

Excitedly, Deborah tore open the envelope. As she unfolded the papers inside, a smaller paper floated out onto the counter where she stood. She picked it up and gasped.

"Sam . . ." Tears began to rise in her eyes. "It's a certified check for forty-seven hundred dollars! Oh, dear Lord! I can't believe it!"

Sam tried to catch her excitement. "I'm happy for you, Deborah."

Deborah continued, having perused the lawyer's enclosed letter. "Mr. Stillwell says he has reserved the money to pay Mr. Farley, but he thought I'd want the rest of the money as soon as possible. He will send me the title to the property the moment he completes the transaction with Farley. Do you know what this means, Sam?"

Sam shook his head, though he was afraid he knew very well what it meant.

"Sam, there is no reason why I can't start for Texas immediately. If I leave this week, I can get there before winter hampers travel. Griff says it'll take about a month to travel there with a wagon and the children."

"But there may be problems with settling before clear title can be established," reasoned Sam. "You don't need that kind of attention."

"I'll have Mr. Stillwell send the title directly to Fort Griffin, which is near the ranch. Who knows—it could arrive before I do. And even if it doesn't, I have the paper Mr. Farley gave you explaining the pending transaction. There won't be any trouble. But, Sam, I'm willing to risk it. I just can't wait another moment! I'm going to leave Monday—as long as Griff, Slim, and Longjim are ready. That will give me one last chance to hear you preach." Suddenly Deborah stopped as reality caught up with her excitement. She had tried studiously not to think of what leaving was going to mean to her friendship with Sam. She found little comfort in the fact that this was the first time in her life that she chose to leave a relationship rather than the other way around. It hurt almost as much. This was her choice, and she was going to something wonderful, but she still felt the emptiness of facing another loss.

"Oh, Sam, I am going to miss you!" The brimming tears spilled onto her cheeks.

"Texas ain't all that far." He tried to sound like his old, buoyant self. "Why, I've been known to ride farther than that for a camp meeting."

"You will come to visit us?"

"Of course I will!"

"I doubt there will be many churches there on the frontier."

"You'll keep on reading your Bible and praying, won't you?"

"Oh yes!"

Sam opened his mouth to speak another superficial remark, but stopped. In his mind, he heard Griff's voice:

You're a durn fool for letting her go.

How could he tell her to pray and read her Bible and leave it at that? How would he ever know the answer to the real question that burned in his heart until he asked it? What did it matter if she refused him; he was losing her anyway.

Hurriedly, before he lost his nerve once more, he blundered ahead. "Deborah, I know maybe I'm speaking out of turn, but with you thinking about leaving so soon I figure I best speak now or, as they say, forever hold my peace. It's just that . . . well, I care for you an awful lot, Deborah, and I'd be right honored to marry you." He paused, took a ragged breath, and stole a glance at her.

"Oh, Sam . . ." The very tone of her voice, both sad and regretful, told him before anything else what her answer was going to be.

"I knew I should have kept my mouth shut," Sam said, hoping to spare her from having to utter difficult words.

"This takes me so completely off my guard."

"I guess I thought you might feel a little bit the same for me—"

"Sam, you know I care for you deeply. It's just that my love for Broken Wing has not faded enough to free me for another. I know I do not speak of him often, but that is not because I have forgotten him, but rather because of the Cheyenne tradition of never speaking of the dead. I realize now that is a superstition that may not fit in with my Christian life, yet I feel that out of respect for who Broken Wing was, I must honor him in this way. Perhaps when Sky is older I will be bound to give this up in order that my son may learn of his father. But for now, it is all much too near to easily shake.

"Nevertheless," she continued, "even though I don't speak of Broken Wing, his memory still occupies the largest part of my heart. The pain of his loss is never far from me. For that reason alone, I am not ready for marriage. But there is more and, though I am ashamed to admit it, I must be honest with myself and with you. I simply cannot bring myself to the place where I can risk loving another, especially in that way. We have spoken of this before, Sam, and I have not changed. I pray about it often, because sometimes I fear this weakness in me also hinders my relationship with my children. I can't let them go far from me for fear of losing them. Sometimes I see this causes terrible rebellion in Carolyn, who is every bit as headstrong and independent as her mother. I try to let go, but I can't.

"So, you see, I must somehow deal with my children because I have no choice. I doubt I could do so otherwise. But I could not go *willingly* seeking this kind of risk. Sam, could you promise never to die on me?"

Sam lowered his eyes. He could not look at her as he shook his head. "I wish I could, Deborah, but you know I can't."

"I know . . ." she murmured, in a tone as regretful as his. "Maybe someday God will heal this weakness in me."

"I believe He will, Deborah. And in the meantime, He will use it to make you strong, for remember, in our weaknesses we are made strong."

Weeping, Deborah threw her arms around Sam and kissed his cheek. Sam, taken aback by her completely unexpected gesture, just stood there. But he knew that in a moment it would be over and Deborah would be as good as gone from him, perhaps forever. Thus, before the moment was lost, he lifted his arms, feeling stiff and wooden, and wrapped them around her also. He didn't return her kiss, though he yearned to.

When they fell apart, he was out of breath, and he noted that she looked somewhat flushed, but neither of them said anything. They both knew there was nothing else to be said. The time simply was not right for them; perhaps it never would be. Then again, maybe someday it just might work out—at least that's what Sam, always hopeful, always optimistic, thought as he left the Sutler's store.

———

True to her word, on the following Monday Deborah and her little party of migrants made ready to depart Fort Dodge. Slim, with Deborah beside him, drove the covered wagon, filled nearly to the brim with supplies purchased from Hardee. The children were nestled into a cozy corner at the front of the wagon where they were near their mother and could look out through the opening at the passing scenery. Griff and Longjim, on their own mounts, flanked the wagon, which was drawn by four sturdy stock horses. The gray stallion and Slim's pinto were tied to the back of the wagon.

On the ground stood Sam and Hardee, both looking rather forlorn and dejected. Hardee had hugged each of the children about ten times and shed more tears than he was willing to admit to when Deborah embraced and kissed him. Sam had also hugged the children who had over the months become dear to him, and he had given each a bag of hard candy to amuse them on the long trip. He and Deborah exchanged only verbal goodbyes. Sam feared that if he embraced her again, he'd never let go.

Slim was about to spur the horses into motion when a uniformed figure, loping across the parade ground, waved and called to them.

"Mrs. Graham, hold up!" It was Lt. Godfrey.

All out of breath, he came to a stop on Deborah's side of the wagon. "I'm glad I caught you," he said. "I've been out on maneuvers for a week and just this morning heard of your departure."

"I'm glad you came by, Lieutenant," said Deborah. "I hoped I could tell you goodbye. I will not forget your kindness."

"And likewise, ma'am, I'll never forget you!" He paused, then suddenly seemed to remember he was not empty-handed. He held out a bow and a deerskin quiver of arrows. "One of the men took this from the Washita encampment after the . . . battle." He hesitated a moment over the awkwardness of the topic, then continued. "I know it isn't a time any of us are fond of recalling, but I just thought that since you lost everything there, you might like something as a reminder of the Cheyenne people you loved. It isn't much, I know, but maybe when your boy is older he might like to have a real Cheyenne bow."

Godfrey thrust the bow and quiver toward Deborah, but she hesitated before taking it. She recognized the bow immediately as one made by Twelve Trees, one of the best bow makers in the village. It was an excellent specimen of his work, and Broken Wing had had one very similar to it that had been buried with him. This was a prize and a memento she ought to accept eagerly and cherish, yet part of her rebelled against accepting such a gift from a man who represented those who had killed her husband and destroyed her beloved home.

Before the passing moment grew too awkward, however, Deborah chanced to look directly into the lieutenant's eyes. There she saw such sincerity and open entreaty that another part of her began to stir—the part that sought, though sometimes unsuccessfully, to live her life according to how her new Lord would respond. And she knew that Christ would not have refused such a well-meant offering.

She reached out and took the gift. "Thank you, Lt. Godfrey. It will be a treasure to me, as will your friendship."

He grinned with relief and pleasure. "Godspeed, Mrs. Graham. And one last word of advice—be careful of Indians after you cross the Red River. We've had recent word that there are several renegade tribes operating quite freely in Texas."

"Thank you, Lieutenant. But I am certain that, as you said, God will speed us along safely."

Then with a loud "Geeyup!" Slim got the wagon moving, and the party left the security of the fort. Deborah waved vigorously to her friends until they faded from sight, and continued to glance backward at the fort until it also disappeared from view. Her parting looks were not entirely from regret, nor were they from doubt. Even if Fort Dodge had little to recommend but its dust and crude, unkempt soldiers, she knew she was leaving a special part of herself behind in that sprawling, rough place. There, she had met her very Best Friend, her Savior and God; there, also, she was leaving the best friend He himself had given her—Sam Killion.

But while sadness tugged at her from behind, anticipation and hopefulness drew her forward. She was on her way to her very own home! Where a new life awaited her, where her children could grow and be nurtured, and where she herself could continue to become the kind of person God intended her to be.

PART 7

NEW BEGINNINGS

66

DEBORAH REINED HER MOUNT as she topped a small rise. The gray stallion, recently christened "Pepper" by Carolyn because of the smattering of black hairs in his coat, whinnied and stamped his foot impatiently at stopping when there was such an inviting stretch of flatland on which to run. He had only just begun to stretch his strong legs.

Glancing over her shoulder, Deborah smiled at the cloud of dust raised by her military escort. The gray whinnied again, and Deborah was certain he, too, glanced back.

If it was flat terrain that the gray wanted, then he should have been more than satisfied in Deborah's new home. These lands on the northern Brazos in west Texas were one flat plain after another, with hardly a tree or a plant interrupting the grassy expanse. Only the azure sky overhead was more extensive in its reach. This rise on which Deborah now paused to survey the countryside was likely the tallest hill around. She supposed, by some estimates, the land was monotonous, even barren. But she never failed to be thrilled by it. Perhaps part of that was because as far as her eye could see, this particular stretch of real estate belonged to her!

And tucked safely in her saddlebag was indisputable proof of that fact, obtained just yesterday from the postmaster at Fort Griffin. But the deed from Mr. Farley, now legally bearing her name, represented only a part of her acquisitions. Immediately upon arriving at the fort last November, she had begun purchasing other land in case the deal with Farley somehow fell through. Land was cheap, and she quickly learned that much more was needed to support even an average size herd than she had imagined. By various means she had come into possession of another five thousand acres and was working on a deal to purchase four thousand more. With Farley's land, it would give her a total of fourteen thousand acres—a sum that continually astounded her, being many times larger than anything even imagined in Virginia. If she started riding at dawn, it would take her until noon to cross her property at its widest point.

Deborah realized, of course, that by Texas standards her tract of land was only average. Under the best of conditions, she could graze no more than five hundred head of cattle on the entire portion, but the open range gave her additional space. She was not blind to the reason why the land had sold so cheaply. Not only was the land relatively barren, there were also the Comanche—though, thus far, since her arrival, she had encountered no trouble with them.

Nevertheless, the commander of the fort had upbraided her soundly for the foolhardiness of settling that far west, reminding her, as if she didn't know, that the fort was forty miles away, and it would easily take two full days to summon and receive help from that source.

Deborah recalled her most recent visit to the fort, from which she was now returning home. The commander, a Captain Ludlam, still managed to find opportunity to browbeat her.

"You don't mean to tell me you rode here all by yourself!" he had exclaimed upon seeing her.

"I did."

"I thought you was maybe a mite crazy before, but now I see you're just plumb *deranged*. What were you thinking of?" He waved his hands in the air with frustration. "We got hostiles out there, Mrs. Graham. Why, just a week ago, Comanches raided a homestead east of you. Everyone, to a man, was killed—not just killed, but butchered. Do you understand? Men, women, and children, excepting for a little girl they took captive. God only knows what'll become of her!" He paused, suddenly realizing the impropriety of his words spoken to a lady. But deciding this stubborn woman needed to be shocked, he forged ahead. "I buried them folks myself, ma'am. I been fighting Indians for years and I have never beheld the horrendous atrocities that were performed upon those poor souls. So maybe you'll excuse my fit of temper when I hear you've been prancing over the plains like you owned the world."

"Listen, Captain Ludlam, what you have told me about the raid makes me heartsick," said Deborah with intense sincerity. "But it also makes me more certain that I did the right thing in coming alone. I have three men working for me—all crack shots—and a Mexican woman caring for my children. She could handle a gun if need be. However, one of my men is down from a snakebite; I nearly lost him. That leaves two men—possibly three in a pinch—and a woman to defend my place and my children. There is no way you can convince me I should have taken any of them from the defense of my home and family."

The captain clamped his mouth shut, ceasing any further protests. Deborah continued. "I have a horse that can outrun any Comanche mount on these plains, and I am a pretty fair shot myself, otherwise I would not have taken such a risk."

She no doubt left him thinking she was just as crazy as before, but she had noted a new respect in his voice as he concluded the interview.

"I will be happy to dispatch six of my troopers to accompany you back home, Mrs. Graham."

"Thank you, Captain; you have made me nervous enough to accept."

The troopers were trailing behind her now, two of them looking rather disgruntled as they trotted up next to her. Having heard her boasts about the gray, they had challenged her to a race and were now regretting their cocky bravado. The fact that two trained cavalry troopers had been beaten by a woman would be a hard defeat to live down.

"Mrs. Graham," said one of them with the utmost respect, "now that we are so far distant from the fort, I feel it would be wise to ride in close formation."

"All right, Sergeant Butler, I'll try, but sometimes it is hard to hold Pepper back."

Of course, her statement was pure bunk. She had complete control of the gray even when they were galloping full-tilt over the plains, but she couldn't tell these soldiers, who were only following orders and trying to be helpful, that their company made her as nervous as riding alone in hostile Indian territory. She wondered if she would ever feel quite comfortable around bluecoats.

But while she was at the fort, it hadn't been the soldiers that had disturbed her most. Rather, it had come from a group of settlers gathered in the Sutler's store, similar to the one in Fort Dodge. One man in particular had seemed bent on harassing her—a man named William Yates. He was tall and husky, and no doubt had earned his nickname of "Big Bill" Yates for that reason. He was in his mid-thirties and had a broad, round face toughened by years of outdoor labor. He started in on Deborah barely a moment after she entered the store.

"Ain't you that woman that bought the Farley place?" he asked, though the tone of his voice and the glint of his cool gray eyes indicated his words were a demand, not a question.

Deborah was immediately put on her guard. But these men were her neighbors, even if some of them were more than a day's ride away from her, and she felt it necessary to be friendly.

"Yes, I am. I arrived last winter. I don't believe I have met you, sir. My name is Deborah Graham."

"Name's Yates. I came here a year ago." He stated this as if it were of great significance that his arrival predated hers.

"I am glad to meet you, Mr. Yates." She extended her hand, but Yates ignored it. She spoke again, tightly, but still determined to be neighborly. "Whereabouts is your place?"

"North of you."

Much to Deborah's relief the conversation temporarily waned and she took the opportunity to place her order with the storekeeper. But Yates wasn't through with her.

"You the one with the half-breed kid?" he asked, or rather barked.

All of Deborah's Christian virtues could not prevent her from rankling at this, but her tone remained even as she answered, "I have a son who is half Cheyenne."

"Well, I'm going to be blunt with you," he said, as if this were news. "I was neighbor to the family that was just massacred by them murdering Injuns. I knew Pete Cook personally."

"You have my sympathies, Mr. Yates. The whole incident is simply dreadful." Somehow, though, Deborah did not think it was sympathy that Yates was looking for.

"I don't like Injuns, Mrs. Graham. I hate them. I'll kill any on sight and ask questions later. You understand?"

"I don't know why you are telling me this."

"You just keep that Injun kid of yours in tow. He'll get nothing but trouble here if he tries anything."

"My son is two years old, Mr. Yates!" exclaimed Deborah with utter revulsion.

"Ma'am," said another man, "we don't mean to be un-neighborly, but these days we're all pretty touchy about Injuns. We just figured you'd want to be fairly warned."

"Warned—!" Deborah's fury momentarily tied up her tongue and she could not speak.

"We don't blame the boy," said this new speaker. "It ain't *his* fault what's in his blood—" This was spoken with such haughty self-righteousness that Deborah began to sputter again, but to no verbal effect. "Especially seeing as how the boy is just a baby," the man continued. "But he ain't going to be a baby forever. And so you might say we're just concerned about the future."

Deborah had absolutely no ready response for this. She wanted to tell them what foolish bigots they were, what imbeciles. She wanted to accuse them of being the cause of all the Indian problems. She wanted to scream, she wanted to physically attack them. But she did none of these things. Instead, she spun around on her heel and left the store.

It had taken half the ride back home for her to simmer down after that encounter. She had welcomed the race with the soldiers as a much-needed release of her pent-up emotions. And she had to admit she had gloated in her victory more than she normally would have.

The sun was low in the western sky when they crossed onto Deborah's land. They had left the fort at dawn, and it would be another hour before reaching the ranch house. Deborah realized more acutely than ever how isolated she was. Seven well-mounted riders could make the trek in a day at a brisk pace; an entire company, with provisions, would take two days at best. Besides the fort, Deborah's nearest neighbors—two brothers and their wives, with a handful of children—were twenty miles away. She had sought isolation and found it, but with it came risks as well.

The afternoon sun had dropped out of sight when they passed a scraggly post oak that stood as a landmark of sorts indicating only five more miles to the house. There, Deborah first noticed that the sky was becoming streaked with gray. She thought it was the sunset, or perhaps one of those sudden spring storms the area was so famous for.

Sergeant Butler drew up next to her, his nose twitching in the air. "You smell something peculiar?" he said.

The gray stallion had been growing progressively skittish, but Deborah attributed this to the nearness of home. Now, she also sniffed the air. It was definitely a pungent, burning odor. Deborah glanced at Butler, perplexed and alarmed. They rode on at a brisk pace, Deborah and Butler now several lengths ahead of the others. Then they heard it.

Gunfire!

Deborah gave no thought to consequences; all she heard echoing in her mind were Captain Ludlam's words: *"I have never beheld the horrendous atrocities that were performed upon those poor souls."*

Her children were in danger, perhaps already at the mercy of raiding Comanche. That the continuing sound of gunfire indicated her men were yet giving fight provided little comfort. All she could think of was her children in the midst of battle and fire, just like Washita. They had been spared then, but what would prevent them from being taken now?

"Oh, God . . ." she cried. "Not now, God. . . !"

She dug her heels into the gray's flanks, and as the stallion responded to her urging, Deborah drew her rifle and charged as if she were the entire Tenth Cavalry. Her six companions were galloping right at her heels, rifles and Colts also drawn and ready for action.

67

TWO DOZEN COMANCHE WARRIORS surrounded Deborah's house. Half a dozen Indian bodies lay fallen in the yard.

As Deborah galloped onto the scene and saw the fierce warriors, she was in no frame of mind to make a rational count of her enemies. There could have been a hundred of them, or merely ten. What mattered was that they were attacking her home, her family! They had already set the barn ablaze and the flames, as they licked up toward the cloudless sky, had ignited a fire in a corner of the house.

Deborah fired five shots in rapid succession, loading her Sharps breech-loader each time faster than a single breath. Two Comanche braves fell, but she couldn't be sure if it was due to her fire or that of the bluecoats, who were now lending a lethal support to the battle.

The arriving reinforcements placed the Comanche in a precarious position. Previously they had been assured of victory. Another torch to the house, if only the staunch defenders would allow them to get close enough, would have sealed the end of the battle. But suddenly the Indians found themselves sandwiched in on two sides. Moreover, they had no idea if the arriving cavalry were the vanguard of a larger force. In moments they could well find themselves facing an entire company!

Their only hope was to recover to a more advantageous position. But Sergeant Butler, a seasoned veteran of the Indian wars, second-guessed the Comanche. He realized a divided force was usually weakened, yet he also knew a two-front battle was just as tenuous. Surmising immediately that the defenders of the besieged house were excellent shots, and the risk to his men of being cut down by "friendly fire" was minimal, he decided to maintain his position and literally put the squeeze on the warriors.

Two more Indians fell, but the gunfire from the house was also diminishing. They could well be running out of ammunition.

It became a battle plan that had to be measured in minutes, not hours, for soon the Comanche would realize no more white reinforcements were coming. If the Indians were not routed quickly, both the soldiers and the residents of the house would be lost. Butler and his men, with Deborah's able support, returned a ferocious barrage of fire in the next five minutes. They were free enough with their ammo to further encourage the assumption that a larger force of soldiers was on the way.

Three more Comanche lay dead, but one of Butler's men also fell before the Comanche made good a hasty retreat.

A loud whoop rose from the soldiers and Deborah could hear cheers from the house also. Without pausing for a breath, Deborah galloped to the house where the residents were already filing out of the smoky quarters.

"Children!" Deborah cried, leaping from the gray's back and racing on foot the rest of the distance to the house.

"Mama!" they called in unison.

Sky first ran into her anxious arms, with Carolyn right behind her brother.

The girl was weeping as she clung to her mother. "Mama, why were the Indians shooting? Don't they know we are friends?"

The simple question burned into Deborah's heart. "I know it's confusing, dear, but . . ." That was all she could say, for it was too complex even for Deborah to comprehend.

In the meantime, the soldiers, with the assistance of Griff and Longjim, were busy dousing the fire in the house. A frustrated Slim, immobile from a snakebite, had been able to sit by a window and lend gun support to the Indian battle, but he was helpless to assist in the cleanup. The barn had already burned to the ground. But fortunately, by the time the last flame was quenched, only a quarter of the house had been lost. The kitchen and front of the house were intact. A bedroom in back, the only other room in the house, had been totally destroyed. Yolanda, Deborah's nurse for the children, quickly set about wiping away the ashes from the kitchen and began preparing supper for the household and the heroic soldiers. With this task in good hands, Deborah turned to more grievous work.

Leaving the children with Yolanda, she headed out to the barn. Griff was already there, shaking his head miserably.

"We were pinned down when they torched the barn, Deborah," he said remorsefully. "I tried to get out to save the horses but..." He paused, wiping a hand across his grimy, sweat-streaked face. Deborah noticed blood running down the back of his hand.

"Griff, you're wounded!"

"Just grazed a mite. Ain't nothing. It's the loss of the horses that hurts more."

"All of them?"

"Except for Longjim's. He was out on the range when the shooting started. He rode in and slipped into the back door of the house; I reckon—leastways I hope—his horse wandered off somewhere and is safe." Griff's voice was tight with emotion. Deborah had never seen him like this. "Deborah, I had that palomino of mine for a lot of years. Why, he was a better friend to me than most humans!"

"I am so sorry, Griff."

"I coulda killed every one of them Injuns for that alone."

"Oh, Griff..."

Suddenly ashamed because of his harsh words, Griff quickly added, "Forgive me, Deborah. I forgot for a minute how you feel 'bout Indians."

She gave a sympathetic shake of her head. "I could have done the same, Griff, when I saw my children and my friends in danger. God forgive me, but in an instant I forgot all those years of love."

"It's only natural." Griff tried to comfort her, but with little success.

"I'm confused, Griff. I hadn't let myself think of it until now, but I *have* made myself the enemy by moving here, by taking over Indian lands. I've done to these Comanche just what other whites did to the Cheyenne."

"Now you ain't being fair to yourself at all!" argued Griff. "You're entitled to land and a home, too. There's plenty for everyone."

"But don't you see? I just came and took it over. Why didn't I ask them first—"

" 'Cause you woulda been scalped and murdered before you even opened your mouth! That's the difference between the Comanche and Cheyenne."

"I don't believe that. The Comanche were allies of the Cheyenne by a treaty that has lasted more than a quarter of a century. I know the Comanche are a lot more brutal in their ways, and I don't condone their barbarous acts. Even the most primitive peoples must have an innate sense of right and wrong. Yet, I believe much of their behavior

362

is retaliatory; and if they are treated with respect, that is what they will give in return."

"Now don't go and tell me you plan to go prancing up to their hideout in the panhandle and make a private treaty with 'em."

"I realize it is too late for such gestures. I do value my scalp, whatever you and the U.S. Army may think."

"So, what are you planning to do?" asked Griff suspiciously. "You ain't going to sell out, are you?"

"That thought has crossed my mind." At Griff's gaping stare, she hastened to add, "But I believe what you said before is right, Griff. There is room for everyone; we just have to learn how to live together."

"Now, you're talking sense. And I'll tell you, Deborah, if you leave here, another white is just going to move in who ain't going to give a hoot about respecting Indians. So, in the long run, the Comanche are better off with you here."

"I just have to convince them of that," Deborah said with a determined glint in her blue eyes.

"Yeah . . ." A wary wrinkle etched Griff's brow.

"Griff, I suppose the wagon was in the barn." When Griff nodded with a perplexed scowl, Deborah continued. "The soldiers' horses will have to do. Come on, Griff. We have a lot of work to do, and as it is, we'll be working after dark."

———

The moon had risen full in the sky and lent an appropriate, dolorous light to the conclusion of Deborah's labors. With the help of Griff and three of the soldiers, she had loaded the bodies of the fallen Comanche on the army horses—given none too cheerfully by the soldiers whose own comrade lay in a freshly dug grave—and carried the dead Indians to a remote pasture some three miles from the house. There, the soldiers, at her instruction, laid all thirteen bodies on the ground in a careful row.

The soldiers then watched with mixed awe and disgust as Deborah proceeded to prepare each body for a proper Indian burial. The scarcity of wood allowed no scaffolds to be built, so the ground had to serve as a bed, but she had brought along all the Comanche weapons left behind at the battle site. These she distributed among the bodies which she had carefully groomed and painted for war. She knew only the Cheyenne rituals, but she hoped there were enough similarities so that this would suffice. She hoped, if nothing else, that when, and if, the Comanche returned to retrieve the bodies of their brothers, they would see and apprehend the meaning of Deborah's gesture of respect.

When the bodies were all arranged in the most suitable and honorable repose, she stood back and sang a Cheyenne burial song. Then she murmured the traditional words that still made her heart ache:

"Nothing lives long, only the earth and the mountains."

And, because she had no hides, she covered the bodies with prairie grass.

A few hours ago she had been fighting these men; her own bullets might well have killed some of them. Yet they were not her enemies. An innate respect for human life, nurtured in her by Broken Wing and brought to its fullness through her relationship with Christ, could not be so easily crushed even by fear for her loved ones. Perhaps she was caught in a confusing dichotomy, but the love that God had placed in her heart was constant. It would in the end conquer the hatred and misunderstanding of others. Last fall when she left Fort Dodge, Lt. Godfrey had given her the bow because she had come away from Washita with nothing. Now she realized she had, by the grace of God, carried away all the best things in her heart.

Before Deborah lifted her head, she was prompted to offer a Christian prayer, not so much for the dead, who were beyond her prayers, but for those who remained and for whom there was still hope.

"Dear God, these fallen warriors are your creation; they belong to you and their fate is in your merciful hands, as is that of Private Haley who fell so heroically in our defense. Give us the strength to love our enemies, to avoid falling victim to the hatred and distrust that so abounds in this world. Somehow, dear God, make this ranch a haven for your peace and love in a complicated and confusing world."

As Deborah lifted her head she noted that all the men standing beside her, even Griff, had bowed their heads and removed their hats for her prayer. Maybe there was hope after all. The small party of mourners then mounted their horses and rode in a solemn silence back to the ranch house.

No one saw the lone mounted figure in the distance silently observing the proceedings. The Comanche warrior had, indeed, returned to discover the fate of his fallen comrades, one of whom was his younger brother. He had been shocked at what he saw—a white woman laying out the bodies of the dead warriors as if she were their grieving sister. It had so stunned his senses that he completely forgot about the rifle gripped in his hand ready for use.

68

IN THE NEXT TWO MONTHS, UNHAMPERED by further Indian raids, Deborah worked tirelessly to make her ranch productive. While Griff and a much-recovered Slim labored at rebuilding the destroyed barn and portions of the house, she and Longjim, whose mount had survived the fire, concentrated on replenishing the most grievous loss of the horses, for without them they could round up no cattle.

In this part of Texas, herds of mustangs still roamed freely in large numbers. Deborah quickly envisioned a profitable business in breaking these fine, wild animals and selling them. First, however, they had to be captured. It took two days of hard work to bring in a small herd of eight, but she and the men had been choosy, since these would be for their own use. Deborah spent the better part of one morning coaxing in a particularly grand filly with a dun-colored coat and black mane and tail.

She and Longjim drove the herd triumphantly into the yard and were greeted with whoops and cheers from the others. Carolyn ran right toward the herd and was saved from being trampled only by Slim's quick intervention.

Too young to realize the danger she had been in, she continued to struggle in an attempt to escape from Slim's confining arms.

"Horses!" she cried with glee. "Mama, I want a horse!"

Deborah was torn between scolding her errant daughter and laughing with pleasure at their shared love of horses. She dismounted and went to her daughter.

"Carolyn, you may choose one of these for your own, but first Griff and Slim get to have their pick." She turned to her friends, "Go ahead, take your pick."

Slim chose a roan and white pinto that looked almost identical to the one he had lost in the fire. Griff went right for the dun filly.

Deborah smiled at his choice, for she had thought of him when she was toiling to bring the animal in.

But the minute he flung his rope around the filly's neck, Carolyn began to shout, "That's the one I wanted! It's mine!"

"Carolyn!" Deborah scolded. "You are being rude and selfish. That will be enough!"

Griff only laughed. "The girl knows good horseflesh just like her mother!" He led the filly to where Carolyn still sat perched in Slim's arms and handed her the rope. "Here you go, sweetie—a present from your Uncle Griff. Only thing is, you gotta break her yourself."

"Griff, she's only four years old," protested Deborah.

"Well, maybe I'll help a mite," added Griff. "That a deal, Lynnie?"

Carolyn nodded vigorously. She already knew how to ride and felt completely confident in her ability to tame the mustang. When she and Griff shook hands, her tiny, delicate hand nearly buried in his big rough paw, a bond of friendship was formed between the two that would survive many years.

True to his word, Griff helped Carolyn—or Lynnie, as he was fond of calling her—with the filly, which she christened "Bunny" because she had once seen a rabbit on the prairie with similar coloring. Deborah had to admit that Griff was good with this strong-willed child who seemed to think she already knew all there was to know about breaking a horse. Griff did what many parents would not have had the patience or nerve to do—he let her do it her way. After only ten minutes of this, Carolyn was contritely calling to him for help, and she listened to Griff as she never would to her own mother.

In a way, Deborah was glad her daughter had someone she could admire and go to for help, which she came to do with Griff in other matters besides horse-breaking. Yet it grieved her because that someone wasn't Deborah herself. She had noticed for some time that Carolyn had begun to draw away from her mother. It was subtle at first, like when she declared she was too big to sit in her mother's lap, then turned around and sought out Yolanda's lap. Or, when Deborah was showing her daughter how to make a rein out of a length of rope and Carolyn would glance at Griff or one of the other men to verify the accuracy of the teaching.

Deborah had no idea that this gradual pulling away had been greatly intensified as a result of an incident following the Comanche raid. That evening after supper the family, including Griff, Slim, Longjim, and Yolanda, were unwinding with the five soldiers. They were all engaged in an innocent conversation, and one of the soldiers

had inquired about Deborah's time with the Cheyenne and compli-
mented her on what a fine lad Sky was.

This was too much for Carolyn, who had no reticence around her
elders, and she piped up petulantly, "I am Cheyenne, too, you know!"

They laughed at this. "Why, there ain't a drop of Injun blood in
you, child, and that's obvious," said a soldier.

"My brother is Cheyenne; I am Cheyenne!"

"It don't work that way, missy, when you got a different pa."

"That's not true! Tell him, Mama."

Deborah hesitated. She had hoped to have had more time before
having to confront this dilemma, yet she should have known that with
a child like Carolyn she had only been fooling herself. They had
talked in deliberately vague terms about the physical differences between Carolyn and Sky, but there had never been cause to go beyond
this. And, Deborah was not anxious to do so.

Sensing the immediate tension, the soldier added quickly, "I ain't
spoke out of turn, have I, ma'am?"

"No," said Deborah. "Not at all." She skirted away from the subject
by offering more pie to her guests.

Later, when they were alone, Carolyn brought the subject up
again. "Wasn't my papa Cheyenne, Mama?"

"No, dear, you had a different pa than Sky. He was white."

"Tell me about him like you tell about Sky's nehuo."

"There's really not much to tell, Carolyn."

"Was he a warrior like Sky's pa?"

Spoken so simply, yet fraught with such youthful yearning, the
question made Deborah wince. And at this moment Deborah did
what she was sure to regret in later years; she began to perpetuate
the great lie about Carolyn's dead father. She did so with the noblest
of motives, believing that even God would forgive her for trying to
give her child some positive memories to cling to. How could she
tell her innocent child that her own father was a mean-spirited, abu-
sive animal, who had succumbed to foul play, and that Carolyn's own
mother stood convicted of the man's murder?

But she kept her explanation simple and vague for, even then,
she did not wish to become caught in a tangled web of deceit.

"Your father was a rancher. I did not know him well and he died
... suddenly. He was a ... good man, Carolyn, but there isn't really
much to tell about him."

Since this was the first she had ever heard about her dead father,
it seemed to satisfy Carolyn. Yet, she was puzzled at the chilly tone
in her mother's voice as she spoke of the man; it was so different

from when she spoke of Sky's father. Perhaps for this reason alone she did not ask about him again for a long time. She was a little afraid of what else her mother might say. Yet it began to undermine her security in her little family. She was too young to *know* that something was wrong, but even a four-year-old can sense such things.

———

With horses to make them mobile, Wind Rider Ranch could move forward and flourish. Once the mustangs were saddle broken, all four adults—except Yolanda, whose job it was to keep a vigilant eye on the children and the house—began to round up cattle. Like the mustangs, the famous Texas longhorns roamed the prairie freely, and many an industrious cattleman would make a fortune off this free gift of the plains.

By August, Deborah had rounded up some five hundred head. Griff calculated that they would bring an easy twenty thousand dollars at the railhead in Abilene. The only problem was getting them there.

Because the Comanche were still raiding the frontier settlements, and with no guarantees that the Wind Rider Ranch would remain unmolested, Deborah did not feel she could spare her men from the defense of the ranch. Yet if they didn't soon sell some cattle and bring in money, the ranch might cease to exist, anyway. Deborah and the men had many discussions over this dilemma.

Griff went to Jacksboro, a town about a hundred miles east of the ranch, to see about hiring a trail crew. There he met a colorful fellow named Reverend George Webb Slaughter, a circuit rider and rancher from the Fort Worth area, who was well known for preaching his fiery sermons while packing a six-shooter as protection against Indians. Griff was leery about getting mixed up with another preacher, but Slaughter's expertise with cattle and his upright business dealings received such abundant praise from all that Griff could hardly ignore the man. Moreover, Slaughter was willing to take another herd on consignment.

"I got four hundred head already tagged onto my bunch from a rancher south of here named Stoner," said Slaughter.

Griff immediately perked up at this. "Stoner, you say?"

"Yeah, you know the old buzzard?"

"Caleb Stoner?" When Slaughter nodded, Griff said casually, almost disinterestedly, "Naw, just heard of him."

The conversation quickly drifted to the cost of Slaughter's services, and Stoner was forgotten for the time being.

Slaughter loaned Griff three of his cowboys to take back to the ranch to help drive Deborah's herd to Jacksboro, as long as she was willing to use the preacher. She was more than agreeable to do business with Slaughter, especially after Griff's assurances of Slaughter's skill and integrity.

Griff said nothing about Stoner, deeming that such news might only cause Deborah undue distress. Stoner was a world away—well, at least several hundred miles away. It seemed highly improbable that he could ever give them any trouble. But it was kind of ironic that their cattle would be mingling nose to nose for a couple of months on the trail. According to Slaughter—a fact that slipped out in a later coversation—the Stoner outfit was so big that Stoner never personally accompanied his cows north, and his son only did so occasionally. This present four hundred head were just a drop in the bucket for them, and they were only sending them north because in a few months they'd be too old and rangy to bring a good price.

Griff drove the cattle to Jacksboro, and the drive north began by the first of September. Deborah would not hear from Reverend Slaughter again until well into December.

In the meantime, Deborah concentrated her efforts on reinforcing her mustang herd. The commanders of Fort Belknap, Fort Richardson, and Fort Griffin assured her the army would purchase practically anything she brought to them. Thus she rounded up a hundred head and spent the fall breaking the horses. By spring, they ought to fetch a good price from the army.

69

WORD OF DEBORAH'S QUALITY mustang business spread quickly over that part of Texas. True to their word, the army purchased a substantial number and impressed cavalry troopers passed the news of the fine mounts along to their civilian associations. It was very good for business. Perhaps a bit too good.

A satisfied customer rode down to Austin, and when men commented on his fine mount he told them about the lady rancher on the frontier in northwest Texas.

Laban Stoner was in the market for horses and he questioned the cowboy closer.

"You say the army deals with her?" he asked.

"Oh, yeah. Fact is, I found out about her through a trooper. Them army boys live and die by their horses, so if they are pleased, you gotta know there must be something to it."

"Where exactly is she?"

"Don't know exactly. I bought my horse from a fella in Jacksboro. But from what I hear she lives way out on the frontier west of Jacksboro."

Laban ruminated on this during his ride back to the ranch. The man who had been providing them with horses for years was becoming less reliable, and the quality of his stock was diminishing. Laban had been looking for sources by which he could infuse their present stock with new blood. If this female rancher in west Texas was as good as the drifter in Austin claimed, Laban saw no reason not to give her a try. Even the distance would not be a problem if the stock was good. He had always been partial to mustangs—that wild and free breed that roamed the plains with a tenacity that even captivity did not entirely dull. Of course, Laban's father sought the stylish breeds with fancy names and European bloodlines. He cared nothing for freedom.

The reminder of his father made Laban grimace. It brought to mind the dismaying fact that no matter what Laban wished for their ranch—and he used the word *their* in its most general term—everything had to pass the scrutiny of the *patron* before being acted upon. No decisions at the Stoner Ranch, except for those of the most minor nature, were reached without the approval of Caleb Stoner. And Laban felt certain that his own decisions received the most intense examination. Laban knew horses better than any man on the ranch—in fact, many neighbors often came to him for advice—but Caleb always managed to treat his half-breed Mexican son like a novice.

"Someday..." Laban murmured, but he did not complete the thought, for thinking of a future without Caleb seemed futile. The old tyrant would outlive them all; he was too mean-spirited to die. And Laban hated to admit it, but he himself was too spineless to do anything to help nature along ... not that he had not thought of it. But there were practical considerations, the main one being that Laban had never been able to ascertain if he was included in Caleb's will. It would never do to kill the old coot and then find himself disinherited, anyway. He might not be as lucky as that snip of a Virginia girl in escaping the gallows.

The ranch came into sight. The big sprawling house, so quiet, so empty, so forbidding, filled the yard like a shadow. Laban dismounted. His horse made its own way to the stable while Laban turned toward the house. He knocked on the door; he never entered without observing the formalities of a guest. He would never be more than a guest in Caleb's home.

Maria answered the door. "Ah, Señor Laban, it is you."

It had been at least two weeks since Laban had last been to the house. "Buenos dias, Maria. I would like to see Señor Caleb."

"Come in. I will tell him you are here."

"By all means," said Laban acidly. Maria did not notice his tone; over the years Caleb Stoner's youngest son had come to have far more bile in his voice than levity.

The woman, grown rather more portly, with far more gray than black in her hair, waddled away. Laban remained in the entryway, hat in hand, waiting. Would the *patron* honor him with an audience? That would depend on the man's mood. If he were in exceptionally good spirits, he would gladly receive his son for the prime opportunity he'd offer the old man for some choice browbeating. Caleb enjoyed nothing more than making others feel small. But more often than not, the *patron* was in a surly, morose mood; if he received his son then, Laban could expect nothing but the most harrowing experience.

Laban glanced around the entryway, seeming to see it for the first time. It was austere and cold, like the rest of the house, but the library table set against the wall was of black walnut and of sixteenth-century vintage. It was valuable, as were the antique brass sconces that flanked it on the wall. On an adjacent wall was an original Velasquez, a portrait of some Spanish grandee who most certainly must have winced at the blatant arrogance captured by the painter in his subject. No doubt this very trait had drawn Caleb to the painting—and had prompted him to pay a good deal more than he could afford for it.

Yes, there were pieces in this house worth a great deal, and someday they would belong to Laban. Someday he would be the *patron,* the master of the house. He would not have to wait at the door like a beggar, the son of a poor peon. It would all be his. But Laban's patience was wearing thin, and perhaps even his cowardice would not be able to withstand the pressure.

Maria reappeared. The *patron* would see him. Laban wasn't certain whether to accept that as good or bad news.

Caleb was in the drawing room. It did not bode well that he was here, for he seldom, if ever, entered this room. There, six years ago, his eldest and beloved son was murdered. Laban could not restrain an impulse to glance toward the spot where the body had been found on the floor behind the settee, near the french doors. A bloodstain still marked the carpet, stubbornly resisting all of Maria's efforts to obliterate it.

Laban did not have to guess what kind of mood his father would be in now. Caleb only came here when he was feeling sorry for himself and particularly hateful toward the rest of the world, especially toward the son who had the audacity to live while the best son was sacrificed. Laban noted a framed daguerreotype of Leonard sitting slightly askew on a table. He shuddered inwardly and braced himself against the inevitable.

Father and son exchanged no greetings, barely even looking at each other. Laban remained standing, while Caleb sat on the settee, his long legs stretched out before him, but hardly at ease.

"What do you want?" asked Caleb, and the acerbic quality of his tone, almost more than anything else, poignantly emphasized the uncanny resemblance between the patron and his half-breed son.

"I wish to discuss the purchase of new horses," said Laban. "I have heard of a woman in west Texas who has exceptional stock—"

"A woman!" Caleb barked a dry, humorless laugh. "That'll be the day when I buy horses from a woman!"

"What matters is that we get good stock. Bradford's are no longer dependable."

"You wouldn't know good horseflesh from a hole in the wall!"

Laban bit down hard on his lip and said nothing.

"Anyway, what makes you think we need more horses?" continued Caleb. "What we have ought to serve us for another season."

"I only thought—"

"Thank God I'm still around! You'd run this place in the ground if given half a chance. Now, Leonard knew how to get the best out of his stock. He wasn't crying for new animals every time I turned around."

"Still, it is not too soon to contact this woman."

"I will not do ranch business with a woman! It's bad enough now with that greaser woman running the cantina so I have to buy my whiskey from her. And believe me, I'm going to run her out the first chance I get."

"Good horses are good horses," persisted Laban.

"And there are scores of other places to get them," Caleb said with finality, adding ominously, "I forbid you to deal with anybody in west Texas, or even to go there!"

Laban shrugged. If that's how the old man wanted it, fine. Caleb was only hurting himself. The Stoner outfit was big and prosperous, but it could have been phenomenal if Caleb had been less recalcitrant. *But let it be,* Laban told himself, as he had many times before. *I have been patient, but I may not always be so. A man can take only so much before he breaks ... or explodes.*

His impatience made him think of the future, no matter how futile such longings were. Laban was a young man, only twenty-three years old. Caleb was old, and his bitter hatred made him older every day. If there was justice in the world, Laban did have a chance.

Ah, yes! All was not lost.

Someday ...

70

THE NEXT SEVERAL SEASONS WERE prosperous ones for the Wind Rider Ranch. Deborah acquired more land and was soon driving more than two thousand head of cattle to market with her own trail crew of hired hands, led usually by Slim, who had never lost his taste for the wandering life.

Deborah's pride and joy, however, was her equestrian business. She continued to round up the wild mustangs and after breaking them, garnered a substantial profit in sales. With these profits, she purchased, from as far away as England, several animals with impeccable bloodlines, including a fine Arabian mare that she bred with Broken Wing's gray, producing a magnificent black stallion. Her stable was well on its way to becoming famous in the West.

Those early years of the 1870s, however, continued to be marred by the frequency of Comanche raids in the area. The Wind Rider Ranch remained miraculously immune, and Deborah felt certain this was in answer to her prayer over the Indian graves. Yet few of her neighbors chose to follow her example, and some even began to look upon Deborah derisively for her pro-Indian sympathies. Most adhered to the basic Texas Indian policy: expulsion or extermination. And Deborah had no doubt there were many who preferred extermination over the first option.

There came a day, however, when Deborah's sympathies were quite shaken. She had business in Fort Griffin, and Griff needed a new pair of boots. Accompanied by five-year-old Sky, they made the trip together.

A week or so earlier, the Cook girl had been rescued by the army after nearly three years in captivity by the Comanche. Deborah recalled when the child's home had been raided and her family killed not long after Deborah's arrival in Texas.

During her visit to the fort, Deborah went to pay her respects to Captain Ludlam and his wife, and while in their quarters she saw the girl cowering in a corner. She was twelve or thirteen years old now, emaciated, and looking uncannily like a starved wild animal. But this was not the most shocking aspect of the girl's appearance. Her body was hideously scarred and mutilated; several fingers were missing on her hands, while her arms showed scars from old burns and cuts that plainly were not the marks of mourning like those on Deborah's arms. However, it was her face that was most appalling and nearly brought an anguished gasp from Deborah. It had been ravaged so with burns that it was barely recognizable as human, and one eye was completely gouged out.

Captain Ludlam said, "My wife is making a patch for the eye."

Her voice thick with emotion, Deborah said, "This was done by the Comanche?"

"Yes, it was. And those are the scars we can see."

"Why. . . ?"

"Because they are animals," said the captain harshly.

Deborah could not believe this, yet she stumbled from the room confused and sick.

It was a most unfortunate coincidence that as she crossed the parade ground, she ran, almost literally, into Big Bill Yates. He immediately saw Deborah's pallor and, judging by the direction from which she had come, surmised the cause of her dismay.

"So, you seen her, have you?" As usual, his question sounded more like a threat than an inquiry. She didn't have to answer, for he went on without encouragement, in a belligerent tone. "If I ever catch any Injun, that's just what I'm gonna do to them! I got me a little daughter and, by God, I'll shoot her with my own hand before I'll let any of them godforsaken savages near her! But I'll kill plenty of them first!"

Deborah could not respond. She silently pushed past Yates and headed to the Sutler's, where she had left Griff and Sky. She arrived there moments after another member of her family had an encounter with a member of the Yates family.

———

Eight-year-old Billy Yates, it seemed, was as narrow-minded and bigoted as his father. He was also showing signs of becoming just as big. He was ninety pounds of solid muscle, and several inches taller than most of his peers. This combined with a surly personality to make him already a formidable bully.

Sky, at five, was showing definite signs of having inherited his own father's strong, lithe frame, but he was yet a child and still had many finely chiseled childish features. He was a head shorter than Billy and many pounds lighter, but this disparity in size in no way discouraged the young Yates boy from taunting and casting derision upon Sky. In fact, it was very likely an encouragement.

"Whew!" Billy wrinkled his nose distastefully as he approached Sky, who was leaning against a post in front of the store while Griff was inside shopping. "I thought for a minute I was downwind from a garbage heap. But it's just that half-blooded redskin."

Billy's companions cheered him on. "Same thing, ain't it?"

They howled and made sneering faces at Sky, who was turning red with fury.

"You better shut up," Sky said.

"You gonna let him talk to you thataway, Billy?" said one of the other boys.

"Yeah," said another, "he might scalp you in the night."

"Let him try!" taunted Billy. "I'll put him back on the reservation where scum like his kind belong."

Without pausing to consider the hopelessness of the battle, Sky could take no more of the taunts, and he launched himself bodily at his persecutors with a fierce tenacity worthy of any Cheyenne warrior. Both boys fell into the dirt street and tussled furiously for some moments. With surprise on his side, Sky retained the upper hand for about two minutes, inflicting upon his enemy a bloody nose, a badly scraped elbow, and a bruised jaw. After that, sheer size gained the advantage, and in the closing moments of the battle Billy throttled his young adversary thoroughly.

Billy's hulking frame, astride Sky, gave the smaller boy little room for movement. Sky struggled, lurching from side to side, flailing with his fists in an attempt to escape. But Billy Yates was too imposing. His fleshy paws, curled into fists, pummeled Sky's face into a bruised and bloody mess. At one point, Sky managed to summon enough strength for a powerful lurch that threw his attacker off balance. He scrambled to his feet, and although good sense should have told Sky to take the opportunity and flee the scene of his own personal massacre, he instead launched another frontal attack. All he received for his heroic valor was another sound thrashing from Billy, who knocked Sky to the ground and began aiming vicious kicks at his defeated foe. The other boys joined in, and Sky could do nothing to defend himself but throw his arms over his face and curl up in a protective ball on the ground.

No passersby made any attempt to stop the melee, and a few even paused to cheer on the white boys. Finally a sergeant happened along and stepped into the fray, grabbing both Sky and Billy by their collars and giving them a good shake and verbal harangue.

Griff didn't hear the ruckus until it was well advanced. He started to come to Sky's rescue just as the sergeant came along. Griff was about to step outside and take charge of Sky, when he happened to scan the crowd. Without a moment's hesitation, he ducked back into the store and waited until everyone had cleared away before coming back out.

By the time Deborah arrived Griff had cleaned away the worst evidence of the fight. But he couldn't hide it entirely. Deborah was ready for her own confrontation with Mr. Yates, but Griff discouraged her.

"Let's just get outta town, Deborah," he said, "before there's any more trouble."

"I never knew you to shy away from a little trouble, Griff."

"I got good reason. Someday I'll thrash both them Yates varmints myself, but now ain't the right time. Let's get—now!"

He was too determined to allow for argument, so Deborah complied. Besides, she was still too distraught over the other events of the day to be able to trust herself in a confrontation. It would be best for her to speak with Yates when she could be calm and collected.

It did not improve her frayed emotions when, as she and Griff and her son drove out of the fort in the wagon, Sky looked up at her with a resolute gaze that looked more than ever like Broken Wing.

376

"Nahkoa," he said, "I'm gonna be a warrior like my father. I'll fight the whites. And I'll win!"

Questions plagued Deborah all the way home. The brilliant sun in the wide, blue sky; the broad, grassy plains, and the lonely mesquite failed to thrill her as they usually did. Suddenly the prairie she loved appeared dark and depraved. What kind of land was this, that little children must suffer so? Or, that humans, both white and red, were reduced to acting like animals? She had believed that the Indian people needed only to be treated with fairness and respect for peace to become a reality in this country. Was she blind and naive? Were they but savages and, as she had heard one man say, "untamable and treacherous as rattlesnakes"?

But even as the questions formed in her distraught mind, she felt like a betrayer. She loved the Indian people. Her experience with Broken Wing's Cheyenne had given her reason to feel no other way. He had been the most civilized, noble man she had ever known, as were scores of other Cheyenne, Arapahoe, and Sioux she had come to know during her sojourn with the Indians. She realized there were treacherous, untrustworthy Indians, just as there were whites. Intellectually, she knew it had nothing to do with race, but rather everything to do with the condition of a person's heart. Proof of this was the fact that she had for years been spared from further raids by the Indians. She did not doubt that her simple act of humanity, of respect, had in this way been acknowledged by the Comanche. Was it possible that the same Indians who had tortured the little Cook girl had also responded with humanity toward Deborah? She did not know the answer. She only knew that she must not allow herself to be deluded by the prevalent attitudes around her. And she especially must not allow such hatreds to be formed in the hearts of her children. She must remain faithful to the urgings of her heart, the urgings that told her all men were equal in God's eyes. He did not see race or color; and she must do the same, judging men by standards other than externals.

71

GRIFF ALSO EXPERIENCED MENTAL distress after that visit to the fort, although his was of a far different nature than Deborah's. Not one to easily succumb to such mental exercise, Griff allowed it to plague his mind for only one day. He thought about it and ruminated over it all the next day while working out on the range, but by the time he rode into the ranch compound, he'd had his fill of introspection and was ready for action.

While he and Longjim were alone in the stable unsaddling their horses, he vented his pent-up anxieties, though he did so in a low, careful tone.

"Longjim, I gotta tell you something. I been chewing it over since yesterday and don't figure I better keep it to myself no more."

"You been acting skittish all day, Griff," said Longjim. "I ain't seen you take on so . . . since we was being tracked by that gang and their Crow Injun. What in blazes is it?"

"Something I seen at the fort yesterday."

"Yeah, what? A spook, or something?"

"Close enough." Griff paused, looked all around to make sure they were truly alone, then went on. "I seen a fellow I ain't seen for eight years, and woulda been happy if it had been eighty years. Markus Pollard."

Longjim looked blank for a long moment, finding nothing familiar about the name Griff dropped like a stick of dynamite. Then it hit him and he gasped. "You sure it was him, Griff?"

"He was eight years older and looking pretty down-and-out, but I'm sure. It was Pollard all right."

"After all these years, it don't seem possible."

"Texas ain't as big a state as we'd like to believe."

"He see you?"

"Heck no! I ain't loony."

"But no one's interested in us no more, Griff. Why, if they started

378

arresting everyone who's run afoul of the law in Texas, they'd have half the state in chains."

"It ain't us I'm worried about."

"Aw, they ain't gonna go after Deborah after all this time."

"Murder's murder, Longjim. They ain't never gonna forget about that, especially Caleb Stoner. And he's more powerful today then he ever was."

"You think Pollard would turn her in? Is he still a lawman?"

"Naw, he ain't, but he sure looked like he could use a few dollars and wouldn't be above bounty hunting to get it. If he hangs around these parts at all, it's only a matter of time before he runs into Deborah. He ain't likely to have forgotten about a woman he nearly hanged."

"You gonna tell Deborah?"

"I reckon someone's gotta."

"What d'ya think she'll do?"

"Who knows? She's never been too predictable." Griff paused and a hard, cold expression crossed his countenance. "There's one other thing we can do."

"What's that?"

"Get rid of Pollard."

Longjim's eyebrows shot up. He knew Griff well, and though the ex-outlaw wasn't a killer, he knew Griff *could* kill. And he knew Griff's statement wasn't an idle one.

"Let's wait and see afore we do anything hasty," said Longjim. "Let's just keep it under our hats; maybe it'll blow over."

"I won't let 'em destroy her!" vowed Griff.

"I'm with you, Griff. But—"

Longjim cut off suddenly and both men tensed as a sharp sound echoed not far from where they stood. Griff jerked his head toward the direction of the sound, where now all was quiet once more, and he signaled Longjim to circle to the left of the spot while he edged to the right. They both drew their six-guns.

If anyone had heard their conversation, he'd have to be dealt with. Griff always knew he'd kill to protect Deborah, and he was ready to do so now if he had to.

Quietly he approached the stall where the noise had originated. It was the one where the new colt was kept, but it had not been the animal that had made the sound. When Griff was close enough, he aimed his gun and called in an ominous voice. "Okay, whoever you are, come on out before I shoot this stall full of holes!"

"Please, don't shoot me, Uncle Griff!" came a terrified small voice.

"Lynnie! What in blazes are you doing here?" Griff knew it was a stupid question, but he was too shaken to think clearly.

Carolyn slowly stood up, pushed open the stall door and crept out. Her face was white with fear, but in her eyes there was confusion.

"I—I fell asleep with Dusty," she said.

"How long you been awake?"

"A bit."

Griff and Longjim exchanged wary looks.

"What'd you hear?"

Carolyn cast down her eyes. She well knew it was wrong to eavesdrop, and her fear sprang as much from her own guilt as from fear of Griff's drawn gun. But she was too tenacious and headstrong to remain docile and submissive for long.

"Is someone gonna hurt Ma?" she asked.

"Now, Lynnie, don't you give what you heard another thought," answered Griff. "Longjim an' I was just telling tales, you know, 'tall' ones like Slim likes to tell you."

"That ain't so! I'm old enough to know different. I'm almost eight!"

Usually Carolyn's precociousness amused him, but this was too serious to draw even a smile from Griff. "Listen here, Carolyn, there is some trouble, but nothing Longjim an' I can't handle. Ain't no need to bother your ma about it. Can you keep a secret?"

Carolyn thought about it a moment. "From my ma?"

"Yeah, but it'd be for her own good."

"Okay. My ma's got a secret from me, and now I got one from her."

"What d'ya mean?"

"She's got a secret about my pa, and now I got a secret about— What's it all about, Griff?"

Griff shook his head and rolled his eyes. The girl could be downright exasperating at times!

"Something that happened a long time ago and is best forgotten. You hear? *Forgotten!*"

Carolyn nodded her head contritely. It was enough that she had her own secret now.

72

LATE IN THE SUMMER OF 1876, Deborah was working with some new mustangs in the corral. Griff was helping, and Sky, now a strapping, handsome lad of eight, was sitting on the fence rail observing. His attention had momentarily wandered while Griff and his mother were having one of their many discussions on the best horse-breaking techniques, each with strongly opposing views. The boy's gaze, always apt to focus on the distant horizons, peered across the fields, scanning the place where the sky met the grass. All at once he sat bolt upright.

"Mama, Griff! Look! Indians!" he cried with pure excitement and no fear.

The adults immediately looked to where Sky pointed and, sure enough, two riders were approaching, though only Sky's sharp vision could have discerned their Indian garb from that distance. Deborah gave Griff a puzzled, concerned glance.

Two years before this, the Indian problem in Texas had been met head on with disastrous results for the Indians. After the battle of Palo Duro Canyon in 1874 when, as at Washita, the Comanche lost all their homes, food and horses, the bands were forced to finally surrender. Deborah had watched with great sorrow as scores of Comanche and other renegade Indians had trudged through her lands on their doleful way north to Indian Territory. She had recalled Broken Wing's dream and knew this must surely have been what he had seen. And for once she had been almost glad that he had not lived to witness this awful time.

Were these Indians more latecomers on their way to the reservation? Or were they renegades? Rumor said there were still some out there, striking blows for justice.

Griff merely shrugged at Deborah's unspoken concern. "Ain't never had to worry before. Don't see why we should start now."

In another five minutes they were close enough to make out

further details. They were warriors, and though neither held a weapon in his hand, each had a bow and rifle fastened to his saddle. One man was definitely a Comanche and, from his rather ornate attire, was very likely a chief of substantial standing. The second rider, however, most arrested Deborah's attention.

She suddenly gasped and gripped Griff's arm. "Griff! The rider on the right is Cheyenne!"

"I do believe you're right."

They waited in silence. Sky climbed down from his perch on the fence and sidled up to his mother, standing close without appearing to cower behind her skirts. He watched the proceedings with total concentration.

When the Indians rode into the yard, Deborah was further surprised to see that the Cheyenne rider was no stranger. He, too, indicated his recognition of her by a barely discernible faltering in his impassive visage. Deborah, all her previous apprehension gone, stepped boldly forward and greeted the visitors in Cheyenne.

"Hello, Stands-in-the-River," she said. "It is good to see my old friend and brother."

"Wind Rider." He bowed his head toward her, his bearing full of respect. "When they said a white woman had honored the Comanche dead, I did not know if it could be you, but I had to meet such a white woman, regardless. I am glad it is you, my sister."

"Will you dismount and come into my lodge?"

Stands-in-the-River glanced at his companion, who gave a slight shake of his head.

"We think it unwise to tarry in the white man's settlements too long," replied Stands-in-the-River.

"You will always find sanctuary here," Deborah said. "In all these years the Comanche have withheld their hand from my ranch, and I will return such consideration with friendship and peace."

"You have honored our dead," said the Comanche. "We have a name for you in our camp: 'She-Who-Buries-Warriors.' We speak it with respect."

"It is I who am honored," said Deborah. "And by what name can I call you?"

"I am Dark Eagle. I am a Comanche chief." As he spoke he seemed to draw himself up even taller in his saddle. He was a proud man, but melancholy infused his eyes.

"We go to surrender ourselves at Fort Sill in the Indian Territory," said Stands-in-the-River. "My woman and children wait for me."

382

"You have fought a long, hard battle." It was all Deborah could say.

"We knew few victories," said Stands-in-the-River. "We thought the Little Big Horn was a victory. But it was not, for it only brought the anger of the bluecoats down on us harder than ever."

Deborah recalled when a few weeks ago word had come to the ranch of the massacre of the Seventh Cavalry and its flamboyant commander, George Armstrong Custer. She clearly remembered when she had wished that very fate upon Custer, but the passage of years and the work of God had changed her heart dramatically. Now she only grieved the hapless general.

"We now must admit defeat and accept the fate the white man has for us."

"You are a good man, a worthy warrior, Stands-in-the-River," said Deborah with conviction. Though he had been headstrong and sometimes even foolhardy, she admired his courage. "The Cheyenne will need men such as you to help them learn new ways."

"I know only the hunting of the buffalo. How can I teach others new ways when I know none myself?"

"Because you are a fighter, my friend. You do not give up easily." She smiled with confidence as she added, "You will learn the new ways and you will teach others."

"My brother made a good choice of a woman when he married you, Wind Rider."

The mention of Broken Wing brought a small twinge of remembered pain to Deborah, but she immediately realized it was a different feeling from the aching emptiness she had suffered in the months and years immediately following his death. His memory now brought a pleasant joy to her heart also. And she suddenly remembered the small figure standing nearby.

Reaching out her hand, she beckoned Sky to her. His eyes were wide with awe as he came to her without hesitation. Deborah took his hand in hers, aware again of how much he resembled his father. She hardly needed to speak her next words but she did, anyway.

"This is his son, Blue Sky—your nephew, Stands-in-the-River."

Broken Wing's brother looked the boy over carefully, then smiled with approval. "He will be a fine Cheyenne warrior one day." Then Stands-in-the-River lifted an ornately beaded collar from around his neck. "Come," he said to the boy, and Sky immediately stepped forward. Bending low over his horse, Stands-in-the-River slipped the necklace over Sky's head. "You are *naha,* son to me," he said solemnly. "I shall be your *nehuo.*"

Sky gazed intently up into his uncle's eyes. He not only fully understood the man's Cheyenne, for Deborah had been careful that he did not lose his father's language, but Sky also fully comprehended the deep significance of the moment. This man was of his father's people, and he was now accepting Sky as one of them. It would be a moment that would stand out in his life as a brightly shining star, never to dim or fade from his memory.

"Thank you, Nehuo," Sky replied in Cheyenne.

Stands-in-the-River nodded. "Be proud always of who you are and of who your people are."

Then the Cheyenne brave straightened in his saddle and looked once more at Deborah. He said, "Perhaps our trails will cross again; if not, I have been made greater in knowing you."

"And I also," said Deborah. "Greet Stone Teeth Woman for me and tell her I continue to hold her in deep affection. And, if you see Gray Antelope Woman, tell her"—a lump formed in Deborah's throat as she realized she had far too much to share with her dear old friend than could be conveyed in a single message—"tell her the same."

"It will be done," said Stands-in-the-River. "Goodbye, Wind Rider Woman."

"Goodbye, my brother," said Deborah, then, turning to Dark Eagle, "And to you also, Dark Eagle. May God travel with you!"

They reined their ponies around and trotted away, leaving only a cloud of Texas dust in their wake. More than dust, however, remained in the hearts and memories of both mother and son as they stood watching the departure of the warriors.

For Deborah, the appearance of the two Indians was a fitting affirmation of the importance in her life of those special years with the Cheyenne. After so many years away, the polish on her memories had begun to dull somewhat, but this encounter made clearer than ever the fact that she would always have two noble heritages to treasure.

For Sky, the visit was burned into his young mind. This was the first tangible link, within his memory, to his heritage, and its impact went further than all of Deborah's stories in impressing upon him that he was not only different, but that his was a noble, laudable difference. Later, when faced with inevitable bigotry because of his Indian blood—such as he had already experienced at the hands of the likes of Billy Yates—he would be able to look back upon that moment in the yard of the ranch. Recalling his uncle, mighty and fearsome even in defeat, Sky would hold his head up with pride.

73

CHRISTMAS OF 1878 BEGAN AS LITTLE different from the many previous holidays at the Wind Rider Ranch. That week had been marked with typically icy wind and frost and a severe hailstorm. Christmas morning, however, dawned with a pale blue sky and a paler sun struggling to warm the crisp air. The children had opened their presents in a flurry of highly energized excitement, followed by the traditional gathering of the ranch hands for a festive breakfast of ham, flapjacks, eggs, and Yolanda's delicious *sopaipillas* with raspberry sauce and honey. Carolyn and Sky then distributed the family's gifts to each of the hands and to Yolanda.

Later in the day a family dinner was planned that would include Yolanda, Griff, Longjim, and, hopefully, Slim. Slim and two of Deborah's hands had accompanied Reverend Slaughter on the fall cattle drive and were expected back any day.

Deborah often smiled to herself when she considered the irony of the three ex-outlaws becoming "family" to her and practically father figures to her children. They were coarse, roughhewn men, truly Western men who carried their six-guns wherever they went and who were far more at home on the backs of their horses than in Deborah's simple drawing room. They were hardly spiritual men, but they were God-fearing in their own way, and Deborah would be the last to judge them for their more uncivilized habits. She prayed for each of them daily that they would allow God to take complete control of their lives. Until that prayer was answered, she believed that each nevertheless had a good deal in the way of practical wisdom to impart to her children.

While she fed Carolyn and Sky their spiritual food, these men taught them how to live in the West, and for the most part, a balance was achieved. Both children could ride, handle a gun, break horses, rope and brand, and drive cattle. In fact, though Deborah hated to admit it, they were far more proficient in ranching than in Christianity.

And Deborah knew she was to blame for this weakness because she could only teach them what she knew, and her own knowledge was limited to what she could glean for herself from the Scriptures. There was no church within a two-day ride from the ranch, and a circuit rider came through once, maybe twice a year. Besides their religious training, Deborah was responsible for their regular schooling as well, since no school was near enough for the children to attend. All this had to fit into the rigorous labors of running a large ranch.

Thus, Deborah had lately been giving this matter over to much prayer.

Yet, as oddly mixed as it was, the three ex-outlaws and Deborah and Carolyn and Sky and their dear old Mexican housekeeper, Yolanda, were indeed a family with strong bonds of love and loyalty forged between them. So it was not surprising that on that Christmas Day, the children asked several times if Slim would get home in time for Christmas dinner. Sky was worried because Slim's present, a leather vest that Sky himself had picked out was still unopened. Griff was worried too, and several times Deborah saw him glance up from his work and gaze off into the distance. They should have been back two weeks ago. There might not be much of an Indian problem anymore, though there could still be a renegade or two loose; but the plains were rife with other hazards—rustlers and outlaws, not to mention natural dangers like storms and swollen rivers and rattlesnakes.

After working in the corral for a while, Deborah returned to the kitchen to help with the finishing touches for dinner. The roasting wild turkey Longjim had shot two days ago was filling the house with a lovely aroma, along with the scent of apple and pecan pies. Carolyn had taken great pains to set the table with the best dishes and silverware and Deborah's best tablecloth.

"It all looks beautiful, Carolyn!" Deborah said.

"I wish we had holly to make a centerpiece for the table," Carolyn replied.

"I almost forgot!" Deborah went to the oak sideboard in the kitchen, opened a drawer and removed a package wrapped in newspaper. Spreading apart the paper, she spoke again. "I bought these in Jacksboro the last time I was there and put them away for the holidays. I wonder what else I have stashed away and have forgotten all about!" With a triumphant flourish she lifted two red tapers and two white china candlesticks from the wrapping.

"They are nice, Mother," said Carolyn. "At least they are better than nothing."

Deborah tried not to reflect on Carolyn's subtly twisted compliment. She was happy to get any compliment at all from her moody thirteen-year-old daughter.

Just as they were turning from admiring the table, Sky burst into the room followed by a gust of cold wind that nearly destroyed all Carolyn's handiwork.

"Mama! Riders are coming from the east!" he yelled between breathless pants. "Three of 'em, Mama, just like the Wise Men in the song."

Laughing at the apt analogy, Deborah followed her son out to the porch. Carolyn trailed after them.

"Do you think it's Slim, Mother?" she asked.

"I hope so."

The riders were galloping toward the ranch now, waving their hats in exuberant greeting. But when the middle rider took off his hat, Deborah gasped as the dull rays of the sun distinctly reflected off the rider's red hair.

"It can't be!" she breathed.

"That's Slim, all right!" Sky said with a whoop. "And Reverend Slaughter. But who's the other one? It ain't one of our hands."

"It *isn't* one of our hands," Deborah corrected instinctively, though she was hardly thinking of grammar at that moment. She fairly skipped down the steps and ran to meet the riders as they galloped into the yard.

"Sam! Sam, I can't believe it's you!" Deborah cried.

Sam leaped from his horse before it came to a full stop and scooped Deborah into his arms, lifting her two feet off the ground.

"Glory hallelujah!" he exclaimed. "You ain't forgot me!"

"Not in a million years!" Deborah almost giggled in her excitement.

Their faces came within inches of each other, and neither knew that in that instant the other's heart skipped a beat. But, suddenly flustered, Sam set Deborah once more on her feet.

"Wherever did you find him, Slim?" asked Deborah once her balance had returned.

"Just where you'd expect, preaching the eyeballs off them poor cowboys in Dodge City."

"And how did you put up with each other all the way from there?" asked Deborah, laughing.

"Oh, I got a tough hide," said Slim, who was already giving each of the children a hearty embrace.

"You'll never convince me of that," said Sam with a good-natured chuckle.

"You always was an old diehard."

"They been going on like this for weeks," said Reverend Slaughter. "If Slim here ain't converted, it ain't for lack of trying!"

"You men must be tired and hungry," said Deborah. "And you are just in time for Christmas dinner."

"What'd I tell you, boys?" said Slim. "I knew we'd make it."

"Sky," said Deborah, "would you please take their horses out to the barn and see they are tended?"

"Yes, Mama."

"My goodness!" exclaimed Sam. "This here ain't that baby I last saw eight years ago! Why, he's practically a full-growed man now. I reckon you don't remember me at all. But if this pretty young lady here is Carolyn, maybe she'd recollect me some."

Carolyn smiled politely but shook her head.

"This is Sam Killion, children," said Deborah. She turned to Sam. "I guess they will have to get to know you all over again—that is, if you plan to be here long enough for that."

"I talked him into pulling up stakes in Kansas," said Slaughter.

"It didn't take much talking," added Slim. "The minute he heard about all the heathens here in Texas and the few number of preachers, no one coulda stopped him."

"I was starting to feel kind of useless back there in Kansas," said Sam. "There's two new circuit riders in the area and churches with ministers springing up everywhere."

"So . . . you're here to stay awhile?" said Deborah, barely masking her eager hopefulness.

"I reckon so."

"What a Christmas we have to celebrate this year!" An excited flush glowed from Deborah. "And we better come on in and get started before we freeze."

Within days, Sam began to fit in as one of the family at the ranch. If the children did not at first remember him, they soon became enamored with his warm and exuberant nature. Even Carolyn softened enough to eagerly await his visits and beg for one of his wonderful stories. Though he stayed in the bunkhouse with the men when he wasn't riding the trails ministering to the scattered settlers, he often took supper with Deborah and the children, and after the meal he never failed to have some entertaining tale to tell. Often these were Bible stories told with such interesting vigor that more than once he had to pull out his Bible to prove to the children that they were actually in there. But when Sky and Carolyn learned that he had once been a Ranger, they hounded him relentlessly with requests for accounts of his Ranger adventures. He proved to be more reticent with these, but during the telling of one, another of his avid interests was discovered.

"What's the Alamo?" Sky asked when Sam happened to mention the famous mission.

Sam turned to Deborah with mock dismay. "Why, Deborah, what have you been teaching these poor children?"

"Only their letters and numbers, and a bit about George Washington and Thomas Jefferson," she said apologetically.

"Well, if these children are going to be Texans, they got to know about the Alamo!"

"Tell us! Tell us!" begged the children.

"The Alamo is one of the most important places in Texas," said Sam, needing little more encouragement. "There, a bunch of brave men fought and died for freedom. They could have quit and saved their necks, but they chose to stick it out, even though they were all doomed to die. They believed freedom is the most important thing a person can have. 'Course, that's one kind of freedom and it is worth dying for, but there's another kind of freedom that only one man had to die for, and that's the freedom of living for and in Christ. I always hope most of them fellas had both kinds of freedom. I know at least one did."

"Who was that?" asked Carolyn.

"That was my pa. He was there at the Alamo, and maybe that's why I figure every true Texan ought to know our history."

"He must have been a brave man," said Carolyn.

"I reckon he was, though I never knew him. I was born in the fall of 1836, after the Alamo, but my ma named me Sam, just like my pa wanted."

"Was his name Sam?"

"No, his name was Benjamin Killion, but he wanted his son to be named after Sam Houston. I wouldn't be surprised if every boy born that year in Texas wasn't named Sam."

"Is your pa dead?" asked Sky innocently.

"Yeah, he is." Sam paused reflectively.

"So is mine," said Sky.

"I know that, Sky," Sam replied, placing an understanding arm around the boy, "but I can tell you're the kind of boy who would have made your pa proud, just like I hope my pa would have been of me."

"My pa is dead, too," Carolyn interjected pointedly. "He was a war hero."

Silently, Sam gave her a slight, vague nod, then drew her to him in his other arm. He couldn't resist a glance toward Deborah, but she was looking down at her lap, so he received no response from her.

"Was your ma and pa born in Texas, too, Sam?" asked Sky.

"Oh no. My pa came from Kentucky and my ma from Pennsylvania, and I can't imagine a more different pair falling in love and getting married than them—though they almost didn't."

"What happened?"

"That's a mighty long story and it's getting late. You remind me another time and I'll gladly tell it to you."

Not only the children enjoyed Sam's presence. Deborah monopolized almost as much of his time as did her children. The very moment her eyes had beheld him, she realized he had come in answer to her prayers. At last she had the fellowship of another believer, and Deborah wondered how she had survived the last years without him. She realized quickly what a dear friend he was and what a gap his absence had left within her. They spent hours together, riding and talking, walking and talking, eating and talking. That there was enough of Sam to go around, between Deborah and the children and his quickly growing flock among the settlers, was a miracle in itself. But he never tired of any of them, especially not of Deborah. He sought her out whenever he could, as much for spiritual enrichment as for the sheer pleasure of her company.

It had been a long eight years. Many times in Kansas and the northern territories where he rode circuit, Sam had seriously considered quitting his ministry there and racing as fast as a horse could carry him to Texas and to Deborah. But always, his impulsive yearnings had been held in check by the stark need for his services. About four years ago he had been all packed up and ready to pull out when a distraught father rode up to Sam's door. The man had traveled two days searching for a minister to give a Christian burial for his wife and two children who had died of the cholera. Sam could not refuse him, and the incident impressed upon him what his priorities must be. He had decided long ago to put God first and had to trust that somehow God would honor his faithfulness.

When so many new ministers began to filter into the area, Sam wondered if he might soon be "called" to another ministry, perhaps even to Texas. He put the matter to fervent prayer and gradually sensed his time in the Northern Plains might be drawing to a close.

When he asked where he would be sent next, the only answer he received was, *I will show you.*

Soon, everywhere he turned he was meeting someone from Texas, or reading and hearing something about Texas. One preacher friend of his told him he ought to return and minister to his home state, which was quickly gaining a reputation for its wild and violent ways. Then Slim showed up. And a sense of uncluttered assurance had immediately filled Sam. He knew this unexpected meeting with Slim after so many years was no coincidence.

What he hadn't known, however, was if this call to Texas also included Deborah.

The answer to that should have been clear the first moment they set eyes on each other. She hadn't looked at Griff that way when she saw him in the Sutler's store that first time after *their* lengthy separation. Was it possible that she was ready to give her heart to another?

He knew there was only one way to find out, but having been rejected once, he was understandably cautious. Thus, it was the spring of the new year before he found his nerve, and that came from a most unexpected source.

74

SAM HAD JUST ARRIVED AT THE RANCH for his usual Sunday supper with the family. He had his own place now, a line cabin loaned to him by one of his converts that was more central to the region. He was unsaddling his horse in the stable when Griff ambled up to him. The ranch foreman obviously had something on his mind.

"We ought to be building another stall here for that horse of yours," Griff said in a friendly but pointed tone.

"I reckon he does spend a lot of time here."

"Sure does."

"I didn't think it was causing anyone a problem, though."

"Naw, that's a real good horse you got there."

391

Sam hoisted his saddle over a rail. "I guess I've been spending a sight of time here, too."

"That's a fact."

"Does that bother you, Griff?"

Griff scratched his chin thoughtfully. "I guess I just ain't figured you out yet, Preacher. Some of the time you irritate me worse than a saddle spur. But some of the time I like you, too—"

"When you ain't drawing a gun on me. . . ?" interjected Sam with a wry grin.

Griff responded with a more sheepish grin. "Aw, you ain't never gonna let me live that down, are you?"

"Someday I will, but you gotta admit I've been at the wrong end of your gun more times than is healthy for most men."

"But I ain't never killed you."

"Not yet."

Griff laughed, then he peered, suddenly in earnest, at Sam. "Why'd you really come back to Texas, Killion?"

"To save heathens like you, Griff," replied Sam in fun.

"It had nothing at all to do with Deborah?"

Now Sam returned the earnest gaze. "I'd be lying if I said it didn't."

"So, what in blazes are you dragging your feet in the sand for?"

"Can I ask what your interest in all this is?"

"I'm interested in Deborah, pure and simple."

"You mean—"

"Sam Killion! You were a durn fine Texas Ranger, and from what I hear, you're a pretty good preacher, too. But you sure don't know nothing about love! You see, I do love Deborah, but not in the way you're thinking, so get that hang-dog look off your face. I'd do anything for that woman. I'd take a bullet for her, and I'd kill for her. I'd kill anyone who tried to hurt her, and that includes you! So, if you don't want to be at the wrong end of my gun again, you'd better decide what you're gonna do about her, and do it. Both of you ain't getting no younger."

"Are you saying I'd have your blessing to . . . well, to court her?"

"Heck no! After eight years, I think you better forget the courtship and go right to the wedding!"

Sam smiled, not without a hint of relief. "You surprise me, Griff, you truly do!"

"Well, what're you gonna do?"

"I guess what I been wanting to do for eight years and more." But Sam paused, still not fully convinced. "Since I've come back, Griff, she's never said anything to encourage me, to give me even a small clue that she's ready for marriage again. That's one reason why I've been reluctant."

Griff shook his head derisively. "Anyone that's been within a mile of you two these past couple of months don't need ears if they got eyes to see. Besides, I saw her every time she'd get a letter from you over the years. Why, the happiness in her eyes could light up the entire prairie."

"Really?"

Griff rolled his eyes. "Go propose to the woman, man, before I propose to her just to spite you."

———

While Sam and Griff were talking in the stable, Deborah was sitting in the old oak rocker in her room. The open book in her lap had long since been forgotten as her mind wandered to the person who had been on her mind so frequently of late. She not only *thought* of Sam Killion, but she dreamed about him at night and even imagined hearing his voice when he wasn't there. If she did happen to see him unexpectedly, her heart was likely to skip a beat, and when she really did hear his voice, she got such a tingly, warm feeling inside that it embarrassed her. She was, after all, a matron of almost thirty-three, who had been married twice before and had two children. Yet these peculiar sensations had all the earmarks of schoolgirl puppy love.

Was she in love with Sam Killion?

She knew she did not even have to ask. Her love for Sam had never really been in question. She had always been aware of her feelings for Sam, but the deeper they became, the more she wanted to deny them. For Deborah, love had almost always been synonymous with pain.

Perhaps now, so many years removed from her grief, she could be more objective. If her attempts at love had always ended in grief, had they not also been associated with her moments of most profound happiness? Would she want to relinquish her dear memories of her friendship with her brother, or of her father's tender wisdom, or of that special camaraderie with Jacob Stoner? If she had known that Broken Wing was to be taken from her so soon, would she have turned her back on their love, on the joy and contentment of those few short years together?

Never.

To do so would be to deny the very essence of life. Love, hate, joy and sadness, happiness and grief—God had used them all to make her life complete and, she hoped, to make her the kind of person who could respond with true empathy to the needs of others. She had been blind to that fact for so many wasted years, but now she could see it clearly.

Oddly, the only time she had become involved in a loveless relationship, she had known her greatest misery. When the terrible experience with Leonard seemed as if it would completely snuff out any desire to venture into a relationship again, especially with a man, God had brought Broken Wing into her life, perhaps to prove that life is nothing without love, that even a woman who has been wounded almost beyond repair yearns for the fulfillment it brings.

And now, Sam had come back.

Was this God's way of telling her she had languished in her fear and reticence long enough? That it was time to take another step toward growth by trusting God to continue to use and work His will in her life? He was so patient with her! Could He be ready to take her further in her walk with Him if she would only take this new step of faith?

"I don't want to be afraid, Lord," she prayed. "Sometimes I think I could be strong enough to face the death of another loved one. Yet, at other times, the mere thought makes me want to curl up into a ball and hide some place far away from all possible hurts.

"I want to step out. I love Sam so much that the possible hurt from losing him through my fear is almost as unbearable as his loss through death. But my Cheyenne people taught me that nothing lives long . . . all things must die. That, too, is a part of life."

Sighing, Deborah closed the book in her lap. Sir Walter Scott would have to await another time to capture her interest. Instead, she reached for her Bible lying on the table next to her bed. It was the same Bible she had found in Hardee's store—a cheap edition, really, and its boards had long ago begun to fall away from the binding. But it had ministered truth to her the same as any expensive leather-bound version, and had served as a pool of clear water in the spiritual desert of her Texas home. She opened it to the gospel of Mark where she had left off last night, but in the present flightiness of her mind, she absently began thumbing through the pages until she came to the first epistle of John. There, she stopped and smiled. She had heard these little books, or letters, referred to as the "love" books, and it was appropriate that she should read them now when love was so strongly on her mind.

She read for a few minutes until one particular verse seemed almost to leap out at her. She smiled again, then laughed out loud and reread the verse.

"Oh, dear Lord, you are so good to me! Thank you for showing me once more how real you are!"

75

SAM KNOCKED AT THE RANCH HOUSE door just as Deborah closed her Bible. She found him chatting with Yolanda.

"Hello, Deborah," he said.

This time Deborah did not try to ignore the thrill that coursed through her body as he greeted her. "Hello, Sam."

"I'm a mite early."

"That's fine. It'll give us more of a chance to talk while the children are gone."

"Would you like to walk outside a spell?"

"Yes, I would."

"Better get your shawl, though. It's pretty out there, but that wind has a bite to it."

They were silent for some time as they walked, each filled with a tumult of thoughts and emotions and no easy way to express them. It was so unlike the usual flow of conversation between them. Perhaps it would have been different if they had realized they had been gently led by the loving hand of their Father in heaven to this very moment; that Sam's conversation with Griff and Deborah's reading in John's letter had been planned to coincide perfectly by Him who sees both the beginning and the end of a matter. But of course they were too close to the situation, too wrought within their own temporary insecurities to see quite that perceptively.

They had strolled for about half a mile when Deborah saw Sky and Carolyn off in the distance riding their horses. She briefly reflected that not too long ago such a scene could not have been possible because of the trouble with the Comanche. But what really struck Deborah as she watched the two young people race across a length of flat pasture was how like herself and Graham they were becoming. So remote from their neighbors out here on the frontier, there were few other children for them to play with, so they had been forced to nurture a closeness to each other that might otherwise not have happened. They would be better for it, as Deborah now knew she was.

"Those two sure can ride," Sam commented as he noted the focus of Deborah's attention.

"It's a matter of survival out here."

"You've done a good job with them, Deborah."

"I suppose I have made my share of mistakes. Carolyn can be mighty headstrong when she wants to be, but all in all, I really can't complain. I do enjoy them. They are growing up fast, though."

"Kids have a way of doing that. Blink once, and poof! They're all grown with kids of their own."

"Oh, please, not that fast!" laughed Deborah. "But you are right. Soon they'll be off on their own."

"What'll you do then, Deborah?"

"I haven't thought much about it. Thanks to the Lord, I am fairly content with the way my life has turned out. I love the ranch, and I certainly have the independence I have always wanted. But, to tell you the truth, Sam, it isn't always enough. There are still some empty places left in my heart that need filling."

"God is able to fill them."

"Yes, I know that. But I think that if He doesn't fill them directly, He often sends us people that do some of the filling, as He has done with my children, or as He sometimes does by sending a husband or a wife."

Sam stopped suddenly as she spoke. He was so astounded at her remark that he could barely force out his own response. It came in a kind of gasp. "You ain't saying you might be considering marriage, are you, Deborah?"

"You know well enough how I have felt in the past about that," said Deborah.

"You've been afraid to risk loving someone because of all its potential for pain."

"Something like that."

"Well, Deborah, maybe you could marry for friendship and companionship and forget all about this love business?" He knew it was a foolish idea, even if it were possible. No one, especially someone as sensitive and compassionate as Deborah, could so detach herself from a relationship. But he hoped his comment would make the path easier for him, if not for her.

"Aw, Deborah!" he threw up his hands in frustration. "It's no use trying to be subtle. I'll just tell you right out that I'd be pleased to be your companion in life. I haven't changed from how I felt in Dodge. In fact, I suppose I've felt that way from when I first set eyes on you in Griff's hideout. I couldn't get you out of my mind after that; and when I saw you in Black Kettle's village, I was awfully confused, though I was happy for you, too, and glad you'd found yourself a good man. Then there was Dodge. And when you went to Texas, I had to stay where I was. I guess the timing was never right for us—except I have to remind myself that we are part of God's timing, so it must've been right. Anyway, here we are now and I'm making a fool of myself again, but I just have to say these things because I think that's a big part of why I've come to Texas."

He paused and took a deep breath, hoping all the while that she would break in on his babbling. But she didn't, and so he went on, for good or ill. "What I'm trying to say, though not very well, is that after all these years, I'd be satisfied to be your companion. I suppose, in a way, it's what I've been these last few months, anyway—only, if we got married, I wouldn't have to go home at night."

"Would that really be enough for you, Sam?"

He gazed deeply into her eyes. He wanted nothing more than for her to love him in the same way he loved her, and part of him believed that she did love him, even if she was afraid to admit it. Yet he believed he could be happy with her even if the words of love were never spoken between them. He wanted to believe it anyway.

But before he could respond, Deborah spoke. "Oh, Sam! *I* am the fool. I don't even know why I asked you that question, except that I'm still trying to protect myself, even though I know it's not necessary. You see, Sam, it doesn't have to be enough."

Sam's bushy red eyebrows shot up. "What do you mean?"

"I mean, it would be impossible for me to marry you just for companionship—at this point, that is. What I mean is . . . it's too late for that. I love you, Sam!"

"You ain't just saying that, are you, Deborah?"

Deborah smiled. "Do you think after all these years, I'd say it if I didn't mean it?"

Sam threw back his head and laughed out loud. Then he scooped Deborah up in his arms and swung her around, dancing joyously in the tall prairie grass.

"Praise the Lord!" he sang. "I knew it!"

"Then why were you sweating so?" laughed Deborah.

"Well . . . maybe my faith did weaken there for a minute."

Deborah grew solemn. "I've wasted so many years with my fear," she said. "I was so afraid of losing you that I might have lost you, anyway, because I was too afraid to admit my feelings."

"What changed you? Or, I should say, how did God change you?"

"It happened just a couple of hours ago, really," said Deborah. "I was reading my Bible when a verse simply jumped off the page at me. I must have read that verse many times before; but today I really *read* it, I suppose, because it did something special inside me this time. It changed me."

"And what verse was it?"

"The one in First John that says, 'There is no fear in love; but perfect love casteth out fear: because fear hath torment. He that feareth is not made perfect in love.' I had the feeling as I read it that it had been written for me alone."

"It was, dear Deborah. . . . It was!"

Sam bent toward Deborah's upturned face. His lips met hers, and his arms enfolded her in a fervent embrace. Deborah sensed as he held her that this great risk she had feared for so long was no risk at all; rather, she was now more secure than she had been in a very long time. And this was a security that came not from independence or self-sufficiency but from knowing her path was within the will of her Lord.